A CHANGING LAND

Also by Nicole Alexander

The Bark Cutters

Divertissements: Love, War, Society – Selected Poems

A CHANGING LAND

NICOLE ALEXANDER

BANTAM

SYDNEY • AUCKLAND • TORONTO • NEW YORK • LONDON

A Bantam book
Published by Random House Australia Pty Ltd
Level 3, 100 Pacifi c Highway, North Sydney NSW 2060
www.randomhouse.com.au

First published by Bantam in 2011
This edition published in 2012

Addresses for companies within the Random House Group can be found at
www.randomhouse.com.au/offices

National Library of Australia
Cataloguing-in-Publication Entry

Alexander, Nicole, 1965–
A changing land / Nicole Alexander

ISBN 978 1 86471 230 8 (pbk)

Country life – Australia – Fiction.
Families – Australia – Fiction.
Inheritance and succession – Fiction.

A823.4

Cover photograph of woman © Masterfile
Cover photograph of landscape © Photolibrary
Cover design by Blue Cork
Internal design and typesetting by Midland Typesetters, Australia
Printed in Australia by Griffin Press, an accredited ISO AS/NZS 14001:2004
Environmental Management System printer

To those who have gone before us:
the pioneers

PROLOGUE

≪ *Spring, 1987* ≫

Wangallon Station

Sarah stared at the headstones, at the ageing monuments silhouetted by the rising moon. The clearing was strangely quiet and she wondered whether the spirits of Wangallon were welcoming her grandfather, Angus, at some other sacred place on the property. Lifting the latch on the peeling wooden gate, she stepped through grass grown long by recent spring rains. Twigs and leaves crackled beneath her, the soft soil creating an imprint of her passing. The familiar pounding of a kangaroo echoed across the narrow stretch of water that formed the twisting Wangallon Creek, and with their movement a flock of lorikeets squawked in a tall gum tree before resettling for the night.

Sarah stopped first by her brother Cameron's grave, and then at the freshly turned mound that covered her beloved grandfather. For the first time the enormity of his passing settled on her slight shoulders. To have lost him, of all people, was incomprehensible, yet curled about her grief like a shroud was a sense of responsibility almost too great to imagine. She was now the beneficiary of a thirty per cent share in their family property, Wangallon. She was, as her father pointed out, the only legitimate Gordon left, apart from himself; nearly everyone else was buried here within the arms of the property that her great-grandfather, Hamish Gordon, founded in 1858. Sarah looked at the ancient headstones: grandmother, brother, great uncle, wives, young children and Hamish Gordon. He that had amassed what was now one of the largest privately held properties left in north-western New South Wales.

Years ago Sarah had wished for such an opportunity, dreamt of it and could admit to resentment at having been passed over because of a chance of birth. Then Cameron died and Anthony– the hired help as her mother called him – eventually became manager. Now everything was different. As a direct descendent, Sarah knew the fates had anointed her as custodian of Wangallon and she felt ill-prepared for the future. She shook her head, hoping to clear a little of the fatigue and grief that had seeped into her veins over the last week. Soon they would be booking the contractors up for lamb marking, soon they would . . . but she couldn't recall what was scheduled next, she was too tired. Leaning against the trunk of a gum tree, Sarah rested her palms on the bark beneath her. Through the canopy of leaves above her, the sky was gun-metal blue. There were few stars, for what elements could compete with the moon that now blanketed her in a mantle of silver.

'Sarah?'

Anthony's voice startled her. She'd not heard the Landcruiser approach and was unsure how long she had been weeping beneath the moon's glow. Anthony took her hand and helped her to her feet, brushing the soil from her clothes.

'I didn't want to leave you out here any longer. I know you needed to say goodbye without the hordes that were here earlier but –'

Sarah kissed him on the cheek. 'It's okay. I'm okay.'

He looked at her tear-stained face and cocked an eyebrow.

'You've barely slept this last week.' He knew, for he had laid beside her and floated on the memory of sleep as she tossed and turned through each successive night. 'You should get some rest.'

Sarah allowed herself to be led from the graveyard, listened as the latch on the small gate clicked shut. Moon shadows followed their progress.

Anthony placed a supportive arm around her slight waist. His girl had lost weight in the week since old Angus's death. Anthony was worried about her. 'We need to sit down and work out the management plans for the next twelve to eighteen months. How does that sound?' Sarah looked at him blankly. 'We've the lambs to mark and . . .' He could tell she wasn't listening; her gaze was fixed somewhere out in the darkness of the countryside. 'Don't worry, I'll handle things until you feel more up to it.' Leading her around to the passenger-side door, Anthony helped her into her seat. 'Look, I brought a little friend for you.'

Sarah stroked the shiny fat pup Anthony placed in her lap. It was Bullet, one of the pups by Angus's dog Shrapnel. She hugged the little dog fiercely. 'Grandfather wanted this one.'

Reversing the Landcruiser away from the cemetery, Anthony headed in the direction of Wangallon Homestead. 'He's yours.'

Sarah rested her hand on Anthony's thigh.

'Everything will be fine, Sarah.' His grip tightened on her fingers.

The words were so familiar. Anthony uttered them after Cameron's death, after the flood of 1986, after her parents retired to the coast and once again when her mother went into respite care.

'Really, everything will be fine,' Anthony repeated.

Once is a comfort, Sarah thought, pressing the warm, wiggling pup against her cheek, twice is not.

As they drove away a lone fox moved stealthily through the ageing monuments. The animal padded carefully through tufts of grass, pausing to sniff the air. Finally he located the freshly turned soil of Angus Gordon's grave and curled up beside the mounded earth.

Tucked up in her bed, with Anthony's rhythmic breath marking out the long hours of the night, Sarah tried unsuccessfully to sleep. Her heart seemed to have taken on a life of its own and it fluttered erratically. At times during the night she found herself clutching at her chest, her breath catching in her throat, her eyes tearing in fright. She knew grief and uncertainty were causing the symptoms she experienced, yet common sense didn't ease her distress.

As the night dragged and the moon spread its glow through the open doors leading out onto the gauze verandah, Sarah watched dancing shapes flickering about her. Outlines of branches and leaves jostled for attention like paper puppets against the cream bedroom wall as she drifted through snippets of conversation shared with her grandfather. This moment was akin to the passing of her brother, for it heralded both unwanted change and an unknown future. Who would guide them now the wily Angus Gordon was no longer with them?

Near dawn Sarah felt a numbness begin to seep through her. With a sigh she rolled on her side, only just conscious of Anthony rising to meet the working day. As the morning sun penetrated the calming dark of the room, she pulled the bedclothes over her head and closed puffy eyes against all thoughts of her changed life. The house was quiet, too quiet. A scatter of leaves on the corrugated iron roof competed with morning birdsong. Sarah huddled further down beneath the covers, tears building. She sensed movement on the verandah and tried to calm herself with her grandfather's words: *It's only the old house stretching itself, girl*, he would say. Now more than ever, Sarah doubted his words. She was one of the custodians of Wangallon now and the spirits from the past were well aware of a newly delineated present.

Part One

Autumn, 1989

Wangallon Station

Forty emus raced across the road, their long legs stretching out from beneath thickly feathered bodies as their small erect heads fastened on the fence line some five hundred metres away. Sarah couldn't resist going up a gear on the quad bike. She pressed her right thumb down firmly on the accelerator lever and leant into the rushing wind. Bullet, her part-kelpie, part-blue cattle dog, pushed up tight against her back, squirrelling sideways until his head was tucked under her armpit. She swerved off the dirt road in pursuit of the emus, the bike tipping precariously to one side before righting itself. A jolt went through her spine as the quad tyres hit rough ground. Then the bike was airborne.

Bullet lost his balance on landing. He gave a warning yelp as Sarah grabbed at his thick leather collar, managing to drag him up onto her lap. Despite the urge to go faster, she slowed the bike down, the brown blur of feathers dodging trees and scrub to outrun her. Sarah loved emus, but not the damage they did to fences or the crops they trampled. Chasing them off Wangallon, albeit onto a neighbouring property, seemed a better alternative to breaking their eggs in the nest to cull numbers. She poked along slowly on the quad until she reached the fence. A number of emus had managed to push their prehistoric bodies through the wires, while the rest ran up and down the boundary trying to find a way out. Bullet whimpered. Sarah reached the fence as the last of the mob disappeared into the scrub, scattering merino sheep in their wake.

'Sorry.' Sarah apologised as the dog jumped from the bike, turning to stare at her. Bullet never had gone much on losing his footing and it was clear Sarah would not be forgiven quickly. He walked over to the nearest tree and lay down in protest.

Two bottom wires on the fence were broken and the telltale signs of snagged wool and emu feathers on the third wire suggested this wasn't a recent break. Sarah walked along the fence, stepping over fallen branches, clumps of galvanized burr and a massive ants' nest of mounded earth a good three feet in height. Eventually she located the two lengths of wire that had sprung back on breaking. Taking the bottom wire she tugged at it and threaded it through the holes on the iron fence posts until she was back near the original break. She did the same with the second wire and then walked back to the quad bike where an old plastic milk crate was secured with rope. Inside sat a pair of pliers and the fence strainers. Grabbing the tools, Sarah cut a couple of feet off the bottom wire, then interlaced it with the freshly cut piece until it looked like a rough figure eight. She pulled on it, feeling the strain in her back, until it tightened into a secure join, then she attached the strainers and pulled back and forwards on the lever. The action tightened the wire gradually. Once taut, Sarah used the pliers to join the ends. More wire was needed to repair the bottom run but at least it would baulk any more sheep from escaping.

Whistling to Bullet to rejoin her, Sarah followed the fence for some distance on the quad before cutting across the paddock. Little winter herbage could be seen between the tufts of grass. The rain long hoped for in March and April had not arrived and May was also proving to be a dry month. It was disappointing considering the rain which had fallen in early February. Within ten days of receiving nearly six inches, there was a great body of feed and then four weeks later, with a late heatwave of 42 degree days, the heavy grass cover sucked the land dry and the feed that would have easily carried their stock through a cold winter began to die off. The pattern of the next few months was trailing out before her like a dusty road. In one month they may have to begin supplementing the cattle with feed; in two they may have to be feeding the sheep corn. By mid-July they would begin the search for agistment or perhaps place a couple of mobs of cattle on the stock route.

Mice, lizards, bush quail and insects all disturbed into movement by her bike created a sporadic pattern of scampering life amid the tufts of grass. A flat expanse of open country lay ahead, punctuated occasionally by the encompassing arms of the wilga and box trees that dominated the landscape here. Ahead, the edge of a ridge was just visible; a hazy blur of distance and heat shimmering like an island. Soon the rich black soil began to be replaced by a sandier composition, the number of trees increasing, as did the birdsong.

The midmorning sunlight streamed into the woody stand of plants, highlighting saplings growing haphazardly along its edges. They were like wayward children, some scraggly and awkward in appearance, others plump and fresh with youth. Sarah drove the quad slowly, picking her way through the ridge, passing wildflowers and white flowering cacti. The trees thickening as she advanced deeper. The air grew cooler, birds fluttered and called out; the cloying scent of a fox wafted on the breeze. The path grew sandy and the quad's tyre tracks became indistinct as the edges collapsed in the dirt. Above, the dense canopy obliterated any speck of the blue sky.

Sarah halted in the small clearing. The tang of plant life untouched by the sun's rays filled the pine-tree-bordered enclosure. She breathed deeply, revelling in the musky solitude. Through the trees on her right were the remains of the old sawpit. The pale green paint of a steam engine from the 1920s could just be seen. It was here that her grandfather Angus had cut the long lengths of pine used to build the two station-hand cottages on Wangallon's western boundary. The sawpit, long since abandoned, also marked the original entrance to Wangallon Station. Long before gazetted roads and motor vehicles decided the paths that man could take, horses, drays and carriages bumped through this winding section of the property, straight through the ridge towards Wangallon Town.

Sarah continued onwards. Soon the tall pines began to thin out, the air lost its cool caress and within minutes a glimpse of sky gradually widened to a view of open country. She weaved away from the ridge through a tangle of closely growing black wattle trees and belahs, the thin branches whipping against her face.

She was in the start of the swamp country where a large paddock was cut by the twisting Wangallon River in one corner. The area was defined by scattered trees and bone-jarringly uneven ground. A ridge ran through the paddock and it was here that sandalwood stumps spiked upwards from the ground. Sarah stopped the bike and alighted.

Years had passed since she'd last been in this area alone. It was almost impossible to believe that her beloved brother had died here in her arms over seven years ago. Kneeling, Sarah touched the ground, her fingers kneading the soft soil.

In snatches the accident came back to her. His ankle trapped in the stirrup, his hands frantically clawing at the rushing ground, and then the sickening crunch as he struck the fallen log and the spear-like sandalwood stump pierced his stomach. Sarah swiped at the tears on her cheeks, her breathing laboured. Closing her eyes she heard the shallow rasp of his breath, like the rush of wind through wavering grasses.

Anthony caught up with her a kilometre from Wangallon Homestead. Sarah could tell by the lack of shadow on the ground that she was late. His welcome figure drew closer, just as it had when he had come searching for her and Cameron all those years ago. At the sight of him the tightness across her chest eased. As the white Landcruiser pulled up alongside her quad Sarah leant towards him for a kiss. Her forefinger traced the inverted crescent-shaped scar on his cheek, the end of which tapered into the tail of a question mark. Sometimes the eight years since his arrival at Wangallon only seemed a heartbeat ago.

'You're late,' Anthony admonished.

Sarah sat back squarely on the quad seat. *So much for the welcome*.

'I was worried. What's with all these long rides around the property?'

'It's his birthday.'

'Oh.' Each passing year Cameron faded a little more from Anthony's memory. He gave what he hoped was an understanding nod. 'Been fencing?' he nodded towards the milk crate. 'You don't have to do that stuff you know, Sarah.'

If she expected a few words of comfort, Anthony was not the person to rely on. He rarely delved past the necessary. She gave a weak smile. 'I am capable of fixing a few wires.'

'I don't want you to hurt yourself,' Anthony replied with a slight hint of annoyance. 'And what's with taking off and not letting me know where you're going or how long you'll be away?'

'Sorry.'

He scratched his forehead, the action tipping his akubra onto the back of his head. 'Well, no harm done. Let's go back to the house and have a coffee.'

'Would that be a flat white? Latte? Espresso?'

Anthony rolled his eyes. 'How about Nescafé?'

Bullet barked loudly. 'Sounds good.' Sarah pushed her hat down on her head and sped off down the dirt road with Bullet's back squarely against hers. She slowed when they passed some Hereford cows grazing close to the road. 'G'day girls,' she called above the bike's engine. Bullet whimpered over her shoulder and gave a single bark as they crossed one of the many bore drains feeding their land with water. These open channels provided a maze of life for Wangallon's stock and Sarah never failed to wonder at the effort gone into their construction nearly a century ago under the watchful command of her great-grandfather Hamish. Shifting up a gear, she raced through the homestead paddock gate to speed past the massive iron workshed and the machinery shed with its four quad-runners, three motorbikes, Landcruisers and mobile mechanic's truck. Weaving through the remaining trees of their ancient orchard, Sarah braked in a spurt of dirt outside Wangallon Homestead. She smiled, watching as Bullet walked through the open back gate, pausing to look over his shoulder at her.

'I'm coming.'

Bullet spiked his ears, lifted his tail and walked on ahead.

Spring, 1908

West Wangallon

Hamish Gordon, immaculate in a dark suit, matching waistcoat and necktie, walked his black stallion along the edge of the empty bore drain. He was travelling westward across country that he'd begun to amass nearly fifty years ago and the sight of the black soil radiating from beneath him eased the ache in his lower back. Tree-filtered light dappled the track ahead and splatters of dew danced on fine spider netting nestled between tufts of grass. A breeze parted the glistening leaves of the trees, the noise like the soft shaking of linen, and he felt the breath of life on his face.

Hamish kept the reins taut on the stallion as he surveyed his land. Having once doubted if it were humanly possible for Wangallon to ever mean more to him, this year proved otherwise. His son Angus was now eight and, having fought off the various ills of childhood, Hamish was convinced that at last he had a worthy successor. When the time came, and he supposed it must, although he would fight death like every other foe, Angus would take his father's place. There was still much for the boy to learn and although Angus retained a child's capacity for foolishness, Hamish knew anything and anyone could be moulded.

The stallion started at something in the grass. The animal, a flighty newcomer to Wangallon's stable, backed up at the slightest movement and was yet to take a liking to both bridle and bit. Hamish was determined to teach the horse a measure of respect, for he intended gifting the animal to Angus at Christmas and expected the stallion to display all the attributes of a highly domesticated animal. If he didn't he'd be gelded. The horse wound its way steadily through the thick stand of ironbark trees. Hamish noticed the lack of grass growing in the densely timbered area and decided at once to have them felled. They could use the timber for a planned dividing fence while simultaneously increasing the stock-carrying capacity with the increase in grass coverage.

'We'll use this timber for the fence,' called Hamish over his shoulder to Boxer, Wangallon's head stockman.

Boxer rode with his rifle resting across his doeskin thighs, the edge of his pale coat flapping against the chestnut mare's back. 'Righto, Boss.' Spitting out a well-chewed wad of tobacco, he ran his tongue around his mouth, the pink tip of it flicking unsuccessfully at the dark juices dripping down his chin.

Hamish dropped his shoulder to skim the sticky boundary of a bush spider's domain. The large bulbous body scuttled sideways in useless anticipation as the distant bellowing of a bullock team and a series of whip cracks announced the end of the morning's ride. A speck of movement appeared in the hazy distance, growing on approach to resemble men. Hamish and Boxer drew level to follow the open channel mounded on each side by dirt. It was a tributary of the main drain that ran east to west and would eventually rejoin another arm some six miles on, watering two grazing paddocks in the process.

The bullock team was dragging a wooden one-way plough along

the predetermined path of the drain; behind it a wooden tumbling tommy scoop, also bullock drawn, gathered up the loose dirt. Hamish and Boxer rode past the drain-making contraptions. Both plough and scoop would need to make a series of passes before a usable channel appeared. Some distance ahead a team of men straddled the breadth of the drain's proposed passage, their faces red with fatigue. The rhythmic swing of axes and the dry strike of shovels gave off dull thuds as the men removed the numerous trees and fallen timber that lay in the path of the oncoming machines. Nearby a campfire expelled a stream of smoke into the cold air. Hamish could smell damper cooking.

Boxer rode across to the foreman and there was a gruff order to down tools. The men turned as one to slowly walk forward. Employed specifically to work on the drain, Hamish noted the men were a motley assortment of varying ages. Jasperson, Wangallon's overseer, had assembled a team of misfits. One wore a stained patterned waistcoat, another sported trousers sheared off roughly below the knees, three wore mismatched trouser braces, while most of their shoes were tied up with twine to stop the soles coming off. The sight of these bedraggled men took Hamish back in time to the steps of The Hill Hotel & Board over forty years ago. Filthy from days spent in the saddle, mourning the loss of his younger brother on the goldfields, he too had experienced the hollow-eyed despair these men carried with them.

Dismounting, Hamish walked across to the campfire, leaving his horse in Boxer's care. The doughy scent of coal-baked bread competed with skin unaccustomed to water and soap. It was a heady aroma.

'You the boss then?' The high-pitched voice came from the waistcoat wearer. The lad fiddled with potatoes in a saddlebag, shifted his eyes like a food-scavenging goanna. Later the potatoes would be wrapped in wet newspaper or bundled into green bark and rested among the fire's embers for their lunch. The lad was younger than he looked, Hamish surmised. A lathering of dust and sweat covered a line of pustules that ran down the left-hand side of his face like a scar. The lad suffered from the Barcoo rot.

'I am,' replied Hamish.

The men jostled uncomfortably. Hands left or entered pockets. There was a low murmur. Hamish knew the look of criminals well enough. He'd seen the chain gangs working at cutting through the heavy rock to build roads down south; winced at the smack of leather against flesh. Some of them stared with open hostility at Boxer. A black with a rifle remained an uncommon sight in these parts and the distrust was plainly evident.

'If any of you are looking for work after this job is completed, speak to Wangallon's overseer, Jasperson.'

A murmur spread out from the group like uncomfortably stored flatulence. Hamish would send one of the stockmen out this afternoon with a side of mutton and a couple of extra plugs of tobacco. There were basic ways of ensuring a measure of loyalty. Springing easily into the saddle, the stallion automatically bucked in displeasure. Hamish tugged on the reins, the horse backing up like an unruly child.

'A man has already offered us work. Doing this,' the youth pointed at the open drain.

'What's your name, boy?'

'McKenzie.'

'McKenzie. You would be from Scotland then?'

'Aye. Born in New South Wales. My father's family is Scottish.'

'And your mother's?'

'Irish. She died with the having of me, Sir.'

Hamish took another good look at the lad. He was not surprised. 'Well, McKenzie, which man are you talking about?'

'He came from over there.' The boy pointed towards the blue hazed scrub. 'Said if we was of a mind to head west and cross a big river, we'd be on his boss's land.'

Hamish knew immediately that the youth referred to Oscar Crawford. His neighbour across the river owned Crawford Corner. The family settled in the area in the 1840s, some years prior to Hamish's arrival, and as such treated him like a brash newcomer; however, it now appeared they were quite happy to try to poach his men and quite likely his stock as well. This was a subject Hamish knew much about and it would only be a matter of time before they were caught, for they mistook their own arrogance for pride.

'And you like this work, do you?' Hamish countered. 'Breaking your backs every day. Reliving the memory of working under the lash?' Some of the men glowered at him. 'I can offer you work if you are able. I've fences to be checked and repaired, trees to be felled, cattle and sheep to be mustered. In return you'll be paid, housed and given your share of station rations. If you can't do the work then you must leave. We don't beat or punish our hands, but if you wrong me I'll shoot you straight.'

The oldest of the group, a grey-haired man with a matching chest-length beard that carried the scraps of previous meals, pushed his way to the front. 'Youse can't shoot nobody these days.'

Hamish patted his moustache as if he were at a Sunday picnic discussing the price of wool. 'Really?' The word hung in the air with the threat he intended. Wangallon had a picket-fence-enclosed cemetery for those that carried the Gordon name and hollow logs and shallow diggings for the less compliant. 'Let Jasperson know of your interest or otherwise.' He turned his horse, secure in the knowledge that Boxer waited with his rifle at the ready. The old black was a crack shot and would drop four with his carbine before they knew what direction the bullets came from.

'What is it?' Hamish recognised the strained look on Boxer's face. It was a look that in the past had signalled a coming bushfire, a black woman's murder and the finding of Hamish's first wife, Rose, dead at the cemetery in the bend of the creek. 'Well?'

Hamish waited a few impatient seconds. A shadow the shape of wind-blown cloud crossed Boxer's broad face. 'Well?'

Hamish struck his spurs against the stallion's flanks and rode ahead of the ageing black and his unfathomable superstitions. Perhaps the steady crawl of age was beginning to impede the astute intuition relied upon in the past. He should put the old black out to pasture and replace him with one of his sons. Mungo was not Boxer's eldest son but he was reasonably civilised and certainly benefitted from the many months traversing the great inland stock routes with Hamish's own son Luke. Aye yes, now there was a manageable arrangement, Hamish decided; although Luke, the boss drover of Wangallon's cattle, had sent no word as to his progress these last two months. The boy had inherited the same unmanageable attitude as that of his long dead mother and it was a tiresome characteristic to put up with. At least, Hamish reminded himself, he had another son who would inherit Wangallon. In the great scheme of things that was all that mattered.

Autumn, 1989

Wangallon Station

Sarah lay flat on her stomach, a Pentax camera resting precariously on a log. This was her third attempt at photographing a lone wallaby and it was proving a far more difficult task than anticipated. Having first seen the wallaby some days ago when she and Anthony were returning on horseback from shifting a mob of sheep, she had revisited the spot twice. It was certainly a secluded setting. The remains of timber sheep yards were partially obscured by shady green peppercorn trees and the area backed onto a sandy ridge dense with radiata pine trees. It was the perfect environment for the notoriously shy wallaby.

Sarah's initial shots showed shafts of sunlight running horizontally through the branches of a peppercorn tree. The sun's rays gave an almost other-worldly feel to the broken timber railings, chest-high clumps of spear grass and red budded cactus trees in the distance. Unfortunately every time she moved to take the picture the wallaby ducked. Anyone would think you were camera shy, Sarah mused, as the light flattened out. Slowly she eased herself up from behind the log and looked through the viewfinder of the camera. The day was diminishing and with the transformation, a spindle of pink gold triangulated its way through the peppercorn's leaves. A flutter of butterflies rose from the grass and the wallaby, intent on chewing a long stem, turned its small inquisitive head towards Sarah.

Her finger clicked the shutter. The wallaby gave a small noise much like a growl and hopped away. 'Excellent.' Sarah jumped up, did a little jig in celebration of capturing what she hoped would be a Kodak moment, and then slipped the Pentax safely back into its carry case. The growl sounded again. Sarah spun around. She was half-expecting to see a wild dog or a pig or maybe even a drop bear, the mythical bush creature Anthony so loved. The noise sounded once more and she looked up to see a koala in a tall gum. Angus, her grandfather, had seen koalas during his lifetime but this was Sarah's first, and the idea that these sensitive creatures still roamed Wangallon thrilled her. She managed to get a single shot before the koala clambered higher amid the branches.

'So you found one?' Anthony appeared astride his horse, Random; so named because it was purely chance if the gelding didn't try and throw him once a month.

'You scared me.' Sarah draped the camera over her shoulder.

Anthony slid from Random, who nibbled his shoulder in an effort to court attention. 'Sorry.' He plucked a long blade of grass, tickling her ear. 'I haven't seen a koala for ages.' They peered up through the foliage. Anthony draped his arm about Sarah's shoulders and together they watched the koala scramble higher. Random snuffled their hair and tried to wriggle his head between theirs.

'What is it about this horse of yours, Anthony,' Sarah asked, scratching the gelding between the ears. 'I think he's suffering from a lack of attention.'

'Well I know how that feels,' he countered, giving her a kiss on the forehead. 'So I see you've taken up your hobby again.' He touched the camera strap.

Sarah patted the camera case. 'Actually I've missed my photography. I think I got a great shot today too. Remember that wallaby we saw?' Sarah pointed to the peppercorn and the broken timber railing. 'I captured him just there and the light was magical.'

Random gave a whinny of impatience that set Sarah's horse Tess to striking the sandy ground with a hoof. Anthony smiled. 'Well I'm pleased you're back into photography again. You always loved it. There's no reason why you can't enter a few more competitions like you did before –'

'Before grandfather died?' Sarah completed his sentence. 'Didn't feel like it before now.' She walked to her horse.

Together they rode through the peppercorns and out into the cloud-streaked sky. The evening star had risen and it was towards this bright glow that they spurred their horses. They rode side by side; diverging from the normal dirt road back to the homestead to follow one of the many sheep trails that crisscrossed Wangallon. Sarah often wondered what these trampled single-file dirt paths would look like from the heavens; leading to and from watering points and feed.

'Nice action,' Anthony commented as Sarah trotted through a gate in front of him.

She could tell by the directness of his expression that he wasn't talking about her riding ability. She pouted cheekily. 'Interested in seeing it up close and personal?'

Leaning from the saddle, he chained the gate closed. 'Before or after dinner?'

'Hmm. Depends on your appetite,' Sarah replied, breaking Tess into a canter.

They rode back to the homestead, reaching the stables as the horizon blurred between day and night. The coolness of autumn seeped upwards from the ground as they unsaddled Tess and Random. Anthony did the honours with the curry comb, giving each horse a quick brush down as Sarah put a ration of feed in their stalls. Having planned on a leg of mutton for dinner, roasted with some potatoes, carrots, pumpkin and lashings of gravy, time-wise it was looking more like spaghetti bolognese, with that special sauce only she could concoct: straight out of a jar.

'Done.' Sarah bolted the half-gate on Tess. Contented munching sounds echoed through the still air. 'Shelley's flying up this Friday. You didn't forget?'

Anthony extricated his shirt sleeve from Random's teeth and gave a final shove to the stall gate, bolting it closed. 'Geez, you're getting an attitude,' he commented. Random turned away from Anthony in disgust.

'You did forget, didn't you?' Anthony seemed to have relegated her city life into the wastepaper bin. Whether it was due to her time in Sydney being associated with her ex-fiancé or purely because he disliked the city and couldn't relate to it, she'd never been sure.

'Is she coming with or without the suit?' A glimmer of mischief crossed Anthony's face.

The suit in question was a fast-talking advertising executive, Robert, with an ex-wife, a brand new apartment and a walloping expense account that suited Shelley, aka recently crowned Lady-Lunch-a-Lot, just fine. 'Without.'

Even in the half-light she could tell he wasn't disappointed.

'Well even without him that buggers up my recreational activities for the weekend. Guess I better make up for them now.'

Sarah found herself thrown uncomfortably over Anthony's shoulder. 'You Neanderthal.'

He laughed, smacking her hard on her backside. 'That would be me.'

Sarah flung open the double doors of her bedroom and breathed in dawn's chill. The air caught at her throat and lungs, pinching at her cheeks. Young Jack Dillard, their jackeroo of twelve months, had taken particular care in fertilising the lawn during spring and summer, the result obvious in the prolonged green tinge carpeting the expanse of garden around the homestead. Within a week, however, the lawn like the rest of Wangallon's garden would begin to shut down for winter. Sarah grinned happily as she scraped her hair from her face, twisting it nonchalantly before securing it with an elasticised band. Every season on Wangallon was filled with wonder. The crisp breath of frosty mornings, birds ruffling feathers to warm themselves and bush creatures foraging amid sleeping trees were just as welcome to her as the new shoots of spring.

Rubbing sleep from her eyes, Sarah waited until a glimmer of the new day appeared in the east. Rays of red-tinged light infused trees, grass and geranium-filled pots until finally the ancient bougainvillea hedge with its straggly trails of flat green leaves and desert bright flowers of pink and red were saturated with light. *Pink in the morning*, Sarah thought, *shepherd take warning*. Her grandfather would have predicted a shower of rain within three days at the sight of this morning's sky. *Let's hope so*, she murmured, for this morning they would begin to discuss their winter feeding plans. Selecting a rusty brown sweater from the cedar wardrobe, she slipped it on.

'Morning,' Anthony said groggily.

Sarah's eyebrow lifted in amused accusation. Shelley and Anthony had gone for the *pass the port* routine after dinner last night. Sarah, never having liked any type of fortified wine, stuck with her preferred poison, a soft merlot, and consequently was feeling pretty healthy. 'Choice of beverage not agree with you, honey?' Sarah covered the few short steps to the side of the bed and planted a kiss on Anthony's sun-brown cheek. He struggled up from beneath the warmth of the bedclothes, his arms folding quickly across his bare chest.

'What's with the blast of cold air?' He frowned, glancing at the alarm clock.

'What's with the sleep-in?' she countered, softly nuzzling his neck.

Anthony squinted against the morning glare, focusing on the antiquated dresser belonging to Sarah's great-grandfather, Hamish. It was an ugly old thing made out of packing cases with large cut-off cotton reels for handles. He'd never liked it. 'We need a blind on that verandah.' He tweaked Sarah's nose playfully before trapping her in a great bear hug. 'Better still, let's move into Angus's room. It is bigger, plus it has an ensuite.'

Sarah, recalling last night's intimacies, found her thoughts quickly grounded. 'We'll survive.'

He buried his face in her neck. 'You smell of sandalwood. You always have.' He held her, his strong hands clasping her shoulders, his fingers lifting to trace her cheek. Knowing how easy it was to succumb, Sarah placed her palm against the warmth of his chest and then ruffled the rusty brown sheen of his hair. Their usual weekly meeting was due to start in half an hour. Anthony, as if reading her mind, glanced at the alarm clock.

'No,' she said strongly.

'Hey.' Anthony picked up her ruby engagement ring, twiddling it between his fingers. 'It's about time this ring had a gold band to sit beside it.'

Taking the ring, Sarah sat it back on the bedside table. His grandmother's ring and two hundred thousand dollars represented Anthony's share of his family's property and she knew he deserved every penny. 'Come on, it's a work day.'

Padding down the hallway in her socks, Sarah glanced into her grandfather's empty bedroom. On impulse she entered, drawing the heavy burgundy curtains aside. Instantly a rush of light leapt into the room. Crystal ornaments and a silver-backed hairbrush sitting on the mahogany dressing table caught the light, refracting myriad dancing squares across the still life of hydrangeas hanging above the king-sized bed. On the hardwood bedside table a picture of her grandfather with his half-brother, Luke, caught her eye. The yellowing image showed her great uncle on horseback. Her grandfather, far younger in age, stood beside him with a rifle and a brace of ducks over his shoulder.

Next door Anthony could be heard moving about their bedroom. Cupboards closed noisily, drawers stiff with age creaked on opening. Anthony's own belongings, including a number of antique items left to him by his grandmother, were still sheet-covered in one of Wangallon's many spare rooms. At some stage she would need to find homes for them, although with the house already stuffed with Gordon furniture, each piece a tangible link to their history, she was at a loss to know where they'd go.

Glancing again at the dressing table, Sarah opened one of the drawers and placed the silver hairbrush safely inside. It was a small step towards accepting that her grandfather was never going to use these items again. She made a promise to herself that during winter she would open the wardrobe and pack his clothes away for good. It was time, Sarah decided. Outside the bedroom window a willy-wagtail fluttered against the glass. The small bird, intrigued by his reflection, hovered momentarily before darting between the glossy green leaves of the hedge. Sarah turned slowly, silently wishing some of her grandfather's wisdom would seep into her.

In the months of instability and grief following her grandfather's death, Sarah worked at keeping busy. They all did. There was much to come to terms with. Angus Gordon's passing left a deep hole in their lives. It was as if a great tree had been rooted out leaving everyone without both direction and stability. Sarah didn't know when she'd awoken from grief's stupor. It was as if each new day brought with it a renewed clarity, allowing her mourning to settle into a livable although still tender state. What she did appreciate was the sense of growing maturity within her. She felt ready to embrace the next part of her life, ready to lead Wangallon into the future. In this future there would be children, heirs for Wangallon, and Anthony would be their father: A fifth generation on Wangallon. Sarah knew her ancestors would be pleased.

Late Spring, 1908

Central Western NSW

Luke Gordon hunkered down in his swag and dug his side into the rocky ground beneath. A rock poked at his hip and he thought of his father. He expects the old man would be up by now, his boots striking the wide verandah of Wangallon Homestead as he strides towards the stables. He imagines his bed still warm, a fan of hair with the black–blue gleam of a crow's wing dark against sun brightened sheets. Though it is still some hours from piccaninny daylight, Luke has been awake intermittently through the night. Aborigines have been following them and despite the steady crawl of exhaustion, he stays alert. Mungo, Boxer's son, is standing guard with two others. Out there Mungo never sleeps. He stays awake to keep the dark at bay, thinks of the girl he loves and would lie with if given the chance.

Luke hears a rider approaching the camp side of the mob. There is the crackle of twigs and the rustle of leaves as Mungo's companion arrives to wake the horse-tailer, Percy. There is the familiar sound of boots being pulled on, a coat shrugged into and the splash of urine in dirt. The fire's still hot and soon Percy is slurping his tea, his swallowing mingling with the lowing bullocks and the tethered night horses tramping the ground.

Percy's footsteps are clearly heard as he leaves the camp and heads past the night horses to where the day horses are camped. Luke opens his eyes reluctantly. He can smell fresh beef frying as the old cook coughs his lungs up. It is the thought of another thick frost that has him rising quickly to dress; boots, hat and coat. He rubs crystals of sleep from his eyes, stretches the knots in his lower back and relieves himself. A tin basin of water, iced over, sits on a log nearby. Luke cracks the ice with his pocket knife. The water stuns him awake, droplets run like ants between his neck and shirt as dawn begins to rob the countryside of its black silhouettes. The sky grows grey. It will be sometime yet before the sun takes hold of the rim of the earth and tugs itself upwards and into view.

There are grunts as five slumbering forms stir, roll up their bedding and pull on boots. Some drag their bedrolls to the fire's rim and sit silently beside the warmth.

'Food's on,' the cook calls at the top of his voice.

As boss drover, Luke takes the first plate and pours himself tea, adding two lumps of sugar from the sack where the provisions are stacked. He squats in the dirt, chewing slowly, his pannikin resting on the rocky ground before him. They are past halfway through the trek southward to market. In a month or so he plans to be feeding the bullocks in the valleys. They've done the hard part, the real snap of winter, although the mountains tend to curry favour with wind and ice and he will be pleased to be free of their cold shadow. With luck he and his team will reach the markets safely. So far in the near five months they have been on the stock route, their losses have been minimal: six dead, including the one that dislocated its shoulder crossing the gorge yesterday. Luke chews on the hunk of beef, relishing the juices. It's a fine change from salted mutton. He has told Cook to render up some of the fat for dripping, promised him another day in this same spot.

Behind him the men are silent, concentrating on waking and eating simultaneously. Luke clears small rocks from the dirt, draws a bit of a map with a greasy forefinger. By his reckoning they are about one hundred and fifty miles south-east of Ridge Gully. He's never been to this town where his mother, Rose, was born, never met his grandmother. Maybe after Christmas he'll postpone the yearly drive south, venture down that way. If he doesn't go soon his grandmother will be dead. He thinks about her emporium. It has been like a cool drink on a hot day for most of his adult life; someday the emporium will be his, then he will have an option other than this. Wiping his fingers on his doeskin trousers he remembers his dead brothers, his beloved mother. He loves droving, yet hates it. It gives a man too much time to think.

Percy returns with their horses. He has fifty-two under his watch. With eight men on horseback and two horse changes alone in daylight hours, his job of caring for their team is the most important. The men saddle up, bursts of steam rising like small clouds from their horse's nostrils. Eventually the men straggle off in the direction of the mob.

'Feed 'em into the wind,' Luke advises, knowing the stock would walk into the southerly naturally. 'We'll water them at Ned's Hollow.' Luke does a quick check of the wagon, counts the pack horses. 'Supplies right, Cook?'

The grey-haired poisoner, as the men call him, salutes. Luke takes a drag of his roll-your-own, blows the smoke clear of his eyes. Cook was in the army years ago, so he says. The men hint at a convict past. Luke doesn't care, he just needs someone who can cook without killing anyone, although there had already been sore stomachs aplenty this trip. He looks at the mountains to the east of them; great monolithic tombs of stone that block the view of the flat country on the other side. He is restless for the open plains of Wangallon, knowing full well that once he gets there he will feel the need to leave. It has been like that for a very long time; the wanting of the property, the need to be on Wangallon soil, then the reality of what it means to stay. With a final sip of his tea, he tosses the remains in the dirt, turns the collar of his coat up against the nippy southerly, the tread of 1500 cattle filling the air.

Luke turns his horse Joseph north towards the rear of the mob as the cattle walk slowly southwards. Mungo is hunched in the saddle, his hat pulled low over his dark skin. He smiles the smile of a long lost brother.

'Time for some food, Mungo.'

'Fresh cooked by a woman,' Mungo answers as if there was a choice. 'Black duck, mebbe some potatoes.'

Luke laughs. There is beef at their camp, however Mungo is more concerned about the cook who would feed him, in particular a black-haired girl Luke has never seen. 'She'd be lucky to have you.'

The Aborigine grins. Luke slaps him lightly on the arm. He has told Mungo that he's in love although his childhood friend refuses to agree with him.

'She was promised to an elder. He died. Probably by now she is promised to another.'

Luke understands his friend's feeling of frustration. 'What will you do?'

Mungo shrugs. 'She would leave the tribe.' His voice is shaded with disbelief. 'Her eyes are soft as a rabbit's, but her heart is strong. She says that this is not our land anymore. I say it is not for the owning.' He glances over his shoulder to the line of dense trees behind them. 'Them fellas out there, Boss. Might be they come too close.'

There had been little trouble with Aborigines this trip, apart from the usual skirmishes and a bit of bartering for safe passage.

Luke glances at the trees behind him, pats his carbine rifle, gestures to Mungo with a quick incline of his head. They have been followed these past two nights. Both of them have been waiting for the blackfellas to appear. They have sat under trees drooping with coldness, hugged rawhide gloved hands beneath their armpits and wiped at their snotty noses between sips of tea and snatches of conversation. Luke wonders about his friend's woman. He wants to tell Mungo to speak to his father, Boxer, who is an elder. He doesn't for fear of offence and the cautionary thought that it is blackfella business.

The familiar red and white of a bullock's hide flashes through the trees. Mungo looks knowingly at Luke as a loud bellowing announces trouble. The tail of the mob are a good three hundred feet from the tree line. Luke doesn't feel like an altercation today. Having woken a little less stiff than usual and with a portion of Wangallon beef stuffing his belly, he was hopeful of a more leisurely start. Instead he finds himself following Mungo.

They walk their horses into the timber, ten feet, twenty, thirty . . . Luke pulls quietly on Joseph's reins, Mungo points to the right. They walk single file through the trees, Luke with one hand on his rifle. There is the crashing noise of a large animal charging through the dense woody growth. The sound echoes loudly for long minutes. An ambush is a distinct possibility, especially here where the trees grow so tightly they appear to have been planted in rows. Another thirty feet on, Mungo heads left. Luke grimaces at the noise of hoofs on leaf litter, his eyes searching for a patch of sky in the canopy above. Joseph pricks his ears and halts mid-stride. Three Aborigines block their path.

Two of them wear torn white men's clothing. Renegades from a station, Luke assumes. The other is tall with a long spear in his hand and alert eyes stare from within the roughness of bark, like skin. He has a wiry beard and a narrow, bony chest, which carries a number of scars thick with age. A possum skin coat, the fur next to his skin, is dragged over one shoulder. Behind the trio a freshly speared bullock kicks its last amid the trees. Luke draws his forefinger tight against the rifle's trigger, lifts the weapon very slowly. He is ready to shoot. Mungo climbs down from his horse and lifts his empty hands towards the trio. The two renegades carry nulla-nullas. One blow could crack a man's head. Luke knows he and Mungo are in a precarious position. Yet his old friend is talking softly and taking a step towards the warrior with the raised spear.

The black answers with a string of unintelligible words, his eyes a yellow white pricked by brown. He points at Luke as if he were a leper, the horizontal crack of his mouth spitting anger. Luke would rather shoot the man dead. They are wasting time and his gut tells him that this is one black that should be put down. Mungo is still talking when the spear is raised and thrown. Luke manages to fire off a single round at one of the renegades, then his flesh is pierced and he is thrown back out of his saddle as Joseph rears in fright.

≪ *Autumn, 1989* ≫

Wangallon Station

In the kitchen Sarah made coffee for three, strong and black, adding milk and sugar to soften the bite of her own cupful. She couldn't imagine Shelley showing herself for at least an hour, so Sarah decided to wait to have breakfast with her. On the old pine kitchen table she placed a notepad and pen, a blue and white bowl filled with apples and mandarins and waited for Matt Schipp, Wangallon's head stockman, to knock at the back door. The kitchen wall clock struck 7.15 a.m. exactly as Matt's thick knuckles struck the doorframe. By the time Matt was seated, coffee in hand and his signature laconic grin in place, Anthony was already halfway through a crunchy red apple.

'I was about to ask Matt –' Sarah began, after they'd all commented on the fine morning.

'Can we just discuss a couple of staff issues first, Sarah?' Anthony interrupted, biting the core of the apple in half and devouring it in two bites.

Sarah leant back in the wooden chair. Clearly it hadn't been a question.

'I was hoping young Jack was ready for a step up the ladder.'

'He is,' Matt answered, swallowing a good mouthful of his coffee. 'Good kid. Listens well, takes advice.'

'I'm pleased to hear it,' Sarah agreed. Only last week she had complimented the young jackeroo on the fine job he'd done with the garden. She would be sorry to see him go, even if he was only asked to spend one workday a week giving her a helping hand. 'Perhaps he could come and help once a fortnight –'

'Take him out with you next time, Matt.' Anthony spoke over Sarah. 'Maybe put him in charge of moving that next mob of ewes.' He reached across the table for another apple. 'I can't promote the kid and then send him back into the garden, Sarah.'

Matt looked from Anthony to Sarah, before reaching for a mandarin. His blunt, perpetually saddle-oil-stained fingernails mangled both the skin of the mandarin and the soft flesh of the fruit.

'I had a look at that fence over at West Wangallon,' Anthony continued. 'It must be nearly fifty years old. I thought we could make it one of our winter projects.'

'Matt doesn't do fencing.' Sarah winked conspiratorially at their head stockman. Her grandfather hired Matt just before his death and his continued employment on Wangallon hinged on the verbal promise that he would only ever work with stock. Anthony frowned. 'Matt knows you don't get to pick and choose your jobs in the bush, Sarah.'

'I'll send one of the boys over to check the fence,' Matt offered peaceably, while effectively extricating himself from the job. 'I'm thinking we'll need to open the silage pit in a fortnight, start feeding the cows. The early oats we planted will last the steers out until sale time, but we can't risk shortening their fattening time by adding to their numbers. Probably be worthwhile selling a couple of hundred of those late weaners. And now would be the time to do a pregnancy test, then cull any cows not in calf. As for the sheep –'

'Sounds good to me, Matt,' Sarah interrupted. It was exactly what she had been thinking over the last few days. 'I've found some corn, we can get it delivered next week and –'

Anthony scraped his chair back. 'I'll think about it. I'm not convinced that we can't put fifty or so more steers on the oats and I'm not in favour of opening the silage up too soon.'

A slight frown crossed Matt's weathered face. 'Any cow in calf needs to begin receiving supplementary silage in a fortnight – in fact the sooner the better. Unfortunately, mate, there's not much we can do about it.'

'Leave it a week or so longer.' Anthony drained his coffee. 'The old girls can scrimmage around for an extra ten days or so. Feeding the silage out should be a last resort.'

Matt shook his head, pursed his lips together. 'We don't know when it's going to rain and nothing's going to grow during winter. If you're hoping that the silage will see us through, it may not; besides, you just can't feed them that, there are not enough nutrients in it. And if it doesn't rain then we'll have to truck weak cattle out on agistment. Sorry, I really think the pit should be opened.'

Sarah expected to hear a small explosion going off, or the voice of her grandfather telling these two young quarrelling pups to wake up to themselves. Instead she spoke across the tensing silence, explaining that the stock route would be a good option, that they could delay the opening of the pit by five days and then plan to put some of the cows on the road, sixteen hundred or so. The rest could be spread around Wangallon to safely calve, assured of enough feed to get them through until spring when hopefully it would rain.

'There's no one on the route around here at the moment. And although it's mainly dry feed, there's a lot of it and the watering points are all good.' Sarah gave an encouraging smile to the two silent men.

Matt was the first to speak. He begrudgingly agreed and offered to call a drover he knew of in Queensland, then he excused himself. Sarah was left facing Anthony across the table.

'Was that necessary?' Anthony asked, pulling a red cooper's notebook from his shirt pocket and noting down some figures with a stubby pencil.

'I'm sorry?'

'We were talking about the right time to open the silage, now you have us on the stock route in a matter of weeks.'

Sarah clasped her coffee mug. 'You can't try to feed all the stock here, Anthony. We need a contingency plan and waiting until the last gasp when we're out of feed and the cattle are weak is not an option.'

Anthony tucked the notebook back in his pocket. 'Well, you suddenly seem to have developed very strong opinions.'

Sarah placed their coffee mugs on the kitchen sink. Had she? It seemed like common sense. In her heart Sarah knew her plan was good. And if it stopped Matt and Anthony from agreeing to disagree, there was an added bonus. She thought back to their opening conversation and Jack Dillard's promotion. 'So I'm expected to handle the garden as well?' Sarah rinsed their mugs out and sat them on the sink. She knew he considered big bush gardens a waste of space, time and water. Especially as they rarely had time to enjoy it.

'It amazes me that old Angus employed Matt. He is becoming more like a manager every day and Wangallon doesn't need two of us.'

'He's head stockman,' Sarah reminded him. She wanted to add that Matt wasn't going anywhere, but now wasn't the time to explain Matt's employment terms. Sarah could only imagine the look on Anthony's face. 'The man has almost no dexterity left in six of his ten fingers.' Having caught his fingers in a grain auger years ago, Matt had turned his original agricultural interest from dry land farming to stock work.

'And doesn't he let us know it.' Anthony was on the back porch pulling on his riding boots.

Sarah was ready to launch into a polite reminder of her place in the Wangallon feed chain. She was not prepared to give up paddock time to look after the garden and both Anthony and she were meant to be sharing the managerial responsibilities; however the telephone was ringing and Matt could be heard on the two-way radio talking to another stockman about straying cattle. Picking up the telephone, Sarah put her hand over the receiver. There was little point staying annoyed with him. 'What are you up to this morning?' The back door slammed in reply. 'Well great, just great.' Thank God Shelley liked her sleep-ins. 'Good morning, Wangallon,' Sarah spoke into the telephone, sounding happier than she felt.

Late Spring, 1908

Central Western NSW

Luke is not sure what part of his body hurts more. He raises his hand and touches the back of his head where it hit a knobbly tree trunk. His skull is sticky; blood and brown hair glaze his fingers. Struggling into a sitting position, he looks grimly at his shoulder. The spear has been pulled free of his flesh. Mungo has worked quickly, pouring liquid from his canvas waterbag to clean the wound, which is bleeding freely. Blood mixes with the brown tinge of creek water.

'It's not so bad,' Mungo grins.

Luke flinches at the pain as he staggers to his feet. One of the blacks lies a few feet away. The other two have vanished into the trees.

'They'll be back,' Mungo advises, gesturing with a quick nod of his head at the dead animal. 'Come.' Mungo helps him onto Joseph, leading him back towards the clearing.

'They're hungry,' Luke says stiffly, breathing through the throbbing pain.

Mungo scratches his chin thoughtfully. 'He's a warrior. I've heard of him further north.'

'He doesn't stay with his people?' Luke, now painfully aware of how fast a spear can fly, considers his team's vulnerability.

'Some of my people want to return to the old ways. They want their land back.'

The mountains hover above them. Luke shivers at the chill of the wind. In this land everything is about ownership.

At the camp the cook's indistinguishable monologue deteriorates into a string of concerned abuse. Luke checks once on the herd before sitting by the fire. They are feeding out happily. 'Once everything is watered and rested for an hour or so, we'll walk them onwards. It's another seven or eight miles to the next night camp, Mungo.'

Mungo looks at a grey tail of cloud snaking above, as if questioning Luke's timing.

'You'll make it. Once the herd sniff the water at the Hanging Hole there'll be no stopping them.' Luke knows Mungo hates making camp at this spot where blackfellas and whites fought last century. When they camp there Mungo hears screams and yells, sees their shadowy forms in battle under the glow of the moon. The worst of Mungo's doctoring is yet to come and Luke grimaces at the thought of their isolation. Although it is Mungo's unstated role to converse with the dark peoples that roam the bush, Luke is aware of a feeling of responsibility towards his old friend. For that reason alone he is pleased to be the one injured.

Mungo flashes his teeth as he pulls Luke's riding coat free of his shoulder and rips open his shirt. A small comb, such as those made for a woman's hair, falls to the ground. Mungo picks it up with a bloody hand, his scraggly nails dark with congealed blood. 'I tell you about my woman and you?'

Luke gave a pained, lopsided grin. 'I dream.'

'Then maybe you keep with you until the spirits answer.' Mungo stuffs the comb inside Luke's coat pocket and frowns as he directs his thoughts to his ministrations. There is a short bladed pocket-knife already positioned in the glowing embers of the fire. The cook, not much for talking now that his morning peace has been ruined by a bloody wounding, pulls a cork from a rum bottle and offers Luke a swig. His eyes watch Luke's bobbing throat. He retrieves the bottle, then, licking his lips, thinks better of it and takes a long swig himself, his eyes white as Mungo lifts the knife from the fire.

Luke turns his head from the glowing blade and grits his teeth. He thinks of the money this sale of cattle will bring; of the supplies that will be purchased. Was a man's death a fair exchange for the continuation of his father's dream? Instead of answering his question Luke thinks of the excitement that would greet the mail when a bolt of fine dress silk or a length of cream-coloured lace arrived. She was the reason he always returned to Wangallon, and why he had become a drover, to get away again.

Mungo pours rum on the open wound and then presses the blade down harshly to cauterise the flesh. 'You visit your girl in Wangallon Town,' Mungo suggests as a diversion.

Luke growls; he has no girl. The stench of burning skin fills the air as Luke passes out amid a contorted grimace. The cook grunts in disgust and swills more rum. Mungo's pink-tipped tongue flicks with concern as he prods at the red skin surrounding the wound. He looks up at the cook and grins, his teeth a flash of righteousness.

Summer, 1908

Wangallon Station

Hamish stalked the verandah, pausing occasionally to puff irritably on his pipe. An unseasonal mist, thickened by moist air and cooling temperatures, hung stubbornly about him, obliterating his world. The gravel driveway, the wavering trees, even the flowering shrubs that hedged in Wangallon Homestead were barely visible. From his waistcoat he retrieved his gold fob watch, impatiently noting that only a paltry ten minutes had passed. With a disgusted puff of his pipe he sat heavily in one of the wicker chairs lining the verandah, listening to the household. The distant clang of pots and the stacking of crockery carried sharply in the still air above which hovered the maids' muffled giggling and the deeper intonation of Mrs Stackland, their cook and housekeeper. The combined noise was akin to the drone of a bee. The scent of baking bread was the only agreeable aspect to his sensory disturbance.

'Hamish?'

Claire is dressed in white muslin from neck to ankle, a fine brocade wrap about her shoulders. Walking sedately behind her is a rather overfed cat, a tabby that Hamish detests. He glares at the cat, knowing the feeling is mutual.

'The weather is most unusual,' Claire allows the cat to settle comfortably on her knees.

Hamish scowls. The cat purrs loudly in defiance.

'It is a nice respite from last week's heat and wind.' Claire's rhythmic stroking makes the tabby's contentment even louder. 'I seem to recall similar weather conditions led to a poor start last year to the season.' She plucks at a loose strand of cotton on the buttoned wrist of her blouse. She had been born in this most unfathomable of countries, yet fifty-six years on, her daily life, her very subsistence, still depended on the vagrancies of the heavens. To be held to ransom by the gods of the sky had, she decided, been a most humbling experience since her arrival at Wangallon. 'It is nearing half-past six, Hamish. Soon this slight fog will burn off and Jasperson will be here to drag you off to some distant part of Wangallon. Why don't you eat something?' Hamish was gazing beyond the silhouette of a native tree. Her fingers touched the hard darkness of his hand. He was looking at her like someone awoken from a deep sleep. 'Take a little tea and some fresh fruit loaf,' she continued. 'Lee has managed to plead his way into Mrs Stackland's kitchen.'

Hamish pulled his hand free of her touch. Claire smoothed her skirt over her knees, disturbing the cat, who growled softly in reproach. 'It has been a year of firsts for our great country,' Claire began, hoping there was some suitable topic in which they could both engage. 'How I would love to have witnessed the great fleet of the United States of America visiting our shores, or seen the first surf carnival held at Manly Beach.'

Hamish stared stonily ahead.

'And how wonderful an explorer is Douglas Mawson', she persevered. 'Imagine climbing a 13,000 foot high volcanic cone in Antarctica of all places.' The mist was lifting. Streaks of blue were interlaced with fluffy balls of white cloud. 'I've received correspondence from Mrs Oscar Crawford.' Surprisingly, at this, Hamish actually turned his attention to her. Claire seized on the opportunity. 'My dear, it would seem their eldest, William, has completed his law degree and is travelling north to visit his father. Oscar Crawford has been ensconced next door for the last six months. I do find it strange that he does not hold some gathering to which we might attend. In Sydney they are quite the fashionable couple. Still, perhaps he feels ill-equipped to entertain without the advices of his good wife.'

Hamish rubbed at his moustache. Having already made an offer to purchase Crawford Corner not twelve months prior, he was beginning to see the virtue in Claire's relationship with the Englishman's wife. 'Mrs Crawford must despair of his ever returning to Sydney.'

'Indeed, one must wonder at his desire to remain on his holding with his younger daughter now married, his dear wife in Sydney and his sons with little interest in the property.'

Hamish stretched his neck and shoulders. Perhaps the time was at hand to approach the man again. 'I must agree with you on that account, Claire.'

Claire tucked a stray tendril of hair behind her ear. Perhaps later in the day she would wash her hair and perfume the final rinse with a few drops of lavender water. Then when the sun drew close to its midpoint she would fluff the long strands dry in the growing heat before retiring to the drawing room and her quilting. She should discuss dinner with Mrs Stackland. It was possible there was some tasty treat the woman could conjure. While she was not a fan of jugged wallaby, Hamish's favourite dish, she was partial to roasted stubble quail, and a refreshing jelly would be a nice cooling dessert. In the midst of her thoughts Lee shuffled onto the verandah, a large tray clasped between his bony fingers. His knees, bowed by age, stuck out like those of a stick insect from beneath his tunic and he moved like a man who, although having seen too much, considered it an honour to have done so.

With the tray finally deposited on the wicker table nearest Hamish, he took one sandalled step backwards and grinned. A silver teapot and a fine blue and white patterned cup and saucer sat next to a bowl of sugar, a pad of rich yellow butter and two thick chunks of fruit loaf.

Claire gave Lee a grateful smile. 'It would seem Lee had similar thoughts regarding your sustenance.'

'You like?' Lee asked, all grin and horizontal wrinkles. His long bony fingers twisted in and out from beneath each other like garden worms as he snarled at the cat, which, in turn, hissed back. Claire showed her annoyance at this unnecessary exchange by placing her hand proprietarily on the tabby's head.

Hamish prodded the bread, cut a slice in half and smelled it appreciatively before spreading a generous amount of butter over the loaf. He devoured it quickly, licking his fingers as Lee poured the tea. 'Excellent. You are an extraordinary cook, Lee. Mrs Stackland should be forever grateful for your presence.'

Claire clutched at the cane under her hands. Sometimes she believed her husband cared more for the Chinaman than his own wife. Lee was not an employee, although Hamish provided for his every need. When it pleased him to oversee the kitchen he did just that; if he decided to spend days tending his formidable vegetable garden, that too was acceptable. If Lee was adamant about churning the butter, ensuring it was turned and well-aired in the pantry with the right amount of salt to taste, it was to the household's good fortune and if he chose, as he did, to remain in a one-room bark hut beyond his vegetable patch instead of accepting a more comfortable iron roofed dwelling, well that was his decision too.

Lee snarled at the tabby twice for good measure, bringing his hand down in a chopping movement. The cat jumped from

Claire's lap and Lee's eyelids flattened as his features elongated into a treacherous grin.

'No, Lee,' Claire reprimanded. Lee bowed his head and took his leave. She was sure that were it not for her presence, cat stew would be on the menu. 'Will Luke return in time for Christmas?'

'Of course,' Hamish placated, aware his eldest would be holed up at the Wangallon Town Hotel for a time, no doubt dipping his wick before returning for Christmas.

'And may we obtain some greenery with which to decorate the verandah's wooden posts? And can we have our own tree, Hamish? As long as it's green and sappy when freshly cut', she argued, 'it could be carefully trimmed with coloured paper and candles.'

'Yes, yes.' Why did women need to unburden their minds with every morsel of what comprised their heads? Did he really look that interested? As if cued to relieve him of such tedious examining, his son Angus raced out of the house. His violet eyes flicked to the freedom of the garden and beyond, then he was running towards them, his sandy-coloured hair plastered to his brow with beads of sweat, a slingshot in his hand. Claire placed a restraining arm on Angus, drawing him to her side. Already the child was dishevelled, his hands grimy with dirt. 'Walk if you please, Angus,' Claire reprimanded. 'And don't fire at the maids or the cat,' Claire reminded her son.

'It's like father's,' Angus responded proudly, holding the slingshot towards his mother.

Claire had long since learnt that her husband's early years in the highlands of Scotland did not lend themselves to idle hours of play. They were spent carrying rocks to build fences, shovelling cow manure from their dirt-floored hut during the winter and burying his small sisters, brothers and finally his mother. No wonder he had left his homeland.

'Come, Angus.' Hamish got to his feet. Angus followed his father without glancing back.

Left alone on the verandah, Claire fluffed her skirts. Her husband and son shared a bond Claire could never be a part of. There was a knowing within them both, an understanding of each other's role within their respective lives. As a mother she knew how fortunate they were to have such a relationship. As a woman it was almost as if she had been abandoned on a barren island, even though she knew their behaviour was not meant to cause pain.

Autumn, 1989

Wangallon Station

Sarah and Shelley were chopping down jade near the back gate. The plant was overgrown and it was taking quite a lot of muscle to saw through the thick woody stems. Bullet sat nearby, occasionally looking up as if to join in on the conversation.

'So it's that serious then?' Sarah asked, wiping perspiration from her forehead. It was a mild 20 degrees yet by midafternoon a southerly change would be upon them with the temperature due to drop to six degrees overnight.

'Serious enough to be talking marriage.' Shelley was almost coy.

'Marriage,' Sarah squealed. Extricating a wrist-thick trunk of jade she threw it on top of the pile in the wheel barrow and gave Shelley a hug. 'And it took the whole weekend for you to tell me?'

Shelley removed her black sweater and retied her recently dyed hair. This year blonde was her colour of choice and considering she was finally in a great relationship and had been promoted to senior consultant at the recruitment firm where she worked, clearly it was the pick of the five different shades she had road-tested over the last three years. 'Two reasons. Firstly I figured it was bad luck to say anything before I was officially engaged.'

'Couldn't help yourself?' Sarah teased.

'Secondly, well, I don't want a long engagement.' Shelley hesitated, 'I don't think it's necessary, not if you really love someone.' She looked pointedly at Sarah as her friend began sawing through another fibrous branch.

Sarah passed her the saw. 'Here, you have a go.'

'Please don't get angry, Sarah, but are you happy? Really happy?' Shelley stared at her, the saw dangling from her hands.

'Of course, silly. I just don't see the rush. We're not exactly over the hill. I'm not quite twenty-five.' Retrieving the saw Sarah attacked another section of the jade. Shelley always managed to push her buttons. 'Besides, there's been a fair bit for me to come to terms with and I just haven't been in the right place to go forward.'

'But I heard you arguing this morning and you rarely come down to Sydney anymore and what happened to your photography? It was your profession and you were damn good at it. I don't want you staying here for a bunch of ghosts,' Shelley said sullenly. Her closest friend was like a frog in a sock and she didn't even realise it.

'I'm not an employee, Shelley.' Sarah snapped. 'Look, Wangallon is a big business and I'm in charge.' Taking a breath, she calmed. 'Actually I've just started taking a few shots again.'

'Well good, but what about the visits to Sydney? Why can't you leave Anthony to mind the fort? He's been running the place for long enough and he's as obsessed with this pile of history as you are.' If Sarah didn't stop sawing there was only going to be a stump left. She touched her arm. 'Well?'

'I'm not going anywhere, Shelley. There are only a couple of months to go before we know the property is safe. Believe me, I've done my best not to think about Grandfather's will since his death but with spring only a matter of months away I feel like I'm one of those bomb disposal experts who suddenly doesn't know whether they should be cutting the red wire or the blue.'

'I'm sorry. With all the time that's elapsed I forgot about the inheritance debacle. What does Anthony say?'

'Nothing. At least nothing helpful since we argued about it eighteen months ago. *The morally correct thing* is his standard answer. We haven't talked about it since. Frankly it's been easier for me to bury it and I'm still hopeful it will go away.'

Bullet rushed out the back gate. Matt and Anthony were trotting up the road on horseback. Sarah looked up, frowning. 'Something's wrong.' She took off her gardening gloves and moved towards the men.

There was a dog lying across Matt's lap; a ten-year-old kelpie christened Ferret, because of his habit of sticking his nose into everything. Anthony slid off his horse, took Ferret from Matt and both men strode up the back path.

Shelley looked at the blood dripping onto the cement path. There was a spreading stain of bloody wetness on Matt's thigh and his face was set like cracked concrete.

'He needs a vet,' Shelley stated, hanging back from the rush to get the hurt animal inside.

'Sarah, I need to set the leg. It's busted. Plus he needs to be stitched up. He's lost a lot of blood.' Anthony's face was creased in concern as he took the back steps in a single leap.

'Righto.'

With the dog on the kitchen sink and water boiling, Sarah sterilised the needle while Anthony washed the wound with Pine O Cleen. Ferret whined softly, his eyes never leaving Matt, who, with Shelley's help, was slicing a piece of thick plastic tubing lengthways.

'What happened?' Sarah asked as she mopped blood around Ferret's wound while Anthony sewed stitches into the dog's hind leg. The air was taut with unsaid words. Clearly Ferret's accident hadn't lead to any mutual bonding.

'He jumped off my horse into some long grass,' Matt answered. 'Shouldn't have had him on there what with his arthritis, but he loves it. Don't you, old mate?' Matt stroked Ferret between the ears.

Anthony glanced at Sarah. 'Reckon that's how he busted his leg. The cut came from the bore pig he was chasing. He's got some buggered tendons here by the looks of it.'

Shelley peered over Anthony's shoulder. 'Are you a vet?' She grimaced at the ooze of blood and stringy muscle.

Anthony frowned at her. 'No, but I have a brain.'

'*Sorry*.'

'Damn pigs.' Sarah rethreaded the needle. 'The bloody lot of them should be culled. Sure you don't want me to take him to the vet, Matt?'

Matt shook his head, his pale eyes glassy and tired-looking. 'Tendons buggered in one leg, the other busted up. He's as good as lame. The best I can do is tie the old fella up under a tree for a month or so and see how he heals.'

Anthony placed a thick smear of Rawleigh's salve over the wound and then bandaged it up, smearing a globule of the gooey antiseptic on his jeans.

The broken leg was a far less messy affair. Matt held Ferret as Anthony gave the dog's hind leg a rough yank. There was the click of bone and a whinny from Ferret. Then the dog was silent.

'He's dead,' Shelley sniffed. The only dead thing she'd seen recently was a cockroach in her apartment. She experienced an urge to reach out her hand and poke the dog in the ribs. Instead she watched as the restraightened leg was bandaged. Matt then proceeded to slip the thick rubber tubing around the break. It was a snug contraption held in place with black electrical tape. 'There you go, boy.'

Shelley was stunned when the dog lifted its head as if in gratitude.

With Ferret on the back porch wrapped in a blanket, the mess tidied in the kitchen and Sarah's offer to care for Ferret accepted, Shelley was surprised when coffee was refused by both men.

'Something I said?' Shelley asked as she watched Matt and Anthony walk down the back path to their horses. She had to admit it she was admiring more than the cut of their jeans. 'Cute buns.'

'Thought you were about to be engaged.' Sarah cut two wedges of thick cheese and plonked them on a couple of crackers.

'Well you know what they say. It doesn't matter where you get your appetite from as long as you eat at home.'

'Those two have a bit of a love hate relationship going on at the moment.' Sarah took a bite of her cracker. 'Actually, they're like young horses that both want to lead.'

Shelley sat down at the kitchen table and peered knowingly at Sarah over her coffee. Someone couldn't see the forest for the trees.

Summer, 1908

Five miles north of Wangallon Town

Hamish escorted Claire to the picnic rug that lay beneath the spreading arms of a gum tree and deposited her next to the bank manager's wife, Hilda, and her two daughters, Henrietta and Jane. A picnic after their fortnightly church service was a regular event during the warmer months and the one held in honour of Christmas was a mildly entertaining one. It surprised him that Claire, always complaining about the dearth of social opportunities, never attended these gatherings with more enthusiasm. The grouping was select, with invitations only extended to six families, a communal picnic table set up for all to enjoy. Hilda Webb inclined her chin coquettishly at Hamish as only a woman assured of her position in society could do. She fluttered eyelashes grown sparse, Hamish surmised, from overuse and bade him a fine day. As bank manager, her husband Reginald scaled the hierarchy of social class in terms of importance and Hilda dictated that it was only proper she and Claire sit together.

'You'd be looking for rain,' Reginald stated when Hamish

managed to extricate himself from Mrs Webb. 'I, myself, am grateful for the dry conditions.' He took a pinch of snuff from an ornate royal blue and sterling silver box and snorted the powder up each nostril. 'I must say I do believe that doctor in Sydney was correct. This dry air has improved my lungs substantially.'

'Indeed, although I doubt your current seat can compare with the sandstone edifice of the Bank of New South Wales,' stated Hamish. 'However, in answer to your question, yes, I do hope for an early break to the season.' Hamish sated his thirst on the rather sickly punch sitting on the white clothed wooden table and waited for the maids to unpack something a little more suitable to his temperament.

'And how's your son Luke?'

Hamish embarked on a detailed description of the herd's trek southward, relying on his own past experience and not the detailed reportage Luke refused to write him. 'I've been thinking of approaching Crawford again,' Hamish revealed, reliant on Reginald for any snippet of information. The bank manager carried the fateful trait of honesty, which assured Hamish of correct information. However, it also meant that Crawford would eventually hear of Hamish's renewed intentions.

Reginald took a sip of punch. 'The man's employed a new stud master, Jacob Wetherly. So I doubt he'd be interested. However I believe there is a settler's block coming up again to the east of your holding. Shall I investigate?'

'Yes, do. Wetherly, you say. The name is familiar.'

'Yes, he should be joining us today. Wetherly's highly regarded in the sheep breeding business although he's a southerner. Don't go much on them myself. The further one travels south in this great country of ours the more the landed become enmeshed with delusions of grandeur.' Reginald slurped his punch and patted his moustache with a snowy white handkerchief. 'Damn awful stuff.'

Hamish accepted a French brandy and a dry cracker from a maid and ensured Reginald was attended to. 'That's better,' Hamish announced, finishing the glass and calling the maid back for a refill.

'Indeed,' Reginald agreed. 'Crawford's determined to increase the greasy fleece weight of his flock. The market's certainly holding its interest.'

'A trend only,' Hamish remarked. 'The competition that has been growing among producers will weaken eventually. Those Vermont imports from Spain will soon go out of favour. The greasy wrinkles in the skin make the battle with flies interminable. We never had those blasted green maggoty blowflies before the Vermont arrived in this country.'

'Still,' Reginald reminded him, 'greasy fleece weight is where the money is and Wetherly was getting results until he embarked on his own mating program.' He narrowed his eyes for emphasis.

Hamish was not one to go against the vagaries of the market when said market was paying top dollar. Besides which, his last clip had topped the selling season. As for Crawford's plans for his flock, nabbing the highly regarded Jacob Wetherly would put an end to that. And while employing Wetherly may not increase the chances of Crawford selling up, it was an opportunity to remind the Englishman of the undeniable benefits of the open market, especially if Oscar Crawford persisted in living next to Wangallon.

The maids began laying food on the table. Hamish and Reginald eyed parrot pie, small damper rolls, sliced mutton, potatoes, the usual fatty dish of fried fish provided by the minister's household, and a duck and quail casserole. Hamish poured more brandy as the women came forward to be served. He greeted Hilda Webb and her red-haired daughters, chatted to the minister's wife, Mrs Ovendale, and even felt gracious enough to comment on the storekeeper's recent business investment into timber. A mill to service the demographic increase of Wangallon Town was a common-sense plan.

Five miles north of Wangallon Town

'Here is Jacob Wetherly now,' Reginald announced as a dapper figure approached the parkland surrounds on the banks of the creek. 'Of course Crawford can never be persuaded to venture forth for an outing.'

'Pity,' Hamish agreed sociably, although personally the opportunity for information gathering was the sole reason he bore such engagements. Wetherly tethered his horse to the branch of a shady gum. 'I believe I will offer him a position,' Hamish announced to the bemused bank manager.

'A position? I doubt that he would . . . but of course, come then,' Reginald offered, 'let me introduce you.'

Hamish was askance. Did the man think he would follow? 'You can bring him to me,' he stated formally, picking up a plate and dishing up some of the quail and duck concoction. He never was one for mixing meats, but one had to make do occasionally.

Claire tired of Hilda's ongoing description of how markedly fine her daughter's matching set of hair tongs, curlers, shoe buttoner and shoe horn were, and looked with disinterest about the scattered picnic rugs. The shopkeeper's family, the Stevens, sat with an English couple who owned a pleasing amount of land to the south of Wangallon Town. Further away reclined the minister and his family – the three sons of whom were off, no doubt, making mischief with Angus. Sally Foster laughed delightedly at an anecdote shared by Mrs Ovendale. Claire would like to have extended an invitation for Sally to join her, however, having married a Baptist some years ago, she'd fallen foul of Hamish who believed that a Scot's Presbyterian should stay with their own.

Claire brushed at the line of ants crawling across the picnic rug and shifted her position. Her whalebone corset was troubling her today, a usual occurrence during summer, and she pined for the coolness of her bedroom. She untied the chiffon scarf securing her curved brimmed hat and let the air waft about her.

'Mr Stevens has invested in timber,' Mrs Webb began by way of conversation, cutting through Claire's daydreams. 'I find the very concept of a trade abominable. Do you not, Mrs Gordon? The very thought of such a life, well,' Mrs Webb gave a convulsive shiver. 'Some say he is clever. Who can be clever in a small town is my response, for there is none to compare the man with.' She ate a morsel of salted mutton and sipped at a warm glass of punch. 'I find him altogether too shrewd, particularly as the foundations for another hotel are being laid almost diagonally opposite the current one. Besides which those that own a general store always know who has money and who does not. To my thinking that is most unpalatable.'

'A big fish in a small pond?' Claire remarked.

'Exactly.' Hilda patted Claire's gown. 'I saw that very ensemble in the Grace Brothers' catalogue. I myself have never been one for all white.'

'Mother thinks it decadent,' Henrietta stated prettily. Jane took a bite of her parrot pie, the pastry crumbling down the front of her somber grey blouse. 'Decadent,' she repeated as if the food she ate had somehow intrinsically weaved its way into her vocal chords.

Claire, having never seen Hilda in anything other than black, patted the older woman's hand. 'Nonsense, white would suit you very well.'

Hilda gave a dimpled smile and then pounced on the arrival of Jacob Wetherly. 'My dear husband promised us some entertainments today, did he not, my girls?'

'Yes, Mama,' Henrietta and Jane answered with the synchronicity of rehearsed obedience.

'A fine style of a man, Mrs Gordon,' Mrs Webb observed. 'He's been employed down south on a highly regarded property for some fifteen years. They say he fell afoul of the owner.' Hilda leant conspiratorially towards Claire. 'There is talk of a liaison with no other than Mrs Henry Constable.'

'No,' Claire whispered. 'How impossibly salacious.' And not at all surprising, Claire decided, as both she and Mrs Webb lifted their fans and under cover of much fluttering stared blatantly at the new arrival. 'Mrs Henry Constable must be –'

'Forty-five in the shade my dear, with five children. Oh he is a fine form of a man,' Hilda said breathily.

Claire couldn't disagree. Jacob Wetherly was tall and wore his clothes well. Dark-haired and straight-backed with a becoming dark tan to his skin, his was a welcome addition to their gathering.

'There is also the whisper of an estate in England.' Mrs Webb tapped Claire on the forearm, 'although there is disagreement as to his actual worth. It would seem Mr Gordon has taken to him.'

It was true, Claire observed, fascinated as Mr Webb provided introductions. Hamish led the man aside, gesturing with his hands animatedly. Claire had witnessed such persuasion before although at the moment she was unsure as to the nature of this particular exchange. Jacob Wetherly's expression alternated from surprise to interest to momentary quiet. Finally the two men shook hands. Claire lowered her fan. Mr Wetherly was looking directly at her. She averted her eyes, for once grateful of Henrietta and Jane's prattling and her curved brim hat. Claire busied herself with the fried fish Mrs Ovendale helpfully suggested was for those with a tendency towards overheating.

'They are coming over to join us,' Mrs Webb announced with an excited tremble to her voice.

Claire dabbed at her greasy lips with a white linen napkin. Hamish and Mr Wetherly were indeed walking towards their shady retreat, with Reginald following.

'Sit up straight,' Hilda advised her daughters. 'Don't say anything silly,' she challenged Jane. 'Remember you are both unmarried and it is a disappointment to me,' she patted Henrietta's arm, '*but* it is a disappointment that could be rectified with effort.' Henrietta plastered on a serene smile. Jane brushed crumbs from her bunched skirt.

Jacob Wetherly declared himself honoured to be included at their picnic and commented on the becoming nature of Mrs Webb's daughters, who in turn dropped their mouths open so that pink tongues and white teeth became the extent of his remembrances of them. It was only after pleasantries were exchanged that Claire enquired as to his visit to Wangallon Town.

'New and I might add unforeseen prospects,' he answered mysteriously. His eyes were grey, made more intriguing by a deep scar etched on his forehead and an aquiline nose a debutante would die for. Claire was positive a wink escaped in her direction, but unsure as to whether this was a premeditated manoeuvre or some undiagnosed tick she took refuge behind her fan. She could not, however, escape the brushing of his lips across her hand, nor the positively languorous way in which he released his grip. It was proving to be an entertaining afternoon, she decided.

'And what are your plans for Christmas, Mrs Gordon?' Mrs Webb enquired when the men strode away to another group of picnickers and their foursome had calmed themselves sufficiently enough to accept Jane's offer of slices of apple pie. Claire was pleased to find herself discussing her thoughts of a large scrub turkey with roasted vegetables.

'Yes, and mutton,' Mrs Webb added. 'We can look forward to mutton chops for breakfast, roasts for dinner and cold cuts for tea before it is salted, cured and placed in the meat safe. Oh, when do you think we will have one of those glorious ice chests such as the city folk enjoy? Now that is something the shopkeeper should be investing in, not timber.'

'We could have ices, Mama,' Henrietta suggested.

'Oh yes, with fresh lemon cordial.' Jane sprayed her sister with morsels of apple and pastry.

Henrietta brushed at her blouse. 'You are not fit for polite society.'

Despite her best intentions Claire found herself glancing in Jacob Wetherly's direction, before drifting off as Mrs Webb began an extended explanation on the digestive benefits of stuffing and gravy.

Reclining on her side, Claire was beginning to doze in the afternoon sun when a disturbance awakened her.

'Oh, what has happened?' Mrs Webb enquired, reaching for her smelling salts. Henrietta perched on her knees in anticipation. 'Well go on, Jane,' Mrs Webb pointed her sharply closed fan in the direction of the kerfuffle as Jane ran off to investigate. 'Come back instantly once you have ascertained the drama of the event.'

Minutes later the minister and Mr Wetherly marched the three young master Ovendales and Angus Gordon out of the timber bordering the clearing. The minister had a firm grasp of Angus's collar and all four boys were covered with mud from their short pants to their feet. The rest of the picnickers were agog with interest, quickly forming a tight circle and blocking any further view.

'It is Angus,' Jane spluttered, looking apologetically at Claire. 'He tied one of the boys up a tree. Mr Wetherly said it was at an impressive height.'

Claire gave an indulgent sigh. 'I've no doubt.'

Winter, 1989

Wangallon Station

Anthony drove along the edge of the bore drain. In the distance he could hear the mechanical rumbling of the excavator as it scooped out the two feet of packed earth that sealed the fodder inside the silage pit. About to head in the direction the excavator was working, his attention was diverted by a cow bogged in the bore drain. She was an older cow. One who'd managed to sneak in a calf before she could be sold, and was now struggling to maintain condition due to the combined effects of age and the simple fact that she was cooking for two.

After only a few hours in the cold water of the drain, the cows usually lost strength and movement in their hind legs, any longer and hypothermia set in. Anthony took one look at the old girl, with her wild-eyed stare and shaking head, and thought she was a goner. Mud was piled up around her from repeated struggling and the bore water ringed the dark red of her hide. Taking a heavy chain from the Landcruiser's tray, he attached it to the vehicle's roo bar and approached the cow. She bellowed and snorted, twisting her head repeatedly so that every time Anthony tried to loop the chain around her horns, he missed; the chain dropping into the mud of the drain. Finally he managed to get the chain secured. He reversed the Landcruiser slowly. The chain grew taut, the cow bellowed. Anthony kept reversing until the cow was clear of the drain, then he drove forward quickly to slacken the chain, jumped out and removed it from her horns. To his surprise she clambered to her feet, snorting mucus into the air. Her scared eyes met his, her body shook uncontrollably and in an instant she was charging him. Anthony scrambled into the tray as she looked at him for a long minute before finally walking away. Further along the drain a calf appeared and mother and child were reunited.

Brushing mud from his hands, Anthony continued towards the pit. They would have to start regular drain runs to ensure they didn't lose any other cows, which meant, he begrudgingly admitted, that they should have opened the pit earlier. Sporadic trees punctuated the otherwise open country and within minutes he was nearing the silage pit that rose like an ancient burial mound from the flat landscape. The sky was dulled by cloud and out towards the west, a mist of rain fuzzed the tree line.

Outdoors everything seemed so simple. The bush was labour intensive yet it rewarded you if you weren't averse to risk and you were savvy management-wise. So why wasn't his personal life as easy? On his arrival at Wangallon as a young jackeroo, Anthony had found himself drawn to Sarah and her brother, Cameron. And while his self-esteem grew commensurate with his journey up the management ladder, from the beginning a sense of belonging permeated his days on Wangallon. It was his desire to remain on the property that helped salve his dismay at Sarah's leaving after Cameron's death, and his attachment to the Gordon's great mass of land almost compensated for Sarah's long absences from the property. Once or twice he considered leaving, although the property had seeped into his veins. And then there was Sarah and the simple fact that one day she might return.

While Anthony could never fathom Angus Gordon's manipulative personality he did understand the magnitude of good fortune that lay in the shape of the thirty per cent share of Wangallon bequeathed to him. He was very much aware of his responsibilities and had been running a tight ship for a number of years now. He could only see disaster ahead if Sarah began questioning his management style and Matt continued on his 'delusions of self-importance' path. Matt was a good bloke and capable, however he was only an employee. Taking advantage of Sarah's weak spots to further his management aspirations, or wangling his way out of station work by pleading a perpetually useless hand weren't endearing qualities.

Anthony pulled up some feet away from Matt's vehicle as rain flecked the windscreen. Matt couldn't wait for the fine weather expected tomorrow. He had to prove a point. The excavator had removed the top layer of dirt from the pit and was now filling two tip trucks with chopped sorghum. The scoop swung from the mouth of the pit across to the first truck and dumped its load in the back. The truck shuddered at the weight, the rear tyres bulging and then resettling.

Matt walked around the side of the tipper, kicking at the rear tyre as if checking the air pressure, his signature cigarette looking like an eleventh finger. Anthony nodded at the spits of rain. They couldn't afford for the silage to get wet. 'There are tarps in the back,' Anthony pointed over his shoulder, 'and you'll need some tyres to secure them.' He didn't bother to remind Matt that waiting another day for the fine weather predicted would have been a better alternative than having tippers and excavators sitting down.

Matt took a drag of his cigarette. 'No worries.' His voice carried over the two-way radio in the Landcruiser as Anthony drove away. 'We'll have to knock off until the rain passes,' he advised everyone.

In the rear-view mirror a line of bulbous grey–blue clouds appeared in the distance. It would be raining tonight although Anthony didn't expect much out of this cold front moving through. The vehicle bumped over a stock ramp, jolted through a series of potholes on the road and then turned towards a gateway. There were some early calving cows to check on, and then a number of telephone calls to make. Anthony opened the gate, pausing to reflect on what he was about to do. He'd been deliberating over an idea for some months. A project which he was convinced would ensure Wangallon's continued longevity and prosperity. Having been on the verge of mentioning it to Sarah he was now loathe to, especially after the stock route and silage pit argument. He tapped his fingers on the aluminum frame of the gate. Sarah wouldn't be happy. Ahead a bore drain twisted away to the right, to his left a startled emu appeared from amid dry grass and bolted from a nest in an effort to lead Anthony away. Anthony pulled his akubra a little further over his eyes; this was one project that couldn't be delayed.

Sarah stared glumly through the kitchen window at the misting rain, her fingers entwined around her morning coffee. She thought of Shelley, imagined her planning her Thursday night out and briefly wished there was a nice little restaurant around the corner where she and Anthony could go to. She was finding the station book work a chore and it was her own fault. The bookkeeper had been let go a few months after her grandfather's death, at Sarah's insistence. It seemed silly to pay for something she could manage herself and there was no better way of understanding the running of the property. Unfortunately the task of keeping the station office running required a good two and a half days a week and once summer arrived the constant watering the garden required would take up any spare moment. She felt her paddock time being gradually eroded.

Outside the lemon-scented gum's trunk was streaked with rain. Sarah watched as a topknot pigeon huddled its head on its breast, a puff of white and grey clinging to a branch. Things were changing. She could feel it as surely as if a new door were open before her, yet a niggling sense of annoyance was competing for her attention. Last Monday's meeting lay as an unsubtle reminder of her discontent. Maybe Anthony was right and she had suddenly developed an opinion – one she wanted heard. And wasn't that how things should be? She certainly didn't want to cause an argument, yet sometimes he made her feel like a bystander in the running of her family's property. And being relegated to second-tier management was beginning to sit uneasily with her. Now she had added reasons to be upset. One of this morning's accounts was for twenty-eight thousand dollars; two new loading ramps and a set of portable cattle yards. She sipped contemplatively at her coffee. She could live with that; however, the equipment finance loan application for one hundred thousand dollars worth of a body cattle truck was getting a little out of hand. Sarah rubbed her forehead; neither of the items were mentioned in the station diary as possible future purchases.

In the office Sarah sat down at the large oak desk and looked out the casement window to the garden. This side of the homestead held her grandmother's cuttings and herb garden. Grandma Jessica had died of an asthma attack out there. The bush she adored had killed her through the combination of an environmental allergy and isolation. Angus had been out mustering at the time, returning to find her lying in the garden unconscious, her wide straw hat and wicker basket lying by her side. The garden was her passion and encompassed a small area of dirt once tended by a Chinese man. His vegetable garden supplied much of the homestead's requirements for nearly forty years until his death. Then there had been extensions and renovations to the rear of Wangallon in the twenties, fifties and the eighties; an office, kitchen, pantry and a walk-in cool room with adjoining fridge and commercial-sized deep freeze now covered the majority of the garden he once tended.

At various stages during the year the vegetable garden boasted rows of neatly planted cabbages, tomatoes, pumpkin, carrots and cucumber. Not particularly adventurous fare, but easy enough to grow, at least. Parsley, mint and rosemary completed the herb section. It was not that Sarah didn't care for the garden, indeed pottering around the moist beds amid the wavering trees was amazingly therapeutic; it was simply that she loved what grew beyond the back gate more. Out there was the rich soil that ensured their survival. Out there was the land that her people had lived and died for.

Clearing away images of a pigtailed man digging up the Wangallon soil, Sarah returned to the remaining unopened mail. There was the monthly fuel account, the molasses statement for the supplement they fed to the cows prior to the spring calving and the usual junk mail. Throwing the flyers for the supermarket cut-price specials and furniture store deals in the wastepaper bin, she jumped when the telephone rang.

'Sarah, it's Dad. I'm afraid I've got some bad news.'

She waited for the tremble in his voice to subside. There were only two things he could be calling about.

'It's your mother.'

Relief flooded through her, quickly followed by guilt.

'She's declined a bit over the last day.'

Sarah wondered if she should jump in the car and begin the long drive north. 'I'm sorry, Dad. Is it bad?'

'Well, the doctor can't give me any specifics. How about I let you know if there's any change.' The cheery tone in her father's voice sounded forced.

'Okay. And you're all right?'

'I'm fine.'

Sarah turned their conversation to the weather and the opening of the silage pit. She was concerned for her father, however this wasn't the first telephone call over the last couple of years heralding her mother's increasing ill health.

'Hey, honey.' Anthony strode into the office, his jeans bloody. 'Can you find me a syringe? One of the cows aborted and she's prolapsed. I need to give her a shot of penicillin.'

'Gotta go, Dad. I'll speak to you later.' She hung up the phone and selected a syringe and a sixteen gauge needle from the stainless steel cupboard. 'The penicillin is in the cool room. I'll go –'

'No need.' Anthony took the syringe and needle from her hand. 'I'll get it on the way out.'

'I'll come.' Sarah walked from the office to the back porch where her riding boots were. She'd had enough of being indoors and figured being outside might give them both some perspective; especially when it came to discussing the purchases she'd not been told about.

He turned to her, kissed her forehead. 'There's no need. I can handle it.'

'But I want to come.'

He took her by the shoulders. 'It's messy, Sarah. You don't really want to see it.'

For a moment Sarah stared after his retreating figure. He made her feel ill-equipped to handle something that she had viewed on more than one occasion. 'Anthony? Wait.' By the time Sarah pulled her boots on and ran down the back path, the Landcruiser was driving away. As she turned back towards the homestead, Bullet sat squarely in the middle of the back path, his head tilted to one side. A few feet away Ferret sat uncomfortably beneath the above ground rainwater tank, his pipe-encased leg thrust out awkwardly to one side.

'How are you going, Ferret?'

The dog gave a whine. Bullet nudged her leg as she squatted beside him. The rain had eased and a cold southerly stung her eyes. Sarah snuggled up against Bullet. Despite the best of intentions, her thoughts turned from cattle ramps, trucks and Anthony to her mother.

Summer, 1908

Wangallon Station Homestead

'Morning.' Jasperson dismounted stiffly from his horse before wrapping the reins around the hitching post that ran parallel to the verandah. By his side was the lad known as McKenzie. Hamish ignored Jasperson's newest recruit. Having plucked the boy from obscurity, the lad's length of tenure at Wangallon depended on his ability. Jasperson looked peaky. In hindsight, Hamish recalled, not much different to the day over fifty years ago when they had come upon him camped alone on the banks of the swollen Broken River. There had only been the three of them after Hamish's brother's death: Hamish, Lee and Dave. They had buried Charlie on the goldfields, headed north and found Jasperson. Jasperson, an uptight Englishman with a penchant for young boys, had given some cockeyed story about having lost everything and everyone. Yet Hamish saw in him the same attributes as Dave; they were men who could follow orders and keep their mouths shut and men like that were damn hard to find and replace. It was a pity Dave finally succumbed to his own mortality. Hamish had thought his willpower was stronger than that.

'Well, what news?' Hamish swigged down his tea. If a month traversing Wangallon's western boundary had not caused the Englishman to hanker a little for conversation, nothing would. There were miles of fences to check, boundary riders to locate and rotate to other parts of the property and general observations on the state of the grazing country to be recorded and passed on. Hamish was usually on horseback by now, the rising sun in his eyes and an image of the country he'd acquired over many years beckoning like a pitcher of water. Instead it was nearing seven o'clock and his impatience was biting at his stomach.

Hamish tapped out his pipe. 'Well?' A glance was exchanged between the pustule-faced boy and his overseer. Hamish knew that look. Their relationship had clearly been settled one night out on the western boundary. Money and terms had been exchanged and Hamish suspected McKenzie had dropped his trousers by a glowing campfire. It was not the first time such a favour had been extracted, nor would it be the last. Hamish narrowed his eyes. This Scottish boy with his flickering gaze and willingness to accommodate Jasperson was looking for advancement. No doubt he believed that the top of the great tree that was Wangallon was poorly stocked with fruit not yet grown or apples souring and ready to fall. Well this one would be at the receiving end of a ready lesson if he diverted from a path directed by Jasperson.

'Luke's about a day's ride away,' Jasperson began. 'The cook's already at the Wangallon Town Hotel. Reckon's the boy got speared a few months back.'

Hamish considered this snippet. 'He's not maimed?'

Jasperson shook his head.

'Good. Take yourself into town and report back to me when he arrives. Is his whore still there?'

'The Grant girl? Yes.'

McKenzie's expression grew attentive. While the question was directed at Jasperson, Hamish sensed annoyance. The Scottish boy was peeved. He shoved his hands in the pockets of his trousers and scuffed at the dirt with the toe of his boot.

'If she be your whore too lad, my advice would be to find another.' Hamish couldn't have his own son sharing a woman with the likes of this boy. 'What else?' he demanded of Jasperson.

'The big river dried up down near Crawford Corner a few weeks ago. The boundary rider moved the cattle south in an attempt to get them to the main drain but it was dry.'

'What do you mean dry? It's a damn artesian bore. It can't simply have dried up?'

Jasperson scratched irritably at his crotch. 'The cattle took off into Crawford's. There's water in that big hole on their side so that's where they headed.'

Hamish considered the relevant facts. He had no water. Crawford did. 'And the drain?'

'I reckon they blocked it off.'

Hamish looked at his overseer: Filthy trousers, dust-covered boots and a clean shirt; the man's one concession to a modicum of respectability. 'You reckon?' he repeated. Such a word didn't exist in his vocabulary.

'The boundary rider –'

Hamish took a sip of tea and uncrossed his legs as he lent sideways in his chair as if looking behind Jasperson. 'I don't see the boundary rider. I didn't ask the boundary rider.'

McKenzie fiddled with his horse's reins. Jasperson spat a globule of something wet and chewy on the ground. 'It's blocked. Crawford's dug a trench to divert our bore drain water into the waterhole on the river.'

Hamish's eyes narrowed. 'And my stock?' he enquired slowly, his dirty fingernails drumming his thigh.

'Fifty or so head are running on Crawford Corner.' Jasperson subtly directed any anger back towards the rightful owner.

Hamish slammed his fist into the palm of his hand. So this was how it was going to be. But he had him this time. He had Oscar Crawford for no less than stock theft. 'Get my horse, Jasperson.'

'Boss?'

If they left now they could reach the river at noon and wait out the hottest part of the day. Hamish paced the length of the verandah. Oscar Crawford needed to be taught a measure of responsibility. The man had grown insufferable. He'd shown uncommon bad sense in refusing Hamish's over-generous offer to buy him out. His veins buzzed with anticipation.

'Boss,' Jasperson scratched thinning hair at his temples, 'the drain's been unblocked and the ditch filled in and hadn't we best wait till after Christmas?'

Hamish stopped walking. 'Yes, all right,' he agreed dourly. He forced his legs to return to his chair. 'Christmas.' He glared at the Scottish boy, who, in response, quickly remounted his horse. 'Well, we have his highly coveted stud master.' Hamish's hands grasped the wicker armrests and the fine cane cracked beneath his grip. His lips curled. 'Let Crawford have his Christmas. Let him stuff his English belly on Wangallon meat. Eventually,' he looked directly at Jasperson, 'he will choke.'

The overseer gave a thin-lipped smile.

Summer, 1908
Wangallon Town

Lauren Grant lent further over the hessian bags of potato, flour and sugar in the small storeroom and steadied herself against the hard sacks. In between two of the stacked bags closest to the timber wall was a small gap where a brown mouse was sedately nibbling his way through one bag. The mouse tracked from one bag to another and Lauren imagined the little rodent tasting potato and then sugar in a delightful method of belly stuffing that would render him exhausted in the growing heat. Silently she concentrated on the mouse eating his fill as Mr Stevens proceeded to satisfy his own hunger. With her skirts thrown up about her waist, Lauren mentally began counting Mr Stevens's panting. He was not much on ceremony and could be relied upon to conclude his business with a modicum of fuss.

Mr Stevens, a rangy man with a deep-set brow and a bony, finicky wife who was no doubt the cause of the deeply entrenched furrow between his eyes, gave a series of loud, breathy gasps. Lauren counted and then smelled eight exhalations of onion and the remnants of teeth-rotting food. Once he got to twelve she needed to brace herself against the wall, however today the hessian sacks were stacked in greater numbers and although she extended her arms, her fingers refused to touch the uneven timber wall before her. Instead Lauren found herself staring at the daylight seeping through the cracked timber and then, as her eyes gradually adjusted, into two pairs of eyes. The eyes giggled and kicked the outside wall before running away. 'You scallywags,' she berated as she was pushed forward onto the sacks. Mr Stevens gave a long sigh and then farted.

God's holy trousers, Lauren thought with disgust. If ever a man knew how to ruin a perfectly harmless transaction it was this man with his less than fine personage, only just adequate dick and a voice like a squeaky wagon wheel bumping over a dirt track.

'Good. Good girl. Take what you need.'

A triangle of light entered and left the storeroom. Lauren heard footsteps travelling the length of the narrow store and then a soft flipping sound, which signified the open/closed for business sign being adjusted. Picking herself up from where she had been so roughly shoved, Lauren patted her skirts down and tidied the wisps of hair that were matted with her sweat and the onion breath of the shopkeeper. She wanted more than potatoes and bread today, if you please. She had a hankering for eggs and a length of calico for a new skirt. Lauren peered around the uneven timber slats of the door. Mr Stevens expected her to leave by the rear window. To actually hitch up her skirts like her tabby cat of a sister Susanna and crawl from his sight. Well not today. Today was the last of such escapades. Though she'd been quite good, for recently only the ugly Scottish boy, McKenzie, and Mr Stevens had been regular.

On her reckoning Luke Gordon could be due in Wangallon Town at any moment. Lauren wiped at the line of sweat on her brow. Despite the morning's undertakings she felt rather jaunty. The months of waiting were now behind her and she expected better things for her life in the new year. 'Best be starting now,' Lauren decided, firming her mouth and straightening her back. 'Ouch.' She pressed at the muscle in the small of her back, pinched her cheeks, although she doubted she needed the colour, scooped up a handful of potatoes and walked from the storeroom, her head high.

Hilda Webb and her two daughters were arguing over their account at the long wooden counter, giving Lauren time enough to select a bolt of green material from the shelf. She snatched up a reel of cotton and a length of pink ribbon that she fancied and dropped them down the front of her loose fitting blouse, and then with a cursory glance at the rather cheap-looking shoes on display, she carried the material to the counter. Her presence immediately raised the ire of the women who were of the social conviction that one should not mix with the daughter of a washer woman.

'Perhaps, Mr Stevens, you wish to serve this person. Then we can complete our business in private.' Mrs Webb held scented pomade to her nose.

Lauren dumped the potatoes on the counter and rested the material alongside. 'This person has a name, Mrs Webb,' Lauren announced, summoning her best toff's voice that she decided was quite wasted in Wangallon Town, 'which you know well enough seeing you can't keep staff for more than a few months due to your own ill-humour and it's me own mother who washes your dirty smalls.'

Mrs Webb opened her lips only to discover that embarrassment and anger rendered her silent. The older Miss Henrietta Webb took her mother's arm and, pulling her aside amid whispers and furtive glances, the two women busied themselves examining some handkerchiefs of very poor quality.

Lauren winked at Mr Stevens, whose permanent brow furrow had mysteriously smoothed with shock. 'A length for a skirt, if you please, a dozen fresh eggs, a tin of condensed milk and I'll be having a couple of those,' Lauren pointed at the boiled lollies. The shopkeeper was staring at her as if she were some criminal straight off the boat from the mother country. 'How is Mrs Stevens?' Lauren wet her forefinger, her saliva marking a line across the dusty counter. 'You'll be needing a cleaner next, Mr Stevens. You ask Mrs Webb. People what are incapable of looking after themselves always need someone handy. Me, for example, I could give those pipes of yours,' she pointed at the wooden smoking pipes on the shelf behind him, then glanced at his crotch, 'a real good blow out.' Lauren enjoyed herself by standing stock still as her material was cut and wrapped and her purchases bundled into a paper bag. 'And I believe I would still have credit.' With her belongings pushed across the width of the counter, Lauren held out her palm. 'I could check with Mrs Stevens?' Lauren snavelled up the coin thrown onto the counter.

Mr Stevens cleared his throat. 'You don't have credit here no more, Miss.' He looked at her meaningfully.

Lauren tucked the bag under her arm and winked. 'Neither do you, Mr Stevens.'

With her business completed, Lauren walked slowly past the three Webb women. The eldest girl, a peaky, skinnier version of her own cat's-bum-mouthed sister, considered herself above the inhabitants of Wangallon Town. 'I'll give Mr Luke Gordon your best, Mr Stevens.'

Lauren didn't bother to look back, though she felt like one of those blue–green blowflies, sticky with interest. She needed to wash, eat and then position herself at the old box tree on the edge of town as if she were going for a walk. Of course it was possible that Luke wouldn't return on this very day, but last year he had. Four days before Christmas when the sky was near white with heat and dust and the birds stopped flying for fear of fainting and a person lost their shadow, well, that was the hour Luke Gordon had walked his horses, pack horses and his blackfella mate into town. Lauren itched at the moisture gathering at her waistband and pushed a boiled sweet into her mouth.

For midmorning the main street was decidedly quiet. There were only three horses tethered to the hitching post outside the two-storey hotel and a black sulky. At the sight of the minister's sulky Lauren decided to take the longer route home by crossing the dusty street diagonally. This direction would take her through Mr Morelli's vegetable garden and past the Gee's chook house before sneaking through the backyards of three rather cantankerous women. Lauren was almost in too good a mood for a fight; however, if necessary she could shout just as loudly as the next old hag. Besides, she figured no good would come of crossing the path of a minister, what with her having committed one mortal sin already this fine day. She didn't think God would mind about the cotton and ribbon, after all it said nothing in the Bible about it being wrong for a woman to look her best. Lifting her skirts, Lauren kicked at a stone with her worn lace-up shoes and walked swiftly across the road. The air was already thickening with heat and swirls of dust spun up from the road like spinning tops.

Hoisting the paper bag beneath her arm, she was about to walk through the shabby remains of Mr Morelli's sun-withered garden when she heard her name called. She turned slowly, loath to be held up yet intrigued as to the voice that addressed her. Riding up the main street was one of the Wangallon men; the ugly Scottish lad, McKenzie. Lauren lifted her eyes heavenwards. *God's holy trousers*, she muttered. Why couldn't they space themselves out a bit instead of all fronting up like half-pint scallywags bobbing for apples. She waved briefly and then continued on. He was a good paying lad who treated her well enough, however business was over for the day and a girl couldn't go for bread and dripping when a joint of beef was soon to walk into town.

Winter, 1989

Wangallon Station

Matt Schipp walked the ewes along at a leisurely pace. He'd given Jack Dillard the run of things today and so far the young jackeroo was proving capable. Angling his backside into the saddle, Matt fidgeted around in the pocket of his oilskin for his rollies. His free hand found the papers and with a quick lick of his lips a thin oblong sheet was soon dangling from his mouth. He fumbled once again, removing the pouch of tobacco from his pocket, and manoeuvred a wad of the dried plant between his fingers. It had taken months for him to reach this stage of proceedings after the accident. Months of swearing and arguments and useless comments from useless doctors until eventually his woman had walked out, leaving behind a paltry eleven years of fair-to-middling memories. Matt dropped the reins for a moment while he used his four good fingers to roll the tobacco within the paper. Finally the roll-your-own dangled from his lips. He pushed his wide-brimmed hat up off his face and searched his pockets for his lighter.

'Come behind, Whisky,' he called out to his dog as if he was addressing a naughty child. 'You know better than to stir the old girls up.' Matt was pleased he'd only brought Whisky out today. There were another seven dogs tied up down the back of his yard and despite their pleading expressions, he'd known Whisky would be fresh enough to do the work of two dogs.

The short-haired border collie ran from where he'd been stalking the tail-end of the mob and headed back towards his master. The mob padded quietly onwards, their cloven hoofs leaving myriad tracks and raising dust in their wake. Ahead young Jack was wheeling a recalcitrant ewe back towards the mob. Having tried her luck by dashing off across the paddock, she was now experiencing the brunt of a young man on a good horse with a fast kelpie. The ewe twisted and turned in various directions, stopping occasionally to stamp irritably at the dog if it came too close, before attempting another path of escape. Finally she gave up, diving into the safety of the mob.

Matt took a long draw of his smoke, a curl of a white line tracing through the air as he exhaled. As if on cue his horse, a black gelding named Sugar, started off into a slow walk. Matt let himself be lulled by the steady gait, his eyes straying from left to right, automatically checking and rechecking the progress of the sheep in his care. They had left the Wangallon sheep yards at daybreak and walked due east, passing within a couple of kilometers of West Wangallon. Now it was time for smoko and they still had a good six clicks to go.

Tethering their horses in the shade, they unpacked their saddlebags and settled down for a break. Matt hollowed himself a nice little piece of dirt at the base of a leopardwood tree, which formed a good backrest, and watched as young Jack perched himself on a log. Soon they were drinking steaming black tea from a thermos with lumpy spoonfuls of sugar. Jack handed Matt a corned beef and pickle sandwich.

'Doesn't get much better than this,' Matt said aloud. His teeth dug cleanly through the fresh bread, his tongue savouring the bitey onion of the pickle. It'd been near five hours since breakfast and Matt's stomach lived for regular meals. He was like a baby; five meals a day and a bottle at night.

'So are they going to advertise for a new jackeroo then?' Jack asked, between slurps of tea. He knew the drill. He'd been at Wangallon for over twelve months, had always done what was required of him quickly and efficiently and if he didn't know or understand something, he asked.

Matt let the boy squirm a bit. A few years back and young Jack would have been a jackeroo for at least a couple more years, but the pastoral industry was changing and a kid with ability like this one couldn't be left doing menial tasks and spending every Friday in the station garden.

'Thought you liked gardening?'

Jack's eyes narrowed slightly with concern. 'Very funny,' he responded when Matt couldn't keep his top lip from stringing out into a smile. 'I don't mind it. I like to see things grow. Used to help my mum a bit. And Sarah's real nice.' He slurped at his tea, scowling at the heat. 'What was her grandfather like?'

'Tough as bloody nails and damn smart.'

'And Anthony started as a jackeroo?'

'Hand-picked, they reckon, by old Angus himself.' The boy fell on his feet all right; Matt couldn't deny that. Not that Anthony wasn't capable.

Jack took a long slurp of his tea. 'He seems really good at managing.'

'He'll need to be.' Matt picked a string of meat from between his two front teeth. Somehow he didn't think Anthony's management capabilities would be restricted to Wangallon. He was living with a Gordon, one who probably wouldn't stay docile for much longer. She couldn't. It wasn't in her blood. Besides, he reckoned the girl had pretty much done with the mourning of old Angus; she was starting to express a few opinions.

He himself had only agreed to work for Angus because he was old school. Properties like Wangallon couldn't go on into infinity unless owner and staff understood each other and Angus Gordon and Matt Schipp had understood each other. With a satisfied belch, he squared his shoulders against the knobbly bark supporting him and rubbed his shoulderblades contentedly.

'Is it true Wangallon was built on stock theft?'

Matt peered out from underneath his hat. One thing he didn't believe in was repeating gossip. He flicked a good finger at a large black bull ant traversing the length of his jeans and considered the boy's question. 'I'd say pretty much anything could have happened out here one hundred and forty years ago, Jack. The thing is…' he paused for emphasis, 'we will never know how much is talk and how much is actual truth.'

'It's just that everyone in Wangallon Town has a story.'

Matt pictured the general store, pub, single tennis court, hall and school. There were ten houses in its four streets. 'I'll bet they do.'

By late lunch the ewes were holed up in their new paddock, camped from the day's heat under the nearest group of trees. Matt shut the twelve-foot gate after them, marvelling at how quickly they could settle. They rode back in tired silence. Jack occasionally whistling snippets from unrecognisable songs, in between talking to his kelpie, Rust, to get him to keep up.

'You'll have to spend a bit more time with that horse of yours. Get him to wear young Rust there.' Matt looked over his shoulder at the tiring dog. In another half a click he'd be foot sore and straggling, ruined for a full day's work tomorrow.

Matt's own dog, Whisky, a surly collie with a grudging respect for Sugar borne of two skin splitting kicks to his muzzle, sat gingerly in front of Matt, his front paws extended in a gruesome lock across Matt's thigh.

Jack looked at Whisky's mournful expression.

'Want to give your young mate a ride?' Matt asked Whisky roughly.

Minutes later, Whisky was walking alongside Sugar at a neat pace, his now alert gaze looking up to check on Rust, who was clamped close to Matt in a vice-like grip.

'What's on tomorrow?' Jack asked, noticing that his dog had a distinctly human expression on his face that could only be described as being scared shitless.

'We'll move the steers from the 4,000 acre road paddock onto the oats. I've got a couple of contractors coming out to give us a hand. Then we'll drive over to Boxer's Plains.'

Matt had been checking the feed situation on Boxer's Plains every Sunday for the past three weekends. The 20,000 acres had been stocked to the eyeballs for over six weeks and the feed would begin to cut out if the block wasn't destocked soon. He was a little surprised when his querying received an *it's under control* comment from Anthony. It may well be but on his reckoning they had a month before the country was chewed out. Matt's finger probed irritably at a hardened lump of wax in his ear. Every time he offered some management advice, Anthony was all over him like a fat lady at a buffet. And ever since their disagreement in the Wangallon kitchen and the early opening of the pit, their once cordial relationship had disintegrated into feigned politeness. Nothing worse than a young manager with an attitude and Matt had seen his share of them.

There were a couple of young people at the helm of one of the most well known pastoral properties in New South Wales and Matt had a suspicion that one of them had his own agenda. Cripes this was going to get interesting. At least the third owner of Wangallon hadn't shown his face yet. That in itself was a blessing. Matt walked his horse through the house gate en route to the stables.

'I'm sure glad Sarah likes her cattle and sheep. I wouldn't like to be spending my time driving headers and tractors.' Jack watched in amusement as Matt picked Rust up off the saddle by the scruff of his neck and dropped him on the ground. The dog landed securely on all four paws.

'Me neither, Jack,' Matt replied.

Wangallon was built and would continue to thrive on stock. They still had a few thousand acres sown to oats every year to fatten their cattle and cull sheep and they sowed barley, which they crushed in a mill to feed out as a top-up supplement to the steers, but that was the extent of the farming operation. Some of their neighbours had embarked on carefully mapped-out land clearing exercises and had enjoyed the monetary benefits of big cash crops of wheat, barley and grain sorghum but, like any commodity, grain growing was subject to the vagrancies of both the weather and the marketplace. Farming was an expensive business and Wangallon had always made more out of grazing.

At the stables Matt unsaddled his horse and began brushing Sugar down with a curry comb. Sugar stood quietly like a woman at a beauty parlour getting her hair done.

'I guess I'm a bit of a tree hugger, Matt,' Jack said almost shyly as he undid the girth strap on his own mount and dragged the saddle free.

Matt clapped the lad on his shoulder. 'I know exactly what you mean. We're stockmen, not tractor jockeys.'

Sarah, Matt and Jack were unloading their horses from the float at the road paddock when a flashy white and yellow trailer pulled alongside them.

'You're late,' Matt admonished as the two men walked towards them.

'G'day. I'm Toby Williams.' The taller of the two shook Sarah's hand. He was slightly built with broad shoulders and budgerigar blue eyes. 'And this is Pancake.'

'Pancake,' Sarah repeated, unsure if he referred to his horse or the squat roly-poly man beside him.

'Pancake,' the shorter man clarified, 'on account of when I take me hat off, me hair's always squashed flat like a –'

'Pancake,' Toby grinned, zipping up his jacket.

'Okay then.' Sarah knew it was going to be one of those days.

Toby and Pancake opened a number of mesh dog cages and a bedraggled assortment of working dogs escaped. The horses reared and whinnied, the dogs barked and peed on every tyre they could find, twice, and then completed a number of quick dashes around both horse floats. Finally the entire crew settled into work mode. Sarah looked at Bullet, who stared back with a look of disdain. He never had taken much to working with strangers and was just as likely to bite first and bark later. Sarah waggled her finger at him to behave.

'Knew your grandfather. Wily old bastard, Angus.' Toby lounged nonchalantly in his saddle, his right leg hooked up as if he were sitting in a chair.

'Thanks.'

'Now he was a grazier. Old school-like.' He gestured towards Matt. 'Wasn't surprised when I heard he got the run of things down here. Reckon Angus had everything all sorted by the time he kicked the bucket and that's the way it should be if you've got any nous.' He gave Sarah a slow head-to-toe glance. 'So how are you going being boss of Wangallon?'

Sarah experienced the unusual sensation of being mentally undressed. 'It's great.' Her fingers pulled at the zip on her jacket until it reached her throat.

Toby's mouth crooked itself up at one corner until an unnerving grin gradually spread from his cheek to a fan of sun-created wrinkles at the corner of his eyes.

'We'll split up.' Matt gave brief directions on how he wanted the paddock mustered. He pointed out a 30 acre clump of belah trees that ran in a belt across the southern tip of the paddock that could easily hide a canny mob of steers, and gave directions for gateways. Before he'd finished his last sentence, Toby was already cantering away from them, Pancake and a menagerie of dogs in pursuit.

'Where's Anthony?'

Sarah hunched her shoulders. He'd left the homestead early that morning without a word and was strangely quiet the night before over dinner. If she'd been in the mood for an argument she would have mentioned the accounting problem, but she knew him too well. Anthony's quiet mood was indicative of a problem and she wasn't going to add to his angst, at least not until tonight.

Standing up in the stirrups, Sarah whistled at Bullet. Excitement had got the better of him and in an effort to slow the 50 or so steers that had broken from the main mob he had raced to the front and was now hanging off the nose of one of the steers. Touching her spurs lightly against her mare, Tess, Sarah galloped across the paddock towards Bullet, aware the main mob was eyeing the runaways with interest. Bullet's one-man war was beginning to look very one-sided and a moment later the dog was airborne as the steer he clung to flung his head from side to side, tossing him skywards. Sarah watched as Bullet picked himself up out of the dirt and then raced back into the fray.

Behind her came the crack of a stockwhip and yells of abuse. The thousand-strong herd of 450 kilogram-heavy steers had changed direction. Intent on joining up with Bullet's escapees, they rushed the ground, closing the 600 metre space within seconds. Sarah galloped alongside the mob, urging her horse closer to the steers in an effort to turn them to the right. Tess obeyed the tightening rein, Sarah's leg brushing the hairy hide of one of the steers before a large log forced Tess to jump and veer to the left. Jack's dog, Rust, sped past Sarah as she straightened herself in the saddle and then Moses, Matt's musclebound blue cattle dog, appeared.

'About bloody time,' Sarah yelled as the dogs disappeared into the dust. Ahead she could see a figure on horseback. Her horse edged closer to the lead. Bullet was still out there and a quick flash of Whisky's black and white coat suggested Matt was the lone rider up front. Sarah squinted through the midmorning winter glare as Toby galloped past her with five dogs following. There was a break in the mob and he galloped his horse directly into the fray, momentarily diverting the oncoming cattle with a crack of his stockwhip. Then he was out skirting the edge of the mob, riding wildly to the front.

The cattle were beginning to turn as Sarah stuck to their left flank with Pancake and Jack. Ahead she spotted Matt. He was sitting right in the path of the steers, horse and rider as unmovable as statues. Sarah gritted her teeth. There was enough beef heading his way to pulp him into a meat patty. He cracked his stockwhip once, twice, three times from the saddle and Sarah held her breath.

Toby Williams appeared like a wraith out of the dust and a blur of red and white hide. Standing tall in the stirrup irons, he cracked his whip above his head until Sarah felt her own arm grow tired from the effort of watching him. His horse spun and reared upwards, then, satisfied that the mob was calming, he cantered back to the wing. A few minutes later he trotted past Sarah, acknowledging her with a flash of white teeth and a tip of his hat.

Within the hour the now sedate steers were trotting through the gateway and onto the oats, snorting air and panting. Sarah joined Matt at the gate as a dozen or so exhausted stragglers brought up the rear with Jack, Toby and Pancake behind them. Dogs littered the dirt track like bowling alley pins.

'Toby Williams, where's he from?' Sarah asked Matt after she'd taken a quick swig from her water bottle.

'The Territory. Big run. Fell out with his older brother over a girl, so he's down here for six months or so until the storm subsides.'

'He's handy.'

Matt nodded. 'He's your drover.'

Sarah watched him approach from under the brim of her hat. 'And Pancake?'

'Victorian. Mountain Country bred: Probably the better rider of the two, just not as showy.'

'Got the buggers,' Jack said when they all met at the gateway.

'Good dog that,' Toby commented to Sarah. Bullet was standing on his hind legs, his paws on Sarah's boot. Toby slid off his saddle and passed the dog up to her, his hand managing to rest briefly on Sarah's thigh.

'You'll be his friend for life,' Sarah commented as Bullet settled himself on the horse as if he were on a rug.

Toby looked at her and winked. 'Hopefully.'

They headed back slowly in the direction they'd mustered, the dogs trotting down the dirt road in front of them. Matt caught her eye. 'Gardening and office work isn't what it's cracked up to be.'

Sarah tore her eyes away from Pancake, Toby and Jack who were all laughing loudly. 'You can say that again.'

Summer, 1908

Wangallon Town Hotel, en route to Wangallon Station

Luke Gordon relaxed one arm behind his head where he lay on the bed. On the first night he had enjoyed the novelty of lying a few feet above the ground, but now in this narrow room, upon a lumpy mattress almost wrecked by his exertions, he longed for freedom. In the gathering light he could see his belongings: swag, boots, strewn clothes and saddlebags on the floor beneath the casement window. The remains of his money, a paltry sum he was sure, would still be beneath the leather inside his left boot. Hopefully the cook would manage some eggs and perhaps some thick bread with a good dollop of mutton dripping – aye, that would set him up for the day.

The water splashed loudly. Droplets from the dampened cloth ran in rivulets over her bare shoulders. The beads of moisture moved downwards, tracing the length of her spine until it gathered in the soft folds of the chemise pooled at her waist. Gradually the wetness began to darken the material, forming patches of variegated colour. It was an uncommon sight to watch the female form bathing in the still of morning. Especially this girl, for she was careless. Her skin shone moistly from her endeavours, her long brown hair dripped onto the wooden floorboards. The curtains, drawn wide to reveal a brightening sky, illuminated the few scattered objects in the room. Bed, washstand, table, chair and the girl. Barefooted, her long underskirt swung almost tiredly as she moved her hips from side to side, the washcloth sweeping perfunctorily beneath an armpit. Somehow, her morning routine had suddenly become too familiar.

Standing, Luke stretched into his nakedness, feeling the pull of his thigh muscles and the dull pain of his back. There was more to these aches than the many hours recently spent freeing his mind and body from months of isolation. Age gave him twinges and pains, headaches and stomach aches. It stung him when he thought of his 46 years. And now he carried another wound to add to his list of scars. Although his shoulder was usable he could no longer lift his arm above his head. Somehow he could not imagine making old bones.

The floorboards squeaked as he walked towards the girl. Lauren twisted away from his grasp, pulling up her chemise in an effort to cover her nakedness, giggling as he touched her breasts. Her fingers scrambled into the armholes of her clothing, plaiting swiftly at the ribbon lacing at her cleavage. Luke relented quickly, shifting sideways until half the room separated them. He could not understand this coyness, not after nights spent in a bed paid for by him. Suddenly she looked downcast as if she had been willing all along. Luke gave a brief grunt. He was not interested in histrionics.

'Do you have the makings?' She pinned her brown hair roughly into a bun at the nape of her neck.

Luke found a tin of tobacco and papers in his doeskin trousers and passed them into her calloused hands. She rolled the tobacco quickly, effortlessly and then encased it in a strip of thin paper plucked efficiently by thick, short fingers. Once finished she placed the makings on the washstand and backed away as if trading an object for peace. Luke, pulling on his trousers and slipping the braces over his shoulders, helped himself to the water in the porcelain bowl, adding the remains of the matching pitcher. The homemade boiled soap carried the tracing of fat almost too rancid for use, yet it scrubbed into an excuse for lather and he doused his face, arms and chest vigorously.

'It's Christmas tomorrow.'

He wanted to ask her what this statement was meant to mean to him; instead he did what came the most naturally – he ignored her.

'You don't talk much.'

What the fig was there to talk about, he wondered. When he had completed his brief ablutions he rolled a cigarette and lit it, throwing the matches in the general direction of the girl. With a slowness borne of repetition he took a long, relaxing drag and then coughed up a mess of yellow sputum. He swallowed the lumpy parcel. Through the window Luke glimpsed a bullock dray ambling down the dirt road. From the hallway he heard footsteps, groans, and a woman's yelp. On his reckoning he'd been in Wangallon Town for near three days. It had to be three for he was feeling imprisoned this morning, like some brumby chased down and yarded after months of roaming free. He was also pretty positive that he'd seen Jasperson skulking about the place not two days ago. Trust his father to send the weasel out to check on him.

Luke listened absently to Lauren as she talked of the green tree in the church, of hymns she had heard sung last Christmas, of the joint of mutton she hoped to eat with her family on the morrow. He was looking forward to some decent food, to Lee's ramblings and his young half-brother's infectious enthusiasm. As for Christmas, well, it was a day like any other day; besides, other matters weighed on his mind. His fingers brushed the small tortoiseshell hair comb purchased in Sydney.

'Tell the cook I've need of some breakfast.' Luke jingled the coin in his pocket, settled another coin on the edge of the wash-stand. A thin curl of smoke angled from the corner of the girl's mouth.

'You don't have to do that.' She bit at her bottom lip, gave a teased-out smile.

Perhaps he'd paid her too much? Certainly it had been enough for a week's service. Scooping up the coin he pocketed it before opening the door. He gestured with his arm for her to leave and then began gathering his belongings. Lifting his bedroll, he sat it on the lumpy mattress.

'When will I see you?' the girl asked. 'I've been good to you, Luke Gordon,' she argued, clutching her hands against her breast. 'Haven't I been good to you? And I waited and I lay with no other all these months you've been roaming the bush.'

Luke gathered her skirt and blouse and watched the girl dress. Patting her rounded behind, he gave her a gentle shove out the door. Strangely enough the lass looked as if she might cry.

'Take me back to that station of yours.'

'I promised you nothing.' Luke shoved his hand in his pockets.

Lauren stood on the bare floorboards of the hallway, her cheeks flushed. She wiped at her nose. 'I'm a respectable girl, I am.' She straightened her neck and shoulders. 'You were pleased to see me.'

Luke tried to shut the door, finding a foot and palm quickly wedged between him and silence.

'I'm a polite and proper young lady. If my father hadn't fallen prey to the demon drink I'd be strolling down the main street in a swish new skirt with a matching parasol if you please.'

Luke pushed at the door and with a final shove managed to close it in the girl's face.

'You'll be back, Luke Gordon,' she called from the hallway. 'You'll be back.'

Wangallon Town Hotel, en route to Wangallon Station

Not two miles from Wangallon Homestead, Luke's attention was drawn to the flicker of movement. He was on the final leg of his journey, having almost completed his progression through the winding track that led through the ridge. It was a route cut by his father forty odd years previously and it connected Wangallon Homestead with Wangallon Town, the settlement which had sprung to life in the early fifties. Now as he ducked to miss an overhanging branch, the stillness of the surrounding trees brought into relief the outline of two figures. They were on the very edge of the ridge where the pine trees thinned gradually before being dwarfed by an open plain of grassland.

Luke reined in his mare, and steadied the other two horses he led. He squinted against the glare made more ferocious by the recent shelter of the ridges' thick canopy. His eight-year-old half-brother Angus was struggling with a black boy a good foot taller in height. Luke leant back in his saddle and grinned in amusement as Angus managed to free himself from the boy's grip. A sharp chase followed. Angus ducked and weaved away from the older boy but Luke was soon clicking his tongue in disappointment as the black boy dived, catching Angus around the ankles and bringing him crashing to the ground. Luke touched the flanks of his mount, walking forwards. The boy's hijinks had developed into a good scuffle. The wiry black boy now had Angus pinned by one shoulder and as Luke neared the twosome he could see Angus's legs kicking out fiercely as he screamed furiously. The black boy was rubbing sand in his face while Angus spat, kicked, yelled and spluttered.

Seconds later, Angus was whacking his torturer in the ear with a broken belah branch. Luke winced at the sting the raspy, thin plant would deliver. Finally Angus managed to push the boy off him. He took advantage of the altered odds quickly and straddled him long enough to deliver two sharp blows with the branch, but the win was slight, for soon Angus found himself receiving a series of hard shoves that sent him reeling to the ground. Luke was beginning to think better of his decision to wait for the final outcome. The black boy was laughing and mimicking Angus as he dragged himself up from the ground. Luke's fingers felt for the rawhide stockwhip curled at his side. He broke his horse into a trot. Boxer's tribe in the past had always been fairly reliable, however now they were no longer comprised of the pure blood relatives of past decades. Intermingling had occurred and, as the inhabitants of Wangallon had discovered, such mixing of blood could and did lead to violence. The black youth was dancing around Angus now, kicking sand in his little half-brother's face, his straggly limbs dancing wildly as if he were partaking in some type of deranged corroboree.

Feet away, Luke dismounted and unfurled his stockwhip. Angus was throwing something and Luke could only watch as the black boy, struck in the face, tottered on his spindly legs and then fell to the ground.

'Angus!'

Angus lifted his fist above the fallen youth, a smooth rock clearly visible in his grasp. Luke cracked his stockwhip. The sharp snap echoed loudly through the ridge. Birds, stilled in the noon day heat, flew with a rush from nearby trees. Kangaroos camping beneath the shade of a nearby gum tree hopped away. Angus dropped the rock immediately and turned in the direction of the whip crack.

'What do you think you're doing, boy?'

Angus's face turned from a concentrated red to a wide grin as he left the boy lying on the ground and ran towards him. 'Luke, Luke, you're back.'

Luke held the eight-year-old at arm's length. Beneath the filthy clothes and grimy face the boy had grown during his eight-month absence. His arms and legs were reasonably thick for his age and his young frame had all the makings of the barrel chest that marked the Gordon men. 'What are you doing out here?'

Immediately the boy grew defensive. 'Nothing.' Angus kicked at a tuft of grass. Feet away the boy was beginning to stir. He straggled upright into a sitting position, obviously dazed. A line of blood oozed from a cut above his right eye and one side of his face was slashed red by the belah branch.

'I'd get a move on if I were you,' Luke said good-naturedly to the youth. 'I'm reckoning the boss, Mr Gordon,' he emphasised, 'won't be too pleased when he hears about this.'

Angus drew a mouthful of spittle into his cheeks and spat in the dirt. The boy glowered back.

'Go.' Luke backed his words with a gentle flick of the stock-whip. As the black boy walked off, Luke pointed to one of the pack horses. 'Hop up, Angus.'

'That's Willy. We had a fight. He stole my slingshot.' Angus held the slingshot proudly aloft.

'Ah.' Luke ruffled his kid brother's hair. Angus tucked his head deep into his shoulders to escape. 'The spoils of war. Well next time I'd be doing the fighting a little closer to home, just in case you need a hand.' Considering the height and speed advantage of young Willy, Angus's win was impressive.

'I would have managed,' Angus answered petulantly.

'With a stone? You think killing the boy would have been the answer?' They were riding side by side, Luke's three spare horses trotting obediently on a lead behind his mount.

'They're only blacks. They're here because father lets them be here. He feeds them, clothes them, gives them work to do. Jasperson says that if it wasn't for father they'd still be savages.'

Luke thought of the bullock speared out of hunger while droving some months back. 'Did Jasperson also tell you that they were here before us, before Wangallon?'

The boy rode on sullenly.

'That's what I thought.' They rode on silently, reaching the trampled earth that marked the beginning of the final approach to Wangallon Homestead. To the right, the track forked out across to the creek where the blacks camped. Closer lay a row of timber huts housing the black stockmen. A few miles to the left lay the woolshed and adjoining yards and the huts that housed the white stockmen on the property. Ahead the iron roof of Wangallon shimmered in a haze of heat. The early mist had been deceptive; by midafternoon it would be hot. Christmas Day promised to be a scorcher.

'Luke.' Mungo called out loudly as his horse trotted from the direction of the creek. 'Where have you been?' His blue shirt flapped about his waist where it had come loose from his trousers, a curled stockwhip hung from his shoulder.

'I'm hoping you don't need a description.' Luke reined in Joseph on his friend's approach as Angus cantered away, scowling.

'Ah,' Mungo raised his eyebrows knowingly and grinned. 'Same girl?'

'Same girl for the last time,' Luke replied, watching as Angus entered the Wangallon Homestead yard. 'Eventually they all become a problem. How's your mob?' He dipped his chin towards the camp on the creek.

'Boxer is a bit old now.'

It was true. Those that were at the founding of Wangallon nearly fifty years ago had long left their youth behind. 'Like Hamish.'

'The Boss? I don't call him old. I call him the fox.'

Luke laughed. Joseph moved his hoofs restlessly in the dirt. 'And your woman?'

'She becomes my father's cousin's woman.'

He'd hoped that as Boxer's son, Mungo would be the recipient of greater consideration. 'I'm sorry.'

Mungo looked ahead to the homestead. 'It is the second time in her life. She doesn't go to him until the next full moon. Until then she works in the big house.'

Luke smiled. 'The big house, eh?'

Mungo pointed at Luke's shoulder. 'It is good now, I think.'

Luke moved his arm up and down slowly. 'I owe you.'

Mungo grinned. 'I know.' He flicked his reins, turning his horse away. 'I must catch her between old men.' With a swish of his hat Mungo galloped off, riding to a stand of box trees where a slight figure in a pale dress waited. The girl's long black hair swayed as he helped her up to sit behind him on his horse. Luke lifted his hat in salute.

Winter, 1989

Wangallon Station Homestead

Sarah took special care with the evening meal. The old family dining table, the scene of Gordon mealtimes since the 1860s, was set for two people. Solid silver cutlery shimmered amid the turn of the century English dinnerware and the cut crystal stemware. She moved the heavy silver candelabra to the opposite end of the table and gave the five-foot-long gleaming mahogany sideboard, with its glass decanters, silver salvers and ancient punch-bowl, a quick polish. Then she boiled potatoes, mashing them up with butter and full-cream milk, and added a teaspoon of honey to the freshly steamed carrots.

'Smells great.'

Anthony's hands gripped her shoulders as he kissed her lightly. He waited as she plated up the juicy T-bone steaks.

'Want me to set the table?'

'I thought we would eat inside.' She sensed his frown, knowing his preference would be a can of beer in front of the television.

'What's the occasion?' Anthony followed her into the dining room.

'Do we need one?' For a moment Sarah considered forgetting her concerns. 'I helped Matt and Jack muster the steers this morning.' She sat the plates on the table. Anthony pulled out her chair so she could sit. 'You should have seen Bullet. He was the star, after Moses, of course.'

Anthony rolled his eyes. 'Moses isn't the wonder dog Matt likes to think he is.'

'I met Toby Williams, our drover.'

'Toby Williams? Now there's a name I haven't heard for a while.' He poured red wine into both their glasses. 'He's a bit of a ladies' man, but a damn good drover.' He raised his glass. 'To us.'

'To us.' Sarah took a large sip before cutting into her steak. 'How do you know Toby?'

'He's been around for a while. Actually he did quite a lot of work for Angus in the seventies. There was talk of him being a descendent of someone who worked here on Wangallon in the early 1900s.'

'How intriguing. I wonder who?'

'Don't know. I mentioned it to Angus one day and he told me not to listen to gossip. Anyway we'll have to be on the lookout when we start mustering. Toby's a bit of a tear-arse. You know, move the stock by the quickest route and if that happens to be through a few fences, tough. Angus always said he was a good stockman but reckoned you needed a clean-up crew after he'd been on a property and he's a bugger for leaving gates open.'

Sarah took a sip of wine. 'So where were you today?'

'I had a few things happening early,' Anthony said evasively. 'I did come back for smoko and lunch. I wondered where you were? I thought there were enough men to handle that job.'

'I like working outside, Anthony. I do it because I want to.' She gave a weak smile, acknowledging how defensive she sounded.

Swallowing her mouthful, her eyes came to rest on the formidable oil portrait of her great-grandfather, Hamish, hanging above the sideboard. He was depicted sitting, his fine dark suit and waistcoat failing to detract from his barrel chest and uncompromising violet-eyed gaze.

'Fair enough. It's just that we do have staff and I thought you had enough to do already, what with the book work and the garden.'

'Actually I'm considering rehiring our old bookkeeper. I'll still do the basic stuff.'

'Why?' Anthony took a sip of wine.

'I would rather be outdoors.'

'But your time is better utilised doing the things we don't need to employ more staff for.'

Sarah sighed. 'Then you take over the book work and the garden.' He didn't answer her. Great, she thought. Did she treat this as a stalemate or go ahead and rehire the bookkeeper? It struck her that perhaps there lay part of the problem. Had she been deferring to Anthony a little too much? 'You've made some purchases,' she began, uncomfortably aware that either way, she was about to ruin the evening.

Anthony nodded, his jaw finishing off a mouthful of tasty homegrown beef. 'The panels of course and the new loading ramps we discussed. This is great.'

Sarah took a sip of wine, her eyes straying to her great-grandfather. 'We didn't.'

Anthony paused, his fork midway between his plate and mouth. 'I'm sorry?'

'We didn't discuss the purchase of the panels, cattle truck or the ramps.' Her fork mounded her serving of potato into an Everest-type sculpture.

'Sorry, thought we did.' His eyes met hers.

'There's nothing in the station diary either.'

Anthony put his knife and fork down and took a large sip of wine. 'And?'

Sarah gave the mashed potato one final stroke before destroying its peak with the flat of her fork. 'Well, I've noticed that you seem to be forgetting to tell me things, important things.'

'They're only panels and ramps, Sarah.'

'Twenty-eight thousand dollars worth.'

'So you're concerned about the cost?' He looked relieved. 'I have been too. These couple of dry seasons have knocked us about a bit, although I've been doing the budget projections on a project that will pretty much pull Wangallon out of debt.'

'What project?' Sarah asked dismissively.

Anthony pushed his chair back, his hand straying to his partially drunk glass of wine. He sipped at the glass, his eyes peering at her from over the rim. 'What's bothering you?'

'Don't get angry. It's just that you seem to be making major financial decisions without consulting me.'

'I didn't realise I had to.'

With precision-like movements Sarah cut a piece of steak, added a sliver of carrot and chewed thoughtfully. The last thing she needed was for Anthony to become defensive. 'Even our weekly meetings have descended into you talking over the top of me.'

'That's not true. Actually I seem to recall you and Matt bonding over coffee and pretty much ignoring my suggestions.' Anthony finished his wine and looked irritably at his congealing steak.

'What's the matter?' she finally asked.

'I don't like my decisions being questioned like I'm the hired help.'

'And I don't like being left out of the loop when I'm the bloody Gordon.'

So there it was. The two things that neither of them had any control over. In Anthony's mind part of him would forever be the jackeroo. 'Maybe,' she suggested slowly, 'we could look at this a different way.'

'What way? Would you like me to report to you every morning now that you suddenly have decided to become fully involved in the running of Wangallon?'

'Bloody hell.' Sarah banged the top of the table with her hand, before taking a deep breath. 'Look, I don't like change, okay? You of all people should know that. There has been too much of it in this family. I don't want to move bedrooms or put awnings on the main verandah. I don't want Matt Schipp disgruntled because you want him to be more than the head stockman and I don't want things purchased or Wangallon's management style changed without us discussing it first, jointly. I'm entitled to have an equal say in the management of Wangallon.'

'Fair enough. It's just that since Angus's death you have holed yourself up in the office a fair bit. I thought you were happy with the way things were going.'

Sarah ignored the tight line of annoyance between his eyes. 'It was important for me to get the feel for things. You know cashflow and budget forecasting. And yes, I've been really upset. Angus's death is the like the passing of an era on Wangallon.'

Anthony rolled his eyes. 'It's nearly two years, Sarah, time to let go and move on.' He cleared his throat. 'We should be discussing the one thing you've been avoiding since Angus's death. You can't keep burying your head in the dirt. Jim Macken was left a thirty per cent share and –'

Sarah held her hand up. 'I don't want to talk about it. Not tonight.'

'You can't ignore it. Angus stipulated that Jim had two years to be informed of his will. And fair enough. They have a lot to come to terms with.'

'*They* have a lot to come to terms with?' Sarah's knuckles whitened.

'Sarah.' Anthony leant forward in his chair. 'All I'm saying is that the two years are nearly up. You have to prepare yourself. Jim Macken has rights.'

'The illegitimate son of my father has rights?'

They ate silently for some minutes, although Sarah's appetite was gone. 'It was great to see Shelley so happy.' Sarah knew her words sounded double-edged.

Anthony pushed his chair out abruptly and stood. 'Yes, it was. Is that going to be us, Sarah? Two years is a hell of a long time to be engaged.'

Sarah closed her eyes briefly. 'Aren't you happy?'

'It's not the same.'

'Nor is saying you're willing to work as a team and then running off and buying expensive stuff without consulting me. There are other people involved in the running of this property. And in case you've forgotten, we actually do work to a budget.'

'Personally I think the main problem here, Sarah, is that my surname isn't Gordon and you want to make sure yours stays that way.'

How on earth did a conversation about his attitude morph into the personal? Sarah wondered.

'Every argument we have invariably involves Wangallon and your heritage. You don't have anything to prove, and I'm not trying to supersede you as far as the running of the property is concerned. How can I possibly do that when you are the fourth generation Gordon? Yes, I was left a thirty per cent share in the property as you were, but you forget; I've been here for eight years. During that time you moved to Sydney, became a photographer, fell in love with someone else and got engaged. It was your grandfather and me running Wangallon. Now after holing yourself up in the station office for months, you seem to have decided that I've taken on too much responsibility and you feel threatened by it. Well I know what has to be done and how to do it. So bloody well let me.'

He left her sitting alone with the remains of their unfinished dinner. Sarah glanced up at her great-grandfather, finishing her wine in two long sips. This was one argument that she couldn't see being won by either of them. In a way she guessed she should have known this would happen. From Anthony's viewpoint he was the one who had put in the hard yards on the place. Yet having both received a thirty per cent share in the property from her grandfather did not make them equal in his eyes, for in the end she was the surviving Gordon, both by name and birthright. She may well have been the second choice following her brother's untimely death, but the mantle was hers.

Sarah cleared the dining room table. She stacked the plates and left them on the kitchen sink and then poured herself another glass of wine. Glass in hand, she walked outside and sat on the top step. The air was cold and crisp; the dome of the sky bright with stars. A slight scuffle announced Bullet as he struggled out from beneath the elevated rainwater tank. He stopped to look over his shoulder at Ferret, the one dog he appeared agreeable to sharing his special camping spot with, and ambled slowly down the cracked cement path towards her. He took up position on the cement step, his head in her lap. Sarah stroked him, examined the dried blood on his nose. He wriggled, wagged his tail, and then opened his eyes briefly to look up at her. He smelled of cow manure and dirt. She ruffled the dog's back and leant against the door. Surely Anthony could see that for their relationship to work he had to let her be totally involved in the running of Wangallon. Even the knowledge that her father intended to leave his ten per cent share in the property to her on his passing didn't really change things. The two of them had to live, love and work as a team. There was no other way, for things weren't perfect and she had a feeling that time was running out. Anthony was right, although Sarah hated to admit it. Jim did have the right to claim a share in Wangallon. It's just that no one knew if he planned to.

Two days later Sarah was back in the office reconciling the previous month's accounts. The mail would have been delivered by now and it would take Anthony only ten minutes or so to drive down to the boundary gate and collect it. The last few days had been difficult. Their conversation was still limited to only the very necessary. At least her mother's condition had stabilised, although Sarah was unsure as to whether that was positive or negative. It was hard to feel much for a woman who'd barely tolerated her when she was growing up and then conveniently slipped into mental oblivion after her son's death. Sarah almost succumbed to discussing her mother with Anthony, but they'd never been friendly and Sarah was still angry enough not to want to admit to needing his support. Instead she reconciled herself to a trip north at some future stage, if only for her father's sake.

In the office Sarah flipped open the paddock book, her fingers running along each line as she checked the stock moved to various paddocks during the last two weeks. The steers had been moved to an oat crop, 6,000 ewes due to lamb in September had been walked 15 kilometres south to the black wattle paddocks, the bulls were on oats taking a well deserved holiday from their breeding duties and . . . Something was wrong. Sarah flipped back through the pages of the paddock book: Stumpy, Ridge, Back, Stud, Corner, all recent paddocks involved in stock movements. She checked and rechecked dates, mobs of sheep and herds of cattle. Boxer's Plain was overstocked with both sheep and cattle. Well it was pretty clear which mob would be first out on the stock route. Boxer's was prime grazing country. A good third of it was comprised of a flat expanse of grassland. That was the last block she wanted to see eaten out. It took too long for the grasses to regenerate when the rain finally did come.

Anthony returned with the mail, his signature slam of the back door reverberating through the house and causing Sarah to frown. He dropped the bundle on the edge of the oak desk and surprisingly gave her a light kiss on the top of her head. He was wearing a brown cable-knit jumper that made him look totally huggable.

'How's the office secretary going this morning?'

Sarah dearly wished that she didn't have to wipe the smile off his face, especially when there hadn't been one there for quite a few days. Pulling the rubber band from the rolled up newspapers and envelopes, she sorted through the pile quickly.

He leant against the desk. 'I'm sorry we argued.'

Sarah passed him the rural newspaper and gave a shrug. 'It's inevitable, I guess. There will always be something happening that one of us doesn't agree with.'

Anthony rolled the paper back into a long tube and began tapping one end of it into the palm of his hand. 'And? I can tell by that matter-of-fact tone that something else is wrong.'

'I don't want us to have another argument . . .'

'Which pretty much means we will.' His smile vanished, replaced by a flat look of defence.

'I'm worried about Boxer's Plains. It's overstocked. We'll have to move some of them immediately. As it is we've probably lost carrying capacity over the winter. Those cattle will have to be the first to go on the route and –' A raised palm made her halt mid-sentence.

'I did mention at dinner the other night that I was working on a project that would assist in helping Wangallon recover from the drought.'

'I sort of remember,' although Sarah wondered what it had to do with overstocking.

'Well, before you start running off about Boxer's, perhaps you could wait a couple of days. I'll have a better idea of the cost by then.'

'Great, just great,' Sarah repeated, shuffling the mail like a deck of cards as Anthony walked out. She didn't like the sound of this cloak and dagger project, especially when he was sounding defensive. Here she was with sweaty palms and the dull thud of a coming headache and she was no further advanced. She looked disinterestedly at the mail. When the knock came at the back door, Matt Schipp's voice boomed loudly across her thoughts.

He stood with his hat in his hands, one riding boot resting on the step. Ferret, having limped to his side, rested his head on his boot. Matt gave him a pat. 'You're a spoilt little bugger aren't you? Up here at the big house.'

Matt looked as if he'd already worked more than a full day and although it was only nearing eleven in the morning, Sarah speculated that he probably almost had.

'Are you free to come out with me, Sarah?' His expression was unreadable, his voice quiet. 'We have a problem.'

Summer, 1908

Wangallon Station Homestead, Christmas Eve

Hamish trotted the gelding up the gravel drive of Wangallon Homestead, wheeling the horse to the right and left. He was a stubborn animal. Even after castration and months of continuous riding, the horse chewed disconsolately on the bit and would move to a gallop as soon as the reins were loosened. At the paling gateway Hamish turned the animal back towards the direction of the house, fighting the gelding's inclination to break for the grassland beyond. The horse pawed the ground and reared on its hind legs, whinnying in annoyance. With one gloved hand on the reins, Hamish dug his knees into the animal's flanks and struck the horse on its rump with a short riding crop. 'You damn recalcitrant.' Immediately the gelding yielded, trotting almost amiably back towards the house where Angus waited.

'Up you get.'

Angus did as his father bid and, with a stirrup in the form of his father's hands, was hoisted atop his new horse. He grabbed the reins tightly, pulled his knees in towards the gelding's flanks and waited for directions.

'Well then,' Hamish gave an almost imperceptible nod of his head as the gelding's nostrils flared, 'you've been complaining for days since you learnt he's to be yours. Let's see if you can handle him.'

Angus flicked the reins and the horse moved forward with an unsteady jolt. He grinned at his father, sat his bum squarely in the saddle and dug his heels in. The gelding snorted and pigrooted across the width of the gravel drive, and Angus was launched up into the air to land solidly on his backside.

'Again,' Hamish commanded, ignoring the boy's look of wounded pride. 'Think about what you did wrong.'

Angus climbed back into the saddle with his father's assistance and flicked the reins. The gelding stood stubbornly still.

'Oh do be careful, Angus.' Claire watched from the verandah, her quilting dangling from her fingers.

Hamish held his right hand up for silence. Angus squeezed his knees against the gelding and was rewarded with a gentle trot. The boy was endowed with a good seat, Hamish noted, and a straight back without a hint of a slouch. Boy and horse began to trot around the perimeter of the garden. Hamish watched as his son relaxed into his mount's gait, the reins drooping, a barely perceptible slouch appearing in his lower back. Cupping his hands behind his back, Hamish readied for his son to receive another grounding. As if on cue Angus dropped one hand free of the reins in imitation of his father, dug his heels in and was quickly launched over the horse's head, his arms flailing in the wind. He landed with a thud to sprawl at the base of a bougainvillea hedge. The gelding snorted and kicked out its back legs before calming.

Claire ran down the steps of the verandah, clutching at her skirt. Hamish barred her path.

'He is not a child, Claire, and you are not his father. Please tend to your domain and I will tend to mine.'

Claire frowned in annoyance and looked to where her young son walked gamely across to the gelding. He led the horse to the paling fence, climbed up on it and half-jumped half-pulled himself into the saddle. The horse immediately bucked him off. Claire shook her head at her son's determination. Angus brushed the dirt from his hands and approached the gelding once more.

'He is as stubborn as his father,' Claire announced, as Angus led the horse back to where his parents waited.

Passing the reins to his father, Angus positioned himself to be helped once more. This time the gelding didn't even allow his young rider to be seated. Hamish extended his hand and pulled his son up off the ground. 'We'll try in the yards tomorrow, Angus.' The boy's cheek was grazed and a layer of dirt and grass clung to his clothing. 'Both hands on the reins at all times, no sudden movements, heels in. And keep those knees of yours gripped against his flanks. Lastly, make friends with him,' Hamish instructed.

Angus patted the gelding between the ears. 'He's quiet enough now, Father.'

Father and son discussed the gelding's merits standing side by side, their hands clasped behind their backs. Hamish could only imagine how the boy's backside felt. By comparison he knew exactly his wife's temperament, her feet managing to make an inordinately loud noise on the verandah.

'Wetherly is dining with us on the 27th,' he called over his shoulder. Claire halted on the doorstep, straightened her shoulders and then, lifting her skirts, walked softly indoors.

'So then you managed to find your way back,' Hamish said between puffs of tobacco as Luke appeared around the corner of the homestead.

Luke ran his hands across the gelding's flanks, the horse side-stepping in response.

'You should have been back earlier,' Hamish continued with a studied puff of his pipe. 'Take the horse back to the stables, Angus.'

'Yes, Father.' They watched Angus depart. He was limping slightly and, thinking himself out of sight, rubbed at his backside.

'After months in the saddle I would have thought I'd earned some rest.' Luke undid the leather saddlebag strung across his shoulder. From it he retrieved a sheath of paper marked by rain, grime and saddle grease. He passed the bill of sale to his father. 'Besides, I'm sure Jasperson reported on my whereabouts.'

'The cattle were obviously in fair order. They fetched a good price, although you had some losses.' He scanned the paperwork with interest.

'Unavoidable losses,' Luke was not interested in giving a detailed account of the trip. His father rarely asked for one. 'They did well. Better than I expected.'

'You always have erred more on the conservative side, Luke.'

'Not everyone can survive on risk alone.' The silence between them signalled the beginning of the weeks ahead.

Hamish stroked his moustache thoughtfully. 'How's your shoulder?'

Luke slung the saddlebag back over his shoulder. 'I'd keep Angus away from that Aboriginal boy. I caught them fighting.'

'Willy is Boxer's nephew,' Hamish explained, 'and if Angus gets knocked about a bit, well, he'll just have to learn from it. As we all do. He's eight and he's not had the cosseting your own mother gave you.'

Rose could hardly be charged with being over protective of her children, Luke thought. His own childhood had been much like Angus's until he'd been all but orphaned through childhood illness, accident and his mother's death.

'You better get yourself cleaned up. It is Christmas apparently.'

'So I've been told.' So that was it, eight months droving and their conversation limited to a handful of minutes.

'By the way, Luke, your grandmother died recently. She never woke from her sleep.'

'I see. And the emporium?' An image of the George Street Emporium he'd visited recently sprang to mind. It was crowded with every conceivable object: hammers and pickaxes, through to sacks of foodstuffs, men's clothing and material for women's things. He'd been intrigued with a set of finely carved men: six tiny Chinamen with poles strung across their shoulders and buckets dangling from fine cord at the end. The owner of the emporium reckoned they'd been carved from ivory. But Luke hadn't settled for that, he'd purchased the tortoiseshell hair comb instead.

His father shrugged. 'No doubt we will receive correspondence in that regard.'

Walking around the side of the house Luke paused to take a swig from the canvas waterbag that hung from a hook under the eaves of the meat house. It was freshly washed down. Clearly there had been a kill in celebration of Christmas. Black flies buzzed incessantly as water dripped from the large wooden chopping block, a hefty tree trunk four feet wide by three feet high. Butchers knives and buckets stood washed on a low wooden table and the tampered dirt floor showed semi-dried puddles of water. Over all came the pungent scent of chloride of lime.

'Luke, Luke, Luke!'

Luke found himself caught up in a great hug by Lee and was soon following his pigtailed, bow-kneed form past the old man's large vegetable garden and into his hut. It was dark inside. Dark enough for streaks of daylight to show through myriad unevenly joined planks of wood. Luke counted three candles burning wanly in makeshift holders, a broken china cup, a saucer, a mound of earth. Beyond that he could smell incense burning. He sat cross-legged on the floor. The flare of a match broke the almost other-worldly feel of the room. A deep chuckle followed.

'Young fella come back, eh?'

Luke followed the voice to a male form sitting some feet away. It was Boxer. Lee turned the flame up on a kerosene lamp.

'So this is where you old people get to when my father's calling,' said Luke.

Boxer coughed a little, drew a deep breath. 'Special occasion, young fella come back.'

Luke accepted the small glass of watered down rum and threw the liquid down his throat. 'And Mungo. He's a good stockman, Boxer.'

The old black coughed again. 'Better be.'

As Luke's eyes grew accustomed to the light the hut came into focus. At the opposite end there was a handmade wooden chair, a bench holding cast iron cooking pots, small sacks of dried goods and a clutch of quails' eggs. Along one length was a narrow bed and across from it, Lee's altar. It was from here that the smell of incense originated. A streak of smoke rose into the air from a ceramic holder. It sat surrounded by a collection of small bowls holding offerings. On the wall behind, tacked up with two nails, hung a torn banner inscribed with Chinese characters.

'My grandmother died,' Luke said slowly, drawing his eyes away from the remnants of Lee's lost culture. 'You remember her, don't you, Lee? My mother's mother? She ran the emporium. What was she like?'

Lee's dark eyes were sunken as if beginning to withdraw from this world. 'At Ridge Gully, yes, yes.' Lee was tempted to tell Luke that the woman liked the pleasures of the flesh. That she paraded her daughter around like a bag of jewels until Master Hamish swallowed her up. 'One should not speak of the ancestors,' he cautioned, dipping his finger into the murky contents of his glass and sucking at his dirty nail.

'You have much sadness?' Boxer asked as he dragged heavily on his pipe.

'No, not much,' Luke said truthfully. 'I never met her.'

'Her daughter was like a scared rabbit,' Boxer continued. 'I remember; too pale, not strong enough for the spirits of this country.' Boxer sucked again on his pipe.

'Not strong enough for many things,' Luke agreed, his finger flicking at an ant. 'All my family are dead now, except for Hamish and Angus.'

'And you,' Lee pointed his wiry finger directly at him.

'Sure, I'm still around.' Luke got to his feet, marvelling at how old bones could sit cross-legged for hours on end when he could barely last a few minutes. 'I admire your loyalty to my father, both of you.'

Lee bowed his head.

Boxer stared at him. 'Mebbe it's easy to follow those who do not forgive. The Boss's path is undivided and for some there is strength in such a life. And remember,' he chewed on the thickness of his bottom lip, 'the Boss is favoured by the old people,' he glanced skywards, 'for he looks after mother earth who is home to us all. As for those who do not walk the earth now,' Boxer continued, 'well perhaps they did not wish to do so; or mebbe Wangallon didn't want them.'

'Come, come,' Lee bustled Luke from the hut. 'You come back later.' Alone with Boxer, Lee hunched his shoulders, pulling a plug of tobacco from the pouch at his waist. 'The boy thinks he is alone in the world, that all that were of blood to him are dead excepting his own father and the boy, Angus.' Lee stuffed his wooden pipe with the tobacco, clamped it between the remains of his teeth and looked at Boxer. 'He is not. There is another.' He sighed heavily. 'There is always another.'

Boxer's wide forehead halved in size as the whites of his eyes increased.

Winter, 1989

Wangallon Station

The Landcruiser lurched across the paddock. Matt never did mind the odd bump and Sarah found herself clutching at the hand bar on the dash as the vehicle found its way into every pothole on the rough track. A heavy dew was only just starting to dissipate and silvery cobwebs crisscrossed the grass. Beneath the tufts the soil was almost bare. Thanks to the lack of rain there was no clover or herbage, winter feed coveted by both cattle and sheep. From the branches of scattered trees, birds fluffed and preened themselves, silver-crested cockatoos competed with the brilliant red and blue plumage of bush parrots, while small bush budgies darted for insects. Sarah smiled, despite the drying countryside. Ahead the road forked into two. One track led to the creek and the family cemetery, with a wider road diverging off it towards the cavernous woolshed and sheep yards. The other bypassed the ridge and paddock where Cameron had been killed, to circumnavigate the boundary of Wangallon. Matt turned down the latter and stopped at the first of many gates, grinning cheekily. 'It's the first of twelve.'

Sarah wasn't surprised when she guessed their destination. She just hoped that the overstocking problem she'd envisioned had not decimated the block too much. Boxer's Plains had been the last property purchased by the Gordons. For that reason it retained a special place in the family's collective history. When her father, Ronald, suggested purchasing more land in the late 70s, Angus made it clear he wasn't interested in following the expansionary vision of his own father, choosing instead to embark on a major improvement plan. Money was spent on renewing ageing fences, building cattle yards and renovating staff accommodation; trees were thinned out to allow an increase in natural pasture growth and in turn the stock-carrying capacity of the country increased. Angus Gordon's legacy was that of a highly efficient property, with excellent infrastructure and a stock-per-acre ratio that was envied by neighbours, especially during periods of drought when his management skills weeded out the men from the boys.

Finally reaching the Wangallon River, they crossed the army bridge Angus purchased and erected in the fifties. A wide stream of muddy water moved sluggishly beneath them as they rattled over the wooden boards, disturbing two grey kangaroos on the bank below. Old box trees marked the line of past floods, while a track leading down the steep bank to the water and reappearing on the other side was a reminder that this waterway could easily be crossed in times of severe drought.

It was unlike Matt to be quiet for so long. Although a person of uncommon calm, Sarah knew that prolonged silence in the man usually meant something significant was weighing on his mind. She settled into a guise of steely resolve that she'd been told on occasion was expected by a Gordon. Frankly she didn't quite think those characteristics were particularly well developed in her.

They drove through a stretch of lignum, the thick, woody plants cloaking their view both left and right. As always, Sarah felt unsettled visiting this part of Wangallon. It was as if she were entering another country, one cut off from the world, and imagined it was the wide river boundary that set the block apart. Then the road broadened out to run beneath a canopy of trees before revealing an open expanse of sky and land. Sarah heard the metallic hum of machinery as Matt pulled up under the shade of a box tree and handed Sarah a pair of binoculars.

'You'll get a better view of things if you stand in the back,' he suggested.

Stepping up into the Landcruiser's tray, Sarah raised the binoculars to her eyes. For a moment she felt she was part of a dream. Two large tractors were pulling heavy discs behind them, cutting and turning the rich black soil beneath. To their left a shimmer of metal caught her attention. 'My God!'

'Yep.' Matt joined her and together they stared out across the wrecked paddock in the direction of the two D9 bulldozers. Sarah heard a crack and then a second later a tree tumbled to the ground.

'They started two days ago,' Matt volunteered. 'They reckon we'll get about 2000 acres of cultivation where these offset discs are working. No trees to knock down so it's pretty cost-effective.'

'Cost-effective,' Sarah repeated. All she could think about was the beautiful grassland that was being ruined and the trees on the horizon that had provided shade in the summer and protection in the winter for their sheep and cattle. 'Where are the ewes? The cows?'

'Out there somewhere,' Matt waved a hand in a vague northerly direction. 'Pushed up against the far boundary, I reckon, trying to escape the intrusion.'

'It was overstocked.' It was more a statement than a question but when Matt nodded Sarah couldn't help herself. 'Why didn't you say something to me?'

Matt frowned. 'I queried Anthony on two occasions about the

stock numbers. And I've been out here the last couple of Sundays to check on things. Actually I intended to tell him today that we would have to start moving stock out, and then I saw this.'

'But Matt, this is too much. Are you telling me Anthony did this?' What a stupid question. Who else would it be?

Matt studied the moonscape before them, avoiding the ticklish situation of an emotional woman. He began the painstaking process of rolling a cigarette. He could crack a snake's back like a stockwhip and hang onto a snarling wild cat by the tail, but a slow discharge of sadness was beyond him. 'I couldn't go to you on a hunch, Sarah. Nor can I play favourites. I'm a hired hand.'

'Jesus, Matt, first and foremost you work for Wangallon.' Sarah jumped out of the back of the vehicle. 'Drive over. I want this to stop immediately.'

They moved slowly across the uneven ground, once or twice bogging down in the freshly turned earth, Matt accelerating to bring them clear. Only when they drew level with the dozers did Sarah see the extent of their work; great trees and stringy saplings all bowed down between the great lumbering chain linking the dozers together. The metal links, each as large as a football, crawled across the ground collecting everything in their wake.

'The country will be far more valuable once it's cleared, Sarah.'

'Not everything is about money,' she snapped back, instantly regretting her tone.

'Maybe not, but even if Anthony didn't intend to farm it, imagine the increased stock numbers we would be able to run once the dozers get into that heavily timbered country. He is doing very selective clearing. Once the trees are gone the grasses will grow back tenfold.'

Sarah considered Matt's comments. He was not one to speak idly. 'Well, Matt, I don't agree with this, especially considering the way it's been handled. Besides which, it's being ploughed up.

Where the hell are we meant to run the cattle and sheep that usually graze here?' She ran irritated fingers through her hair. 'Then there is the monetary side. How much is this going to cost?'

'Upwards of two hundred thousand dollars, with the work to be done in two stages. At least that's what the contractor tells me. I haven't spoken to Anthony about it.'

Sarah felt physically ill.

'His intention is to clear all of Boxer's Plains eventually. Personally I don't think it's a good idea. Farming is costly. You've got spraying and machinery and the vagaries of the weather. Then there is the infrastructure: you need silos to store seed, trucks for cartage to the rail lines at harvest . . .'

'The list goes on.'

'Pretty much.' Matt drew up to the side of the one of the dozers and got out to speak to the driver.

In an hour these men would be hunting down Anthony, querying him furiously as to why a stop-work mandate had been suddenly imposed on them. 'This is going to be difficult,' Sarah admitted as they headed back to the homestead. 'Can we get those cows from Boxer's Plains out on the stock route pronto?'

'Sure thing, Sarah.'

'Good. And the sheep?' They drove through the house paddock gate.

'They'll be right. We can feed them out there.' Matt's knuckles were white, gripping the steering wheel.

'I'll get the corn delivered asap. We can store it in the portable 25 tonne silo and then fill up the sheep feeder when needed.' Sarah knew that like her, Matt was mad as hell. Yet beyond her anger lay something far more distressing; there was a terrible unravelling within her. Anthony had broken her trust.

High Summer, 1989

Northern Scotland

Jim Macken finished reading the file and closed the manila folder. He glanced uneasily at his mother, who smiled at him nervously. He knew her opinion. She believed he should be leaving well enough alone. With her usual quiet movements she walked into the kitchen and closed the door. Jim heard the rattle of the water tap as it came to life and the solid click of a kitchen cupboard. She would be making tea, strong and hot, perhaps pouring a nip of whisky into hers to ward off the melancholy that stalked her these days. It was true that his mother wished Sarah Gordon had never come to their country. And it was equally true that neither of them would have believed that he could be heir to land in Australia.

'The place has been willed to you fair and square by Angus Gordon himself,' said Robert Macken, chewing on the stem of his pipe.

Jim flicked back through the folder. 'I still can't believe you waited so long to tell me.'

'Probate took some time, I told you that, lad; and there was a clause in the will that gave us until next month to respond. I was not of a mind to use it, but your mother insisted. She didn't want to rush things. We only want what's best for you,' his father persevered.

'Do you?' Normally his father would begin arguing. They had always argued and the past that grows between father and son is always difficult to erase, no matter whether it has been good or bad. Yet their relationship was now altered. For three weeks Robert had not been his blood father and although Robert knew of his wife's pregnant state before they were betrothed, the revelation of Jim's natural father caused a marked alteration in their reasonably contented existence.

'Now what type of a question is that?'

It was one Jim decided was plain enough, for he knew where his mother's preference lay. She would sooner see him a pauper than open himself up to grief. As for his father, or his Scottish father as he'd mentally begun addressing the man who'd clothed and fed him, he was beginning to see the makings of what pride could do when there was the opportunity of mixing it with a little revenge.

'You owe them nothing, lad. Think of the money.'

The sentence was punctuated by the re-entry of his mother, carrying a white plastic tray. Her eyes met his as she placed the cups of tea on the wooden table with a slight clatter of crockery. When she sat again in the wooden rocker that once belonged to her own mother, her hands were wrapped securely around the hot tea. Her cheeks were tinged a becoming red, her eyes soft. More than a nip had been consumed, of that Jim was sure.

'Jim's existence has been acknowledged, surely that is enough.' She blew carefully at the steaming tea; the rocking chair ceased its gentle sway. 'Besides,' his mother continued softly, 'it is Jim's decision.'

Robert huffed loudly, the noise of his teeth chewing at the pipe filled the room. 'This is a will, woman. There is no decision. I know we've all had much to come to terms with,' he nodded in his son's direction, 'but it's past the time for waiting. It's not fair to them –' his large thumb pointed at the folder – 'nor us. This is a lot of money. The whole family could benefit from it.'

'And what happened, Robert Macken, to being happy with our life? How many times in the past have you sat at this very table and told Jim not to wish for greater things, to appreciate his life,' she held up a quivering finger to his obvious desire to interrupt, 'and I agreed. We have food and a roof over our heads and the things that have been most blessed to me remain so. My family, this place where I shall live and die, sleek cattle, the pungent scent of peat . . .'

Robert gulped at his own tea. 'Don't be idiotic, woman. Your son is a descendent of the Gordon clan. He is entitled to his inheritance. How, as his mother, could you possibly ask him to ignore this?' He waved a typed letter in the air, the thick creamy paper crackling with the action.

'The money doesn't belong to you, Jim.' His mother continued sipping at her tea.

Jim admired how a woman of such impoverished birth could turn down the chance of wealth, yet it also surprised him she remained so adamant.

'Rubbish.' Robert folded the letter carefully, placing it on the narrow mantlepiece above the fire.

Part of Jim wished that Sarah Gordon had never visited his country; for it was only through their chance meeting and friendship that they both eventually learnt of his blood ties to her family. At moments it had been too much, his wayward mother, the father who was not his father, every important element in his life had been controlled by someone, even the timing of when he should learn of his real father's identity and the contents of Angus

Gordon's will. Jim listened as Robert and his mother argued. It was no longer just about the will, it was about lost love for his mother and the harbouring of resentments for Robert.

'Think of the money, Jim. It is rightfully yours,' Robert argued, gulping the scalding tea as if his mouth was lined with asbestos.

To Jim it was money borne of sadness. His clearest memory of Sarah was the day they walked in the heather, gradually ascending one of his favourite hills until, at the rocky summit, they had looked out into the distant lochs below, stringing out like small puddles of water that a child could jump. For indeed that was how he felt. On first meeting the Australian he'd experienced the most comfortable of sensations. It was like coming home after a long journey. 'It doesn't feel right. It's like something the English would do, taking over something that isn't rightfully theirs. Like here where they've resumed land and forced us to eke out a living on these tiny blocks; generational Scots relegated to bed-and-breakfasts and scrounging for a living.'

'Then do something about it,' Robert interrupted with an impatient wave of his fist. 'The Gordons are worth millions. You've been offered a thirty per cent share. Get your money and come back and do something positive. Stop you and yours from bowing at the feet of the likes of Lord Andrews and his family.'

Frankly Jim could see little that was positive. He'd spent three months pining for a girl who turned out to be his half-sister. And even though loneliness had made him believe he cared for her, it didn't stop him from feeling stupid and uncomfortable at the prospect of sharing in her inheritance.

Jim's mother shook her head. 'You love Scotland, Jim, almost as much as I do. You don't need to say anything, I can see it in your eyes. You smile at the wild landscape, feel the comfort of home when you step upon her springy heather and breathe in the bracing air when the wind blows across the loch. How you feel for your country, how you worry for the people of the north is what makes you Scottish.

Remember that, for if you go to Australia and take your share, you will be destroying Sarah's home. Imagine how she will feel.'

'Enough of your melancholic women's tales.' Robert was on his feet, tugging at his homespun woollen jumper. 'Regardless of your inclination, the facts remain the same, lad. You only need direct the solicitor to give you the value in cash. Either you make the call or I will.'

'I'd imagine Sarah would have to sell a part of the property.' His mother's softly persuasive tone resonated through the cramped confines of their living area.

'And who are you most concerned about, Sarah or her father?' Robert left the small crofter's cottage, slamming the door behind him.

Jim looked from his untouched tea to his beloved mother. Having already discussed the possibility of him flying to Australia, it was now becoming increasingly important to him as the days progressed. He would prefer to have never known about his true parentage, yet he needed to meet his real father. And there was another part of him, he guessed the Gordon part, that wanted to see the land that a Scot managed to carve out for himself over one hundred and thirty years ago. If only his mother were not so against the idea.

He walked outside to a day grown bright. From their small house on the edge of the hill, patches of heather extended outwards, interspersed with rocks and dirt. The landscape extended downwards towards the loch that shimmered invitingly in the midmorning light. Hands shoved deep in the pockets of his corduroy trousers, Jim walked the slight distance between house and water, his sturdy lace-ups crunching pebbles underfoot. His mother was right – he did love this land.

He was unaware of her presence until her warm hand linked itself through his arm. Together they stared out at the loch, at the treeless hills surrounding the water's grey beauty.

'If you go to Australia you may get your inheritance, Jim,' she touched his cheek gently, 'but you will lose your Sarah forever and you will never be the same on your return.' She squeezed his arm tenderly. 'She won't be able to forgive you if she is her father's daughter.'

His mother's voice trembled. Jim patted her hand. 'Yet he is my father as well.' *And you loved him* he thought sadly. He leant down to select a smooth pebble at his feet. 'He wronged you.' He turned the pale grey stone in his fingers, weighing the cool rock carefully. There were unsaid words within his mother's pale eyes. He sensed a need for her to unburden. Jim waited for her to speak, imagined a shifting of memories, a sorting of explanations dulled by time and censored by a mother's love. The moment was blown aimlessly away by a lift in the morning breeze. Angrily he flung the pebble expertly across the loch's surface. The rock skipped effortlessly across the face of the wind-rippled water, and on the fifth bounce it sank from view.

Summer, 1908

Wangallon Station Homestead, Christmas Day

Mrs Stackland shooed the two maids out of her way and opened the oven door on the cast iron stove with a thick piece of towelling. She swiftly turned the loaf of bread and cinnamon biscuits out onto the wooden table; the aroma of freshly baked goods circulated with the scent of burning wood. Mrs Stackland prodded at both bread and biscuits, a slight smile the only indication of her pleasure. With a beckoning nod of her greying head she gestured to the younger and less clumsy of her helpers, Margaret, showing the girl how to prise the warm biscuits off the baking tray and place them to cool on a wire rack.

'Mind you don't break any. We don't serve broken biscuits at table,' Mrs Stackland reprimanded her newest recruit as the thin, agile fingers placed the biscuits carefully on the rack. She dabbed at her brow with the length of her apron, uncomfortably aware of the moisture soaking the back and front of her bodice. 'Butter and dripping, Margaret, and be quick, girl.' The kitchen would be a furnace by midday if she didn't have the majority of her menu prepared by eleven. There was little time for dawdling.

A large scrub turkey, plucked and ready for roasting, sat wrapped in a swathe of calico. Lifting a heavy pan from a side table she unwrapped the freshly killed bird and sat it tenderly in it. She surveyed the pile of vegetables to be peeled, then there was the plum pudding that had to be reheated in the steam boiler and an apple pie to be baked, for Mr Gordon demanded pie twice a week, Christmas or not. And Lee, Mrs Stackland realised with some irritation, was late with the preserved lemons for the custard and the bush quail she intended making into a tasty pie. She cut the fresh bread smartly in two and placed half the loaf onto a large tray, adding a plate of the biscuits. From the shelf above the stove she took the teapot and added a good handful of tea-leaves and then water from the steaming kettle. A quick glance confirmed the near completion of sizzling meat in a large skillet. Martha, the older of the maids, poked at it disinterestedly, as if she had something better to do than to ensure Mr Gordon's meat was perfect.

'Come, come. Hurry up, girl.'

The rebuke was addressed to Margaret, who was returning from the food safe located on the shady eastern side of the homestead. 'Did you top-up the trays?'

'Yes Ma'am.' The girl held a pad of butter in one hand, a container of dripping in the other.

'Good.' The safe was constructed like a cupboard with hessian walls sitting in drip trays of water. The water soaked into the hessian and if a light wind blew, it created a remarkably cool atmosphere. Trying to explain the importance of keeping food cool and unspoilt, however, was a daily challenge. 'And I think of those city folk with their fancy ice chests. Why they've no idea.' Mrs Stackland set the butter on the tray with the bread, biscuits and tea. 'Right you are then, lass. Take that into the Master and Mrs Gordon and do try not to slop anything.'

'Yes Ma'am.'

'And do stand up straight.'

'Yes Ma'am.'

Mrs Stackland observed the girl's studied concentration and slightly wobbly progression with undisguised concern, before turning her attention to the skillet. With a bustling movement of her wide hips, she sent the sullen Martha in the direction of the vegetables. Wrapping her towel around the burning hot handle, she served up the meat.

'Have I not told you to tidy yourself before entering the dining room?' Mrs Stackland tutted irritably at Margaret on her return. Dabbing at the girl's shiny face, she set the plates on the tray and handed it to the girl. 'They don't wish to have their meals served to them by a maid dripping in sweat. Mr Gordon first and then Mr Luke and then –'

'I'll be having mine right here,' Luke announced, lifting a plate from the tray.

'Right. Well, then,' Mrs Stackland stammered in surprise as her kitchen found itself with the unusual presence of a male who was neither Chinese nor child. Luke Gordon, gone near eight months, was a rare sight at Wangallon indeed.

Luke, aware his intrusion had momentarily thrown the usual precision order of the kitchen into disarray, winked jauntily at Wangallon's cook, then grinned at the maid. Clearly she was a half-caste, for her lighter skin contrasted obviously with the ebony of her companion. Her large brown eyes cast him a direct glance and then she was gone, her footsteps padding lightly across the polished cypress pine floorboards. Luke cocked his left eyebrow. The girl was a new addition and a pleasant one at that. Positioning himself at the far end of the table, he cut into the mutton chops with relish, appreciatively nodding at Mrs Stackland as she sliced two pieces of bread for him. He dropped the bread onto his plate, scraping the thick crusty dough through the juices. Adding a slice of meat, he chewed hungrily, reaching for the dripping to smear a thick layer of it onto his second piece of bread.

'The missus says the biscuits are good.' Margaret directed the statement to no one in particular as she re-entered the kitchen, although she made a point of looking at Luke.

Shooing the girl back with a wave of her hand, Mrs Stackland gave both maids firm instructions as to how the peel the vegetables. 'And make sure there is a good dollop of dripping in the pan, but don't put them on until I tell you. I want that bird half-cooked before they go in. Yes, Margaret you can put it on now. Well, Martha, don't stand there like a dumb cluck. Open the oven door. For goodness sake use some towelling or you'll burn up so bad you'll lose the use of your hand. And tie back that long hair of yours.'

Luke glanced at Martha. She was a bigger build than her lighter-skinned companion, with rounded hips and breasts and a slow way about her movements. He figured this was Mungo's woman, with her long dark hair and newness to the tasks required of a maid.

Mrs Stackland poured tea for both of them. 'I confine myself to two glasses of water a day,' she admitted. 'The first laced with a little cod-liver oil for the digestion –' she looked across at the maids and lowered her voice – 'the second with a teaspoon of brandy for the constitution.' She held up a tin of condensed milk. 'Truly this is the greatest of inventions.'

'Merry Christmas.' Lee appeared, dumping two full cast iron buckets on the wooden table, the movement shuddering the table's contents; rattling cups and saucers, pots and skillets and spilling the tea in Mrs Stackland's cup.

'And Merry Christmas to you too, Lee,' Luke replied as the maids screeched at his unannounced entry and the cook admonished him for disrupting her domain.

Lee, appearing to ignore the remarks, began to empty the contents of the two buckets. There were two glass jars, one of preserved lemons, the other oranges, two small cabbages, some potatoes, carrots, onions, two plucked quails and an assortment of wilted-looking herbs. Lee separated the clutch of herbs, dirt spilling out from the furry roots onto both table and floor. He pushed the quails and a bunch each of sage and parsley towards Mrs Stackland. 'Put inside,' he stated, waving a scrawny finger from the herbs to the quail.

'We're having pie,' Mrs Stackland answered as she meticulously sorted through the fare as if she were selecting goods from a street vendor in George Street, Sydney.

'Put inside,' Lee repeated, the long nail on his pinkie finger extended at the birds.

'Thank you for the lemons,' Mrs Stackland said brusquely. 'They will do nicely for my custard.'

'Put inside.' Lee smiled, forcing his cheeks into circles of puffy flesh.

Luke slurped down his scalding tea as their argument continued over the herbs and then moved on to the caterpillar-chewed cabbages. He watched Margaret select two cut lengths of timber from the wood box and place them smartly into the slow combustion stove. Her dark hair was tied back into a thick bun on the nape of her neck and she was a slim, lithe little thing.

'After lunch I want you two girls to busy yourselves beating out the dirty carpets, then sweep the hall and change the linen on young Master Angus's bed,' Mrs Stackland ordered in between her arguing. 'And don't be forgetting the cleaning of the silver and Margaret the copper will have to be fired up for the washing and Martha do clean the flat-iron . . .'

'Oh, Mrs Stackland, are you there?'

Claire's clear, light voice carried sweetly towards the kitchen. Luke glanced at the doorway and thought of the nine months since he'd last seen Claire Whittaker Gordon. All of a sudden he needed air and space. He slipped silently out the back door.

'Mrs Stackland tells me you prefer the company of our staff, Luke.'

Luke heard the rustle of her skirts. It was a sound from his earliest memories of the girl who would eventually marry his father. He left the upturned bucket where he had been enjoying a quiet smoke and stubbed the thin roll-your-own out with the heel of his boot, purposely busying himself with the action. 'I never was one for airs and graces,' he answered flatly, keeping his broad back to Claire. Now she was near him again after so many months, he wished her gone.

'Where have you been? Your father tells me you arrived yesterday.'

'Busy.' He'd never quite seen the point of all the civilising his father enjoyed and his years droving had bred into him a preference for quiet meals with little talk. 'Are you enjoying your Christmas, Auntie Claire?' He did not mean for the words to come out so tightly and he cursed himself inwardly. He turned towards her, steeling himself lest any outward sign of his thoughts should be revealed. She was dressed all in white. The material draped gently over her bust and was inlaid with lace and net chiffon. On her head she wore a large hat with a curved brim. She was a study in decadence for a woman who lived on a remote station. 'I remember you sitting in the schoolroom with that fancy tutor from Sydney,' Luke said, 'learning all those languages and me with my readers in the corner.'

There were fine wisps of grey fanning out from her forehead now and the line of her proud jaw was softening. 'I never thought you would stay, you know,' he continued. The high-spirited teenager with the lustrous black hair and winning smile always appeared so ill-suited to both Wangallon and Hamish Gordon.

Claire gave a small confused frown. 'I never considered leaving.' She removed a finely embroidered lawn handkerchief from the sleeve of her bodice and dabbed at her neck above the high-topped blouse. 'You will join us for Christmas lunch, Luke. Your father would be so pleased.'

'He has you and Angus,' he smiled wryly, 'and Jasperson for that matter. There's no one else coming to be needing me for appearances' sake.' Last year he had argued with Jasperson and he would not on his life ruin another Christmas for Claire. He found the man's company abominable. Luke thought of the men and women who had crossed his path during his life to date. There was always some imperceptible sign that gave their true nature away. An undeserved remark, a lie for self-gain, or the physical reactions of the human body, such as the careless whore in Wangallon Town who, having overestimated her importance, had frowned at the extra coin he'd been prepared to give her. Apart from the man's predilection for young boys, the other hated truth of Jasperson was his meanness of spirit. Luke's fingers touched the tortoiseshell hair comb in his trouser pocket.

Claire sighed. 'Must you always be so stubborn? Come walk with me.'

The warmth of her slim arm through his was accompanied by a bittersweet stab of pleasure. Luke smelled lavender water and the sweet musky scent that was indefinably hers. Claire smiled up at him as they walked through Lee's garden and out into the orchard, which Lee had watered daily for over thirty years. It was a sight Luke would always remember for the patience and sturdy persistence it required; the bow legs and flapping pigtail and the long pole slung over his slight shoulders, which carried the two buckets of water.

Claire was walking in short stilted steps. 'Have we grown so poor, Claire, that there is not enough money to buy enough material for your dress?'

She gave a laugh. 'The fashionable ladies call it a hobble skirt for its lack of movement. And I admit to not being partial to its constraints.'

'Then why wear it?'

'Why, to be fashionable, of course.' Claire gave his arm a quick squeeze. 'It is good to see you, Luke. It has been an abominably boring year. When it stops raining, everyone seems to disappear; no parties, dances, balls. I have given only five soirees, with few attendees, and was staggered to see a number of my companions in last season's gowns. Are things so very bad?'

Luke patted her hand, her skin dewy beneath his calloused fingers. 'Not everyone has the advantages that come from a substantial property such as Wangallon, and there have been a few rumblings with some of the Aborigines a little south of us and you know how quickly that makes folk shun travelling.'

Claire's mouth drooped prettily. 'You think me shallow. It is only that there is no one with whom I can discuss matters of importance. And with Angus growing so quickly time seems to be spreading out before me. Our regular highlight is the interminable church picnic Hamish insists we attend. I'm not being disagreeable; however, I long for interesting, educated conversation.'

They strolled silently beneath the trees in the orchard, dappled light creating moving patterns on their clothing. Leaves, sparse grass and twigs crunched beneath their shoes as they walked first up one short avenue of trees and then turned to walk down the next. Beyond the orchard the open countryside beckoned. A murmur of a breeze stirred the branches above, the scents of the bush growing more distinguishable as they ventured to the end of the orchard. Luke could smell the brittleness of the grasses contrasting with Lee's recently watered vegetable garden and the faint scent of rotting fruit. Claire's arm remained pressed against his and for a moment he considered resting his free hand over hers, his sense of contentment was such.

Wangallon Station Homestead, Christmas Day

'This is for you.' He placed the tortoiseshell comb in the palm of her hand, the pleasure of his giving increased by the delighted smile on Claire's face.

'Oh, Luke, thank you. It's so very pretty.' She tucked the comb into her hair beneath her hat. 'Well, what do you think?' She pirouetted like a young girl.

He searched for a suitable word. 'Very becoming.'

She giggled, took his arm once again. 'You're spoiling me with these yearly gifts you bring. In this household one is lucky if your father even acknowledges the day. I can't understand the fascination the Scots have for celebrating New Year's Day. For me the festivities are over by then.'

Her words broke the quiet enjoyment of the moment. Luke turned abruptly towards the homestead, dropping her arm simultaneously. 'Couldn't we just once have a conversation without my father shadowing everything?'

'I only meant that . . . I'm sorry.'

Luke slowed his pace.

'I'm sorry for the recent loss of your grandmother,' Claire offered, a little out of breath.

He thought of the emporium. 'Well, I didn't know her, so her passing means little.'

'Still, she was family,' persisted Claire.

'There have been greater losses in my life, Claire.' He held her eyes for just a moment, the intonation of his comment creating a bridge between them that Claire's widening eyes acknowledged. What had possessed him to speak of his feelings? They walked on, their companionable silence replaced by awkwardness. What a fine facade this would develop into. Now they would have to continue on as if nothing were said until he left Wangallon for a new life in Ridge Gully. That was it then; clearly his subconscious had made the decision to depart.

'You will be joining us for Christmas dinner?' she asked stiffly.

Thinking of the fine French brandy, roasted turkey and Mrs Stackland's plum pudding, Luke was of a mind to say yes. 'No,' he replied. He expected an argument, a practised pout; instead he was left alone with his adamancy. He watched her gently swaying figure, the lightness of her step, the graceful way in which she caught a handful of her skirt between her fingers to lift it above the dirt of the backyard. He thought of the warmth where her arm lay against his and knew he'd already been back at Wangallon too long.

≪ Winter, 1989 ≫

Wangallon Station Homestead

Sarah crunched brittle lawn under her riding boots as Bullet completed a triple roll on the grass. He trotted back to where Ferret limped slowly from around the corner of the house, gave an encouraging bark and rushed back to Sarah. The grass, fragile from three consecutive frosts, was now pale. Like the surrounding countryside, most of the plant life was dormant. Sarah walked to the far end of the garden where the fence was bordered by towering cacti. Bullet trailed her, snapping at imaginary insects and sniffing at the base of peeling lattice which, in the warmer months, provided support for a trailing potato vine. Turning from the paddock, she looked back towards the homestead. Sarah could imagine her great-grandfather, Hamish, reclining on the verandah. At the thought, her gaze was drawn to the oldest part of the house, the original bedrooms. She shook her head. Only she would imagine a shadow at a window. As if agreeing, Bullet barked and then busied himself snuffling at a group of geranium-filled pots clumped next to a wooden garden seat.

There was no breeze and the trees were quite still. She held her palm millimetres from the surface of a lemon-scented gum and, closing her eyes, sensed the energy hovering beneath her skin. Beneath the ground the tree's roots travelled for many metres, spreading out like tentacles to suck up every available millimetre of water around them. She gazed through the shrubs and hedges, imagining the gravel drive that, up until fifty years ago, had been the main entrance into the homestead. What, she wondered, would her ancestors have made of Anthony's project? Certainly they cleared Wangallon. With teams of men, axes in hand, they had cut a swathe through the more heavily timbered areas allowing grasses to grow, homes, yards and fences to be built, and in return the country became more productive, more fertile.

Sarah's grandfather had referred to this massive undertaking as the civilising of the bush, yet in the same breath he'd laughed at his use of the word. The Gordons knew no one could tame this land. It was intimately tied to the vagaries of the weather. After a small flood in low-lying areas, the belahs would grow up thickly across paddocks already selectively cleared maybe twice in this decade alone. The cost of keeping such paddocks clear of regrowth was both costly and time consuming and if left unattended, would render a paddock useless: The woody plants would decrease natural pasture, decrease stocking rates and ultimately become a breeding ground for feral pigs and the kangaroos that could eat out a paddock in months if they were not culled annually.

Yet the large scale clearing of Boxer's Plains did not sit easily with her. She could see the benefits Matt pointed out, but apart from the all-consuming and limiting factor of cost, large scale cropping wasn't in their blood; conservative grazing was and had been since the property's settlement. That was the reason for Wangallon's longevity. Boxer's Plains was also the last property the Gordons had ever purchased and that made it important in the family's history, although for some inexplicable reason Sarah also knew it was a special place. It just shouldn't be touched. Her stomach knotted. All these thoughts were compounded by Anthony's actions. He'd kept the proposed plan from her and in doing so fractured the basis of their love by destroying the trust between them. Through the fence two wallabies were nibbling grass. They were timid, reclusive creatures, preferring the scrub to the open. For a moment Sarah wished that she too could duck back into the bush to hide.

Anthony walked around the corner of the homestead. His arrival was heralded by Bullet who barked twice.

'I've been looking everywhere for you,' Anthony said with a touch of annoyance in his voice.

He looked harassed. His hat was cocked back on his head and there were hollows beneath his usually clear eyes. Sarah readied herself for an argument as she walked towards him, aware that by now Anthony would know that she had stopped the clearing. They met halfway near an orange tree, the silence magnified as Bullet scruffed the lawn before sitting next to Sarah, his paw resting on her riding boot. Anthony stared at her strangely.

Sarah folded her arms across her chest, all thoughts of discussing the situation rationally disappearing. 'How long did you actually think you would be able to keep your new project a secret?'

'New project?'

Sarah let out an agitated sigh. 'The dozers at Boxer's Plains? Did you honestly think you could get away with such a major undertaking without discussing it with me first, and what the hell would make you launch off and do something like that? Did you not give any consideration as to how it will affect Wangallon? We can't afford such a massive undertaking, apart from the fact I'm not interested in growing bloody wheat!'

'We can't afford not to do it,' Anthony replied soothingly. 'We need to manage this place better and faster to ensure Wangallon continues into the future.'

'Damn it, Anthony. What has got into you? I can't believe you would go off and do something like this. It's almost as if you don't give a damn about Wangallon or my opinion anymore!'

Anthony held up an envelope. 'You and Wangallon are the only things I ever think about.' He passed her the letter. She plucked it from his fingers. It was creased and smeared with a blob of grease. Although unopened it was clear he'd been carrying it around for some time. 'We are in debt, Sarah. You know that yet you seem to be living under the misguided impression that Wangallon can keep functioning as it always has in the past.'

'All big stations work on overdrafts. But we do make a profit most years and we always make our interest payments. Even if we have a bad year the banks will carry us. Wangallon is like a great ship that keeps sailing straight ahead regardless of the weather.'

'Yeah, well,' Anthony nodded at the letter, 'here's your iceberg.'

Her eyes focused uneasily on the airmail letter. She looked at the postmark. It was from Scotland. Sarah felt her stomach turn.

'A good wheat crop would give us a mighty cash injection,' Anthony said slowly, 'if we managed six bags off 2000 acres and if the price stayed at two hundred dollars we would repay this year's development cost in a season. In a couple of years with 5000 acres in and the possibility of a ton we could be looking at a return of . . .'

Sarah looked again at the Scottish postmark. 'Minus tax, minus chemical costs, minus the infrastructure required.' She tore open the letter. 'Minus the fact you didn't bother to consult me about it first.' She read the letter.

Sarah,

Having reconsidered my initial inclination of allowing a solicitor to handle this mess, I have decided to pay Australia a visit.

I do not do this lightly, nor with enjoyment. I do, however, having discovered and reconciled myself to the fact that we are half-brother and sister thanks to the dalliances of your father, wish to visit Wangallon. If you ever returned my sincerity I hope you will welcome me. You have seen my parents' poor crofter's cottage and met the woman that your father deserted. I believe through my inheritance I can put right the wrongs done to her. I arrive on the 8th of next month and have booked a charter flight that will land me at the small strip at Wangallon Town. This I know cannot be a glad reunion, yet I hope for the best.
Jim

'Sincerity?' Anthony was reading the letter over her shoulder. 'Was he in love with you?'

Sarah crumpled the letter. 'A crush.' There was little point denying it.

'I see.'

There was no possible way Anthony would understand. Her trip to Scotland two and a half years ago made in an effort to find herself had unintentionally led her to the place her father Ronald had had an affair 25 years earlier. Sarah and Jim met through chance and spent a week traversing the lochs and hills around the most northerly tip of Scotland. And while Jim developed a crush on her, Sarah had soaked up the joy of being free.

'So sometime between then and now this bloke's discovered that the woman he was keen on is actually his half-sister, his father is not his real father and his mother was unfaithful.' Anthony turned to look about the large garden, his face unsettled by thoughts. 'Then he discovers he's been left a share in a big spread in Australia.' Anthony looked directly at Sarah. 'Well, Jim Macken was named in your grandfather's will. It's all legal as I keep on telling you.'

Sarah crushed the letter into a ball. As the months went by and they heard no word from the Mackens, she truly believed that his Scottish family chose not to reveal his association with the Gordons in Australia.

'Sounds like he's not coming for a social visit. Well, what's he like? Can we sway his mind?' He'd crossed his arms defensively, stuck out his chin a little.

'How the hell would I know? Your thoughts are as good as mine at this point.'

'Well actually you probably have the edge, after all you've met him on his home turf and he didn't fall in love with me.'

For a moment Sarah felt like screaming for everything to just stop. She took a deep breath. 'It's the 8th in four days,' she calculated. 'Shit, I can't believe Grandfather did this to me. Dividing up the place like a piece of cake. It's made everything impossible.'

Anthony stared back at her, shoved his hands in his pockets. 'It must have been a real shock to learn Wangallon wasn't going to be left solely to you.'

They stood for a moment facing each other. A flock of tiny jenny wrens flew past them. Bullet jumped up and chased them into the bougainvillea hedge.

'Well, I'll let you arrange things with the solicitor.' Anthony's voice was flat. 'You do know that we will have to sell part of the property to pay him out?'

From inside the homestead Sarah heard something breaking, like a glass being dropped. She turned towards the noise. They both did.

'Probably the wind,' Anthony stated. 'We'll need to make more money off the remaining property because our debt will remain the same. Have a think about how we might do that before you crucify me for trying to do us both a favour.'

Sarah looked at the crumpled piece of paper in her hand. When she looked up Anthony was gone, Bullet was sitting waiting for her and the house was silent.

That night Sarah lay quietly in bed listening to Anthony's soft snoring. He'd returned late and the whiff of cigarette smoke and stale beer signalled a night at the pub. Sleep eluded her as she struggled with the weight of the past few days. Finally she left the bedroom to walk down the hallway to her grandfather's room. The low wattage light overhead illuminated the room in a yellowish tinge as Sarah sat in the middle of the large bed. It was cold in the room and she felt uneasy, as if she were invading someone else's domain. A light wind blew; it rustled the trailing vine and the hedges outside the window and sent a scattering of leaves across the corrugated iron roof. Sarah was about to pull the thick brocade bedspread about her when a low growl sounded and then a deep warning bark. Quickly pushing up the window she flicked on the outside light. Bullet stood some five feet from her, his gaze fixed on an unknown form among the darkness of the trees.

'What is it, boy?' she called softly, wrapping her arms about her.

Bullet looked briefly over his muscled shoulder. A streak of golden red flashed between tree trunks.

'What is it?' she called again.

A fox appeared from between the trees as if in answer to her question. The animal was large and powerfully built, with a solid body, glossy pelt and penetrating eyes. Sarah blinked under the fox's stare, glad of Bullet who was sitting between them as if on guard. The two animals watched each other for long seconds before the fox finally withdrew, backing into the shadows.

Sarah, discovering that she had been holding her breath, took a gulp of the wintery night air and closed the window. She had the strangest feeling that she was not alone as she drew the heavy curtains closed. She was aware of the creaks and groans within the old homestead, of the spirits that roamed the land that was Wangallon because they loved it so much they could not leave; so what would happen now that one of the chosen custodians was embarking on a project that would change the very face of the property? What would happen now a third Gordon sought his inheritance?

The thought chilled her more than the tiny pinprick goose bumps on her skin and she thought of her great-grandfather. Years ago she'd recognised the cycle of continuity that was Wangallon. In the past it had been fed by the ambitions of her forefathers and their obsessive need to protect the Gordon land, and she'd witnessed this all-encompassing desire for security in her own grandfather's actions. Succession for the Gordons had never been messy. Why was it now? Suddenly Wangallon was being challenged on two fronts and Sarah didn't know what to do.

Returning to bed she huddled close to Anthony, the heat from his body warming her immediately as she cocooned against his back. His warmth sped through her as she aligned limb against limb, traversing each small gap between them until only a breath of air infiltrated the spaces between their bodies. Sarah listened to the rise and fall of his breathing as she wrapped an arm around him. She willed him to wakefulness, praying he would turn towards her encircling arm and gather her up as he'd done so many times in the past. At night there could be a coming together, for surely here within the confines of the room in which they'd grown to know each other so intimately, need would reunite them. It was not possible for Sarah to forgive his behaviour, at least not immediately; nor could she ignore the basic longing that consumed her. This was the man she loved and needed. Anthony was part of the landscape of Wangallon, he was her family. Outside the verandah Sarah heard Bullet's low growl. Anthony gave a loud snore, coughed and then rolled onto his stomach. Sarah moved back to her side of the bed. The flannelette sheets were cold.

⋞ *Summer, 1908* ⋟

Wangallon Station Homestead

'Excellent, Mrs Gordon.' Jacob Wetherly rested his damask napkin on the polished wood of the dining table and twirled the stem of his glass. 'You cannot imagine the pleasure of being at a cultured table once more. And I believe I've not had roasted boar for some time. My compliments to your cook and no doubt to you as well, Mrs Gordon, for a table is only as remarkable as the mistress that rules over it.' He raised his glass and, finding it empty, gave a small frown.

'Our previous stud master, Andrew Duff, will now assume Boxer's position as head stockman,' Hamish announced irritably. 'I advised the men today, Wetherly.' Hamish pushed the crystal brandy decanter across the table to his left and watched as Wetherly topped his glass past the level of decorum. 'Duff is better acquainted with sheep, however he's really too valuable to lose.'

'And Boxer?' Claire enquired.

'He has earned his rest.'

'The man has been indispensable for over forty years, Mr Wetherly. A great mark of loyalty towards my husband,' Claire revealed, sliding a morsel of custard onto her spoon. 'Do you not agree?'

Wetherly nodded politely, his own dessert spoon rounding his shallow bowl with renewed concentration.

'I think we should withdraw to take brandy,' Hamish announced, his hands grasping at the arms of the great carver chair.

So soon? It had been some time since Claire had enjoyed the company of such a cultured guest and although Wetherly was somewhat obvious in his attempts to charm, his was an amusing diversion. She waited patiently as Mr Wetherly passed the decanter back to Hamish, hoping he might be inclined to sit at the table for just a little longer. It was a convivial evening after all and no one could deny the elegant setting. Their candlelit surrounds highlighted a pair of skilfully painted emu eggs perched either side of a French marble clock on the mantlepiece and although her husband's grandiose oil portrait tended to dwarf near everything else in the room, she could hardly complain when her own imperfect rendering hung in the drawing room. She patted at her hair, pleased at the effect she'd managed to achieve without the services of a maid. Built up over strategically placed pads, her dark hair curled and puffed out most becomingly.

'And are there many social engagements one can look forward to here, Mrs Gordon?' Wetherly moved his arm to allow the maid to clear his dessert plate. There was a clatter of porcelain and silver.

Claire took a sip of water. 'I usually hold a number of soirees a year. Unfortunately 1908 has proved exceedingly dull.' She looked directly along the length of the table to where Hamish glowered.

As if sensing the change in his host's demeanour, Wetherly tapped his nose knowledgeably and turned to Hamish. 'There is some wild Aborigine causing mayhem just south of here.'

'A renegade?' Hamish asked, his fingers tapping the table with interest.

'Apparently so. He has been travelling northwards. The constabulary thought they'd caught him at Ridge Gully but the black they'd chained to the tree for three days died before the landholder for whom he worked could vouch for his innocence.'

'Oh dear.' Claire shuddered. 'How terrible.'

Hamish poured more brandy.

'It happens.' Wetherly drained his glass. 'However, Mrs Gordon, if you have suffered for a lack of entertainment you can be sure this savage assisted in the decision of many a hostess this season.'

Hamish gave a belch that carried down the length of the table. Claire turned her nose up distastefully. With that singular announcement he scraped the tapestry-backed chair across the polished wooden floor. 'Yes, well, enough with the pleasantries. If you will excuse us, Claire.'

Mr Wetherly gave a formal bow. 'Delightful, Mrs Gordon. Perhaps in repayment of your hospitality your husband will allow me the pleasure of escorting you about your spacious garden.'

Claire composed her features into a mask of politeness as their dinner guest looked pointedly from her husband to Claire. She could think of nothing more delightful than a stroll with Mr Wetherly, firmly reminding herself that her interest in being alone with him had absolutely nothing to do with the scandalous tidbit of information Mrs Webb had so thoughtfully let escape from her lips. 'I would be delighted.'

'Unfortunately, Wetherly, my wife retires early and you and I have much to discuss.'

'Come, Sir. Ten minutes of your time,' Wetherly insisted. 'The walk will be quite invigorating. You should join us.'

Claire kept her lips pressed together.

'I will leave you to enjoy the night air,' Hamish relented. 'But ten minutes and no more. I am an early riser.'

'Of course.' Wetherly bowed as he left the table.

Claire stepped lightly across the grass as they crossed to walk the length of the gravel driveway. She was pleased with her new evening gown. Having purchased it through Grace Brothers' mail order service, this was only her second occasion to wear it and at the rate fashions were changing, very soon it too would have to be altered. In the space of just a few years women's clothing had gone from the rather S-shaped silhouette that emphasised one's bust and derriere, to a more vertical appearance. Although her figure was contained by the rigid under-structure of her corset, she did like the current fashion of a slightly high-waisted skirt that fluted becomingly over one's hips to sweep outwards at the hem. Claire lifted her skirt just a touch, conscious of the grass, leaves and dirt that would catch on the fringing. An owl swooped. The frightened squeal of a mouse followed. As the countryside bedded itself, the outlines of the homestead and station buildings slid into a glow of sun-settled pinkness.

'It is as if we were promenading along Collins Street,' Wetherly remarked as a wallaby dashed through the grasses beyond the garden.

Claire's arm was linked through his as the evening stretched into darkness. It was a hot night, cloudless, with not even a zephyr to stir the air. It was a most pleasant sensation to be strolling with an amiable gentleman, especially one so becoming in appearance.

'I see you adhere to the latest fashions, Mrs Gordon.'

'One tries.' Cocooned as they were within the twilight embrace of a summer's night, Claire felt her person the subject of intent observation. When Wetherly guided her from the path across the patchy lawn to a wooden bench, his hand moved to the small of her back. It lingered only momentarily, leaving a fleeting impression of genuine care and interest. Careful, she warned herself. Had she not been forewarned of the gentleman's indiscretions?

'And do you enjoy your life out here? You will excuse me, Mrs Gordon, for my forwardness; however, it is a remote, lonely environment for an elegant woman such as yourself to endure.'

'You have journeyed here.' She made a little space between their bodies, moving slightly away from him. It was a warm night and the lace insertions stretching to her high-boned collar itched Claire's upper back and décolletage. 'Life requires adaptability, Mr Wetherly. There will always be fulfilment and disappointment no matter where one resides. Admittedly station life has its own set of difficulties, yet once one grows to understand the parameters of their existence, life tends to become easier.'

Wetherly crossed his legs. 'It is a burden to be endured.'

'On the contrary, it is a challenge. Isolation causes one to be a little introspective, Mr Wetherly. If you are expecting me to pine for the perfect life you will be disappointed. What is the perfect life anyway? I can admit to disliking the dearth of social engagements available, the annoyance of petty conversations and the lack of women of my own elk with similar interests and accomplishments; however, these are petty complaints, I believe.' A swirl of stars began to dust the sky.

'You are not what I expected,' commented Wetherly.

She gave a gay laugh. 'Nor you, Mr Wetherly.' Around them the barest of winds stirred the air. It carried the scent of dry earth and spoke of parched grasses clinging tenuously to lifting soil. 'May I enquire as to whether you have family in New South Wales?'

'Alas, no. The family seat is in Devon. My older brother, Harold, has the good fortune of residing there.'

'So you have come to make your fortune?'

Now it was Wetherly's turn to be amused. 'It is a little long in the making, I fear.'

Claire gave a wistful sigh. 'England. I dream of the coolness the very word evokes.'

'Ah then, I shan't tell you of lush grasses, sparkling streams and the picking of wild strawberries in the summer.'

'Do tell.'

He took her hand, drawing Claire towards him with a delicate slowness. 'If I told you, that brave exterior in which you've cloaked yourself would surely crack.'

His features were barely visible. Claire could just discern the strength of his jawline and the outline of his hair. She could have chosen to be annoyed at his familiarity, instead she wondered at his own charming facade.

'Come.' He extended his hand and they resumed their walk. Claire lifted her tasselled hemline above the ground as they approached the house.

'You are a devotee of this trend in greasy wool, I believe, Mr Wetherly. Can you tell me if it will last?'

'Who knows, Mrs Gordon? We follow market preferences like a child pining for candy.' Within a few minutes they were on the verandah and Wetherly was assisting her indoors. 'Our allotted ten minutes are up.'

He took her hand in the hallway. Claire turned hesitantly towards the partially ajar drawing room door. Hamish was merely a wall's width away.

'Business precludes me from your company, Mrs Gordon, for which I am sorry.' He bent and kissed her hand. 'However I don't believe our parting will be short-lived.'

Claire gave her best smile of understanding as Wetherly strode confidently away to join her husband. As the door at the end of the hall closed and male voices rose in conversation, Claire brushed at a smudge of dust on the hall table, straightened a landscape hanging on the wall above and shook the layers of her skirt free of dust. With those three things attended to there was nothing left to do but retire to her room. In the quieting household the muffled voices of the men carried through the empty rooms. Claire thought back to their conversation and fell asleep smiling.

Winter, 1989

Wangallon Station

Jim pressed his forehead against the oval window of the four-seater Cessna and watched the countryside move beneath him like some great lumbering animal. Having left the mountains some time ago he watched, fascinated, as the land had spread out beneath him in rectangular shapes, growing ever larger as they headed north-west. It was as if he flew above a vast patch-work quilt, where sage greens competed with the full spectrum of browns: coffee, tan and russet. There were long, straight roads heading endlessly onwards, massive trucks towing second trailers, and scattered buildings and livestock massed in some areas like the pebbles on the edge of the loch. He'd not imagined a country could be so vast.

'First visit, mate?'

Jim adjusted the headset, 'Aye.' He wasn't exactly expecting a welcoming committee. In fact he didn't even expect Sarah to pick him up. His father explained that the outback properties employed staff to assist in the running of their businesses, so he expected a car and driver and little else. That in itself was a novelty. His family wasn't used to money, at least not the sort of money the Gordons were sitting on. He didn't know what to expect and the thought made him both angry with himself for making the trip and nervous. He felt like a lowly crofter seeking the assistance of a wealthy Englishman and had to remind himself more than once that he was a blood relation and that the Gordons were no better than him. Jim pushed his shoulders back and straightened his spine in the cramped seat. His mother had only given him one piece of advice upon learning of his decision and that was *to walk tall*.

The plane was descending quickly. Jim pressed his nostrils together with thumb and forefinger and blew to relieve the pressure in his ears. He touched his breast pocket. Inside was an envelope containing the details of a specialist in estate law who would also arrange the transfer of funds to The Bank of Scotland. A scatter of ten houses or so appeared through the window and then disappeared as the plane circled towards the landing strip. They came in low. A rush of trees and gravel sped past them and then they were lifting upwards again.

'What happened?' Jim asked, concerned at the abruptness of the manoeuvre.

'Roos.' The pilot pointed to where eight grey kangaroos were bounding away from the strip and into the bush. 'They come in for the green pick at the edge of the strip. Bloody nuisance.'

The pilot brought the plane back around again and they landed with the maximum of bumps and a screech of gravel that sent them careering off course and into the dry dirt off the edge of the strip. As the plane stopped, Jim was jolted forward. His breath caught in his throat and he decided that when he finally left this blasted place he would get a hire car.

The pilot grinned, his irregular-shaped teeth forming a flashy contrast against the dark tan of his face. 'Sorry about that, mate. The old girl tends to do that sometimes.'

When the billowing dust finally settled, Jim saw a woman standing beside a white truck. He slung his bag over his shoulder as he walked towards the solitary vehicle. Despite his best intentions his chest lurched just a little and he automatically slowed the pace of his walk, conscious of the past. It was Sarah and she was unchanged. Her red-gold hair was tied away from her face, her hands shoved deep in the pockets of her jeans. Jim adjusted the bag on his shoulder.

'Good trip?' Sarah asked politely. She thought back to their first meeting in the ruins near Tongue. Their roles were completely reversed. Now it was his turn to be in a foreign land.

'Aye.'

Deciding against any physical show of welcome she got behind the steering wheel. 'Throw your bag in the back and we'll be off.'

Jim slid into the passenger seat. 'I wasn't expecting you.'

Sarah recalled his brief letter. 'I considered my options, Jim, after you pointed out this wasn't going to be a pleasant reunion. But Wangallon is a working property. I can't pull people off jobs even if I wanted to.'

There it was, the clipped tone of someone who was firmly in charge. Jim recalled Robert Macken's parting words: 'Remember the old man that willed you the money is dead. Them that are left may not have been taught how to share.'

'How's the season?' Jim had heard the line used between two wide-brim-hatted men at the airport in Sydney.

Sarah turned towards him briefly, her eyes narrowing. 'Good enough'. She slowed as they turned down the main street of Wangallon Town, idling the vehicle to a stop outside the Wangallon Town Hotel. 'Thought you might prefer to stay here?' She let the question hang, positive he would agree that sleeping under the same roof was a bad idea.

Jim looked at the peeling paintwork and reminded himself of the purpose of his journey. He was here to meet his father, have a look at the property and then get his money. Although part of him would be happy to escape into the pub, it wouldn't help his cause being stuck here without transport. 'No, thanks. Wangallon will be fine.'

'You sure?' Sarah persevered. Silence answered her. The pub and its wrought iron upstairs balcony disappeared in the rear-view mirror. 'You might be interested to know that this town was built just before my great-grandfather selected Wangallon. My family has been here a long time, Jim. We have a proud history.'

'You forget, Sarah, it's my family too.'

She hadn't forgotten, but she considered the link tenuous at best. He had his own family in Scotland and they were good people. 'I'm surprised your parents agreed to you coming out here.'

'Do you begrudge me the right to my inheritance?'

She wanted to say yes, that he had no right to take something that he did not create himself, that he had never been part of; that he wasn't born to. The length of time it took her to answer betrayed her true feelings. The air grew tense between them. Sarah wound down the window and breathed in the freshening wind. In a month it would be spring. Turning up the radio, she took the back route into the property. It cut through West Wangallon and added an extra five gates to the normal four. She figured the exercise wouldn't hurt him.

'I grew up there.' She pointed out the West Wangallon homestead. 'After mum and dad retired to the coast the place was locked up for a while. Matt Schipp, our stock manager, lives there now.'

'But Ronald's back here, isn't he?'

'Nope.' If Jim had been hoping for a showdown with her father it wasn't going to happen. He looked disappointed and for the briefest of moments she felt sorry for this boy who had travelled halfway around the world thinking he would meet his birth father.

'But you told him I was coming.'

'Nope.'

'Why not?'

'You didn't mention your undying need to meet him.'

'That's a bit unfair.'

'So sue me.' Bad choice of words, Sarah decided.

'I want him told.'

'You don't get to make demands, Jim. My mother's ill and Dad has enough stress at the moment.'

By the time they reached the main homestead it was nearing lunchtime. They passed Matt and young Jack walking eight Hereford bulls into the yards. Sarah didn't slow as she normally would to chat to them. She skimmed her eyes over the lumbering beasts, waving as she continued on to Wangallon Homestead. Wordlessly she parked the Landcruiser and walked up the back path, kicking her riding boots off at the back step. Bullet was there instantly, slithering out from beneath the rainwater tank to give Sarah's hand a quick lick and bestow upon Jim a low growl.

'Nice dog.' Jim reached out to pat him, as he removed his shoes.

'I wouldn't,' Sarah advised. 'He's very loyal.' Bullet wagged his tail at her voice, his head cocked to one side, and then silently began to chew on Jim's rubber-soled footwear.

Inside the homestead they walked through the kitchen and living areas, Jim pausing at the entrance to the dining room to sweep the room with his eyes. The silver gleamed on the mahogany sideboard, the chandelier sparkled and the various side tables, lamps and oil paintings gave off an aura of aged elegance. Having grown up with her family's possessions, Sarah appreciated the years of toil that had led to their accumulation whereas Jim was stepping into a world completely different to his own. Having him to stay in the homestead was her first mistake.

'Who's that?' He pointed to the large oil above the sideboard.

'Hamish Gordon. He founded Wangallon.' Sarah shivered, there seemed to be a chill in the room. She rubbed her forearms briskly. 'The other is his second wife, Claire.'

'She's a good-looking woman.'

'They say she managed to civilise Hamish, at least for a while.'

'Meaning what?'

Sarah hunched her shoulders. 'If you'd stayed at the pub you would have heard any number of stories.'

They continued through the homestead, passing the reading room and music room before turning left from the main hallway. For some reason Sarah decided to put Jim in the oldest wing of the house. The plaster was cracked and crumbling in spots and the dry seasons combined with the earth's movement caused the house stumps to push and pull at the floorboards so that any remainder of a flat surface was in memory only.

'What's through there?' Jim pointed at the end of the hallway where a faded blue and green tapestry of the Scottish Highlands hung.

'It used to lead out past the dining room through to the original covered walkway to the cook house.' Sarah gestured to a bedroom door. 'Sorry if it smells a little stale. It needed a bit more of an airing.' Her apology was automatic and borne more out of politeness than concern. Drawing aside the velvet duck-egg blue curtains, a stream of light entered the room. Everything was blue, the walls, carpet, even the bedspread. It had been her grandmother's favourite room for she and Angus followed the habits of their forefathers and kept separate bedrooms. Before Jessica, Hamish's second wife, Claire, claimed it until her untimely death in an automobile accident.

'Nice,' Jim commented, gazing out the French doors leading out onto the verandah. 'You must have thought Scotland very basic.' He dropped his bag on the floor.

'Actually I loved Scotland. Your houses are built to withstand the cold. Out here we have large spacious rooms to fight the heat.' He was standing with his back towards the French doors, the wintery light of early afternoon silhouetting his solid build.

'You can have a tour of the property in the morning.' Sarah wanted to add that she hoped it may stop him from making any hasty decisions. 'I'll get Matt to take you out.'

'This is difficult. I still remember the day you left. All this seems surreal.'

Sarah took a step back. 'Yes. It does.'

'We were friends once.'

'Jim, what do you expect of me? You're only here for your inheritance, otherwise you wouldn't have bothered coming. Your letter said it all.' He was staring at her, scrutinising her as if trying to understand the person before him.

'You've grown hard, Sarah Gordon.'

'I've grown realistic, which I should, don't you think, considering the circumstances.' Opening a camphor wood chest she took out a thick woollen blanket, setting it on the end of his bed.

'I thought this would be easier, that you would appreciate my situation.'

'What? When you don't *appreciate* mine?' She turned on a gold and cream bedside lamp. 'You know nothing about Wangallon or my life here.'

'Perhaps not, but I do own a thirty per cent share and I would have thought that even you, Sarah Gordon,' he emphasised the surname, 'would *appreciate* that.'

Sarah rubbed automatically at a smear of dust on the dresser. 'You come here after discovering you are related and expect a grand welcome and a golden handshake. Where have you been during the last one hundred and thirty plus years of Wangallon's life?'

'That's a damn unfair thing to say. After all it was your father who decided to keep everything secret.'

'Oh I see, and you were conceived through divine intervention and your mother was physically forced to keep the truth of her child's father a secret. Please don't have the audacity to stand there and tell me it's my father's fault. Your mother obviously never had any intention of revealing who your father was and Dad didn't even know your mother was pregnant when he left Scotland.' Sarah's chest heaved. She could have said much more, although Jim was already looking shocked. 'You didn't know that?'

Jim paled. 'No.'

Sarah thought of her mother's indifference during her childhood. Jim's existence was only part of the cause for it. Sue Gordon had also taken a lover and after his accidental death, she doted on their love child, Cameron. If Jim was intent on recriminations, he could have a lesson in blame apportioning. She could ill afford to feel sorry for him. 'I'll leave sandwiches in the fridge for you.' That was the best she could offer. She certainly wasn't going to do his cooking. 'There's space in the wardrobe if you need to hang anything and if you need water, use the brass tap in the kitchen. It's rainwater. The rest of the house is running on dam water at the moment. We haven't had rain for a while.'

Sarah shut the bedroom door and looked across the hallway. Diagonally opposite were two bedroom doors – one once belonged to her great-grandfather, the other to his first wife, Rose. She opened Rose's door tentatively. Inside was a washstand with a matching ceramic bowl and water jug, an old wardrobe, dresser and a bed. The yellow curtains were drawn closed and the room smelled musty. Sarah sprayed some lavender scent about the room. It was a custom her grandfather had taken to and now the lavender scent in its plastic bottle was a permanent fixture on the dresser. Some months ago she'd found herself walking straight up the main hallway, only to detour into Rose's room. Now the airing and scenting of the room formed a part of her weekly routine. Sarah smoothed the creased pale pink bedspread and left the door slightly ajar to air.

Next door was her great-grandfather's room. Sarah's fingers hovered over the doorknob, before clutching at the tarnished brass to turn it. Nothing happened. She turned it again but the door wouldn't budge. Strange. Intrigued enough to consider placing her shoulder against the aged cedar and giving it a good hard shove, she reconsidered. Only once had she stepped across the threshold into Hamish's room and even then her grandfather had led the way. Sarah recalled an almost overwhelming male scent and glimpses of dark furniture, fluttering curtains and a yellowing photograph hanging crookedly on the wall. Angus had tutted in annoyance before steering Sarah out of the room.

Hamish achieved almost folklore proportions when Sarah was little. To her it seemed that the strength of his person had permeated every atom of Wangallon. The position of every building, yard and fence division had been planned by him, and his painstaking plans and details of the management of the property were all carefully recorded in copious leather-bound ledgers. Angus had packed them away for safe-keeping in an old tin trunk. One day, Sarah promised herself, she would read them. Taking a step back, she glanced from her great-grandfather's room across the hallway to where Jim was. She needed a plan. Any plan. She wondered what Angus would do.

Midsummer, 1908

Wangallon Station

Hamish and Angus walked through the yard of rams. An easterly kept the sheep-refined dirt flying. It sneaked into crevices, swirling into the whorls of ears so that it took a persistent finger to clean out the sweat-moistened gluck. Angus breathed hot air through the handkerchief tied about his nose and mouth and glared defiantly at every ram turning towards him in interest. Having been knocked over last year, he knew the pain of a broken rib. At the gate, he stamped his foot in reply to a ram's cloven-hoofed annoyance and was relieved when they finally approached the drafting race.

A row of peppercorn trees overhung the race, providing some shade, and beneath the largest tree on a rotted stump sat Boxer, sweat running down his face. Boxer swiped his arm across his mouth, took a swig of water from the canvas bag hanging off a branch above him and greeted Hamish with a broken-toothed excuse for a smile. Wetherly jumped the race easily and met Hamish halfway across the yard. Another Aboriginal stockman,

Harry and the Scottish boy, McKenzie, waited nearby. Andrew Duff barely tipped his hat.

Hamish studied the rams pushed tight in the narrow race. The vibe from the men was strained. It was to be expected with the recent changes, however he wouldn't tolerate any attitude – no one was indispensable.

'An ordinary day for classing,' Wetherly noted.

Hamish ignored him. 'No need for you to be here, Boxer,' he said kindly.

Boxer looked around the yard. 'Long time dead, Boss, and mebbe you still need old fella.'

Hamish nodded. 'Maybe.'

'I've always been a firm believer in keeping sheep out of the yards on days such as this,' Wetherly persevered. 'It does a fleece no good to be subjected to such dusty conditions.'

'Then you won't find it a problem ensuring the rams are taken back to their paddock as soon as possible,' Hamish answered curtly. Already the big animals panted and snorted, their curly horned heads catching on their neighbours or becoming wedged over the top of the wooden rails of the race. Hamish walked to the lead.

'I'd be happy to do that,' Wetherly offered, shadowing Hamish as he parted wool over a ram's shoulder.

Hamish brushed the wool closed gently with the palm of his hand. 'I'm classing out thirty of the better rams to be joined with a mob of maiden ewes.'

Angus regarded Wetherly with a doubtful incline to his head and repeated what his father had recently told him. 'They're a particularly good drop.'

'And you're figuring on some growthy lambs by the spring after the ewes are shorn,' announced Wetherly, inserting his foot between father and son so that he slipped in beside Hamish.

Hamish spat dust from his mouth. 'Keep your head clear,

Angus. Plenty of men have been injured in the past, either having been knocked over in the yards, as you well know, or headbutted while leaning over the race.' Behind Hamish, McKenzie followed with the raddle. 'Give it to Wetherly,' Hamish barked. That would take the new stud master down a peg or two. Wetherly marked a line of blue down the muzzle of the selected animal. Hamish parted the wool on the side of a large ram and beckoned Angus closer. 'Good staple length and colour. See that whiteness?'

'Good growthy size and height about him too,' Wetherly added.

Hamish continued on down the race to the end. Boxer then drafted the classed rams out the top end through a pivoting gate, sending the selected rams to a yard on the left and the remainder to the right. Once the race was empty, McKenzie, Andrew and Harry filled it from the adjoining yard at the other end. Hamish classed six pens of rams and, finally satisfied with his selection, ordered them to be walked back to their new paddock at dust. He didn't intend joining them until March but was a stickler for rotating mobs of sheep. He believed rotational grazing assisted with nutrition, disease prevention and stopped paddocks being eaten out.

The men moved the selected rams into another yard. There was little talk between them as they whistled their dogs up, pushing the disgruntled rams through a narrow gateway. The last twenty head ran in the opposite direction, stamping their feet in a combined show of anger and agitation. McKenzie walked in the opposite direction to the way the milling rams needed to head. The sheep ran back and quickly joined the mob.

Hamish gave the slightest of nods. 'Well, McKenzie,' he asked, 'what did you learn?'

'They should be tight in the race so as not to cause injury, Boss. But not so tight that they might go down and s-suff-'

'Suffocate?' Angus finished.

'Yeah, suffocate,' agreed McKenzie.

'There's a bit more to it than that, boy,' Wetherly pronounced.

Hamish looked McKenzie up and down. 'Speak to Jasperson about some decent boots.' Half the sole appeared missing off one. 'And when you get them, polish them. The leather will last longer. And don't leave them out in the sun – quickest way to ruin them.'

'Yes, Mr Gordon.'

'So that will be all?' Wetherly asked with an imperious tone. His face carried a streak of blue from the raddle.

Hamish grunted. 'You, Tambo and Andrew can walk the rams back.' Across the yard one of the Aboriginal stockmen fell over in the dust of the yard. McKenzie was laughing, his stocky leg stuck out like a low hurdle.

Hamish wiped at the dust layered across his face and sat down at his desk. There were papers to be locked away, including the thick envelope on his desk. The letter written with the unstudied elegance of an educated man outlined the circumstances of Lorna Sutton's demise. Luke's grandmother had passed in her sleep, having partaken of a five-course dinner the preceding evening. Hamish lifted his brandy glass in mock salute. It was nearly fifty years since he'd first set eyes on Rose Sutton, Lorna's only child. Mistakenly Hamish believed that the young girl would give him a measure of respectability, instead Lorna had played him at his own game: Rose was the daughter of a whore.

The fabric of their marriage was unceremoniously revealed when Hamish learnt of his mother-in-law's activities and Rose gradually became aware of how her new husband was acquiring his wealth. Yet Hamish still believed the marriage could have endured were it not for Rose's unforgiving nature and delusions of grandeur. And then of course she formed a child's attachment to an Afghan trader.

Leaving his reflections behind, Hamish returned to the letter. The solicitor outlined in detail Lorna's substantial legacy. There was the fine brick residence in Ridge Gully, a large number of household items including solid silver cutlery, candelabra, crystal stemware and no less than two fine English dinner services, as well as a collection of oil paintings. The inventory extended to her immaculately maintained stables: three geldings, four mares and a fine buckboard. Hamish inclined his head upwards to Lorna. His decision to make her the owner of the emporium and provide her with his Ridge Gully home had not been ill-advised. She had been well paid for the service requested of her following Rose's departure to Wangallon.

Hamish reread a copy of the letter he'd made from the original, mailed some weeks prior.

Dear Mr Shaw-Michaels,
I was deeply saddened to learn of the passing of Lorna Sutton. In regards to her last will and testament I would direct that the 3,000 pounds bequeathed to my eldest son, Luke Gordon, be willed instead to Mrs Elizabeth Sutton Russell. These instructions are made on the strict understanding that on no account will my name be brought to Mrs Russell's attention and that to all intents and purposes Mrs Russell was the original and single beneficiary of Lorna Sutton's will. I make these instructions conditional on your firm's continued association with Mrs Russell now and into the future and declare to have no interest now or in the future in Lorna Sutton's will. You will be recompensed accordingly for your services, Sir.
Yours sincerely

John Shaw-Michaels had been Hamish's solicitor for many years and was intimately involved with the particular machinations that built Wangallon. Folding the letters, Hamish unlocked the tin chest in his study and deposited the paperwork carefully inside. If Luke were to receive the measly 3,000 pounds willed to him and not the emporium, he would discover the majority of the estate had been verbally gifted to someone else nearly three years ago. Rose's death had closed a door on that part of his life and ensured an impenetrable succession plan. Hamish thought only momentarily of Luke. His eldest was bound to Wangallon and the future, not a past that could dislodge the natural order of things.

Winter, 1989
Boxer's Plains

Anthony sat the chequebook on the bonnet of his Landcruiser and wrote the figure down carefully. Even though he was convinced his actions were correct, it was a lot to part with, especially when he was taking full responsibility for the project. Tearing the cheque free he passed it to the contractor. They had worked twelve-hour shifts to get the new cultivation ready for planting. All they needed was a good fall of rain. Three inches minimum was required to plant a summer crop. Anthony had already discussed the specifics with an agronomist and although he'd advised to wait until next year, he was determined to plant 1000 acres to grain sorghum and fallow the remaining cultivation until next year. By then Anthony hoped to have more acreage cleared and be ready to plant wheat. He looked at the landscape around him. It was the same over most of Wangallon. The little grass that was left was brittle. What the lack of rainfall started, the cold of winter finished. He needed good rain to plant.

'Thanks, mate,' Colin Harris grinned as his grease-smeared hands imprinted themselves with an inky stain of ownership on the pale blue paper. 'When do you reckon you'll want us back?'

Anthony looked across the freshly cultivated grassland in the direction of where the two bulldozers were working: stage two of his project. Once the trees were knocked down, they then had to be raked into piles and burnt. 'It'll be at least a month before we have a block squared off and ready for ploughing. I'll give you a call in a few weeks and let you know how we're travelling.'

'Sounds good. And everything's okay now?'

Anthony knew Colin was referring to Sarah's instructions for all work on Boxer's to stop. 'Yep, fine. As I said, unless you hear direct from me, Colin, everything goes ahead as planned.'

As the contractors packed up their gear, Anthony drove around the edge of the new cultivation. The offset discs had dug deep into the ground, bringing up buried logs, old branches and sticks. These would have to be picked up by hand, placed into piles and burnt before a sowing rig was brought onto the cultivation. It was another costly job and one that would need a team of good stick-pickers.

At the opposite end of the new cultivation two dozers crawled slowly through the scrub. A clump of old belah trees was left standing nearest him and such groupings were scattered over stage one of the development. There were other spots on this initial 5,000 acres that he'd personally marked out to be left undisturbed. It was pointless clearing ridgy country, for the soil was too hard-packed to be any good for cropping; and it was important to leave scattered stands of trees, both for the wildlife and livestock. He was also conscious of the need to ensure the continuation of as much of the natural habitat as possible, having been reared on the yet unproven theory that trees attracted rain. To that extent belts of trees would be left where possible across the entirety of Boxer's Plains.

From the esky on the passenger seat, Anthony pulled a mutton and tomato sauce sandwich free of its plastic wrap. Since his argument with Sarah in the garden, his vehicle had become both his office and sometime home. He bit hungrily into the doughy bread, pouring black tea from his thermos. A 5 a.m. start borne of a desire not to face Sarah made for a long day, especially when he was waiting for dark before returning. Well, he had his wish. The sky was striped with the colour of cold steel, the paddock darkening as if a blanket had been thrown over the landscape. He finished his sandwich.

The Landcruiser bumped across the bridge, shuddered as a tyre hit a pothole and then swerved to miss a wallaby. Of course Anthony knew he should be going straight back to Wangallon, but the thought of facing Sarah on Jim's first night was more than a little off-putting. Jim Macken was legally entitled to his inheritance. Anthony could only hope that Sarah would be able to come to grips with losing part of Wangallon, for even with this current project underway there was no possibility of borrowing all the money required to pay Jim out. All Anthony knew was that they needed to increase productivity and quickly. The only positive aspect of Jim's arrival was that he would take all of Sarah's attention, so hopefully the work on Boxer's Plains could continue on without further stoppages.

Best they have a bit of time together, Anthony decided. Besides, he wasn't in the mood to meet the man; a man who had as much right as him to be in the Wangallon Homestead. What he really needed was a beer and the bright forgiving eyes of the young backpacker Anastasia Kinder, with her gentle voice and general disinterest in all things farming. Besides which it was $12 roast night at the pub.

Winter, 1989

Wangallon Station

Matt drove away from Wangallon Homestead to the refrain of barking dogs. In the rear-view mirror he watched the Scottish ring-in walk slowly up the back path to the house, his head continuing to swivel from side to side. The boy didn't miss a trick during their morning tour and asked questions of him to the point of exhaustion. Matt continued on past the two orange trees, the remains of the once impressive orchard and the site of an old timber hut that some old Chinese man by the name of Lee lived in eons ago. Jim Macken was not at all what he'd imagined. The boy was tall, broad shouldered and clearly had a bit of nous behind that freckled face. However, he was certainly missing one thing. He didn't have the presence of a Gordon. He blended in with the rest of the population like a soldier ant. Strange that. Dodgy breeding, he concluded. The only thing that would make Jim stand out in a crowd was money, which was clearly why the boy had flown halfway around the world.

Matt was aware of the stipulation in Angus's will regarding the time frame for Jim to be told of his inheritance. Angus had hoped Sarah and Anthony would be married and have consolidated their working relationship on the property before Jim's arrival. Up ahead, two emus crossed the dirt road, their long necks lengthening as they moved from a stately walk to a disturbed trot. They ducked through a stand of box trees and disappeared quickly from view. Matt accelerated, turned the radio up and twisted the knob until a Glen Campbell number came on. He listened to the lyrics for some time until his thoughts took him back to the days after Angus's return from hospital after nearly being killed by a rogue bullock.

They were sitting on the front verandah of Wangallon Homestead, Angus sprawled in an old squatter's chair, his left leg flung out over one of the extendable arms. Matt was smoking, flicking his ash into an ancient-looking brass spittoon, occasionally looking over his shoulder towards the oldest of the bedrooms that led out onto the verandah. Old houses gave him the creeps. He cradled a glass of beer in his injured hand, his mind still coming to terms with what Angus was telling him. The old patriarch had hand-picked Anthony from a short list of possible jackeroos years earlier and his judgement was rewarded with the lad having risen through the ranks to become manager. Angus explained that back then Anthony's selection was about finding a suitable marriage partner for Sarah. Angus knew the girl's strengths and figured that with Sarah and her brother, Cameron, living on Wangallon the place would go on for at least a couple of generations. Fate, however, had interceded and the boy had died.

Angus poured himself another shot of straight whisky and drained the glass. He offered Matt a highly coveted management role on Wangallon.

'I've done my homework, Matt. The Carlyons speak extremely highly of you, as they would after twenty-eight years' service – they were sorry to see you go.'

Matt stretched out his injured hand, recalling how once he could pretty much do anything: Now his ability was limited to stock work, and more managerial at that.

'I knew your father, Matt, honest as the day was long and I trusted him. My solicitor, Frank Michaels, agrees with my decision.'

At the word solicitor Matt straightened his back. He never had taken to men with soft hands who wore suits for a living. He took a gulp of beer.

'After I've gone I need you to watch over the young ones.'

Matt opened his mouth, stifled a belch. Angus quieted him with a shake of his head.

'I need the property safeguarded against the vagaries of youth. There is no one else equipped for the role. My own son is tied to a woman with Alzheimer's, among other problems.' Angus sloshed amber fluid into his glass from a silver-topped decanter. 'Too weak anyway. Never had the gumption. Do you accept?'

Matt struggled to comprehend what was being offered as Angus topped up Matt's beer glass from a long neck.

'As I said, the need may never arise. It will never be yours, though if you watch over her, monitor those who are left to run her after I'm gone, you will be handsomely rewarded.'

Matt felt the stirrings of a cramp in his buggered hand.

Angus leant towards him. 'The thing is, Sarah's smart but she's a woman. Eventually there will be a fifth generation of Gordons and she'll have her hands busy with anklebiters. In my opinion, in a good fifty per cent of cases it's the men who should be rearing the young'uns.' Angus took a good slurp of whisky and belched. 'Never affected the breeding numbers of the emus doing it that way. What was I saying? Oh yes, Anthony's morally strong; probably got too much of a dose in that regard. But, and it's a big but, he's not a Gordon.' He curled his fist into the palm of his hand for emphasis. 'He doesn't have the attachment to the property that a Gordon does and I doubt he could comprehend it.' He picked his nose. 'How could he? One grandfather worked on the Snowy Mountains Hydro-Electric Scheme among other jobs, the other was a second-generation grazier from Western Victoria. He was a superb card player – always the sign of a wasted life – who lost his fortune in the fifties and then promptly shot himself. As the younger of two brothers the Monaro family property wasn't large enough to sustain all of them. Anthony was the one who had to leave. So –' Angus positioned his backside more comfortably in the hard canvas of the squatter's chair – 'although Wangallon is the only job he's ever had and I know Anthony loves the place, I doubt he'd do anything to protect it; at least not the way I want it protected. I'll bet my dodgy prostate on that. If anything he'll always lean towards his moral convictions and put business first, not the land. And therein lies the quandary for Anthony, Matt. You can't have one without the other. I don't want the drive for the almighty dollar to destroy what my family's built. I want Sarah's children to inherit the property in its entirety. The boy's always had an ego. All I'm saying is keep Anthony in check.'

'Ah, that's fairly loose,' Matt replied.

'Loose? In my day loose was a woman on war rations in dark lipstick and too much perfume. Stand them opposite a Yankee officer holding a packet of silk stockings, and that's loose.'

Matt figured that was about all the instruction he was going to receive.

Angus proceeded to explain how he would be paid monthly in his employ as head stockman, but that a separate bank account would also be set up in Matt's name. 'Call my solicitor if and when the time comes, Matt, and remember, if there are any problems you are employed with the mandate to protect Wangallon.'

Matt looked at his injured fingers. In the years to come it was possible his hand would be useless. He was a bush man. He couldn't end up in an old man's hospice, broke and sitting with a bunch of buggered old bastards in God's waiting room. 'Sarah, you mean?' Matt confirmed.

'Yes, Sarah and one other, Matt. You see my granddaughter has a half-brother, and a Gordon can't be turned aside. Frankly I'm at odds with bringing the boy into the fold although I would like to die knowing that I have done the right thing by him. And the acknowledgement of his existence will go some way to purging the mistakes of the past.'

'Mistakes?'

Angus waved a bony finger. 'Some things are best buried with a generation's passing. In this case, mine.'

Matt pulled up outside his house. His acceptance of this job was borne out of both financial need and intrigue; besides, who wouldn't have agreed with Angus Gordon? He merely needed to abide by the solicitor's instructions. Basically he was required to keep an eye on things and make sure they headed in the right direction. So far this current dry spell had been the first test. Quite frankly, being a little more adamant and putting Anthony offside didn't bother him in the slightest. His best interests were served by protecting Wangallon and Sarah. Besides which he figured he could hardly be fired. Matt pushed his hat back off his forehead and scratched at an itch that was part imagination and part a need for action. Then the thought came to him. If he was being paid to ensure Wangallon ran smoothly by watching over the current custodians, was anyone watching him?

Despite his avowed avoidance of all things spiritual, Matt looked up into the winter washed blue of the sky. This is just plain stupid, he reprimanded himself. He needed to call Toby Williams and confirm the mustering of the first herd of cattle for the stock route. Ahead a willy-willy of dust spiralled upwards from the road, carrying dust and bits of spindly blow-away grass. The wind had risen and changed direction. It was heading towards Wangallon Homestead.

Midsummer, 1908

Wangallon Station Homestead

Angus watched his father as Hamish continued writing the day's activities in the station ledger. He'd been standing quietly for some minutes and the very act of not disturbing the scratching noise of ink on paper had made him desperate to move. He concentrated instead on a strip of light as it squeezed its way through the gap in the burgundy curtains. The sliver gradually decreased in intensity and the nearby kerosene lamp overcame the weakening daylight. Having only been in front of his father's wide desk previously, this perspective revealed a new world. He imagined Jasperson receiving his orders here, discussions regarding staff being made and money being counted. It was, Angus decided, a far better side of the desk to be on. Across the room a wall of books, stacked row upon row, reached to the ceiling. There was a wooden ladder with which to reach those books most out of reach, and an old armchair made of used wooden packing cases and covered with a dull red material. His mother hated that chair. She called it an old ugly thing. However there were some things that Angus knew his father would not let go of. There was the armchair, a chest of drawers in his bedroom made from packing cases with sawn off cotton reels for handles, and there was the memory of his brother Charlie, Angus's uncle. These three things, like the founding of Wangallon itself, had come before Angus and his dear mother, Claire. In fact there had been a whole other family before them, of which only his half-brother, Luke, remained as proof that they had ever existed. Angus dropped his eyes to the tin chest sitting next to the battered armchair, its padlock tempting him with a tarnished keyhole grin.

Hamish poured brandy from a crystal decanter into a glass and checked his fob watch. 'How is it possible that –'

Jasperson gave his customary three knocks on the study door and waited for Hamish's voice to enter. 'My apologies, Boss, there was a problem…'

Hamish waved away the explanation. 'Are you listening, Angus?'

Angus nodded, clamping his lips together in his best impression of concentration. It was a look that required much practising and having recently discovered the effectiveness of it he now realised he would have to be careful not to overuse it. Still, it was terribly hard to listen to his father when he could be with Luke, shooting wild ducks.

'This, then, is the area of concern.'

Jasperson and Angus looked squarely at the map spread out on the desk, the curling corners of which were held in place by large polished rocks. Wangallon's boundary was marked by black ink with various paddocks outlined and named in his father's tight handwriting. Their newest acquisition, now known simply as West Wangallon, hung like a small branch off a mighty tree. The purchase of the block had only been completed eight months ago, yet already the extension on the bore drain had been completed, it was fully stocked and a one-room timber hut had been built for the new boundary rider. His father's thick finger drifted to the far corner of the western boundary in the direction of the big river.

'This area here.' His forefinger encircled the area.

'It's not ours.' Angus clamped his mouth shut. He knew that the Crawford family had owned their land before even Wangallon existed, although it was difficult to believe such things, for having been read the Bible by his mother he was of the firm opinion that Wangallon had been created on the eighth day. His father cleared his throat, ran his fingers along the length of his moustache. Angus had never known him to look any different; he remained sun-blackened, with thick lines radiating from his violet eyes, lines that grew deep on occasion like the cracks that appeared in the black soil of their land when the rain was long in coming.

'Crawford tried to poach some of our men earlier in the year. And then at Christmas there were other problems. They cut off our water and they have some of our stock. In any case as you can see our boundary runs here to Crawford Corner where the two properties adjoin. The river runs away from us and this part of Wangallon,' he tapped the map with his forefinger, 'is left to depend on the bore drain for stock-watering purposes. Crawford knows this.'

Jasperson pointed at the map. 'Crawford didn't extend the bore drain on his side of the river, so of course when it gets dry –'

'He steals our water,' Angus said triumphantly.

'Exactly. You're coming to an age, Angus, where you need to have a grasp of how things work in the bush. In the years to come when I'm not around, you'll have to listen to the advice of others. Listen –' he tapped his son's chest, the action sending Angus backwards – 'However, when you are in charge of Wangallon, you make the final decision.'

Angus rubbed his chest as his father rolled up the large map and secured it with a piece of thin red ribbon.

'There is only one simple rule to remember. Look after Wangallon, protect her at all costs and she in return will look after you.'

Angus stood back as the bulky frame of his father removed a long key from his trouser pocket. The creak of metal was the only indication that the chest had been opened, for Angus could not see past his father. Seconds later the creak sounded again and the map had been replaced with a thick book, the Wangallon station ledger.

'You can go now, Angus. Jasperson and I have business to discuss. If you see that brother of yours, send him to me.'

Angus raced out onto the verandah. One of the maids was rushing away, crying, a man's chuckle reverberating with the encroaching dusk. There was a crunch of gravel and Luke appeared. He gave the straggly youth Angus recognised a sound shove, sending him sprawling to the ground, and was astride the prone body in an instant, his fist raised. The sharp intake of female breath broke his momentum. Both Angus and Luke followed the noise to where Margaret watched.

'Luke,' Angus spluttered. Margaret stepped back into the shadows.

Grabbing the youth by the scruff of his neck Luke jerked him towards the verandah. The face before him was of no remarkable feature, except for the line of boils which ran down one cheek. The boy looked at him and gave a sly grin.

'I'm McKenzie.' The youth made a show of dusting himself down. 'I'm employed by –'

'Mr Gordon,' Luke interrupted impatiently, 'considering no one else would likely show at this hour of night without an invitation.' The boy's accent was Scottish, reason enough for his father to employ him. 'I've not seen you before.' Angus joined Luke, clutching at the string of dropped ducks.

'I'm with Jasperson.'

Luke's mouth curled downwards with distaste. 'Don't make the mistake of thinking the blacks on Wangallon are easy picking.' He would have said more except for Angus. The boy stood very close; the ducks at his feet, his hands shoved in his pockets.

'Apologies, Luke. McKenzie didn't know that one was taken.' Jasperson gave a short amused chortle through spindly yellow teeth.

'Careful, McKenzie,' Luke warned. 'My father has no time for troublemakers.'

'Nor I,' Jasperson mounted his horse. 'Half of these blacks should be culled.'

'Who would do your work for you then?' Luke retaliated as the two men turned their horses into the darkening night.

'Who would you be friends with?' Jasperson mocked. Only the crunch of hoofs on the gravel and the creak of oiled leather marked the men's leaving.

'You don't like Jasperson, do you, Luke?' Angus asked. There was a smear of blood on Luke's cheek and the sickly sweet smell of death mingled with the sharp tang of cordite and the staleness of sweat. Angus poked a finger at one of the lifeless birds.

'Luke?' Hamish was standing in the doorway, his frame blocking all but a few stray streaks of light from the hall behind him. 'Come inside.' Angus bolted around the corner of the house.

Depositing the ducks and rifle on the verandah, Luke brushed his hands on his shirt front and followed his father into the study.

The room was musty and hot as Luke sprawled in the packing-case armchair. Hamish offered brandy, swigging his own down quickly. 'Must you start a fight on my front lawn?'

Luke picked at the dried ducks' blood under his fingernails. 'You have a bad habit of choosing debauched employees.'

Hamish let out a deep belly laugh. 'And how is your whore?'

Luke flicked a ball of blood onto the floor. 'I'm not married,' he challenged.

They stared at each other. 'I'll be wanting to drive 1500 head south to market in two months. The feed's cutting out so it would be best to leave a little earlier while the cattle are strong.'

'I'll be wanting news of my inheritance before I go,' Luke countered, lifting his brandy glass towards the light as if a connoisseur.

Hamish screwed his bushy eyebrows together.

'The emporium,' Luke reminded him. 'I expect it to be left to me.'

Hamish laced his fingers together. 'And what would you be wanting with that? You have Wangallon and you're boss drover.'

'*You* have Wangallon now and Angus will have it in the future. What do I get?' He threw the contents of the glass down his throat. 'It's the only thing that will truly be mine.'

Hamish frowned. 'What in God's name do you think I've been doing out here for the last fifty-plus years? You will be running Wangallon after I'm dead, in trust until Angus is old enough to take over.'

'I see,' Luke stood. 'It's a fine plan, father, and probably a good offer for an elder son who's a few years off fifty.'

'Sit, sit. I've a problem with a neighbour. Crawford has stock of ours.'

'You're not accusing them of theft?' Luke queried. 'Things have been quiet for some years now. Let's keep it that way.'

Hamish's eyes gleamed. 'No, no. I intend to make another offer for Crawford Corner. It's a large tract of land with good grass coverage and a mix of mainly black to light soils.'

'I thought we were consolidating?'

'I thought you wanted to be a shopkeeper,' Hamish retaliated. 'The purchasing of the property would enable the rotation of our stock. You know well enough that overstocking is damaging our fragile soils. I'm not of a mind to be forced to decrease stocking rates and lose productivity.'

Luke cared little for neighbours, good, bad or indifferent. 'Well, it sounds like you've made up your mind. You know where to find me.'

Hamish took a sip of his drink. 'Under a tree I presume'.

Winter, 1989

Wangallon Station

Jim took a sip of his beer and cradled the glass in his hands. A fire flamed brightly beneath a long mantlepiece upon which decorative pieces were carefully arranged; two large painted eggs belonging to some type of prehistoric bird that were mounted on gold stands, a pair of vases and a fancy clock. Sarah was twiddling with the stem of her wine glass as Anthony returned with another log for the fire. He dropped it atop the burning wood, a scatter of sparks flying out.

'Be careful of the carpet,' Sarah reminded him, turning her attention from the wine glass to a spot on her jeans. Jim watched as she rubbed at the denim with a determined finger.

They were sitting in the drawing room. One wall held a large hand-painted Chinese fan encased in glass, which was high-lighted by a single spotlight above it. Apparently the item had been purchased by Hamish's first wife, Rose, from a travelling hawker in the late 1850s. To Jim's thinking it should have been in a museum. It was faded in places and fly-spots dotted one side of it. Sitting his beer down on a flowery drink coaster he tried to find a more comfortable position in the plush burgundy velvet of the deep armchair. He was exhausted. Sleep had eluded him for most of the night and when he did manage to doze off he awoke to the sensation of someone standing at the end of his bed. Of course such imaginings were ridiculous, but the image of a tall barrel-chested man with the crinkled face of a raisin was not something his own subconscious had offered up before. Nor was Jim particularly used to waking at dawn to find his few belongings strewn about the bedroom. Although he was not one for believing in ghosts, Jim admitted last night may have been his first introduction. With less than steady hands he took another sip of beer. That same room was waiting for him tonight.

Jim glanced up at the eleven-foot ceilings and crystal chandelier, his sleep-deprived mind less than calm as he digested the recent news that the man sitting opposite him also owned a thirty per cent share in Wangallon. So much for their solicitor's research; Mr Levi had said nothing of a long-time employee who'd managed to ingratiate himself with Angus Gordon.

'So who makes the final decisions when it comes to running Wangallon?' Jim asked when the room's silence reached the uncomfortable threshold.

Sarah crossed and uncrossed her legs.

'Everything is done jointly here,' Anthony began. 'We have weekly planning meetings with our stock manager, Matt, who you met earlier.'

An obvious frown shadowed Sarah's face. She took a sip of white wine.

'Right,' Jim said slowly. Sarah was looking a touch uncomfortable. 'So does that work?' No one rushed to answer him. 'I mean, you're the Gordon, Sarah. Don't you get the final say?' By the expression crossing Sarah's face he had hit on a rather delicate subject.

'The management team works fine here, Jim. Besides,' Anthony moved from standing next to an oval mahogany table stacked with photographs and expensive-looking figurines, 'maybe Sarah hasn't had a chance to tell you, we're engaged. I'll get you another beer, mate.'

For a moment Jim wasn't sure he had heard correctly. He looked directly at Sarah's left hand as Anthony left the room.

'Oh, I don't wear the ring unless we're entertaining or I go to town. Jewellery in the bush can be a bit dangerous if it gets caught in anything.'

'When?' Jim knew it shouldn't matter.

'After I came back from Scotland.'

'I see.' While he managed to develop a crush on Sarah during her short stay in Scotland, Sarah had already been in love with Anthony. And hadn't Anthony made things neat and tidy for himself.

'So what did you think of the property?' Anthony returned, refilled Jim's beer glass and positioned himself on an ancient-looking wooden chair. Another family heirloom, Jim guessed, assessing both the extent and limitation of his inheritance. A thirty per cent share in the land was his, yet he wondered about his rights to the old homestead and its valuable contents.

'There's a lot of it and it looks the same to me.'

Sarah's mouth dropped open in amazement. 'I'm sorry, but I'm not interested in you two sitting here and discussing Wangallon like you're mates. This isn't exactly a social visit.'

'Aye, you're right there, Sarah.' Jim drained his beer. 'I want my inheritance, the full amount in cash.' If he believed there could be a modicum of friendship between him and his half-sister, he was wrong. There was too much at stake.

Sarah turned white. 'But we have to keep the property together, Jim.'

'Why?'

'Why?' Sarah repeated the word, looking at him as if he was an idiot.

'I'm sorry, Sarah, but I've no ties to you or Wangallon.'

'But you could move into West Wangallon Homestead,' she began. 'Couldn't he, Anthony?' Anthony's broad back was turned in her direction. He was gazing out the wide casement windows at the gathering darkness. Sarah turned helplessly back to Jim. She'd had no opportunity to discuss any of this with Anthony. He'd returned late again and left at dawn. She bit her lip. Her only option was to make Jim realise the importance of keeping all the country together, to explain to him Wangallon's significance to the Gordon family, of which he was now a part. She could not bear to see one acre of the property sold. 'We would teach you everything about the property, pay you a partner's salary, you would have a car, be involved in management decisions . . .'

Jim put his beer glass down. 'You honestly believe I want to stay here?'

Sarah spread her hands, palms up. She was desperate. 'Why not?' She gave a weak smile of enticement. She didn't want Jim Macken here any more than he wanted to stay.

'No,' Jim said with finality. 'Just give me my share.'

Sarah steadied herself by taking a sip of her white wine. 'We can't afford to buy you out.'

'I don't need to know the details.'

'You insensitive bastard,' Sarah said angrily, rising.

'Hey, Sarah, cool off.' Anthony tried to lead her back to her seat but she shrugged him off.

'Fine, fine.' She ran her fingers through her hair, pacing the room. 'What about a payment plan? You know, a cash sum every year for say –'

'What? Ten years, twenty years? I don't think so, Sarah. What is the point of dragging this on?'

'But why? Why are you doing this?' Even as she asked the question Sarah knew the answer. He didn't know the history of Wangallon. He had no concept of those who'd lived and died in its creation. It was just a commodity to him. He was too ignorant to appreciate what he was intent on destroying. 'You are no longer welcome at Wangallon.'

'Sarah!' Anthony said loudly.

She folded her arms across her chest. 'Get your things and get out.'

Jim stood. What did she intend to do? Leave him under a tree? 'I'll be staying until I meet my father, Ronald.'

'Ronald has no interest in meeting you,' Sarah seethed.

'Mate, look,' Anthony began. 'Why don't you move into the pub?'

'Don't mate me.' The one thing Jim knew he would not be able to tolerate was any interference from Anthony.

'Fine, work it out yourself,' Anthony retaliated.

'You can bunk over in the jackeroo's quarters,' Sarah finally relented. 'I'll telephone Jack and let him know you're coming. When you walk out the back door, you'll see the lights in the distance. It's about a mile. You Scots are used to walking across the hills and dales, should be a doddle for you.'

'Was that really necessary?' Anthony asked when they were alone.

They were sitting in the kitchen, eating a hastily prepared dinner of leftover steamed chicken with lettuce and tomato. Sarah speared a piece of chicken and chewed on it sullenly. She was in no mood to justify her actions. 'I hear the work is still going on over at Boxer's Plains.'

Anthony, finishing his own meal, drained his beer. 'I don't think tonight is the time to be discussing this.'

'And when should we be discussing it, Anthony? When you have succeeded in wiping out some of our prime grazing country or when our costs escalate from your broadacre farming enterprise and the bank telephones and says, "I'm sorry, but we have a problem"?'

Anthony tried not to take offence at the curt anger in her voice. 'Jim is going to be the problem.'

Sarah shook her head. 'You think?' She carried their plates to the sink.

'Hey, I am on your side, Sarah. The Boxer's Plains project is being done specifically so that we can increase our productivity and therefore our income. Jim is legally entitled to his share and when that happens we will have less country and the same amount of debt to service.'

Sarah dropped the plates loudly in the sink. 'Unlike you, I don't consider Jim's claim to be a done deal.'

Anthony sighed. 'Legally and morally it's the right thing to do.'

'And when did you decide to become a beacon for human rights?'

Jim walked through the kitchen in stony silence, his bag thrust over his shoulder. They listened as the back door slammed shut with a bang that shook the plate of chicken on the sink.

'Where are my bloody boots?' Jim questioned angrily, his voice loud.

Bullet's bark answered. Sarah allowed a grim smile to settle on her lips.

'This is turning into a debacle.' Anthony shoved a split piece of wood into the Aga's firebox.

'You're telling me. I'm sorry but I don't understand what I've done to deserve your sneaking around with the Boxer's Plains thing. While I'm starting to understand the reasons for the new development, I'm hurt and disappointed in the way you handled it.'

'I know,' Anthony brushed his hands free of dirt. 'I just couldn't see any other way of doing it. Wangallon has always been predominantly grazing and I knew you would want to keep it that way.'

'Of course I want to keep it that way. We're not bloody farmers, we never have been. I don't know the arse-end of a scarifier from a set of harrows. And I'm not inclined to learn.'

'Change can be good.'

'Not if it's not required,' Sarah replied quickly.

'You can't stop Jim, you know.' Anthony drew his eyebrows together. 'The law is *the law*, Sarah.'

She stared back at him with the stirrings of the flinty gaze he'd grown accustomed to seeing in her grandfather. 'Maybe if you'd strained yourself to come home at a decent hour last night we could have had some sort of a plan worked out. Instead you deserted me.' The hot water splurted into the sink where it bubbled with dishwashing liquid. Sarah began washing their few dinner things.

Anthony recalled the comforting fug of the hotel with its billow of cold air every time the door opened to allow another stray in. Anastasia cooked him up some sausages for dinner and he'd managed to snavel the corner seat near the wood-fire heater. Later she'd joined him and they'd shared a glass each of rum and warm milk. The evening reminded him of what his life had become and what it could have been and now he felt guilty for it. He wanted to wrap his arms around Sarah, tell her he cared, ask her not to do anything rash. Although from the resolve that was showing in the set of her jaw he figured now was not the time for talking.

Sarah threw a tea towel over the draining dishes and pulled the plug from the sink. 'I may not be able to stop Jim, at least not immediately, but I can make things very difficult for him.' She looked pointedly at Anthony and walked stiffly from the room.

Anthony cringed. Sarah was setting herself up for a mighty fall.

Sarah tiptoed into the bedroom and began packing an overnight bag. Anthony had left one of the bedside lights on and the glow was bright enough to choose a couple of crisp white shirts, a pair of clean jeans and a tailored navy blazer with smart gold buttons.

'What are you doing?' Anthony sat up in bed, rubbing his eyes. 'Geez it's freezing in here.'

'Sorry, I didn't mean to wake you.' Sarah shut the bedroom door. She was beyond feeling anything. From the dresser she selected underwear, the string of pearls once owned by her grandmother and a pair of pearl earrings. 'You told me a couple of days ago that I'd have to sort out the problem myself. Well, that's what I've decided to do.'

Anthony tugged at the bedclothes. 'I didn't mean for you to rush off on some hair-brained –'

'Clearly I have to see a solicitor and as you seem so ready to accept what you consider to be the inevitable, there's no point in you being involved in this particular exercise.'

'I see.' He bashed his pillow into a more comfortable shape. 'So what you're saying is that you're effectively cutting me out.'

Sarah zipped up the bag and sat it on a small chair in the corner of the room. 'Jim arrived yesterday afternoon. Tonight is the first I've seen of you. Look at this from my corner, Anthony. You haven't exactly been the supportive fiancé.'

'Is this your idea of some type of payback?'

Sarah shook her head and sat on the end of the bed. 'Anthony,' she began as if talking to a child, 'this isn't about you, or me. It's about Wangallon. I'm the last direct descendent after Dad – there is no one else.'

'There's Jim.'

Sarah frowned, choosing to ignore the jibe. 'There are spare seats on tomorrow's plane to Sydney.'

'I'd be calling Ronald. It is his bloody mess after all.'

'I can't.' She sat on the edge of their bed. 'Sue's ill.'

'Oh, I'm sorry. I didn't know.'

Sarah wished she didn't feel so alone. 'Well, once again you haven't been here much to support me and when you have we've been arguing.' The expression didn't change on his face. Sarah wasn't the only one facing change both internally and externally; Anthony was developing into the type of person who wouldn't give an inch and she didn't like it. What happened to the man she fell in love with. 'I'll have to go see Dad anyway, and Mum, so I'll tell him then, in person.' She reached out and touched his hand. It had been days since they'd last held each other. 'If I don't try to keep the property together I'll feel like I've failed every one of the Gordons who have come before me.'

Anthony pulled his hand away and tugged the blanket higher across his chest. 'And what about us?'

Sarah sighed. 'Did you consider my feelings when you dreamt up the Boxer's Plains idea? Do you even comprehend how painful it is to me to hear you talk about Jim's inheritance as if it's inevitable? Knowing you feel that way, what is the point of you coming with me?'

'You haven't answered my question, Sarah.'

'And I can't. You are the one who has to answer it. You have to look at the way you've behaved over the past few weeks. Our relationship began on Wangallon and it will end on Wangallon, whether it be next year or in fifty years, but there has to be a Wangallon first for everything else to exist. That's the way I see it.' He was staring at her as if she were a museum sculpture. 'I don't expect you to understand.'

'Good, because I think you're being a bit melodramatic.'

'That's probably because there's not three generations of your forefathers buried here.' Outside the wind rattled the doors leading out onto the verandah. 'When you first came here, this place was just a job for you.'

'That's unfair. I love this place.'

'You do now.' Sarah could feel their relationship taking on a new form, one which would never be quite the same again. 'Wangallon has to continue being run the way it always has. I'll accept the two thousand acres of cultivation, the grassland that's already been cultivated. I have to as it has already been developed. I think that's fair considering how you went about it, but that's it. I want the rest of the project stopped until this mess with Jim is sorted.'

'You're serious? You're actually telling me how you want the property run, after all the bloody hoo-ha about teamwork?'

'I'm making a suggestion that you shouldn't take offence at if you are willing to work as a team as Grandfather intended.' Sarah couldn't believe she was even having this conversation. All Anthony had to do was include her in the decision-making, even if sometimes it was just a courtesy. 'Well, are you?'

'I told you the benefits of the project, that I was doing it for Wangallon, for the future, our future.'

'And you admitted you had gone about it the wrong way.'

He was silent.

'Look, I don't expect you to understand or agree with what I'm saying, but I do expect some consideration. The Boxer's Plains project is stopped indefinitely. Agreed?'

He looked at her evenly.

'I'm trusting you, Anthony. I need to know I can rely on you. I'll fly down to Sydney, see if there's an angle we can work on.'

'And you don't want me to come.'

She busied herself, gathering cosmetics and toiletries together. 'I don't see any point.' Sarah found her black leather handbag and placed her wallet inside. The bedclothes rustled and she turned to see Anthony walking out of the room down the hallway towards the spare bedrooms. She didn't call after him. They seemed to be coming from opposing directions with no possible hope of slowing down before they crashed. Stepping out of her clothes she slunk naked between the covers, moving across to where the warmth of Anthony's body still clung to the pale blue sheets. Sarah scrunched her eyes together. How did it come to pass that she was fighting Anthony as well as Jim Macken?

Summer, 1908

Wangallon Station Homestead

The piano was framed by two curly brass candle holders and a panel of rose-pink pleated silk above the keyboard. Claire had always thought it a lovely piece, even if the silk was faded and the travelling piano tuner never quite got the keys correct. Placing her fingers against the cool of the ivory keys, she began practising scales, pretending to ignore the discordant sound of middle C. Her fingers hit the keys lightly. She persisted for some minutes despite the stuffiness of the room and the perspiration dripping down her legs. Having drawn the curtains early in an attempt to hold the midday heat at bay, Claire was tempted to reopen them in the hope that a slight breeze might take pity on her. As her fingers ran up and down the keys, she tried the beginnings of a concerto.

'Mr Wetherly, Ma'am,' Mrs Stackland announced with more than an air of dislike. Claire would have queried her attitude had not Mr Wetherly already been present. He was dressed in a dark three-piece suit of a wool cotton mix and carried the smell of sheep and manure with him and the chewy aroma of persistent perspiration.

'Mr Wetherly, I'm afraid I am not dressed for visitors,' Claire remarked, straightening her rather drab grey skirt, which was matched with a blouse adorned with black lace inserts. It was certainly her least becoming gown and her hair was piled atop her head in an unflattering bun.

Wetherly gave a formal bow, somewhat overdone for midday. 'My apologies, Mrs Gordon. I was seeking your husband.'

'I'm afraid he is not here.' Claire wished she'd chosen her cream silk gown this morning. 'I could have refreshments sent out to the verandah if you care to wait.'

Wetherly hesitated. It was not particularly appropriate for the stud master to be in her drawing room alone with her. He was, after all, staff and undeniably single. Yet he loitered without answering, staring at her unabashedly until her cheeks flushed under his gaze. 'Thank you,' he replied with a cool slowness. 'I think not. I had –' he cleared his throat – 'better wait outside. Besides, I find my thirst quite sated,' Wetherly answered smoothly. He turned to find Hamish staring at him with uplifted eyebrows.

'I'll meet you at the yards at four o'clock, Wetherly. It's far too hot to be working stock until then.' Hamish dismissed Wetherly instantly, shutting the door quietly. 'The man has a high regard for himself and his abilities.'

'Give him time,' Claire returned to the piano feeling like a child whose outstretched hand had been caught seeking the boiled lolly jar. 'He is very new to Wangallon.'

'I see he has earned your admiration,' he sniffed, removing his jacket and throwing it across the horsehair couch. A puff of dust lifted into the air. 'I don't think it appropriate for Wetherly to be alone in your company, my dear. He has somewhat of a reputation.'

One of the maids entered and, with a curtsey, walked towards the lead fireplace with a dustpan. The girl was reasonably efficient and as yet had not broken any of her knick-knacks, although Claire was not taken with the way she picked up ornaments and inspected them. Hamish walked idly around the drawing room. 'You've been playing?'

'A little. Lemonade, Margaret.'

'For two,' Hamish ordered sternly. The girl bobbed a poor excuse for a curtsey and left them alone. Hamish peered out the damask curtain, flicking at the tasselled fringing. 'New?'

Claire repositioned a hair pin. 'Twenty years ago.' In the past her husband was quite particular about their furnishings; however, time had rendered many things commonplace. This phenomenon did not extend beyond the mud brick walls of Wangallon homestead. Her husband's obsession lay with the land and it spread out beneath him like a great fount of prosperity. 'If you recall we ordered the material during a visit to Sydney.'

'Yes, of course.'

There was little doubt in Claire's mind that Hamish would not remember. Her husband knew every bend in the creek and river, every fence and outbuilding and clump of trees in every paddock. He knew Wangallon so well that Claire was convinced he could start at one end of the property and recall every single detail of the landscape as if he were riding through it on a summer's day. In comparison he ensured his homestead was suitably impressive for the holding it sat upon, although it remained only a dwelling to him. Wangallon was Hamish's love and she drew his focus like a demanding mistress well used to lavish attention.

'Have you seen Luke?'

'No.' Claire retrieved her fan from atop the piano. In truth she was pleased that he'd not come calling, for after their last conversation she had suffered from such a sense of confusion that she doubted her ability to converse properly on any subject at all.

Hamish examined the silver-mounted emu egg and the matching ruby lustre vases on the mantlepiece. 'One of the maids is sweeping the verandah at an unfathomable hour. Dawn and dusk should be sufficient.'

Claire wafted the air with the ivory and lace fan. 'I'll mention it to Mrs Stackland.'

'Good.' He walked to the armchair and, retrieving her quilting, passed it to her.

'Have you received correspondence from Mrs Crawford?'

Claire began stitching a square of yellow material. 'Only that her eldest has arrived to visit his father. Should we entertain them?' Her mind quickly leapt to the table seating. They could invite Henrietta Webb for the younger Crawford's sake, the father, of course and, and Wetherly? Who else was there to make up a suitable number after all?

'We shall see. I would like to call upon you tonight.'

The needle pricked Claire's finger, drawing blood. It was some weeks since he'd come to her bedroom, although Claire was sure he did not lack companionship. She sucked at the bead of blood welling on the fleshy pad of her finger. His back remained stiffly towards her as her assent was mumbled.

Margaret returned with a pitcher of lemonade and two glasses as Hamish left the room. Claire held out her hand and, accepting the poured glass, sipped at it, wincing at the sourness.

'Mrs Stackland says to tell you, Missus, that the last of the preserved lemons are a might tart.'

'Indeed Mrs Stackland is a fount of wisdom,' Claire answered brusquely. 'I would like cold cuts and some tasty vegetables this evening.' She would be needing sustenance, she thought with a smile.

The girl left hastily with the tray. Claire heard a screech and then the smash of glass; Mrs Stackland's taut reprimand followed. She flicked her eyes closed in annoyance before securely closing the door leading down the hall to the kitchen. It was too hot in this room, far too hot. There was a sensation of discomfort in her stomach and she felt the debilitating approach of a headache. Claire opened the window on the southern wall, flinging back the curtains in an effort to stir the air. Her home was beginning to resemble a madhouse. Now she could hear muffled sobbing. Despite the heat and the massing flies, Claire crooked her neck out the window to see who was making such a pitiful racket.

Margaret sat crouched by the meat house, the black skirt of her maid's uniform wet with what Claire assumed to be spilt lemonade. About to slam the window shut, she watched in surprise as Luke approached the girl.

'Are you all right?' He squatted beside her. 'Mrs Stackland will be wondering where you are.' At the mention of the cook, the girl wiped her eyes. 'That's better.' He held out his hand to her. She looked at him as if he were offering something forbidden. 'Here.' He took her hand and helped her up.

Margaret hesitated, her soft mouth opening and closing. The girl was staring at Luke whom, having been distracted by the opening window, was now looking directly at Claire. The maid glanced from Luke to Claire and walked quietly away.

Luke tipped his wide-brimmed hat, his eyes never leaving Claire's face.

Claire closed the window quietly. From the Chinese-lacquered cabinet she poured herself a sweet madeira, drinking the liquid down in three swallows, before placing the glass on a leather-topped table, oblivious to the ring stain seeping into the leather.

It was midnight. Claire swirled the washcloth in the blue and white ceramic basin, wrung the excess water from it and gave a final freshening wipe to the nape of her neck. Dropping the cloth on the top of the wooden washstand she pulled the cotton nightgown over her head, the material catching on the dampness of her skin. The bed creaked.

'I won't be back till dusk. I'm expecting Mrs Stackland to prepare a feast for New Year's Day celebrations.'

A wave of tobacco, brandy and Hamish's rough male scent lingered in the room after he'd left. She could not recall when his lovemaking had been so amorous. It was late and tomorrow she would be tired, bruised and out of sorts. Hamish, once tender and careful in his affections, had grown physical and sometimes a little rough in his infrequent ministrations towards her. She touched her stomach. There was a swelling there and she was sure a flutter of movement awoke her not two nights ago. Could it be possible? Certainly her moods had been fractious recently and her health not as it should be.

During her life Claire had been as reliable as the full moon and although her womb chose to grace her with only one precious child, she now believed it possible there might be another, though why now? She was past child-bearing both in age and enthusiasm. How she wished she could recall her last fertile month. Of course such a condition excused her from her girlish fancies. One could expect to be emotional if they were with child. A convenient excuse, Claire decided, as she fingered the delicate workmanship of the tortoiseshell comb. Often she wondered where life may have taken her if Luke were older. Certainly she was aware of an attraction spanning some years, however Luke's recent innuendo had changed her perceptions. She was past middle age – this was not the time for romantic fancies – and yet here she was thinking of Luke's admiration and the presence of Wangallon's stud master. As for being with child, Claire ran the silver-backed brush through the curling ends of her hair . . . How ridiculous.

Pinning her hair back in a loose French roll, Claire studied her reflection, first the left side, then the right. There was a softness to her jaw, hollows beneath once full cheeks and wisps of grey in her dark hair. She was no longer a girl, no longer gilded by the dewy gods of youth. She pinched her cheeks to heighten their colour as perspiration settled in the hollow of her throat, between her breasts and on the backs of her thighs. She touched her stomach again, hoping it was a phantom of past wanting. Strangely enough she'd never been one for tears. Even now, accepting her loneliness as she had these past few months, the pity of it remained contained within her. Where she once saw space and freedom, she now experienced isolation, and the great untamed wilderness that was Wangallon now seemed savage. One could be grateful for what they received in life and one could also resent it. Claire looked at the pretty hair comb on her dresser and thought of the many times she had wished to go dancing or to dine out or call on a friend or promenade down the street. She was the wife of one of the country's wealthiest graziers. Good fortune was too hard to come by to treat it so poorly.

In bed the hot night brought beads of moisture to her skin. Beside her the bedside candle fluttered. Thank heavens, she muttered, as the slightest of breezes wafted about her face. It was strange how one could look for the most mundane of things: A cool place to sit, water to parch her thirst, and air, any air. Air, a puff, a gust, a draft or a zephyr; how she longed for wind to stir her clothes and blow away the heat of this place. It was as if Wangallon's thirsty soil were reaching for her, its many hands dragging her down. Claire pictured the acres of land emanating from Wangallon Homestead, envisioned the cemetery down by the bend in the creek. She wanted to be buried near her beloved father in Sydney. Not here in this desolate place where few people visited and the sun cracked the ground like a piece of broken pottery. Turning on her side, Claire reached for her book.

Mrs Aeneas Gunn's *We of the Never Never* had created quite a stir in social circles on publication and Claire, determined to converse on the book's merits, had procured a copy via catalogue almost immediately. It did not appeal, however, for who wished to read of a woman's pain, isolation and hardship when one's own life was far from the gentrified circles of convivial female companionship. No, this was one book she would have little problem dismissing, although she kept it by her bedside, for Hamish had once noted his approval. Claire's favourite book, which she was reading for the fourth time and which lay hidden beneath Mrs Gunn's weighty tome, was Kenneth Grahame's *The Wind in the Willows*. Claire smiled as she turned to the next chapter. Sometimes she longed to have been born within the cool green of England's bosom, instead of being conceived on the long sea voyage out to be born in the most distant of countries. She envied Wetherly his English life and wondered at his leaving of it. With a yawn she closed her eyes, her fingers automatically touching her lips where Hamish's kisses had fallen.

High Summer, 1989
Northern Scotland

Robert Macken gulped down the rest of his coffee and wiped his mouth with the back of his hand. 'A fine breakfast, Maggie. Fine indeed.' He pushed the wooden chair back roughly. The legs caught on the rug beneath and he swore softly under his breath. 'Have you heard from Jim?'

Maggie collected the empty cup along with her husband's plate as he stood, stretching his back out. She shook her head.

'I accepted the lad as my own. You know that, Maggie, and I have no problem with him not being mine. I don't know why I tell you this now after so many years.'

Maggie left the dirty breakfast dishes on the end of the wooden table to place a small white hand on her husband's chest. She looked up into his pale eyes.

'I want the lad to get the money that's owing to him and come home,' Robert stated as he brushed her hair with his lips. He lifted his cap from the peg on the wall, flicking at the brim as if new.

Maggie moved to rest her head on his chest. Since Jim's leaving she'd refrained from arguing against the lad's inheritance. What was the point? He'd gone despite her protests. Now her nights were filled with anxiety as she wondered why she'd not done more to stop him.

'There's much we can do with the money.' Robert rubbed his hands together. 'A new sty for the pigs and a John Deere tractor: Aye, not a big one mind. I'd clear that field behind the milker's shed and we'd have to move those rocks.' He adjusted the cap, hitched up his trousers. 'There's a few days' work in that.' He rubbed his lower back at the thought of it. 'Wouldn't I love to see the look on Lord Andrews' face when I tell him that I've no need of his contract?'

Maggie busied herself wiping imaginary crumbs from the table into the palm of her hand.

'You all right then, lass? You're looking a bit peaky.'

Maggie brushed her hand against the floral cotton of her dress. 'Never been much of a morning person, Robert. I expect my age is catching up with me.'

'Rubbish. Steady as a black-faced ewe climbing a rocky hillside you are, my Maggie.' He rumpled her hair, rested a large hand briefly on her shoulder and gave it a shake. 'We'd have enough produce to sell direct to the supermarket. And I was thinking eggs, laying hens. Just enough to sell in Tongue first off and then we'll see how it goes. Once the lad's back we'd be able to manage the feeding of them, and the gathering. When we're established we'll get one of the Childers' girls in to help with the sorting. That would be good for you too, Maggie,' he clucked her under the chin. 'Bit of female company eh?'

'That would be good, aye.'

'Well sound a bit keen about it, lass.'

Maggie untied her apron. She needed some fresh air. 'They're grand plans, Robert.'

Robert winked at her, picked up his wallet. 'I'd add a room to this house too.' He surveyed the tiny crofter's cottage. The ground floor served as kitchen, living and dining area. 'I'd build a new bookcase.' He scraped his socks on the threadbare rug, 'and carpet –'

'You'll be late,' Maggie gently reminded him. Robert was meeting Mr Levi, the solicitor, in Tongue. There was an accountant arriving from Edinburgh to discuss the tax implications of Jim's impending fortune.

Robert kissed her on the cheek and she helped him with his tweed jacket. Although it was summer the breeze from the loch was cold when she opened the door and Maggie shrugged her shoulders into her homespun cardigan as Robert stepped from the threshold.

'It'll be the most pleasure I've enjoyed in years, telling Lord Andrews he can stick his measly wool contract up his ill-gotten kilt.'

Maggie watched her husband drive away in his old pick-up. The vehicle made a grating noise and puffed dark smoke from its exhaust as Robert changed gears to drive up the slight hill to the left of the house. She smelled diesel and added a new pick-up to her husband's list of improvements. She supposed she should be grateful for his excitement, yet she didn't think she could live with someone else's money, especially this money. It was wrong.

The air carried a whiff of moisture as Maggie left the white-washed cottage. The loch rippled at the pebbled shoreline as she turned from the east and followed a low stone wall that ran past the house up the side of the hill. In her youth Maggie dreamt of being a famous athlete, a long distance runner. She would tuck her skirt into her knickers, and run the length of the loch bordering her parents' small block that lay some miles to the east. She had no running shoes then. Her brown lace-ups sped her around the loch as she slithered on pebbles, slippery with the misty breath of the night. If the wind was behind her on those dawn-lit mornings she would lift her arms in freedom, feeling the crick of her ankles as she stumbled with joy. On the weekends when school was done and she could wangle time away from her mother, she would add a scramble up the hill next to the loch as part of her running course. From this vantage point she would catch her breath amid the tangle of green and purple vegetation.

Maggie walked the hill of her home these past twenty-five years, stroking the stone wall that breasted the hill. It was a pleasing aspect, for Robert was a fine crofter. Not one stone wall was in disrepair, not one shingle loose on the roof of their house. Their few sheds were weatherproof, their new potatoes were soft and buttery and there was always a neatly stacked heap of peat for the fire. The cow always gave milk and Maggie still churned their own butter, though their neighbours laughed at her domestic tendencies when a trip to Tongue could supply most of what Maggie grew or made. If she were to ask herself if she were happy, her answer would be yes. Although she also comprehended that she knew no better. How did one judge a life if there was nothing to compare it with?

At the top of the hill Maggie paused by a cairn and collected her breath. Her forty-seven years were now presenting themselves in the form of swollen ankles and a stiffness that did not abide with the passing of winter. Even her breath seemed shallow now, as if her lungs were shrinking with age. Shielding her eyes from the sun, Maggie looked back across their loch. It was a fine view. The water stretched out like a wide yawn to disappear at the foot of another hill. Summer brought a shimmer of heather to the landscape and as the breeze picked up, the landscape shimmied with the vibrancy of a young girl at her first ceilidh. It was a far different atmosphere to the memory of her childhood.

The view from the hill of Maggie's youth took in a wedge of flat country and the village of Tongue. Usually she would reach this hilltop after scrambling up its grassy sides, her calves burning with use. It would be then that the dreadful sameness of her life stared back at her. The thousands of rocks which some cataclysmic event had spewed up from the ruins of the earth; the stagnant pools of water lying dank across the flat country, the B&Bs that signalled the yoke of the English and the measly four acres most crofters were expected to survive on.

Maggie would breathe then, a great lungful of unpolluted air, and cast her eyes across to the adjoining hills at the cairns topping each successive high point, until the furthest mound of rocks looked like an unlit candle on a poorly made cake. The urge to run this route of ancient markers would be so great that Maggie scarcely acknowledged she had made the decision to be punished again by her weary mother. Her feet would take her to one and then two cairns before her brain bargained with her pumping heart to return home.

Was it so long ago? Maggie asked, stooping to place a fallen rock on the crumbling pile. With a sigh she turned downhill. There were still the breakfast things to be tidied, a pair of Robert's socks to be darned and the fish man would be calling. They would be having haddock tonight, probably breaded, for being a Friday Robert would call at the local for a few ales and be wanting a bit of a fry up for his dinner.

She looked at her watch, wondering at the time in Australia. Hoping her boy was with friends; wondering if the getting of the money would be as easy as everyone expected. Jim's silence from the far side of the world set Maggie's memory in motion and her ulcer to flare. Inside the house she poured herself a long glass of milk, her hand only briefly hesitating before pouring a good measure of whisky into the glass. She gulped the liquid down, feeling the fresh cow's milk glaze her tongue and gums with a fatty coating. She hoped Jim would return home soon. With a sob Maggie lent on the kitchen bench, her hands cradling her forehead. The waiting was proving too much for her.

How had all of this happened when she had only wanted a pair of running shoes?

Part Two

Midsummer, 1908

Wangallon Station
Aboriginal Camp

The night dripped with the heat of a long day lingering. There was a closeness in the air; a tight constriction existing beyond the mantle of discomfort left by the sun's blaze. Boxer felt the constraining pressure of the unknown in the droplets of sweat beading his neck, arms and chest. The moisture tracked a path to pool at his stomach, while the wadded blanket cushioning his head from the dirt beneath grew wet from the water seeping along the wrinkled coils of his neck. His hands swiped irritably at the sheen covering the dark skin of his body. The spirits wanted to make their presence known, regardless of Boxer's inclination.

Leaving the woman by his side, he crawled awkwardly from the bark humpy. His knees cursed at the clash of bone against bone, nonetheless he managed to stand, his aged slowness masked by the night sky. As his muscles warmed, Boxer's feet traced the dirt track. He walked nimbly, skirting the edge of the camp, weaving through trees and grass tufts until the creek snaked its scent into his nostrils. When his cracked soles finally sank into the cool, sandy mud he sniffed in recognition. Here, in the dank still of the creek, he breathed in the cloying odour of stagnant water, oozing mud and rotting vegetation. Layered within hovered the remnants of campfires, and the tangy fish scent of mussels. His splayed toes clenched at the sinking softness. The water ebbed at his ankles. If he walked to the left, Boxer knew his feet would be ripped by the mound of opened shells that supplemented the white's food the tribe was given monthly. To the right, further up around the second bend in the creek, was the women's sacred place. Directly opposite across the water was what he'd come for.

Lowering himself to the ground, the skin of his thighs sagged into the sand beneath as he sat cross-legged. Above him the depth of the sky seemed to angle downwards, the glow of the spirits flickering with differing degrees of intensity. He longed for the guiding path of the moon, for the brightness that allowed safe passage in the dark, for fair hunting of both land and water creatures. This night was not that time.

Boxer narrowed his eyes, his gaze directed across sluggish water to the far bank of the creek. There was a deeper darkness there. A murky crevice between the trees beyond that beckoned through wisps of unknown movement. His lips moved in unspoken speech, his mind calmed. They had awoken him with the sweat of their need. As he closed his eyes his skin prickled, the wiry hairs standing upright on his sinewy arms. He nodded then, ready. Once one comprehended their presence, their breath of life in all things, fear borne of ignorance settled like the embers of a fire turned to ash. Boxer breathed with the land in and around him. The great heart of mother earth steadied his vision like a soft caress.

Boxer pictured the great sweep of land that was Wangallon. Far beneath him Hamish Gordon rode on horseback flanked by his men and one black, one of Boxer's own. They were crossing the big river from the land of the Gordon's to another. A chill wind swept along the mighty waterway. Boxer felt the gust as surely as he rode beside his Boss.

He awoke to the scurry of feet and the screech of laughter, to the flick of sand on his face. Women were stoking fires on the creek's bank. Children were rushing into the water, screaming with delight. Great streaming curls of water flashed in the muted greens and browns of dawn. The first tinge of light smeared the space above the tree line red with heat. Boxer scraped the sand of the creek from his drooping cheek before scrambling to his feet. Brushing gritty crusts of sleep from his eyes, his filmy sight followed the smear of red as it grew in the lightening sky. It was true then, he thought despondently as he retraced his steps back to his humpy.

There would be blood.

Winter, 1989

Wangallon Station

Anthony didn't wait to be cordially invited inside the jackeroo's quarters. It was 6.30 am. He knocked twice on the screen door and walked inside. He found Jack in the kitchen, the youth's bare feet resting on the kitchen table where last night's dinner plates jostled for space with a recently consumed breakfast of mutton chops, onion gravy and fried egg. The smells hung in the air, competing fiercely with the stench of cigarette smoke and a blazing wood-fire heater.

Jack was stubbing his cigarette out on the rim of an empty beer can, oblivious to his surroundings. The local FM station was turned up to what Anthony suspected was its highest volume.

'Morning, Jack.' Anthony sat down nonchalantly and hit the off button on the radio. Jack moved his feet immediately and, as if caught having committed a serious crime, set about clearing the dirty plates.

'Sorry, Anthony, I wasn't expecting you.' Jack placed the plates on the sink.

'Relax, kid, where's your guest?'

Jack hovered between the table and the sink, unsure whether he should sit down or start washing up. Eventually he elected to busy himself wiping down the kitchen table with a dishcloth. Crumbs and other assorted bits of food scraps fell onto the floor. 'Having a shower. He asked me if I'd drive him to the airport, but I told him that Matt and I were . . .'

Anthony looked automatically through the open door that led out to the small living room and bathroom. 'Tonight's plane leaves at 6 pm so you have him in town at lunch and then leave him to his own devices.' That way, Anthony decided, he was unlikely to cross paths with Sarah at the airport.

Sensing there was more to this than just a friendly visit, Jack asked, 'Who is he, Anthony?'

Anthony briefly considered laying it all on the line. 'Someone we don't want here.'

'Well, that is a grand way to greet the morning.' Jim, freshly showered and dressed, was standing in the doorway.

'Coffee, anyone?' Jack offered meekly, sensing both men's eyes boring the other's like a drill bit. He might be the jackeroo but that didn't mean he couldn't pick up when two men wanted to bash the crap out of each other. He made a fuss of filling the kettle at the sink, lit the gas cooktop and sat the kettle on top.

'Jack here will drive you into town,' Anthony said casually. 'There is a plane at six tonight. In the meantime, we've got a few things to take care of so you can make yourself at home here, watch a bit of telly or something.'

'Or something?' Jim mimicked.

Jack retrieved two mugs from the beige kitchen cupboard.

'You know I'll get what's coming to me,' Jim stated, pulling on a pair of socks.

Anthony dearly wanted to tell him that pigs might fly. He watched Jack fiddling with the coffee and sugar.

'I just wanted people to be a bit fair about things,' continued Jim.

Anthony had to give the Scot points. He had some nerve with his surprise visit and genuine disappointment with the welcoming committee.

'If I had a written history of the Gordon's at Wangallon,' Anthony said, trying to keep the annoyance out of his voice, 'I'd gladly give it to you to read. Then you might be a little more understanding.'

The kettle whistled. Jack added a teaspoon of coffee, then water to each mug.

'Understanding?' Jim's voice was raised.

Jack held up a container of milk. 'Milk?'

Anthony lowered his voice. 'I don't want to argue with you.' The last thing they needed was a scene in front of the jackeroo. It would be around the district within a few days.

'I'm sure you don't. You can't exactly complain about my rights when you've got your share and you're not even a Gordon.'

At this Jack dropped the mug he'd been about to pass to Jim. 'Bugger.'

Considering the events of the last few weeks, Anthony could barely contain himself. Only Jack's presence stopped him from saying anything further. He walked out of the kitchen onto the gauze enclosed verandah. 'Jack.'

Jack skirted past Jim in a flash. He pulled his boots on and stuck his wide-brimmed hat firmly on his head. Anthony held the screen door open for him as he went through.

'You're not welcome here, Jim, and I'm starting to think that Sarah was right. You shouldn't be entitled to a bloody cent,' Anthony growled. Having spent the night alone and with Sarah now en route to Sydney, Anthony had little time for the Gordon wannabe.

Jim was a nose length from Anthony's face in an instant. They remained that way for several seconds, Anthony opposite Jim, young Jack looking up from where he stood on the cement path below.

'Don't talk to me about entitlements. You've got your share and the grand house and its contents, just for insinuating yourself with the Gordon family. It's me by rights that should be having this conversation with you, mate,' Jim spat, 'not the other way around.'

Anthony's fist collected Jim squarely on his jaw; there was a crack, the force of the blow sent Jim into a flat spin that propelled him through the gauze of the verandah and out onto the small square of lawn where he landed with a thud on his back.

'Damn,' Jack said with reverence, admiring the great gaping hole in the gauze. 'Damn!' He walked over to where Jim lay sprawled on the ground. He was holding his jaw, moaning. *Take that*, Jack thought savagely, itching to throw in the Wangallon Town boot. He didn't know exactly what was going on, but he was on Anthony's side. He ran after him and slid into the passenger side of the Landcruiser.

Anthony stretched his fingers, felt the pain rip into the back of his hand and down his finger and knew his knuckles were broken. The dust spurted out from beneath the Landcruiser's rear tyres. 'We better go find Matt and see when Toby's going to start mustering the cattle to go on the route.'

Jack angled his backside into the seat and smiled. Now this was a good day.

Summer, 1908

Wangallon Station, New Year's Eve

Angus stopped near the entrance to the stables. A brown snake slithered from under a pile of old timber railings, leaving a wiggly track in the soft dirt as it headed towards open country. Its skin was glossy, the body fat. Angus watched until the snake was out of sight. The door to the tack room was open and his father's saddle was gone. He looked over his shoulder to make sure he was still alone and, selecting a bridle from a peg on the wall, headed to the rear of the stables. Willy was in an adjoining yard brushing one of the mares with a curry comb.

'Are you meant to be here?' Angus slipped through the timber rails. He'd not seen Willy since their fight over the slingshot.

Willy turned abruptly, running his hand across a snotty nose. 'Boxer says I'm to brush down the horses.'

Angus walked up to the boy. He was standing perfectly still now, the mare nuzzling his shoulder. 'Do you know where they've gone then?' His hand tightened on the bridle. Jasperson once told him a good stripe with the bit on a bridle would stun any man.

Willy pointed in the direction of the river. 'Mebbe that way. Are you going riding?'

'Maybe.'

They stood staring at each other until Willy returned to his brushing.

Angus scrambled through two lots of railings and walked across hoof-packed dirt. Standing alone, sniffing the wood of the yards, was the black gelding. Angus had christened him Wallace after William Wallace, the Scottish highlander who attempted to free them from the English. His father approved of his choice, reminding Angus that an animal with such a name would not suffer fools. Well, Angus knew that. He still had a bruise on his bum to prove it. Angus had reminded Wallace that his father was also a highlander, not that this shared allegiance made much difference. To date Angus had managed to stay on once out of seven attempts.

Angus slipped through the railings. Wallace trotted away. 'Come on, fella,' Angus called softly. 'Come on.' Having taken his father's advice to make friends with Wallace, he'd spent the last few days, morning and night, feeding and talking to him. Willy appeared on the other side of the railings with a bucket of chaff. 'Here,' he called. 'Try this.'

Reluctantly Angus accepted the bucket. As soon as he placed it on the ground Wallace walked forward and began to eat from it. When the horse lifted his head clear Angus slipped the bridle on. 'Gotcha!'

Willy opened the gate and Angus led Wallace into a larger yard.

'Jump on him here,' Willy encouraged. 'Bareback. You can ride bareback?'

Angus chewed his lip. He didn't much like the thought of falling off again. Willy stared at him, his skinny black hands resting on his hips, his bare toes digging into the sand of the yards. Angus was sure he could see the beginning of a smile. Gritting his teeth, he led Wallace to the railings, climbing up until he was level with the horse's back. The horse was stamping the ground impatiently, snorting and shaking his head.

'Come on,' Willy encouraged. 'Get on.'

Angus hesitated, considered the ramifications of being too scared to continue, before flinging his right leg carefully over the horse's back. His father had warned him of sudden movements and every muscle tightened expectantly in his body as he grimaced. He took a breath. Wallace barely moved. Shifting his bum into the centre of the horse's back, Wallace moved strongly beneath him before wheeling from left to right. Angus dug his knees in as he'd been taught, tightened his grip on the reins and turned the horse to his right. Soon they were walking around the yard's perimeter, his face all gappy eight-year-old grin.

'Faster,' Willy encouraged, perching himself on the top railing of the yard. 'Faster.'

In response Angus touched the horse's flanks. Wallace increased his speed. Soon he was in a trot. Trees in surrounding paddocks began to blur, the railings whizzed past his legs as Angus bounced lightly up and down.

'Me too,' Willy cried out. Without waiting for a response, he jumped from the railings when the horse passed by and landed behind Angus. Wallace reared immediately. Angus felt Willy's hands frantically grabbing his shirt tail, then the boy was gone, Angus clinging to two great handfuls of mane.

'Whoa, Wallace, good Wallace.' Angus calmed the horse and turned to see Willy rubbing his bum. Wallace snorted and whinnied as Angus slid off his back, patted his nose and removed the bridle. 'What did you do that for?'

Willy hunched his shoulders. His arm was bleeding where it had scraped the timber railings.

Angus moved to inspect the injury. 'Come on now.' He pulled a handkerchief from his pocket and tied it around the worst of the deep scratch. Willy watched warily, rubbing at his bum.

'Hard, isn't it?' Angus bandaged up the wound. A few minutes later Wallace trotted up to nibble at his shirtsleeve. In the distance was a horse and rider. The boys ran to the railings and clambering to the top, looked out towards the west. 'Wetherly,' Angus guessed. 'He rides like he's on show, so Father says. But where's he going?'

Willy hunched his shoulders and then pointed towards the orchard. It looked like Mungo waiting beneath the last of the orange trees, his hat cocked back on his head. Soon one of the maids came into view. With a grin, Angus elbowed Willy in the side and they ran from the stables, their feet soon crunching orange and lemon leaves soft with ruin as the morning sun crisscrossed the land. Angus spotted Luke's empty camp at the base of a large tree and dived for his swag, Willy landing partially on him.

'Get off,' he struggled. Ahead Lee was shuffling along the avenue of trees, beyond lay the neatly plotted square of the vegetable garden. One of the maids was in the garden, a basket over her arm. As if on cue Lee began walking towards the maid, his fist flaying the air in agitation, chasing the girl from his domain. Angus and Willy crawled on their stomachs to a tree and then darted to another.

'Ouch.' Willy extracted a prickly burr from his big toe.

'Shh,' Angus frowned.

Margaret's soft voice drifted across to them. They dropped behind a log as Mungo and Margaret sat at the base of a gum, he with his legs spread long and wide and she with her skirts tucked about her ankles.

'I would see you tonight.'

Angus peered above the fallen timber, watching bug-eyed as Mungo took Margaret's hand in his. It was pale next to his blackness.

'I'll be going again soon; in two full moons.' Mungo glanced about them. 'We could meet at the ridge.'

Angus clapped Willy on the head and they ducked behind the log, their hands clasped across each other's mouths.

Margaret removed her hand from his grasp. 'I'm promised.'

Mungo took the girl by her shoulders. 'He is old. He will die soon and then –'

'Then there will be another.'

There were tears in the girl's eyes. Angus saw them swell in size like small quail eggs and then drop, glistening, to wet the material of her dress. Mungo reached for her and kissed her.

Angus jammed Willy's face in the dirt to muffle his laughter.

'I would be with you,' Mungo said softly.

'For one night?' Margaret shook her head. 'It is not enough.' She stood, turning to look at him. 'In here,' she touched her chest, 'I am not black, I am not white. I am me. Do you see me?'

'I too have dreams,' Mungo told her. 'Most of them remain in the sky with the spirit people.'

'That is because you make it so.' Margaret shook her head. 'You are not the one who must lie with an old man. Who must listen to the jibes of the women because my father was white.'

'These are our people.'

Margaret scowled. 'I have not seen you camped by the creek. I have not seen you for nine moons. I think maybe that sometimes you too are white.'

Mungo scrunched a handful of twigs in the palm of his hand and tossed them into the tufted grass at his feet. Margaret walked away.

Angus rolled away from the log. 'Blackfella business.'

'Mebbe whitefella business too,' Willy answered. 'This is bad thing,' he cautioned, 'this wanting.'

Mungo looked like bad meat had entered his belly.

Midwinter, 1989

Castlereagh Street, Sydney

Frank Michaels looked at his appointment book and squinted, as if wishing he were blind. Sarah Gordon was slotted in for 3 pm, Mr Harvey Jamieson, a personal friend and prominent entrepreneur with a recalcitrant wife and messy divorce looming, had a thick line through his name. He would have to take the old boy out for a scotch to make it up to him, Frank decided. God knew he would probably need it. He was on his third wife. Pushing his reading glasses onto the bridge of his nose, Frank studied the facsimile received earlier.

Mr Woodbridge advised he was acting on behalf of one James Robert Macken of the village of Tongue, Northern Scotland and that his client wished to receive his full entitlement as bequeathed to him by the late Angus Gordon. Further, his client wanted a full cash payment and a thirty per cent share of both the livestock and the contents of Wangallon Homestead. James Macken would therefore be contesting the last will and testament of Angus Gordon accordingly. Frank placed the facsimile to one side, removed his reading glasses and leant back in his black leather office chair. Tony Woodbridge was capable enough. The man knew how to argue a case. Unfortunately he was not averse to underhand shenanigans either.

'Ronald, old chap,' he said aloud, addressing Sarah's father, 'you should have kept your dick in your pants, old boy'. Frank wasn't one for dramatics but he felt disturbed by James Macken. In his experience there was nothing worse than dealing with someone who was comparatively poor with a grudge, and it was clear by the Macken boy's demands that he did begrudge the Gordons. His second concern of the day came via another telephone call that caused him to drop his blue enamelled Sheaffer ink pen on the office floor. Were it not for the knock on his door announcing his personal assistant, Rhonda, with Sarah Gordon in tow, he may well have added a little whisky to his morning coffee.

'It's nice to see you again, Frank.'

'And you, my dear,' he replied, composing himself as he cleaned his spectacles. The last time he'd seen Sarah was at Angus's funeral. He adroitly summed up the situation, reading Mr Macken's requests, wondering if the renowned Gordon temper would flare. 'As you can see, he is now contesting the will and if he chooses to go to court, Mr Woodbridge will represent him and . . .' Frank leant forward for emphasis, 'he is very good'.

'Damn it. You know he arrived at Wangallon two days ago?' asked Sarah.

Frank linked his fingers together.

'I can't lose one acre of Wangallon, Frank.'

'Hmm. What does Anthony say?'

Sarah rolled her eyes. 'I'm having a few issues there. His idea is to develop Boxer's Plains.'

'Boxer's Plains?' Frank set about cleaning his spectacles again.

'You know, increase productivity from a decreased holding. I don't want Boxer's ploughed up, Frank, it was the last block purchased by my great-grandfather and it's prime grazing country.'

'I agree.' Frank studied Sarah's tapping fingers. 'I think you had better tell me everything.'

Sarah hadn't really discussed life on Wangallon for quite a while. Even her telephone conversations with Shelley were sanitised versions of her daily life. She told Frank about the management issues, lack of teamwork and Anthony's handling of the clearing project at Boxer's Plains. 'And I told him to stop doing anything else on the block.'

Poor Anthony, Frank thought, the lad did have the foresight to know an increase in productivity was warranted. Unfortunately his timing was lousy, his lack of courtesy towards Sarah troubling and his choice of block unbelievable. 'Well there's only two thousand acres ploughed so far, so not too much harm has been done but I agree the project has to stop immediately. The bank won't lend the money at this point in time to pay for any land development, and –'

Sarah looked at him suspiciously. 'How did you know how much country had been cultivated? Or that the bank won't lend us the money to do it?'

Frank cleared his throat. 'Secondly, there is lobbying going on from the environmentalists to bring in clearing legislation. We don't need any negative publicity coming from that angle and I imagine Mr Woodbridge will do his utmost to paint you and Wangallon in a very poor light. If you decide to contest your grandfather's will, he will make this private matter very public.' And that, Frank decided, could place Wangallon's and the Gordon's reputation in jeopardy.

Sarah ran her fingers through her hair. 'I have to do something.'

Frank wondered if Angus Gordon had done the right thing including Ronald's illegimate son in his will. He and Sarah's grandfather had spent long afternoons discussing his proposed instructions. Every argument produced a counterclaim and more than a bottle of Scotch had been consumed during their diatribe. In the end, however, Angus was not prepared to go to his deathbed without ensuring that the mistakes of the past were not repeated. It was a revelation to see his cantankerous old friend develop a sense of decency at the end of his life, especially considering the number of scrapes Frank only just managed to get Angus through over the years.

Frank cleared his throat. 'You asked me how I knew about the clearing.' He leant back in his chair, made a pyramid of his fingers. 'Your grandfather set a number of mechanisms in place prior to his death. You know how obsessed he was with the property, with its continuation. He wanted to ensure its survival. To that end Wangallon's yearly financials are forwarded to me; I, in turn, discuss them with Wangallon's agribusiness financial advisor.' Frank leaned forward. 'You never would have received approval from the bank for the cattle truck loan.'

Sarah looked at him, dumbfounded.

'My dear, many large grazing properties have trusts in place to run the business until the successor reaches a certain age. Wangallon's arrangement merely keeps an eye on financial matters.'

'So Anthony and I were never in charge?' Even now her grandfather was controlling them from the grave.

'Of course you were, or are, I should say.' Frank pulled out a manila folder, flipped it open. 'Checking figures is not the same as running the property.'

Sarah felt decidedly uncomfortable. There was a lack of trust on behalf of her grandfather that made her feel ill. 'What about the funds needed to pay the contractors for the Boxer's Plains development?'

Frank looked her directly in the eye. 'Sarah, I've seen no budget or projections. Banks just won't lend money willy-nilly, you know, and until your cattle sales start and your shearing proceeds come in next month, you haven't got a great margin to be playing with. And if we go to court it will be expensive. Have you seen any costings for the development?'

Sarah shook her head. Matt had mentioned the inordinate sum of $200,000 plus.

'Well we don't want to place Wangallon in financial difficulty or put the bank offside. I suggest you tell Anthony that you've spoken to the bank and that they're not willing to support the project. In the meantime I'll see if they're happy to increase your overdraft in order to pay for the work already done. Sarah looked peaky. 'Would you like a glass of water?' Frank walked over to the cream sideboard and poured water from a plastic jug. 'Here.' He passed Sarah the glass and perched himself on the edge of his desk. It was unfortunate to have to take such a hard line, yet quite frankly Anthony's clearing of Boxer's Plains could have serious ramifications, not least of all to his own family firm. 'Look, I'm not saying the development can't be done at some later stage, *if* both of you are agreeable to it. After all, increasing productivity through selective clearing increases the value of one's asset base. Although I am extremely surprised Anthony didn't present his plans and budget to the bank.'

Sarah took a long sip of water. It was room temperature and, unlike the sweet rainwater of Wangallon, tasted of chlorine.

'Once you have contacted Anthony and clarified why the clearing has to stop we can concentrate on this inheritance tangle. The development project can be revisited properly next year. But not on Boxer's Plains.'

'Why not?'

Frank adjusted his reading glasses on his nose. He was convinced this part of his body was also shrinking with age. 'Because the block is already extremely valuable in terms of grazing potential.' Which was true. 'Choose an area on the eastern boundary.'

Sarah could only imagine Anthony's response: A directive on

where he could and could not develop, coming from a solicitor.

'My dear, you have just sat there and complained about a lack of teamwork and not being consulted about the development. And I agree with you.'

Sarah looked down at her short oval fingernails, at the pale moons that extended from beneath the softness of her skin.

'You must explain to him why this decision has been taken.' Frank returned to his chair and the comfort of the padded cushion that eased his bony backside. 'By the way, Sarah, Matt Schipp was employed by your grandfather. He is on Wangallon to keep an eye on things as you well know, so if you have any concerns management-wise, speak to him.'

Sarah nodded. If Anthony knew half of the control mechanisms in place she doubted whether his commitment to both her and Wangallon would have lasted beyond the reading of her grandfather's will. 'I guess Matt told you about the development?' Frank gave a dip of his chin. 'Well now he and Anthony are arguing.'

'The man signed a contract. Matt isn't going anywhere.' The girl had the look of a startled deer about her which reminded him that for all her on-farm capability, she was only in her mid-twenties. 'Now you're here for advice, so here it is. You have two options. One, sell thirty per cent of the property to pay out your half-brother, or two, sell ten or fifteen thousand acres elsewhere. With that sale the bank would happily finance the rest of Jim's entitlement.'

'Sell?' Sarah repeated. She had come here for help.

Frank lay his long knobbly fingers on the top of his desk. 'This will only get more stressful and Wangallon is a large property. 'Fulfill the terms of your grandfather's will and get on with your life, Sarah. It's the only logical solution. And stop that development on Boxer's Plains.'

Sarah gulped at the water. She felt like she was going to be sick.

Summer, 1908

Crawford Corner Homestead, New Year's Eve

The first thing one noted when sighting the Crawford's homestead was the impressive lawn that surrounded the building. Established fruit trees were arranged in a grid formation to the front right of the house while a generous patch of herbs sat squarely opposite. The remainder of the substantial space was bare of trees, although immaculately maintained and surrounded by a startlingly white picket fence. The house itself was imposing, rectangular in design, of the same mud brick and plaster construction as Wangallon Homestead, but, Hamish concluded, probably one-third larger in size than his own home. Resting his hands on the pommel of his saddle, Hamish shifted forward a little, the action freeing the cramp in his right calf muscle.

'Big place, Boss,' said McKenzie as they approached. Their horses trailed single file along the narrow dirt road up to the large verandah that encircled the homestead.

'His holding does not match the grandiose view he holds of himself,' Hamish stated with a patronising tone, although he had to admire the English for their ability to add regimented beauty to the Australian bush. 'Jasperson, we are here as friends.'

His overseer raised a grey bristled eyebrow.

Once Hamish had craved success, then respectability, and now he had both. The gaining of it meant deliberation must now replace ruthless action, for the Gordon name needed to be protected. He chewed at his top lip, pulling at the hairs of his moustache; he was suppressing his innate need for revenge with a far more advantageous course of action. It was a pity the event didn't feel more rewarding.

At the hitching rail they tethered their horses and Jasperson turned to survey the grounds. 'Take a lot to maintain this, Boss.'

'Indeed, Jasperson. Although I'm sure the domestics and gardeners will be keen to stay.' At least for a while, Hamish concluded. There was little need for another homestead on Wangallon and the uptake of this one would be costly; besides, there was no one to live in it. Luke was beyond the niceties of a homestead such as this. For the moment he would continue to keep the household running and use it as a base for when he visited the property. It would make the five-hour round trip more bearable to know that there was a semblance of comfort at the end of the journey.

The wide verandah and sloping roof invited the three men into its embracing coolness. Hamish noted two hard-backed chairs, a table with books piled high upon it and an expanse of wooden boards.

'Yes?' A manservant in a black cloth suit, with a pointy chin lifted higher than his position demanded, was standing in the open doorway of the homestead.

Jasperson stepped forward, straightened his shoulders and gave the man his most withering look; a direct gaze of sunken cheeks, sun cracked skin and eyes that spoke of loathing. 'Mr Hamish Gordon of Wangallon Station to see Mr Oscar Crawford.'

Crawford Corner Homestead, New Year's Eve

The manservant took a step back and opened the door wide for the trio to pass. They allowed their hats to be taken although on Hamish's lead they refused to remove their riding boots and spurs.

'Please follow me,' the servant addressed Hamish.

They stood in a twelve-foot-high ceilinged hallway. The floorboards were highly polished, the tongue and groove walls whitewashed and hung with paintings. Undoubtedly these portraits were relations of Crawford. Hamish studied the florid face before him with its chin that resembled a sole dangling from a shoe. It still amazed him that men of this elk conquered Scotland. With a final glance at the dead, Hamish readied himself for business. He tapped dirt-stained nails against the carved wooden frame of the oil painting. Success, he decided, combined with respectability, was boring.

The manservant knocked once at a cedar door and waited until an impatient *yes, yes* answered. Hamish signalled for McKenzie to remain in the hallway outside the office as the door opened and they were announced.

Oscar Crawford was clearly not dressed to receive visitors. He wore a buttercup-yellow silk robe over which was another silk robe of the same quality material, this one in forest green. His remarkable white gold hair was just visible beneath his silk candy-striped smoking cap that gave a slight clownish air to a fair complexion ruined by sagging jowls. There were sheaves of paper to the left of his magnificent leather tooled desk and a number of folders secured with ribbon on his right. Before him sat a silver salver containing a selection of small glass bottles that he was studiously frowning at.

'This is god early for a visitation, Gordon, especially when you come uninvited.'

Hamish sat down in the leather chair opposite, crossed his legs and smiled. 'Might I have some tea?' The servant looked from Hamish to his master.

Oscar removed his smoking cap in annoyance, dropping it on his desk. 'Yes, yes, tea for all. And take this,' he gestured to the salver, which was quickly removed. 'The negative aspect of age,' he said by way of explaining the potions. 'I see you are still in service, Jasperson.'

Standing at Hamish's right shoulder, Jasperson nodded.

'And just as reticent. Well, sit. I don't need another servant hovering around like one of the infernal flies that inhabit this landscape.'

'I'm here to make you an offer to purchase Crawford Corner,' Hamish began, never one to circumnavigate a subject. 'It is my third such offer on my reckoning and it will be the last.'

Oscar sat back in his chair and joined his fingers together in a peak. 'I see. And this, after you have absconded with my stud master?'

'He left willingly.'

Oscar waved his hand dismissively.

William Crawford entered his father's office, dressed for a day outdoors. The boy was fit-looking and tanned, clearly not the bookworm Hamish expected. Indeed his handshake spoke of a determined confidence.

'Crawford Corner is not for sale, although we are of course flattered by your offer.'

'My boy,' Oscar said by way of introduction, 'refuses to be parted from the family seat.'

A surge of annoyance shot through Hamish. 'A lawyer choosing to live up here? On a paltry selection of –'

William's bland face stiffened. The Crawford's have interests in more than *just* land.'

Hamish's forehead creased into a row of parallel lines, each deeper than the first. He had been insulted by the finest; once by an aide to the Governor for sitting prior to the Queen's representative at a state dinner. As Hamish reminded the gilded youth at the time, she was not his Queen and he was hungry. As for this young pup, William, well he had some learning to do. 'And that would be the reason for the selling of 50,000 acres further west some ten years ago to repay a debt for commercial property in Sydney. Yes, I can see how important it is to have interests in more than *just* land.' He flicked an imaginary fleck of dirt from his trousers.

Crawford coughed into a white handkerchief. 'Let us have peace, gentlemen.'

'My profession,' William emphasised, 'allows me a number of choices, Sir, none of which involve selling our land.'

Hamish lifted a formidable eyebrow. 'You don't have to justify yourself to me, William. However, if you do intend remaining on this land I would hope that you will appoint a suitable head stockman in your absence so that the property is properly managed.' Hamish knew he had stepped beyond the boundaries of propriety. For a moment the room was quiet.

William brushed a strand of dark hair from his face. 'I think you have explained the purpose of your visit, Mr Gordon.'

Hamish ignored the boy. 'What do you intend to do to rectify your water situation? Diverting water from the bore drain system is illegal. And I will not tolerate the possibility of Wangallon stock dying of thirst because of it.'

William looked directly at his father. Clearly Oscar had not fully briefed his prodigal son on his recent doings.

Hamish continued. 'Then there is the additional problem of missing stock.'

William's mouth gaped.

Oscar stood, pushing his chair back with such force that it toppled over, striking a small table. Littered with black and white photographs in gilt-edged frames, all fell to the red carpeted floor.

'How dare you, Hamish Gordon! You, who built your holding on deceit and stock theft, come here and have the audacity to accuse me of, of . . . you Scottish upstart. It is an embarrassment to be of acquaintance to you.'

'I expect reparations for the damage you have done me, Sir. The water has already been diverted back to Wangallon, at my own cost. However, you will be in receipt of an account for the cattle I am missing. Some fifty head, I believe.

'I'm warning you, Gordon . . .'

Hamish turned to Oscar's son. 'William, I wish you luck in your endeavours.'

'You damn upstart,' Oscar yelled. 'We should have starved you all out of the Highlands when we had the chance.'

It took only the few ill-judged words of an Englishman to send Hamish spiralling back towards the edge of the loch. Winter was coming. The scent of herbage, the season's last before winter assaulted his nostrils as he looked across at the mounds of stone on the edge of the water. His brothers and sisters lay cradled in the cold clay and rock of his homeland. Beyond him in their one-room hut lay his beloved mother, dead. His family had slaved for the English, died for the English.

Hamish flew from his seat, drew his hardened fist and struck Oscar Crawford in the cheek. There was a crunch, the bruising jar of skin, bone and gristle. The strength of the punch sent the older man tumbling to the ground where he struggled like a floundering yellow-belly, gasping for air. There was a startled gasp from the son. Hamish turned on him at once, readying his fist. Unexpectedly the youth cowered. 'See what you have bred?' Hamish glowered at father and son before exiting the office. Barely halting in his stride, he barged past the returning servant, knocking the salver from his hands. Jasperson followed, sidestepping the spilt tea and smashed crockery.

'Get the horses, McKenzie,' Hamish growled.

When Hamish turned to face his overseer the muscles around his jawline were bunched, a large vein throbbed powerfully in his neck. 'The day I take possession of Crawford Corner,' he spat through gritted teeth, 'I will burn this house to the ground.'

The men mounted as one and rode out of the homestead garden. Jasperson let Hamish take the lead as they cantered off. 'Now you will see how such men are made, McKenzie.' Jasperson's lip curled upwards as he nodded at the rider in front of them.

Midwinter, 1989

Boxer's Plains

The toe of Anthony's boot struck the gear upwards and he accelerated. The Yamaha motorbike sped along the dirt road. Each bump and pothole on the road jarred his body and sent unwelcome slivers of pain through his right hand. Two of his fingers were strapped. Anthony's only regret was that he had not hit Jim Macken harder. He revved the motorbike, swallowing the throb of his hand, wishing the Scot had given him the opportunity of throwing two punches instead of one. At the old army bridge spanning the waters of the Wangallon River, he stopped. Beneath him, a muddy swirl moved downstream. There were waterbirds stalking the furthest bank, a lone wallaby and a number of kangaroos having an early morning drink. Anthony pulled the zipper up further on his oilskin and stretched his leather-and-wool encased fingers. The morning was colder than it had looked from Wangallon's kitchen window.

Restarting the bike he continued on across the bridge and into Boxer's Plains. With two sleepless nights behind him, he'd spent much of the time trying to decipher how things had become so skewed. His reasoning regarding the development was sound and the inevitability of Jim's inheritance made his project one hundred per cent correct. Why then was Sarah so damn determined to stop something Wangallon needed? Stubbornness ran in the Gordon family, of that he'd had firsthand experience, and it was true Wangallon had always been predominantly grazing, but the bush was changing and Wangallon needed to move with the times as well.

He knew his girl didn't like change and in truth, considering the past, he couldn't blame her. But this was different. They were both trying to protect Wangallon, yet Sarah was acting as if he was the enemy. Somehow everything seemed mightily screwed up. The motorbike startled a mob of kangaroos nibbling near the edge of the cultivation. Immediately the animals turned briefly towards the oncoming noise, then they were off, their muscled hind legs powering them forward, leaving small puffs of dust as they hopped quickly into the safety of some wilga trees. Anthony rode around the edge of the cultivation to where the contractors had been working. He followed their metal track marks in the soft dirt, careful not to land in one of the gaping holes where a tree once stood. Scattered branches and large limbs, the debris from fallen timber, lay strewn in every direction and Anthony found it difficult to pick a path through the tangle of branches. More than once he found himself backing up his bike in order to find a clearer passage. The area was heavily timbered and with new tree growth over the last few years, it was virtually impossible to muster stock out. Anthony doubted if many people had ventured this far into the ridge for years. Angus had fenced off a square of about sixty acres right in the middle of the ridge in the late twenties. It was a smart solution for it stopped stock from hiding within the timbered environs, although Anthony was at a loss as to why he'd simply not had the timber thinned out a little.

The bulldozers were clearing on a face of about five hundred metres. Eventually Anthony reached their start point and rode around the man-made boundary. It struck him how easily a landscape could change. On his right, trees swallowed the countryside while to his left timber lay on the ground like fallen soldiers. Eventually a glint of metal caught his eye and soon the unmistakeable shape of heavy machinery came into view. The two dozer drivers were sitting in the middle of their handiwork in deckchairs.

Anthony got off his bike and tucked his hands into the pockets of his jacket. It was damn cold, but these two blokes were wearing short-sleeved shirts and shorts. 'G'day. Working on your cruise tan, Bruce?'

'Almost summery today,' commented Bruce, the older of the two men, unscrewing the lid on his thermos. 'Cuppa?'

'Sounds good.' Anthony squatted in the dirt as the black tea was poured. Soon he was warming his hands around the lid of the thermos.

'Five weeks till spring,' agreed Neville, Bruce's companion, passing Anthony a milk arrowroot biscuit spread with butter and vegemite.

Bruce took a slurp of tea and licked the topping off his biscuit. 'Saw that head stockman of yours this morning.'

Neville poured more tea for himself and spread his legs straight in front of him in order to pick up more of the sun's weak rays. 'Don't like him.'

Anthony took a sip of his tea. He could have stood a teaspoon up in it, it was that strong.

'Yeah, Mrs Kelly wouldn't have let Ned play with him,' Neville stated solemnly.

'He's not that much of a poor bastard,' Bruce replied.

Neville shook his head. 'Met him up at Carlyon's place before his accident. Wasn't too bad then.'

'And now?' Anthony asked, intrigued.

'Delusions of grandeur.'

Bruce poured more tea. 'Well, I don't mind the poor bastard. He's got a busted sandshoe for a face and fingers that are no good to any woman.'

'He's capable,' Anthony admitted, draining his tea. 'And permanent.' He passed Bruce the thermos lid. The three of them finished up and Bruce packed up his esky, tying a narrow cotton rope around it to keep the broken lid on. 'Got the ear of your girl, eh? You'll have to put a stop to that. 'Bout time you two married and had a couple of sprogs. That will keep her busy.'

Neville grinned, displaying a gold front tooth. 'Ahh, ankle-biters. Would have lost an eye for me own little fellas. Course then they grow up and become right little arseholes and you can't give the buggers away.'

Anthony blinked. 'Look fellas, I need to stop the work here for a few days.' It was a tough thing to be pushed into an uncomfortable decision, but if the development was going to cause such a major problem between them, especially with everything else going on, then he would do as Sarah asked – at least for the moment. One of them would have to take a step back before they did further damage to their relationship. Once she returned home he'd talk her around.

Bruce rolled his eyes. 'Again?'

'Yeah, the fuel truck's been delayed,' he lied. 'It's got me buggered, but we're all out of diesel. And they're not promising a delivery this week.'

'Fair enough.' Bruce heaved his burly frame out of the deck-chair. 'We'll go through to knock-off time. Give us a call when you want us back on board. I was hankering for a steak and chips at the Wangallon pub tonight anyway.'

'No probs. Thanks, mate.' Anthony shook Bruce's hand, wincing at the vice-like grip.

'Got yourself a bit of a fencing job,' thumbed Neville over his shoulder. 'Hit a wire back a bit. Old fence?'

'Yeah, it's pretty old. We might use that as a bit of a marker and clear up to that. Later on I might thin it out a bit.'

'No worries. Up to the fencing relic it is,' Neville confirmed with an excuse for a cough and a string of spittle that landed to sit foaming in the dirt.

Bullet was waiting at the back steps when Anthony arrived home. Surprisingly the dog actually stayed still long enough for a brief pat on the head. Ferret gave a melancholy whine.

'Missing her, aren't you, mate?' Anthony commented, scraping his boots off at the back steps.

As if on cue Bullet looked down the back path. Satisfied that his mistress was not following, he ambled back to the rainwater tank and lay down beside Ferret, a half-chewed boot between them.

'I'll tell her you want her home.'

Bullet answered with a snappish bark.

Inside Anthony washed his hands, wondering if Sarah would be back at the serviced apartment where she was staying. He was half-inclined to jump on the next plane to Sydney. He hadn't been to the big smoke for a while and there was nothing like a motel room for rekindling a love affair. He didn't need to agree with her decision to fight Jim Macken, but he guessed a little support might make Sarah more amenable towards the land development. In the office he checked dates in the station diary, noting down flight times from the faxed listing the airline circulated every year. He was about to contact the travel agent when the telephone rang.

'Hey, I was just thinking about you. Must be ESP. How's everything going?'

'Okay,' Sarah said with little enthusiasm. 'Looks like I might owe you an apology. Frank reckons we probably will have to sell.'

Anthony knew it was a bitter blow for her. 'I'm sorry. So you're coming home?'

Sarah sighed. 'No. I need to see Dad. Tell him about everything.'

'Oh.' So much for the trip to Sydney. Anthony flipped the diary closed. 'Good. I don't see any benefit in keeping him out of the loop when he caused the problem.'

'That's a bit blunt, isn't it?'

Her voice was tight. Anthony knew he was doing the right thing by deciding to halt the development in the short term. If only she knew how dogmatic she was acting and how oversensitive she sounded. 'Sarah, I've decided to –'

'If you haven't stopped the Boxer's Plains development, Anthony, I want you to immediately. The bank won't support us. I've just spoken to them. They might agree to increasing the overdraft to tidy up anything owing to the contractors – other than that we're on our own.'

'I see.' He scrunched the airline schedule in his left hand.

'Do you? I can't believe you didn't do any budget projections to present to the bank.' The line was silent. 'The solicitor agrees that you'll have to forget about this development of yours.' Sarah took a breath. She had a foreboding feeling that she was sounding like Anthony's boss and not his partner and fiancée. 'Anthony? Hello? Anthony, are you there?' She looked blankly at the receiver, the line was dead. 'Damn it.' Anthony had never hung up on her before.

Summer, 1908

Wangallon Station, New Year's Eve

McKenzie didn't want to bother Mr Gordon, however intrigue was getting the better of him; that and an empty stomach. Having ridden from Crawford Corner in a flurry of excitement, they soon slowed. The better part of two hours was spent meandering through a grass paddock, after which they trailed the course of the river until midafternoon. McKenzie itched from the heat. When he scratched his hairy arm, dirt caked up under his nails. His stomach was rumbling terribly and his water was near gone. The horses stepped nimbly over fallen logs and then, without warning, they were splashing across a river sluggish from lack of rain. The horses drank for long minutes, slurping up gallons of the brown water, their whiskered nostrils quivering against the liquid.

Oozing mud sucked at their horses as they reached the opposite bank. Then they were urging the horses up the sandy slope and through a path of stringy saplings. A goanna ambling across their path took flight as they approached and scurried quickly up a tree. McKenzie watched the prehistoric beast's progress. The blacks called them overland trout; reckoned they were good eating. Once or twice he'd tracked a goanna when he was near starving. If you were lucky and the lizard crossed loose dirt, its clawed feet and thick tail left visible impressions. He'd never tasted one though. Never been bitten by one either. The rotting flesh between their teeth left ulcerated, festering sores. Looking back over his shoulder, McKenzie's imagined feed disappeared as the trees merged and closed in behind him. He figured there would have been a fair chance of hitting him with his rifle. A wounding would do. He could finish the job with a lump of wood.

The day lengthened, layering shadows of light through the scrub. An hour or so would have them back at the station, so he was more than surprised when Hamish announced they would be stopping. They made camp under a carbine tree, tethering the horses nearby. He gathered wood as directed and made a good blaze of it. For once he was pleased to be camping out – there'd be no favours given this night with the Boss about.

'Have you made a decision?' Jasperson settled his saddle and blanket by the fire. Pulling a ration of flour from his saddlebag, he knocked up a rough damper with a little water and sat it in the coals.

Hamish removed his jacket and sat, trying to find a more comfortable position. 'Yes.' Unfurling a length of calico, he speared a piece of salted mutton and held it over the fire, nodding to McKenzie to help himself. 'We'll be taking back what's ours and a measure of theirs.'

Jasperson chewed thoughtfully on a twig. 'Times have changed a bit, Boss.'

'You lost the taste for it then?' Hamish picked at the shreds of mutton sticking to his moustache.

Jasperson poked at the damper with the twig he'd been sucking.

Hamish spat gristle into the fire. 'I'll not be relegated to the common class by a man such as Oscar Crawford. It's time the Englishman had a taste of what his countrymen did to mine. I will take back my cattle and some of his for good measure and we'll be doing it this next full moon.'

Jasperson speared the damper with a stick and sat it on the blanket. 'We'll be needing Boxer and Luke.'

'Mungo too,' Hamish looked at McKenzie, 'and you, lad.'

McKenzie nodded trying to hide his suprise, his tongue sucking at the dried meat.

Jasperson threw McKenzie a chunk of steaming damper. 'They'll be illegal doings.'

'Are you up for it?' Hamish asked.

McKenzie looked at the man who owned Wangallon. He thought Hamish Gordon was a respectable pastoralist. His own plans for promotion looked amateurish in comparison and he wondered if he had more to worry about than Jasperson's inclinations. He took a bite of the steaming damper, the severe heat of it sticking to the roof of his mouth.

'Well?' Jasperson's thin nose was pinched inwards.

The dough caught in McKenzie's throat. His first sighting of Hamish Gordon occurred at the building of the bore drain. That day the man threatened to shoot anyone who didn't toe the line. The dough slid uneasily down his gullet. 'W-whatever y-you want, Mr Gordon. I-I'm your man.'

A crackle of leaves quieted them. Hamish pointed to the left, making a circling motion with his hand. Noiselessly they walked out into the darkness, edging away from the rim of the campfire, their rifles ready for action. They spent long minutes circumnavigating the camp, only to return empty-handed. The bush was noisy once one listened. The dull thud of kangaroos echoed through the timber, a creature squawked as if under attack, crickets chirped rhythmically.

'Kangaroo?' Jasperson suggested once they were sitting back within the halo of the fire.

Hamish hunkered down in the dirt, resting his head on his saddle. 'You keep watch, McKenzie. The bush is busy tonight.'

'Blacks?' McKenzie propped his back against a tree. Jasperson shifted a heavy night log onto the fire and moved a little closer to it.

'Maybe.' Stars flickered through the trees. Hamish thought they resembled candles sputtering through a mottled cloth of darkening greens and browns. As he drifted towards sleep an image of the miles of flay country extending outwards from the heart of Wangallon came to him. Like a shapeshifter, it merged to form mountains and valleys, easing out over rocky crags and grassy verges to the sandy shoreline of a nation too young to know true hardship. This was not a land like Scotland, where war was waged by those such as the English intent on control. This was not a country where the yoke of suppression had existed for hundreds of years. Hamish's eyes flicked open.

Sometimes he could recall the tangy scent of the Highlands, the slivering coldness of the loch. Sometimes he wondered what it would be like to return. To walk the pebble-strewn shoreline on acreage he would never truly own. Hamish could conjure his mother, carrying water from the loch, pulping their scant supply of oats for the small cakes she made on the hearth. There was dirt on her smiling face, her coarse woollen skirt was torn and her hair greasy. She had died in the winter, sharing her deathbed with their lone cow; her two surviving sons and a husband worrying about taxes. They were small memories, indistinct, yet recently their importance had grown.

Midwinter, 1989

The Gold Coast, Queensland

The corridor leading to her mother's room was long and beige. There were photographs of the Queensland coast between each white doorway and at the end was a soft pink couch currently providing comfort to two young children, who, although having been left with books and soft toys, sat staring straight ahead. Sarah checked the numbers above each door, mentally counting down both the number of rooms left and the months that divided their last reunion. Leaving her luggage at the door, she knocked once before entering.

'Sarah, it's good to see you.' Sarah glanced towards the hospital bed as her father bustled her in, sitting her in one of two comfy armchairs. He looked reasonably well, although tired. His bulky frame was only just beginning to stoop and he filled the room with the unmistakeable genetics of a Gordon male: tenacious, craggily handsome in the later stages of his life with an aura that made people stare on passing. Newspapers were scattered on the wide window ledge and table next to her mother's bed. Sue Gordon sat upright, a cream bed jacket about her shoulders and a vacant stare boring into the blank wall opposite. Immediately Sarah questioned her presence. She could have waited at her father's apartment or gone for a walk along the beach or invested in some retail therapy; although with everything occurring at the moment, shopping didn't hold any interest for her.

'She's comfortable,' her father stated. 'Of course she doesn't know where she is, or who I am.' He cleared his throat. 'I'm sure the reading helps. You know, otherwise she just lies there, in silence.'

Sarah settled herself in the armchair. 'You read aloud to her?'

'Of course, mainly the news, although sometimes I skip to the entertainment page. She always did love the cinema when she lived in Sydney.'

'Dad,' Sarah touched his arm gently, 'you do recall two years ago the doctors said that her mind had basically shut down, so why –'

'Why bother?' Ronald snapped. He began tidying the papers, heaping them into a neat pile at his feet. 'Maybe it makes me feel better.'

There was a bald patch, round and smooth on the crown of his head. The brown of the skin contrasted sharply with the grey-streaked brown hair, yet he still looked younger than his wife. Sarah looked across the small space to where her mother lay. Her father was wasting his life through some strange aberration of guilt. It wasn't as if he'd been driving a car that led to her mother's condition, nor could her mother claim a morally unblemished record.

'Jim Macken has arrived in Australia. He wants to meet you and is claiming his inheritance.' Having planned on a more subtle revelation, Sarah found herself delivering the news like a corner shop spruiker.

Ronald rearranged the pile of papers. 'So you didn't come to visit your mother?'

'Dad, you know we never had a normal relationship when I was young. There's no point pretending now.'

He walked over to Sue and tucked a stray lock of hair behind her ear.

'You did hear what I said, Dad?'

'The doctor gives her a week. She's stopped eating and, well, I can't see the point of putting her on a drip.' He turned to her. 'Can you? Anyway some of her organs are beginning to shut down, something to do with all the medication she's been on over the years. Did you know that she used to down painkillers with her martinis, like they were a side plate of olives? Well, anyway, she doesn't exactly rate for the transplant list.' He pulled the bed jacket a little more snugly about Sue's shoulders. 'She hasn't spoken to me for over a year, although the night nurses say that sometimes she's quite lucid.'

'I'm sorry, Dad.'

'Well, you two never did get on.'

Sarah's eyes widened. 'That's unfair. I have had to live with the repercussions of your extra-marital affairs: both yours and Mum's. Both of you playing favourites with Cameron was one thing, but being relegated to the role of second-class citizen, being the recipient of all Mum's angst, was truly unfair. You're my father, you should have supported me.'

Her father's shoulders slumped just a little. 'I tried to, but no one gave me a manual, Sarah. After Cameron's death, I'd had enough. I'd battled your grandfather all my life, married a woman with a weak mind and tried to see you safe from harm's way with a new life in Sydney. I've failed in nearly everything I've done, including you. You never should have gone back to Wangallon, Sarah. The property should have been sold.'

'Well now it might have to be,' Sarah replied.

Ronald turned slowly from his wife and looked from Sarah to the window. His face was unreadable. Then gradually, as if his emotions were rising upwards to fill a blank canvas, his features tightened, reddened and then settled. 'What is he like?'

'Stubborn and selfish – all he wants is his share, in cash. He feels no attachment to the property, doesn't appreciate what has gone into its creation and was angry when he didn't get the welcoming party he believed he deserved.'

Ronald looked directly at her. 'He's been to Wangallon?'

'Been and gone.'

'I'm sorry. You shouldn't have been left with that mess.'

It took some time for Sarah to explain to her father all that had occurred over the last week. Occasionally the furrow between his eyes deepened to a thick crevice, yet he never interrupted her. For once in her life Sarah had her father's attention. Then the nurse arrived on rounds and there was a checking of Sue's pulse, blood pressure and temperature.

'No change,' the nurse said brightly, tucking the sheets in and adjusting pillows. She nodded in their direction, her gaze resting on Sarah a touch longer than necessary, before leaving the room.

'Your mother hasn't had many visitors since she was moved into this ward. She's more comfortable here though, I think. The nurses are very caring.'

'What do you think we should do, Dad?'

'Well, I'm not surprised Frank Michaels advised to sell. But . . .'

Sarah perched forward in her chair. At last someone was prepared to fight.

'Better to sell another parcel.' Ronald scratched above his ear where his hair was thinning.

'What?'

'We should off-load twenty or thirty thousand acres on the eastern boundary. It's less productive than other parts of Wangallon.'

Sarah sat back, deflated. She'd almost believed her father would provide her with a solution.

'As for Anthony, well quite frankly I'd let him go ahead with a development if the costings work out, but not on Boxer's Plains, Sarah, that's good grazing country. It would be a real waste to plough it up; besides, Dad always wanted it left as is. It *should* be left as is.'

Sarah's eyebrows crinkled together. Was she reading more into this than needed? It seemed as if both her father and Frank Michaels were overly protective of Boxer's Plains. 'We're not farmers.'

'Maybe we should be,' Ronald suggested. 'Read the rural papers, Sarah. There's money to be made in grain. It's a burgeoning commodity and the world needs to be fed.' Ronald patted her arm. 'If you and Anthony are going to marry, you're really going to have to let him manage Wangallon. You can't have two people trying to lead, not when you're in a relationship. Don't look at me like that, Sarah. You don't have to make everything harder than it is, you know. The development sounds like a good idea so go see the bank and find out what they're willing to lend and choose another block to do it on. But first things first. Jim Macken has to be paid out as per your grandfather's terms. He's entitled to his share. I'd suggest selling the black wattle block on the eastern boundary.'

Everyone – Anthony, her father and the solicitor – all of them had the same point of view. Maybe she was being stupid fighting the inevitable. Maybe she should let Jim have his inheritance. Then she could go home to Anthony and Wangallon. 'And what about Jim? He wants to meet you.'

Ronald looked down at her and for a split second Sarah glimpsed the unmistakeable hardness of Angus Gordon. 'I have no intention of ever meeting Jim Macken. To me he exists on paper only and it's best,' he looked directly at Sue, 'that he stays there.'

Midsummer, 1909

Wangallon Town Hotel

McKenzie pulled tightly on Lauren's long hair until her throat stretched out, making her breathless. She could feel her cheeks flush an apple red and she shook her hair free, squinting at the pain. McKenzie gave one final, tumultuous shove and slumped across her sweaty body.

'Get off. You're heavy.' She stuck her raggedy nails fiercely into his arse until he rolled obediently to one side, watching with amusement as she untangled her hair from around his wrist. Lauren wiped at the drops of sweat running down her forehead and fluffed her hair, which was plastered flat.

'You're a plain-featured girl.' He pinched at her nipple, his calloused hands rasping her skin.

'You're ugly,' she retaliated.

He lifted his hand and poked at her soft wet belly, ruffled the brown heart of her before swinging his legs over the side of the lumpy mattress.

He pulled coins from the pocket of his trousers hanging on the end of the bed and added one more than the usual. 'What's your game then?' Lauren asked as he sat the small pile between them on the dirty rumpled sheets.

'Your voice reminds me of a stray cat I once slaughtered for food.'

'It's nice to be appreciated.' She picked up the coins and deposited them on the rickety bedside table. Struggling upwards, Lauren pulled the sheet up to her waist. Her breasts spread to two soft peaks. 'Have you got the makings?'

McKenzie tossed her his tobacco and papers. Shreds of tobacco tumbled onto the whiteness of her chest. She dabbed at them with her finger, popping the bits into her mouth.

'There was a girl once.'

'Where?'

'From where I came from.'

'And where's that?'

'Somewhere you ain't been. Anyway this girl, she followed me about like horse dung stuck to a shoe. She came to my hut, wanting it, and I gave it to her.'

Lauren chewed suspiciously on the tobacco. She wasn't one for conversing about other people's problems. Served no purpose for her.

'Her neck went back like yours did just then. There was this thin line of blue that ran down her neck and I took hold of it and didn't let go.'

Lauren spat the chewed filaments of tobacco onto the floor, her eyes agog. 'You killed her.'

McKenzie hunched his shoulders. 'She'd been wanting it. So I gave it to her.'

Lauren laughed. He was just the type of boy who'd pretend something like that just to make him tougher. He dressed slowly and then splashed water on his face from the bowl on the washstand until his shirt was wet through. Taking a drag of the cigarette, Lauren plucked a stray piece of tobacco from her tongue and flicked it into the air.

This McKenzie was a strange one to want her services in the middle of the afternoon. Even with the curtains drawn tight against the heat, one could not escape the thickness of the air. It was an unholy time for fornication. She stepped into her chemise, sweat dripping down her like a washer woman. That was her mother's occupation and it struck her as funny that on a day such as this they would both be suffering. 'What's it like then, being there on that great property.'

'Good. You want to come and see it?'

'Why?' Lauren asked guardedly. Luke Gordon had sent her scurrying out the door whereas this one was giving her an invitation.

'I'll be getting my own hut out there.'

Lauren knew that meant he wanted someone to cook and clean for him. 'Not much interested.'

'I'm planning to be overseer or head stockman and I figured you'd like that.'

Lauren hunched her shoulders and leant against the walls of the hotel room. She inspected her broken fingernails and took another drag of her cigarette, before dropping the butt in a glass of water on the bedside table. 'You sick of paying for me?'

'There's money in it for you.' He counted out more coins and sat the pile on the edge of the washstand. 'You need a home. I could give it to you.'

Lauren wet her lips. 'At Wangallon? Why?'

Because he had Hamish Gordon's eye and was about to embark on an adventure that would make him indispensable in the future. 'Respectability.' Curled within that one word was Jasperson. Having lost count of the number of times he'd spewed up a day's food after lying with him, he was ready to rid himself of the man. Besides which he needed the other stockmen on side, not laughing at him behind his back. He was no man's whore. It had all seemed easily attainable until Wetherly's arrival. His coming freed Andrew Duff for the role of overseer once Jasperson was out of the way and would bring Mungo back to the head stockman position if needed. There was more than a man too many for his liking. Two of them would have to go.

Lauren looked at him. 'I'm not a whore, you know.'

'What's that meant to mean?'

'That I'm not just for the asking.'

He grinned. 'Well I've asked four times and you've bedded me.'

Lauren pulled on her skirt, did up her blouse. 'Come back soon and we'll see.' She slid the coin from the bed into the palm of her hand and, slipping on her shoes, she left the room.

The wife of a boundary rider, Lauren thought as she walked downstairs. That would be all the boy was offering: Overseer, blah. Still, it was the first offer she'd had. On the landing Lauren looked over the bannister to make sure no one she knew was in the bar, and then she ran lightly across the floor and out the back. The yard was crowded with Mr Morelli's hens, and the remains of his vegetable garden were a wilted testament to summer and the limited novelty of bucketing water from the hotel's well. At the splintered gate, Lauren checked the coins in her hand before lifting the latch and running down the side street to her house.

Mrs Grant was in the backyard, leaning over a fire, stirring a blackened cast iron pot bubbling with water and something grey in colour that Lauren imagined had once been white. The baby, her youngest brother, was lying on the grass balling his eyes out, her sister Annie playing in a patch of mud from used wash water. Mrs Grant was a big woman with thinning blonde hair beneath which were round bloody scabs; some dried, some freshly picked and bleeding. She looked up from the copper and grunted towards a balled-up mess of wet clothes, steam rising from the pile into the hot air. Lauren dropped the bundle into another pot of cold water and swished them about with a wooden paddle before proceeding to pull sheets, long johns, petticoats and towels from the tangled mess to throw over the paling fence to dry. Some of the wet things looked clean, others smelled liked boiled rats. Lauren turned her nose up at the stench. No wonder the clothes usually dried and aired for two days.

'Well?' Mrs Grant said in a husky voice grown deep with steam and heat. 'You missed your sister Susanna. She's gone and got herself with child. Of course the father wants nothing to do with her, called her a slavering whore or some such.' Mrs Grant wiped her dripping nose with the back of her hand. 'Don't blame him.'

The baby was screaming. Lauren digested her sister's shocking news as the baby digested the thick mud his two-year-old sister was shoving down his throat and up his nose. 'Mary, Jesus and Joseph, Annie, but you're a terror.' Lauren, glad to be distracted, rushed to the screeching, mud-covered blob on the ground. 'Mother?' she screamed.

'Dump him in the bucket,' Mrs Grant offered helpfully without looking up from the steaming boiler.

Lauren found the three-parts-filled cast iron bucket sitting under the gum tree. She lifted the now silent baby and dunked him three times by the ankles up and down. He came out purple and crying, which clearly was better than muddy and quiet, for Mrs Grant gave a perfunctory look over her shoulder and nodded. With the subdued, spluttering baby on her hip, Annie sulking in readiness for her mother's sharp backhand, Lauren decided good news was required if she were to have a peaceful night.

'I've an offer of marriage, Mother.'

Mrs Grant dropped the great wooden stirring paddle and, wiping her hands on her apron, trundled across the withered grass. 'Who is 'e?'

'A stockman from Wangallon Station, name of McKenzie.'

Mrs Grant rubbed her red peeling hands together. 'Scottish? Well, the Scots are not bad, you know. Good workers. Serious minded, especially if he be a Presbyterian. Gawd, now there are a mob of churchgoers. And Wangallon, eh? Them Gordons have money. I've seen that Jasperson here at the store buying up like he was the King of England himself. You're not with child? Not that it matters if you're to be married.'

'No and I've not given him an answer . . . yet.'

'What? Are you daft? An offer of marriage from a man who's not a drunkard, a thief or an old man is as scarce as feathered frogs.'

Lauren placed her hand on her mother's muscled shoulder. 'I've said nothing for I'm hoping for a better offer.'

Mrs Grant took Lauren's face in her hand and squeezed her cheeks until her lips popped out an inch from her face. 'Who?'

Lauren shook herself free, prodding her bruised cheeks. 'Another from Wangallon.'

Mrs Grant laughed. A great belly laugh that set the baby to crying. 'What have you been up to, my clever girl?' From a pile of folded laundry she pulled out a white blouse detailed with fine pintucking. 'Here.' She tossed the garment across to Lauren before retrieving a bottle-green skirt. 'Here, the Peters can't pay this week. Want to work it off with eggs and butter. Eggs and butter? What do I want with the likes of eggs and butter when I can have condensed milk and a joint of beef.'

Lauren grinned.

'Men like to be chased just a little, my girl. So you dress yourself up real nice and use some of the money in the jar under my bed to hire yourself a dray and horse. And check the almanac at the store. That way you'll be safely travelling on the night of a waning full moon.' Mrs Grant winked. 'They can't rush you back now can they, if it's too dark to travel at night.'

Lauren swirled across the brown grass with the second-hand skirt and blouse clutched between her fingers. She was going to visit Wangallon and show Luke Gordon that she was a lady, one very much in demand.

Midwinter, 1989

The Gold Coast, Queensland

Sarah opened her eyes to a strip of light. She focused slowly, feeling a crick in her neck. The room was in semi-darkness and the light came from the bottom of the door, beyond which muffled laughter sounded. She straightened slowly in the chair, recalling a late lunch of packaged sandwiches, uncomfortable at her father's insistence at her staying in the room with her mother while he returned home to shower and change. Streetlights lit the drawn curtains behind her, footsteps sounded in the corridor. Sarah wanted to leave, yet she was aware that once she stepped beyond this room where the woman who should have loved her lay, she would not return. This would be the culmination of her long goodbye; one that had started many years ago.

Hesitantly Sarah walked to her mother's side. Vividly she recalled the day of her brother's death. The carrying of his body to the Wangallon dining room table and the outpouring of grief as they stood gazing in shock at his wrecked body. Her mother had blamed her for Cameron's death because it was Sarah who had wanted to go riding that morning. And before that blame had been years of disinterest. Why? Because Sue Gordon loved and lost a man who was not her husband and then she lost her love child.

'You should have loved me,' Sarah said bitterly to her mother. 'You were so caught up in your own world that you lost something precious –' she reached over and flicked on the night light – 'me.' In the soft light her mother looked almost serene. There was a curve to her lips and the vertical lines that fanned from her mouth in a web of disappointment had smoothed. Her eyes were closed, her breathing steady. 'I needed love too. I needed your support.' Her mother's eyes opened so slowly that Sarah imagined her waking from a deep sleep, one that spanned hurt and betrayal and love. Despite the improbability of her mother returning from the mental abyss which engulfed her, Sarah leant forward and lifted her hand as if to test her mother's sight, although she doubted if Sue had any synapses left that could join form and reality.

'She can see you.'

Her father stood beside her, a paper bag of takeaway in one hand, a thermos in the other. 'It's time to let go of the past and move forward, Sarah,' he said wearily. 'You need to do it for all our sakes.' He placed the items on the chair near him.

Sarah wanted to argue with him, yet somehow the words were already dissolving.

Ronald took her by the shoulders, turned her towards him. 'She's not like you, Sarah. She never could be like you. Can't you forgive her?'

Sarah shook her head. 'I can't Dad. At least not at this moment.' Too much had occurred in her life to date to make forgiving or forgetting easy. Maybe when she was older with a family of her own she would come to understand her mother's attitude, but not now. Everything still seemed so raw.

'You will one day, Sarah.' Ronald moved a step closer to his wife's side. 'In some respects I blame myself for your mother's troubled life,' Ronald revealed quietly. 'She never loved Wangallon. She didn't fit into the bush.'

With her father's words Sarah understood the heart of her parents' troubled relationship. Her father loved Wangallon enough to spend nearly his entire life there while knowing his own father would never pass on the reins to the property. And he had loved Sue, wanted Sue, even knowing that his life was not for her. Sue's time on Wangallon had eaten away at her until the final irrevocable loss of her child, Cameron. Sarah suddenly understood that Sue Gordon had no room in her heart for her daughter because it was broken before Sarah was born.

'She was a city girl,' Ronald said fondly. 'Used to parties and socialising and getting dolled up to go out. She was beautiful when we married, Sarah. Fun and vibrant and everything a man could want.' He swallowed loudly. 'I took her out to the bush and from day one she was like a plant that could never get enough water. I think she thought we'd live in the main homestead, have staff like my parents, visit Sydney regularly. Worst of all she grew bored; firstly with station life and then with me.' Ronald glanced at Sarah and then turned back to his wife. Sarah could feel her father's sadness. It filled the room.

Sarah knew her mother was dead. There was a small gasp, like an intake of collective breath at a cinema when the unexpected appears on the screen, then silence filled the room. She looked at the woman before her, watched her close down like a wilting flower. Sarah was ragged with exhaustion, however she wondered what Sue witnessed at her final crossing and who she would meet once she travelled to the other side. It would be Cameron, Sarah surmised, and his father, Sue's lover: Reunited in death with the only people that mattered to her.

'It's for the best.' Ronald sounded unconvinced. He wiped at his eyes and blew his nose loudly. Eventually he took his wife's hand and, kissing it gently, sat beside her on the bed. 'I'll wait,' he said shakily, 'while you bring the nurse. I don't want her to be left alone'.

Sarah nodded. There would be no burial for Sue Gordon at Wangallon. Her mother's wishes were for a cremation and for her ashes to be sprinkled around the rose garden at the crematorium. Even in death she would be apart from the Wangallon Gordons. Sarah kissed her father on the cheek and walked from the room without a final glance at her mother. There was no need to. She had said goodbye years ago. Despite her best intentions tears came to her eyes.

Midsummer, 1909

Wangallon Station

When Hamish did not return by the evening of New Year's Eve, Claire sent word to discover what had become of him. No one knew. Most of Wangallon's stockmen were out in the further corners of the property mustering Wangallon's cattle in readiness for the next drive south. By midday a feeling of nausea had settled in Claire's stomach. She'd never known her husband to miss a New Year's Day luncheon. She berated herself for being unable to eat, seethed at Hamish's selfish, uncaring attitude, and then the vomiting began. She blamed the phantom child for her sickness, and silently willed the brief painful cramps to continue when they stopped. She spent the afternoon lying on her bed, the dull heat layering her body with droplets of moisture. She was thirsty, yet her throat would not take the water she held to her lips. She found herself wishing for Luke, but he did not come. She sent word to Wetherly only to discover he too had vanished. She wished again for Luke and dry-retched at the guilt of it.

Only when darkness stripped her room of light did Claire rise.

She thought perhaps a little moistened bread may help, and a sip of sweet madeira. She wondered why Mrs Stackland had not come to check on her needs. As her bare feet padded on the polished floorboards, the object of her thoughts appeared before her. Mrs Stackland carried a tray of food, her puffy white face registering awkwardness.

'Are you feeling better, Mrs Gordon? I've come twice to check on you and you've been asleep.'

'What's this?'

Mrs Stackland glanced at the tray she carried. 'He does not wish to be disturbed.' Both women glanced at the strip of dim light beneath the cedar door of Hamish's study.' Mrs Stackland was clearly uncomfortable. 'He has much business to attend to.' Her voice softened. 'You look unwell, Mrs Gordon.'

Claire grasped the tray gently. 'I will take it to him.' She smiled gingerly at the older woman. She felt weak from her sickness, yet refused to allow the housekeeper to fulfil Hamish's request or usurp the consolation of duty. Mrs Stackland looked doubtful, yet released the tray into Claire's hands. The housekeeper knocked once on the study door, opening it so that Claire could enter, and then closed it behind her.

Claire sat the tray down on the desk. A lone candle gave off a yellowish light that flickered across a desk littered with papers. There was a lump of dirt sitting in the middle of a handkerchief that may once have been white, Hamish's gold fob watch and an empty cut crystal decanter. The immobile figure of her husband stood vigilant at the window. Beyond him a swathe of stars hung so close that Claire imagined being able to reach out and touch them. 'Where have you been?' She lifted the silver food warmer from the dish beneath. Mrs Stackland had prepared jugged wallaby accompanied by fresh damper and black tea. There was the slightest of noises and the sound drew her to the clasping and unclasping of Hamish's hands behind his back. She cleared her throat. She felt akin to an invader. 'Hamish?'

'I asked not to be disturbed,' he answered tersely. He turned slowly, and Claire caught a shadowy glimpse of his haggard face. The scent of sweat, horses and tobacco wafted across the desk to where she stood; familiar smells grown potent by time, dirt and tiredness.

'I've not seen you these past two days.' Remembering she still held the silver food warmer, she covered the congealing food. 'Hamish, I –'

Hamish struck his hand in his fist. 'That is the dirt from my brother's grave.'

Claire flinched at his tone and supported herself on the armchair nearest her as he pointed to the filthy handkerchief.

'Aye, I can feel your examination, Claire. You wonder that I have not mentioned such a keepsake when the closeness of our lives creates a compulsion in you to share, misguided as that may be.'

'Misguided?' Claire recalled the innumerable times she'd been unable to draw him away from his ruminations and into conversation, into her world. Had her attempts been considered so trifling? She could feel the sickness seeping into her again, and with it a dulling sensation as if a dense cloud engulfed her.

'We are so unalike, you and I, yet we coexist. Perhaps it has been the disparity of age between us, perhaps affection.' His voice faded, sounded unconvinced.

What was he telling her? That he no longer wanted her? While Claire was under no illusion as to the fractured state of their marriage, she was not one to be thrown aside.

He looked at her with the hard stare that would cut through a blanketing dust storm if he so wished. 'You have grown used to the routine of a respectable husband.' His words curled with disgust. 'I tell you now that it is an illusion. It is an illusion that has been carefully cultivated and I myself have tilled the soil. I too wanted respectability, but there are those who will not give it, not to the likes of us at least. And I wonder now at this pandering of ours in the hopes of being accepted by polite society.'

'Hamish, I don't –'

'Lethargy brought on by success has made me forget my reasons for first coming to this new world.' His filthy forefinger prodded the handkerchief. 'I did not come here to reach the giddy heights of society, knowing that our acceptance would be determined by the very people who helped destroy Scotland. I will not live by another's leave and that includes the condescension of those like the Crawfords.' He gave an exaggerated sigh. 'I'm sure you were quite a pretty project for Oscar's wife. I'm sure that she tutted and tweaked with her friends about your less than admirable beginnings and I've no doubt they admire your transformation from settler's wife to Government House invitee. Tell me, Claire, is it not inane to you? It is to me. I have physically and mentally curtailed my nature in order to be accepted by society. Well, I tell you now I will not have it. I have few years left to make a mark on this world I have created and make a mark I will. There are those who will suffer for their treatment. This is a reckoning I will have.'

Claire was staring at him. Despite his disappointing first marriage, Hamish did believe in companionship and Claire was the most resilient and caring of the few women he'd known. Perhaps he'd been too hard on her. Sitting at his desk Hamish considered how to broach the gulf between them. Claire's coddled life should not cause him to feel resentful when he thought of his own dear mother, especially when Claire's greatest gift to the Gordon legacy was their son, Angus. Hamish formulated more kindly words and was endeavouring to articulate them when Claire left his study.

Removing the crystal stopper from the brandy decanter Hamish poured himself a good measure of the amber liquid. He drank the fluid down in one gulp, poured another glass and settled himself in his chair. He stabbed at the jugged wallaby with a fork, slurping at the rubbery juices, pausing to lick his fingers. He hoped Lee managed to provide him with a little entertainment later. He was sorely in need of some. Pushing his tea tray aside, he unfurled a yellowing map that showed the Wangallon River as a series of finely pencilled squiggles, a watery boundary between Wangallon and Crawford Corner. Hamish traced the waterway closely. He added a series of small circles where the timber grew too thick to pass and then drew a line that crossed the river from one side to the other. This was the only known point that was shallow enough to cross. They'd been diligent in their reconnaissance, checking the riverbank and surrounding bushland. Boxer believed there had been rains further north earlier in the month, however Hamish witnessed no rise on their return from Crawford Corner. As long as no more rain fell they were assured of safe passage.

Jasperson, McKenzie and Boxer were already in Wangallon Town. From there they would ride north-west to cross the river at Widow's Nest and continue on until they circumnavigated Crawford Corner. Crawford ran a fine herd of cattle on his far western boundary and it was these animals that Hamish now targeted. Once they managed to get past the boundary riders they would simply drive the mob east. With luck they would be across the river before dawn, before Crawford began berating his unfortunate manservant for his late breakfast. Hamish slammed his fist in his palm, gulped at his brandy in anticipation. He would be waiting with Luke to take delivery of the stolen cattle on the Wangallon side of the river.

With the concentration of a man convinced of the rightness of his task, Hamish took the large almanac down from a library shelf and sat the volume on his desk. He turned the pages, slowly reaching the calendar section that was marked with a silk tasselled bookmark. Beneath the neat squares showing each month's dates, there was a bordered section showing the phases of the moon. It was this that Hamish referred to constantly, for the illuminated passage of a full moon was the only means for man and beast to travel at night. Jasperson and his team had to reach the far boundary of Crawford Corner on the brightest night of the month. It also meant they had little time to waste. Hamish wasn't of the disposition to wait another full month before he could seek retribution.

Tomorrow his men would cross the river at Widow's Nest, by night they would be on Crawford's property and by the almanac's reckoning the night would give them safe passage. Besides which, Boxer was with them, assuring the expedition that at the very least they would be able to find their way back home. Hamish closed the almanac and rested a large thick hand on the cover. Now all that was left to do was to send for Luke. He would want the boy ready to move in four days with the mob. Hamish intended incorporating Crawford's cattle with his own sale mob and no one would be the wiser. With a satisfied belch, he located his pipe and the makings for it and walked out onto the verandah. He was almost ready for a strong cup of tea.

Dawn was still some time away. The scent of grass and smoke from the kitchen hearth mingled in a manner Hamish considered to be quite homely and he walked out across the gravel drive to a stand of box trees. The world had changed, and Crawford was about to learn a lesson or two about the new world he now had the misfortune to inhabit next to Wangallon.

Claire lay on her bed in her chemise. There was a drift of noise seeping through the darkening rooms from the gradually quieting kitchen, the sound of footsteps on the verandah, the shutting of a door. She imagined Mole by an English river, everything so cool and green and fresh, a breeze blowing. She dabbed cologne on her lace handkerchief and patted her wrists and forehead. How she longed for the coolness of a sea breeze, any breeze. Yet finding such relief could only come from a bone-jarring coach ride of many long, tiring days. Something was scrambling on the roof. There was the patter of feet similar to the scattering of leaves. Claire followed the noise with her eyes, imagining the creature stalking backwards and forwards beneath a warp of spinning stars.

The last spasm had left her quite faint. She gazed down over the sloping mounds of her breasts to where the gentle swelling of life she had so rashly hated now lay dormant. It was beyond her as to how the pains could come without a final exiting of her unborn baby.

The unmistakable tap of Mrs Stackland's knuckles was followed by the woman's entry into her bedroom. Without waiting for approval she pushed the door wider with her ample hip and sat a tray on the edge of Claire's bed.

'You'll be excusing me, Mrs Gordon, however it's high time you took a little nourishment. There's mutton broth, a slice of bread and a glass of madeira.'

Claire glanced at the tray and nodded her thanks.

'And I've brought you some Beecham's pills. Now I know you've been poorly, what with the recent kafuffle, and Mr Beecham is just the thing for whatever ails you. Wind, stomach pain, indigestion, insomnia, vomiting, sickness of the stomach, scurvy, heat flushings, liver complaints, lowness of spirits . . .' Mrs Stackland raised a scraggly eyebrow. 'Well here you are then.' She tipped two pills from the glass bottle and handed them to Claire, administering water from the glass on the bedside table as if she were a nurse. 'Now you swallow those. Mark my words, you'll be feeling better in the morning.'

Claire swallowed, the pills catching at her insides all the way down. What if she wasn't with child? What if what ailed her was something far more sinister. Good gracious, she had heard the most unfathomable stories; twisted bowels and blocked bowels and growths in stomachs and troublesome appendix that burst when least expected.

'Are you all right, Mrs Gordon?' Mrs Stackland asked, her pale eyes narrowing.

Claire fiddled with her wrap, hoping she had not been muttering her concerns aloud. 'Of course, Mrs Stackland.'

'You will promise me that you will eat.' The question hung in the air as the housekeeper waited for her response, which Claire gave dutifully.

Later in the night Claire awoke to the sound of footsteps. Her tray, the food partially eaten and the madeira consumed, was gone. Feeling a little better she opened the bedroom door quietly and glanced up one end of the hallway and then down the other to where a candle flickered. Elongated shapes were shadowed against a wall. One of the maids was tapping lightly on her husband's door. Claire caught a glimpse of long dark hair and bare feet. There was the squeak of a brass doorknob and the creak of cedar and then the girl disappeared inside. For a moment Claire was unsure what she had witnessed. She stepped backwards into her room and shut the door, her teeth clenching together so hard they grated sideways. Guessing at her husband's proclivities and witnessing them firsthand was more shocking to her person than Claire could have imagined. While aware that men had certain appetites and, according to Mrs Crawford a devoted family man of Hamish's stature was a rare occurrence, Claire never dreamt his liaisons to be so rudimentary. She drew her wrap around her shoulders and threw Mrs Aeneas Gunn's detestable monument to resilience at the bedroom door.

Midwinter, 1989

Wangallon Station

Matt Schipp waited at the rear of Wangallon Homestead. He was leaning against the fence near the back gate, scruffing the dirt with the toe of his boot, his arms crossed. Anthony figured there had been some balls-up with stock, a broken fence perhaps, which had led to different mobs getting mixed up or maybe one of the new bulls had damaged himself. That was all he needed – an expensive bull with a broken pizzle. 'Problem, Matt?' Anthony called from the back door, trying to curb the anger in his voice. A sleepless night had done little to restore Anthony's mood. He was bloody furious with Sarah. None of this was Matt's fault though, regardless of whether Anthony thought he was overpaid and milking his injury. 'Come in and have a seat.' Anthony opened the screen door. He needed a drink of water and a couple of panadol for his hand.

'No, I'm pretty right. Thanks all the same.' Matt hovered on the back path. He was rolling a cigarette, his damaged fingers having trouble with the tobacco cupped in his palm.

Matt was a quiet bloke yet he always looked a person straight in the eyes, all the time . . . except for now. 'You wanna buy some tailor-mades, Matt,' Anthony suggested, aware of a growing tension between them. 'Make it a whole lot easier for you.'

'Probably. You heard from Sarah?'

Anthony's eyes flickered with interest. If Sarah had called Matt first . . . 'Maybe you better come inside.'

Matt shook his head, looked at him squarely. 'Toby and his boys will be here to muster up the cattle on Boxer's Plains in a couple of days. They want to be on the route by the weekend.'

'Righto. Just make sure they shut the gates behind them as they walk them through. I don't want those young heifers getting out of their paddock in case one of the bulls gets in with them.'

'I'll double-check them myself. I heard about the clearing job.'

Anthony's mouth hardened into a thick immovable line. 'That was quick.'

'Well Bruce was up at the pub last night talking about running out of fuel.' Matt took a puff of his cigarette, shoved his spare hand in his pocket. 'We both know that's a tall one.'

Anthony shrugged and looked blankly at his head stockman. He wasn't inclined to fill Matt in. He was only staff after all.

Matt grimaced, dropped his cigarette on the path and ground it flat. 'Anyway, I just wanted to give you a piece of advice, mate.'

Anthony recalled Neville's words from the day before; something about delusions of grandeur.

'Just let things lie for a week or so, wait till this inheritance thing is cleared up. The Gordons are a rare breed, mate, and once they have a bee in their bonnet, well –'

'I think I know the Gordons better than you.'

Matt looked at him with an air of disbelief. 'It's nothing personal, but you haven't been around for as long as I have, Anthony. Geez, some of the stories I've heard.'

'Yeah and in some of them,' Anthony reminded him, 'I've played a leading role.'

The expression on the older man's face didn't vary. 'Not eighty years ago, not one hundred years ago. You don't get it, do you? It's all about the land. It's only ever been about the land and their control of it. Sarah can't help it.' Matt sorted through the words in his brain. 'It's genetic.'

'And you're the expert?' At this point all Anthony wanted to do was shut the door on both Matt and Wangallon.

'You own a share, Anthony. But you'll never own Wangallon, not the way Sarah does, because the property owns her. It's in her. Look, I'm trying to help. It's not my place to take sides.'

'But you bloody well have, haven't you?'

Matt looked at him for a long minute. He was starting to get pissed off. 'If you're asking me where my allegiance lies, then yes, it is to the Gordons: To Angus Gordon particularly.'

Anthony drew his eyebrows together. 'He's dead.' He watched Matt walk away. He reckoned Neville was probably right about Mrs Kelly. Matt would have been the type of kid you needed to tie a chop bone to his ankle to get a dog to play with him.

Matt walked down the cracked cement path shaking his head as he went. He was annoyed with himself for the way he handled things, but even more surprised at Anthony. He knew Anthony was in an ordinary situation, but if he had a few brains he'd let sleeping dogs lie. Take off for a couple of days until Sarah got things sorted in Sydney. Yeah, that would be the smart thing to do.

Hooking the chain around the back gate, Matt called to Whisky. The dog was camped under the back tyre of his Land-cruiser. He stretched and whined before falling in beside Matt like a well-trained foot soldier. 'Things are starting to get a bit interesting,' Matt commented to his dog, opening the driver's side door. Whisky jumped in first.

'You right?'

The dog positioned himself in the passenger seat, looked briefly at Matt before facing the windscreen.

'Seems everyone has a bit of attitude today,' Matt commented as he drove down towards the cattle yards. The new loading ramp had arrived yesterday and not before time. The previous one had seen thousands of head through it and been in need of an upgrade. The timber structure was so old that recently a charging steer managed to crash though one of the railings and one of the forcing gates that could be slid behind beasts to stop them backing up had broken off its hinges. Matt drove past the yards, admiring the shiny new metal. A good loading ramp was vital. It allowed the ease of movement of cattle in and out of the large road trains that transported them to market and also to various parts of the property when the distance to be covered was too far to walk.

Matt scratched his head, wondering what he'd really signed himself up for when he'd accepted this job. It sure wasn't quite what he'd imagined. Whisky wangled himself across the seat of the Landcruiser, nuzzled in the crook of his arm.

'Righto, mate. We're off.' Despite the situation Matt couldn't stop a smile edging at the corner of his mouth. In a couple of days Edward Truss was due out to inspect some sale steers and tomorrow Jack and one of the contractors were helping to bring in the lambs. Matt wanted them drafted up and moved to a different oat paddock a good six weeks before they were to be sold. This time round he didn't need to have a kitchen table conference about the proposed lamb sale or wait down at the yards until the ram buyer finished his cup of tea at the homestead. Reporting to a couple of young ones almost half his age and taking orders from Anthony remained a daily pain in the arse. Things would be a whole heap easier if Sarah was in charge.

It was true he'd had thoughts of easing his way out of the whole shooting match, as his dad used to like calling avoidable disasters, but well, that day on the verandah pretty much sealed him up as neatly as a brown paper parcel and string. The old fella, Angus, had him by the balls to the extent, Matt mused, that he couldn't even scratch one. All he could do was keep his mouth shut and see what happened next and wait for the payout at the end of the day. He drove slowly back to West Wangallon and was contemplating whether he had time to put a frozen pie in the oven for lunch when he saw he had company.

Tania Weil was sitting on the bonnet of her white sedan. Matt reckoned a good four years must lay between now and the last time he saw her. It was the day he resigned from the spread up north.

'Last time I saw you, my paperback westerns were scattered across the lawn.'

Tania smiled and slipped off the car bonnet. A spray-on pair of white jeans, black T-shirt and white cap emphasised the weight she'd lost. Even her hair was different. It was still the same dull brown, although the curls and length were gone. Short and straight suited her angular features.

Matt walked towards her, avoiding a kiss by holding out his hand. 'How did you find me?'

Tania laughed and, ignoring his hand, managed to kiss his weathered cheek. She rubbed at the smudge of beige lipstick with a glossy white thumbnail. 'Once a month you're in the rural papers, Matt. Buying or selling stock, hanging with your pretty boss or socialising after a sale.' Tania glanced around at the breadth of lightly timbered country, then back at West Wangallon Homestead. 'You certainly managed to fall on your feet.'

'Didn't know I hadn't been standing upright.'

Tania looked pointedly at his hand. 'You know what I mean. How is it?'

Matt held both hands up as if examining a sale item that he didn't want. 'Buggered.'

'You miss me?'

Matt looked her up and down. He had to admit Tania was looking pretty damn good. 'Nope.'

'Sure you did. Invite me in, Matt. You can make me some lunch and tell me if it's true that the Gordons are going to lose some of their land thanks to a father that couldn't keep his dick in his pants.'

Despite a bad sense of deja vu, Matt led the way down the cement path.

Midsummer, 1909
Wangallon Station

Claire walked her horse carefully across the paddock, her gloved hands loose on the reins. The morning sun was bright and hot, offering only a few precious minutes before she would need to retire indoors. She needed to escape the dreadful vision in the hallway and the whiff of illness that still encircled her. Yet barely twenty minutes in the saddle and she was exhausted. Her mind kept returning to Hamish's words, to the black girl entering his room in the dead of night. Once again she wondered if he'd ever truly loved her. She shifted in the side saddle. She was of a mind this morning to pull on a pair of Hamish's trousers and ride like a man, like she used to, thirty years ago. Instead, convention saw her don a riding suit complete with veiled hat, cropped jacket and black-heeled boots. Ridiculous, she now thought, as her legs and back began to ache, her stomach swelled in anger against her tight corset and the perspiration on her skin formed a sticky barrier next to her clothes. A final muscle twinge in her lower back ended Claire's thoughts of continuing on and, unhooking her leg from the side saddle, she slipped off the horse to stand in the tufted grass.

'Claire.'

In the midst of lifting her veil, Claire looked to where Luke was riding towards her. Despite her discomfort and her annoyance at his recent absence, a flutter of pleasure greeted his arrival. His wide-brimmed hat sat laconically on the rear of his head, his hair looked damp and lay plastered to his forehead. Claire lifted her hand to shield her eyes from the glare of the homestead, its white-washed walls shining brightly behind him.

'Morning ride?' It was a rare sight to see a woman on horseback around these parts, particularly one garbed as if she were about to join an English hunt. Luke swallowed his amusement. 'Dressed for the occasion I see,' he drawled, looking down from his horse, although she cut a fine figure with her snug-fitting jacket and jaunty hat.

Claire finished poking the black netting into the grosgrain ribbon banding the hat. 'Where have you been?' They'd not spoken since Christmas Eve, apart from the unsettling glance that had passed between them the day prior to Hamish's departure. Claire was unsure as how to proceed.

Luke dismounted and fell into step with her. 'I went trapping.'

She looked at him suspiciously. Luke tied the reins of her horse to his own. 'I needed you and you weren't here. Nobody was. Not that I suppose it matters.' She sniffed. 'Anyway, we really don't see you when you're here.' Claire began walking towards the homestead.

'Is everything all right?' Half-moons of darkness highlighted her eyes. 'Claire?' She gave a questioning look that made him sorry for his absence and pleased he was needed. 'Is it Hamish?'

'Your father,' she politely corrected him, 'has –'

'Returned from his walkabout?' He wondered if Crawford Corner was now part of the great rural monolith that belonged to Hamish Gordon. They walked on for some minutes, their slow pace enticing myriad small black flies to land on backs, faces and hands. Their horses shook their manes, swished their tails, causing the flies to rise in a mass and then resettle. Claire pulled the netting down across her face. 'Two days he was away, with no word. Then he returns, almost a changed man.' She recalled Hamish's harsh words – they could not be repeated. She stepped slowly through the grass. 'I'm worried.'

Luke laughed – the idea of someone being worried about Hamish Gordon was quite a novel thought and he was sure his father would feel the same way.

Claire cocked an eyebrow. 'Not for him. For Angus.'

'Angus?'

'You wouldn't understand.' She walked on, her body stiffened by resolve. 'Sometimes I wish you were more like the rest of us.'

Luke grabbed at her wrist, slowing her walk. 'What is that meant to mean?' Beneath her riding jacket was a high-necked white blouse with fine pleats running the length of it. The stark whiteness of the material contrasted vividly with the darkness of the jacket and Luke found himself holding Claire's wrist for a moment longer than necessary.

'You've always come and gone as you please.' She stepped over some fallen branches, taking his arm for support. 'The conventions of society – companionship, respectability, social acceptance – these are meaningless to you. While I on the other hand cultivate this family's place in society for the benefit of –'

'Angus,' Luke finished for her. 'And you're wrong, Claire. If things had been different . . .' But what could he say? That he too craved the comforting normality of family? Family was something that he'd only glimpsed and most of the time it seemed as if that life never existed at all. A sheen of moisture covered Claire's fine features. He wondered at how different his life would have been if he'd been boss of Wangallon. 'You're wearing my comb.'

Claire glanced at him, her eyelashes fluttering as she looked away.

'Are you feeling all right?' Luke asked, slipping a supportive arm around her slim waist as she stumbled.

'I will be fine once I reach the shade of the house.' She felt her breath constrict and with renewed energy shook his arm free of her. It was the heat, Claire decided, berating the tightly laced whalebone corset that nipped in her waist and cupped her breasts. 'I know your father is not what people suppose him to be.' They reached the gateway and the gravel path leading through Wangallon's garden to the homestead. 'You know what he once did?' Claire began tentatively. 'The stealing of sheep, cattle, perhaps –' she hesitated – 'worse?' She looked at him directly, searching for the truth.

'Do you really want to know?'

Claire looked towards the house as if someone may hear them. 'Yes.'

'I expect he did what any man did fifty years ago to carve himself a place in this world.' Except, Luke thought, he did it better and more ruthlessly.

Claire lifted her skirts to climb the stairs leading to the verandah. Luke was his father's son and whatever she expected to discover she would not hear from this man. There was no one moment that led to her revelation that Hamish Gordon was not as he seemed. It was more an awakening to the attitudes they received when first they ventured out into society as man and wife. It fell to Claire to cultivate female companionship and, by extension, introductions to those members of society she believed her husband should be mixing with. It was a painstaking, lonely process, filled with small slights, whispered innuendoes and strangely missing invitations. Their ostracism coincided with a number of stillborn children, leaving her in such a state of melancholy that she'd condemned herself to being both childless and virtually friendless. Yet her perseverance eventually paid off some years later when a season in Sydney saw their Centennial Park terrace positively flooded with invitations. Suddenly they were in vogue.

It was a well known Sydney matron who whispered sweetly behind the sanctity of her fan at a ball one evening:

Your husband is most charming, Mrs Gordon. I must compliment you on subduing the brigand of New South Wales.

It was such a short statement, yet that one word carried so much potency that Claire would never forget it. And so she had made Hamish promise that however he accrued his fortune, henceforth she wished to hold her head high in public. Indeed they both did the following year when, at the introduction of the doyenne of society, Mrs Oscar Crawford, they were invited to Government House. To Claire's mind the Gordons' rise in society had taken far too long; however, having been taken under the rather ample arm of Mrs Crawford, their place would not be rescinded. Yet it came too late to be enjoyed for any length of time. Hamish had drifted apart from her. Although they played at their relationship, only in appearance were they successful. In truth she was like a cat scrabbling with an inanimate toy.

'Things have been good for the family, Luke. I don't want anything to jeopardise everything I've worked for.'

Luke slipped their horses reins about the smooth railing and, tying a loose knot, joined Claire in one of the wicker chairs 'You think Hamish has something on his mind apart from the purchase of Crawford Corner?'

'Crawford Corner?'

At Claire's repetition of the property name Luke faltered. 'You didn't know?'

'No,' she replied, smoothing her skirt over her clammy knees. She undid the row of buttons on the jacket of her riding habit, would have escaped to the coolness of her room had she not realised how desperately alone she felt. She'd done her best at being his wife. Rarely had she earned his scorn, except perhaps in the matter of child-bearing. What was it about his man she'd entrusted her love to?

Luke poured her a glass of water from the pitcher on the table, replacing the doily over the top of it to keep the flies out. 'He has always been changeable in character. You know this. The wonder of it is that you have been happy for so long and for the last ten years or so he has behaved himself.'

'In matters of business?'

'Look, the mail has arrived,' Luke diverted. Knowing the delight Claire received from a newspaper or fashion catalogue, he passed her the bundle sitting on the wicker table. As she sorted through the pile he considered telling her of his plans, of sharing his excitement of his proposed new life in Ridge Gully.

'Luke, there is one for you.'

The letter was addressed in handwriting unknown to him, although the address given was that of Ridge Gully. He peered closely at the cramped writing, deciphering the name Shaw-Michaels. His chest tightened with excitement. This then was the news of his new life. At the thought he looked across at Claire.

'They expect Deakin to be elected prime minister again,' read Claire from the newspaper headlines. 'Oh, and Dame Nellie Melba is planning on giving a series of concerts this year.'

He sat forward in his chair, opened the envelope. There were two letters inside.

May God bless you, Luke,

Although we have never met I imagine you strong and fierce like your father and perhaps a little soft like my daughter, your mother, Rose.

Luke glanced down at the signature. It was from his grandmother, his dead grandmother.

'And what do you think about this, Luke, the government of New South Wales is thinking about reintroducing assisted migration.'

I've not been one for travelling nor correspondence so you must forgive me that, as I forgive you. The doctor tells me I've not much time though I doubt his knowledge for it only comes from a book and I've never placed great store in another's words. Still if the learned man is right then I best have my affairs in order. It is important for me to safeguard that which was manufactured by my own hands and you have your own responsibilities. Your father is in agreement.

My Rose and the little ones departed this life so long ago, God bless them. Visit your mother's grave for me, say a prayer lad, say good-bye,

Your loving grandmother

Luke reread the contents before reading a second letter from his grandmother's solicitor. He had been left out of her will. The entire amount had gone to some acquaintance of his grandmother's. Stunned, he reread her letter again. *Your father is in agreement.*

'Did you know?' Luke finally asked when the reality of the letter sunk in. 'Did you know I'd been robbed of my grandmother's inheritance?'

'Inheritance?' Claire let the newspaper drop to her lap. She was just beginning to feel a little better. 'What inheritance?'

'Did you know?' Luke demanded, his fingers scrunching the envelope.

'No, no . . . I had absolutely no idea.' Claire touched her temples.

'You're sure?'

'Of course I'm sure, Luke. What are you talking about?' Yet she didn't want to know, not really. There was already too much in her life. In the space of a week she'd discovered she may be pregnant, wished her baby dead, silently admitted to her girlish infatuation regarding Luke, fallen ill and been berated by her adulterous husband. Now there was another element for her brain to contend with, a loneliness that appeared to have crept up on her like a snake and she could have wept with the realisation that her life was a mirage. Claire took the letter with shaking fingers, managed to read the brief contents though the words shifted and weaved into almost unmanageable forms. 'Your grandmother must have good reason for this, Luke.'

'My grandmother? I think you are mistaken, Claire. It is my father who has had the final say in this matter. Have you not read that properly?'

'Of course I've read it. I just don't believe that your father would –'

'You don't believe it? It's there in black and white!'

Claire read the letter again. 'Luke, I know you're upset, but you have Wangallon. You are a part of Wangallon, it's your home. You can't honestly have wanted to leave here.' How could she placate him? A wrong had been done, but surely it was not Hamish's doing. 'Luke, where are you going?' His riding boots struck the wooden floorboards sharply as he strode away from her. 'Luke, please?' Claire went to follow him.

'This is the person you married, Claire.' He turned, took a step towards her. 'Do you really want to know what he is like? Do you?'

She backed away from his temper.

'He has stolen, cheated and murdered for his own gain!' He flung his hands outwards in exasperation, 'and you worry about respectability, about what people think. You would need at least another generation to dilute what has come before and even then, the name Gordon will always be tainted.'

Ready tears came to Claire's eyes. She willed them back. 'Everything your father has done, he has done purely for the well-being of his family.' In reality she wasn't sure anymore.

'He has done for himself,' Luke said sharply. 'How is colluding with my own grandmother going to help me?'

'How would it help him?' Claire countered softly.

'Look around you, Claire. After Hamish passes, someone is needed to safeguard the property until Angus comes of age.'

Claire couldn't respond immediately. For as long as she had known Hamish, Wangallon came first, before everything.

Luke snorted. 'He cares for his own ambition.'

'That's not true.' Claire walked steadily towards him, took his rough, sun-dried hands in hers. 'It's not his fault that your mother and brothers died,' she soothed. 'As for your inheritance, there must be some good reason why –' She stopped mid-sentence as his hand stroked her cheek. He was very close to her. No man had come closer except her husband. His hand moved to the nape of her neck. His fingers plied the soft skin. Claire, vitally aware of the need to break free, found herself looking into violet eyes of her husband's making. It was there, that steely resolve. The unflinching look of a man who knew what he wanted. Claire's breath caught in her chest. It was not land, money or power that he wanted; at least, not at this moment. Hamish had taught her how to decipher the difference.

'You are his redemption, Claire. You have chosen to see only goodness in the world.' Instinctively his arm encircled her waist. 'Perhaps it is because you were so young when you first came to Wangallon. Or perhaps you feel obliged to him.' He was oblivious to the sharp escape of her breath as he bent his head and kissed her.

This is wrong her mind screamed. *You forget yourself, stop*. Yet she couldn't, not when her arms were pinned so tightly. Eventually she rested her hands against the firmness of his chest and extricated herself from his embrace. Her lungs could barely gather in enough air to speak and she was aware of tears falling to moisten her cheeks, of her lips numbed by pressure and of something far more dangerous, a wanting. She backed away from him.

Luke held out his hand and then let it slowly drop. 'Tell me this, if not for my father –'

'If not for your father,' Claire found herself barely able to draw breath, 'if not for your father, neither of us would be standing here today.' She placed her shaking palm against her stomach. 'Heavens, Luke, what have we done?'

He watched her collapse into one of the wicker chairs, her slim form heaving as tears consumed her. He waited some minutes, unable to decide as to the best course of action. The boundary between them that had been broken would never be crossed again, for he could not stand to see such pain on Claire's face. Luke looked out towards the garden at the gravel road that led him to and away from this woman whom he had loved since his teenage years. He could not have her, perhaps now he did not want her. For like his own father, Claire burdened him with pain and he was angry for it.

'My mother was still very much alive when my father decided to become your secret benefactor. I often wonder what he would have done if Rose had not died prematurely.'

Claire looked up from where she sobbed quietly, smoothed the folds of her skirt and wiped carefully at her eyes. 'What?' They both knew the words did not have to be repeated. The insinuation was clear.

'It's my penance to care for the woman who supplanted my mother.'

With shaking hands Claire removed the tortoiseshell comb from her hair and sat it on the wicker table. If her imaginings had remained just that, she could have gone on. She could have swallowed her pride and somehow set out along the new path Hamish had defined for her. However, she had gone against the natural order of things and in doing so realised that there could be another love beyond husband and wife, beyond right and wrong. Claire straightened her shoulders and walked indoors. The structure of her life was crumbling and she had not the materials to rebuild it.

Luke retrieved his grandmother's letter from where it had fluttered to the scratched floorboards. He folded it carefully, his fingers patiently creasing it into a diminishing square. Finally he shoved it securely into the pocket of his moleskins. He looked out at the trees shimmering in the haze, at the pale lifeless grass swaying meditatively, and experienced the sharp bite of anger that only frustration could create. Removing a plug of tobacco from his pocket, he plied the wad into the semblance of a cigarette, used his thumbs to roll it into a slip of paper and lit it with a flinty match, drawing back heavily. Luke wanted to hit something, hit it so hard that it smashed into a million pieces. The cigarette flared and then calmed itself into a thin stream of smoke. Beside him on the table sat the tortoiseshell comb, his monument to stupidity. He touched the fine prongs, lifted it to his nose and sniffed at the scent of her. Then he let it fall from his fingers to clatter on the wooden boards. Margaret appeared soundlessly and began to gather the discarded newspaper and mail. She looked apologetically at Luke. 'Mr Gordon wants the mail.' 'My father's here?' Luke asked, his eyes flicking towards the study window.

Margaret saw the comb lying on the floorboards, picked it up and held it out to him.

'Mrs Gordon does not want it anymore.' Luke folded her fingers over it. 'Take it.' The girl bit her bottom lip. 'Take it,' he said harshly.

Margaret held the comb close to her chest. 'Thank you, Luke.'

He was reminded of soft rain as she padded, barefooted, away from him, the mail under one arm, the comb clutched to her chest.

Midwinter, 1989

Wangallon Station

The Dash 8 aircraft flew low across the countryside. Sarah studied the landscape as they crossed kilometres of green crops, areas being tilled by large tractors pulling wide machinery, and hundreds of cattle and sheep. There were also open bore drains crisscrossing the country, feeding water across the land, dams and tree-shaded waterways. She pressed her head against the window, mesmerised by a mob of kangaroos bounding off into the bush as they approached the airstrip. The animals left a trail of dust that puffed up into balls of dirt. They skirted past trees, reached a fence line and halted in their progress just long enough to squeeze beneath the wires, then they zigzagged across a paddock before finally disappearing from sight into a clump of trees.

Leaning back in her seat, Sarah squeezed her eyes tightly shut and pictured Wangallon; imagined circling above the sprawling homestead with its large garden. There was the vegetable plot, the remains of the property's ancient orchard and a number of outbuildings, large machinery and worksheds, the jackeroo's cottage. Further away sat the stables with their original bark and timber interior walls and adjoining horse yards. When she opened her eyes again the plane had landed.

She hurried through the one-room terminal, collected her bag and was one of the first passengers to reach the car park. There was a meeting organised with Jim Macken in three days and Sarah desperately wanted to see Anthony. She'd missed him despite their disagreement and she needed to sit down with him, smooth things over and decide what the best option was. The three men currently in her life all favoured paying out her half-brother and saw benefit in a development of some sort. Maybe it was time to stop fighting everyone.

'So you're back?' Anthony was sitting quietly at the table having an early lunch. Sarah shut the back door and dropped her bag. Pleased to be finally home, the excitement drained at his tone.

'Hi.'

'Have you eaten?' His back remained turned towards her.

She'd been ready to swoop on him with a hug. 'No, but I'll get something.' Somehow Sarah didn't think Anthony was going to make it for her. She busied herself carving a few slices of meat from the leg of mutton on the sink and then buttered the white bread that was almost past eating. 'It's good to be home.' Sarah added meat and tomato sauce.

'Nice of you to call and let me know you were coming.' He didn't look up from his sandwich.

Sarah took a bite. The meat was tough and the bread hard. 'What happened to your hand?' The knuckles on his right hand were strapped and a ghastly blue-green bruise spread out from under the narrow taping.

Anthony lifted his hand and turned it slowly, as if only just discovering he was injured. 'Smacked it in the yards.'

'Oh.' She took another bite. 'Well, I visited Dad.' The moistened dough clung to her gums and she ran her tongue across her teeth to free the sodden clumps. 'Mum died.' She rubbed her eyes, surprised that after so many years she felt so sad.

'I'm sorry.'

'It's for the best.' Sarah left the remaining sandwich on her plate. 'She was pretty sick at the end. It's hard to reconcile the person in the hospital bed with the woman who used to stand in the West Wangallon kitchen ordering me about.'

'Some people are just different, I guess.'

'Everyone seems to think we should pay out Jim.'

'Well, it looks like my opinion didn't count for much.'

'Maybe you should have listened to mine, or at least asked it. It cuts both ways, Anthony.'

Anthony wet his finger and dabbed at the crumbs on his plate. Sarah knew it was a waste of time trying to discuss Jim or the development at the moment. 'How's everything going?' There were dirty plates and coffee mugs on the sink and a trail of sugar ants tracking their way towards the toaster.

'Ask Matt.'

'I'm asking you.'

Anthony lifted his plate and carried it to the sink. Their eyes met briefly. 'I'm not much interested.'

Sarah swallowed the remains of the bread and mutton. 'What do you mean you're not much interested?' Tension fizzed between them. 'Well?'

'As I said, ask Matt. Your precious stockman has taken to giving me advice in your absence. Bloody hide of him.' Anthony squeezed his thumb and forefinger together. 'He's this close to getting booted off the property.'

Sarah gasped. 'What? You can't fire Matt.'

'Why the hell not?'

'Because.'

Anthony shook his head. 'Not good enough. He seems to be swinging on your grandfather's coat-tails. I had to remind him that the bloody old master and commander had kicked the bucket.'

What was she going to do now? She could hardly reveal Matt's role on the property without acknowledging she'd kept it a secret from Anthony, and he wouldn't give a squat if she argued that the terms of Matt's employment were part of her grandfather's will. 'You two aren't getting on?' she asked.

'Let's just say that we're not cogging too well. Matt's down at the yards about to weigh the steers. Now you're here you can give him a hand.'

Slightly miffed by the abruptness of his tone, Sarah covered the mutton in plastic wrap and gathered the bread, meat and butter in her arms. 'You coming?'

Anthony picked up the newspaper from the kitchen table. 'Now why the hell would you need me?'

Sarah walked through the side gate of the cattle yards. Bullet greeted her with an excited yelp and she ruffled his coat. 'Good to see you too.'

Bullet gave a low whine.

'I'll tell you all about it later. Now you stay here boy,' she cautioned. Bullet slid beneath the bottom steel railing and took up his front seat position between Whisky, Moses and Rust. They were itching to get into the yards although they were trained sufficiently to know that unless they were called by name, the cattle yards were off limits. Sarah marvelled at the dogs' resolve. Climbing over the rails into the next yard, she waved as she approached Matt and Jack. They were standing at an aluminium table, checking the digital readout on the monitor attached to the portable scales. If Matt was surprised by her unexpected return, he didn't show it. Nor did he mention Anthony's absence.

'G'day Sarah. Nice day for it.'

'Tops,' Sarah answered. There was a biting southerly ripping into their faces.

Jack reattached the leads to the battery. 'Hi Sarah. Is that better, Matt?'

Sarah looked over Matt's shoulder. 'Hi Jack.' The monitor showed minus five. 'It's out 5 kgs,' Matt answered. 'How much do you weigh, Sarah? Jack here put on 3 kgs from the two meat pies he scoffed down.'

'About 62 plus a stale mutton and tomato sauce sandwich.'

'Tasty,' Jack grinned.

Matt cleared the monitor to zero, walked over to the race and opened the side panel. On the ground inside sat the heavy metal scales. 'Hop on.'

Once she was standing in the centre of the scales Matt checked the monitor. 'Spot on 62 kgs. Seems to be weighing okay now. Do you want to do the pencilling, Sarah?'

'Sure.' Sarah slammed shut the side gate and cleared the monitor to zero again, looking down at the clipboard on the dusty table. There were forty-four steers already weighed, a handful of which were bordering on being a bit low for the feedlots specifications. KA International's current market was for milk to two tooth steers weighing between 400 and 510 kilograms a head. 'What do you think, Matt? Knock out the ones under 415 kgs?'

Matt finished rolling a cigarette and lit it. 'Reckon so. I've banged the tails of anything below 415 kg so far. There are a few that are poor. A couple of mad buggers and the rest are just bad doers. I spoke to Edward Truss this morning. He's happy to book in another road train load at the same price in ten days' time if you're interested.'

'I'm interested if the cents per kilogram go up.'

'Same price.' Matt took a healthy drag on his cigarette and gave a rare look that Sarah knew was his excuse for a smile. 'Won't do any better in this market. Anything that's not sold over the next few weeks can be left till late spring. It's a pity we can't hang onto all of them, but if it doesn't rain we won't get the turn off from the oats.'

'Sounds like a plan,' Sarah answered, although she would try and bargain with Edward anyway.

'Well let's get to it. Truss will be here this afternoon to have a look.'

Sarah could barely push the reset button on the monitor her hands were so cold, however twenty minutes later she was in her shirtsleeves, harbouring a cold sweat. Jack spent the afternoon in the forcing yard pushing the steers into the race. Once the race was full and the sliding gate was pushed up hard behind them, it was Sarah's turn to prod the next beast onto the scales. Another sliding gate was pushed behind the scales and the beast was contained just long enough to be weighed.

'480 kgs,' Sarah called, writing the weight down.

'Righto,' Matt answered. He opened the sliding gate at the front wide enough for the steer to stick his head through, then slammed it shut before lifting the head bail under the steer's chin to keep his head up. The beast snorted, grunted and sprayed Matt with mucus as his mouth was prised open for his teeth to be checked. 'He's a baby,' Matt called. 'Milk tooth.'

Sarah put a tick beside the weight, wrote *milk* in the corresponding column while Matt read out the steer's ear-tag number, which was also written down. She waited until the beast had been set free to join those steers already processed, then reset the monitor and prodded the next animal up the race.

By the time Edward Truss arrived a little after 3 pm they were nearly finished.

'Sarah, Matt, Jack.' They all shook hands.

Edward Truss was a short skinny man with knock-knees and teeth on him like a Moreton Bay shark. He was also known for his penchant for size 16-plus women. It was a strange phenomenon, yet women loved him. He had already meandered through three marriages, two de facto relationships and a string of one-nighters, most of which were consummated in Brisbane. In that regard he was quite fussy and rarely paraded his affections locally. *Don't shit in your own backyard,* had been his advice on first meeting Jack. Ever since, Matt made a point of leaving a roll of toilet paper on the top step leading into the jackeroo's cottage if word got out that Jack was playing up.

'What have you got for me then?' Edward scrambled up atop the railings and looked down at the processed steers. 'Nice even line. What are the weights like?'

Sarah scanned the clipboard. '418 to 515.'

'That heavy fella can go in. He'll lose those extra 8 kgs in the yards overnight. The trip up in the road train will fix any kgs left over.' He climbed down the yard slowly. 'Matt told you about my offer?'

'Sounds good,' commented Sarah. 'I'll have to check the competition though, Edward.'

Edward scratched the back of his hand. His sunspots were giving him curry today. He glanced at Matt. 'You won't find better.'

'The rural news is talking up cattle prices,' Sarah continued. 'And as you said they're a fairly good line and there's another four hundred of similar weight ready to go within the next fortnight.'

He narrowed his eyes, pulled out his red notebook and pencilled a few calculations. 'Four hundred you say?'

'Give or take.' She fiddled with the monitor, made a show of checking the leads. 'By October there'll be more coming up.'

Edward scratched his groin, walked over to the processed steers and took another look. 'The spring mob will be on oats?'

Matt nodded. 'These early ones are not quite finished to ensure we've got enough oats for the rest.' He turned to Sarah. 'He won't like to miss out on anything,' Matt whispered.

Sarah rolled her eyes at Jack. There were only fifteen head left to put through but the cattle needed to be walked back to their paddock and she figured the men had been out in the cold long enough already.

'Two cents extra a kilo.' The skin around Edward's mouth puckered. 'Tops.'

Sarah shook his hand. 'Done.' She offered him hot tea and homemade biscuits that she didn't have, knowing he wouldn't stay. He hadn't stayed since her grandfather had passed.

Edward hesitated. 'Next time. I'll be having some of those scones your grandmother used to make.'

After Edward had off with an escort of barking dogs, Matt shook Sarah's shoulder. 'Sharp as your grandfather. But you've started something now. You'll be feeding him for the rest of his life.'

'Maybe not. He hasn't tasted my scones.' Sarah laughed.

Midsummer, 1909

Three miles from Wangallon Station Homestead

Luke made camp down on a bend in the creek. The day's gradual unravelling had been similar to the course of the sun across the sky. Having started softly with a promise of clarity, it had turned poker hot, eventually becoming unbearable. He gathered long strips of bark, prising them free of their sturdy trunks with a small axe. The action helped to calm him. He rested the bark lengthways against a three-piece frame, the centre branch of which was wedged into a gouge on the trunk of a large tree. Each movement helped to dislodge the anger inside him. He pictured it fragmenting, wished it would disappear, knowing how unlikely it was that he'd ever be free of it.

Tying the bark at the top, Luke surveyed his rough dwelling. It was open at both ends and high enough to crawl into, but it was a shelter of sorts. Satisfied, he unstrapped his bedroll from Joseph's rump and tossed it into the lean-to, unsaddling Joseph so he could feed. His two pack horses were not so trustworthy. Ned and Ellie were known wanderers, so having unpacked their respective loads of cooking utensils and stores, he walked them to a grassy verge where the tree-edged creek bank bordered patches of sweet herbage. Here he hobbled them and let them be.

He was just beginning to start the makings of a fire when Mungo appeared like a wraith out of the timber.

'Live here now, Luke?' He pointed at the rough shelter and shook his head disbelievingly.

'It'll do.' He only needed a bit of protection from rain for he was more inclined to sleep under the stars. From around the corner of the creek five women approached, their melodic voices carried by the breath of air hovering above the water. They were bare-breasted, their loins covered in short skirts. At the creek's edge they squatted and began scraping up mud. This they placed in lengths of bark that was then carried to the lean-to. They set about slapping the mud onto the bark, effectively sealing the gaps and cracks with the sludge from the creek. Luke gave his thanks amid a women's gaggle of laughter as they squatted at the creek to wash themselves free of the caking mud, flicking their hands dry before straggling back to prepare evening meals.

Mungo sat cross-legged by the unlit fire after removing his riding boots.

Luke stretched out beside him. 'Thanks.'

Mungo gave a series of slow nods. 'The fox is cunning. He plays with his cubs, teaches them to fight and hunt. But this fox, mebbe he doesn't want to let you go. Mebbe he wants this cub to fight for him.'

The light was dwindling as they crunched twigs and grasses, a flame springing up immediately once a match was held to the dry tinder. Although the sky remained bright, the sun's rays couldn't penetrate the timber bordering the creek and the shadows grew long, the sky a berry-red haze. Luke poked at the fire with a stick, concentrating on the glowing flames, on the coolness of the sand against his palm. 'This will be my last drive, Mungo.' Luke had little choice. He must do the drive one more time to get money in his pocket and then he would look for work elsewhere.

Mungo flexed his toes and then busied himself pulling on his boots, not bothering to brush the sand from his feet. 'And then?'

'Best water the horses.' Luke walked through the timber, found his pack horses by their gritty chewing and led them back to the creek's edge. As the animals mouthed up the brown liquid, Joseph meandered down to join them. Luke scratched his old mate between his ears, rubbed his muzzle, ran a kindly hand along his faithful flanks.

The two men stood together on the creek's edge, looked up at the rapidly darkening sky. When the day grew to the point of ending, Mungo gave Luke a wry grin. 'You'll come back. Boxer says everyone comes back.'

'We will leave when the moon's full next month.' He felt his friend's eyes regarding him.

'Mebbe.' Mungo looked back up at the sky. 'Mebbe I go walk-about. The old people call me.' Luke understood that, like him, Mungo had a need to be free. Both chose to leave their fathers behind and in their own unique ways forge something of a life for themselves beyond the constrictions of Wangallon. This was the true basis of their friendship, a mutual understanding of their respective needs regardless of their father's wishes.

'What about your people?' The air between them drew taught. Luke sensed a constriction of words grown unspoken by disappointment.

Mungo spat on the ground. 'She wants us to leave, to make a life for ourselves beyond the tribe. I fear we will be outcasts. Mebbe it would be all right for me, but not her, not a woman. It's safer here. But to have her I must leave.' He wiped spittle from his chin.

'So you do love her?'

Mungo squished moist sand beneath his leather boots. 'Mebbe,' he grinned, 'I want her.'

'Have you told her yet?'

Mungo gave one sideways nod of his head. 'She goes to the old one tomorrow on the fullest night of the moon. I'll tell her before then. Mebbe we leave then. Mebbe I catch up with you and she come with us on the drive?' His voice faltered at the suggestion.

'Maybe,' Luke agreed. They both knew Luke was against women on drives. 'You're a good friend.'

'And you.' Mungo shook his hand. 'Like brother.'

At the campfire Luke made damper. He mixed flour and water, added a pinch of salt and kneaded the mixture roughly on a tin plate. When he'd formed it into a rough loaf he dropped the dough into a cast iron pot, placed the lid on it and sat it squarely in the embers. He filled his billy from the hessian waterbag hanging from a branch in the tree and sat down by the fire for a smoke. Hunger was a state of mind he was used to controlling. However, experience taught him that an empty belly at bed often led to a ruinous morning. So he would eat the bit of damper when it was cooked, swallow his tea and hope that sleep would come.

Overhead a flock of bats winged their way across the silent depth of water and took up residence in a nearby tree. Their squeaks heightened the solitude of the camp. Luke thought of Joseph contented in a comfy, quiet hollow. He threw a handful of tea leaves into the billy of boiling water, waited a couple of seconds and then, removing his neckerchief, wadded it against the red hot handle, pouring the brew into his pannikin. The damper proved a little more eventful; he dropped the pot and spent some time brushing coals and dirt from his dinner. Finally he sat, chewing his way through his meal, moistening each bite with a swallow of scalding tea. It would have been good to have a brother closer to his own age, Luke decided as he settled himself for another quiet evening; or a sister perhaps. Someone to visit, someone else out in the world living and breathing who was of his blood; it was a small thing to want but it would have filled such a void.

Luke relieved himself a few feet from his camp, dragged a night log onto the fire and splashed creek water on his face before lying down on the sand, his hands cupping his head, the tree-edged sky as a blanket. This self-imposed ostracism would last until they were ready to go droving. Luke knew it was useless confronting his father about his inheritance. What could you say to a man who was obsessed with the land he owned and the protection of it, who was block-brained to the idea of a person wanting something of his own, even his own son? He would leave with the next drive south, not expecting to return. How could he? Not only did he feel totally alienated from his own father, he had broken something that should not be broken. He'd shared one single intimate moment with the woman he loved, his father's wife, his stepmother, and broken the law of what was permissible within one's family. Yet all this meant little when he thought of the unravelling within his heart. He had shattered his life's ideal.

'Luke?'

Someone spoke his name. It was a soft low voice. A voice he barely recognised. The figure appeared across the campfire. Luke's fingers felt the cold metal of the carbine's barrel as he grew instantly wary. Whomever it was squatted before the campfire, the outline thrown into relief by the glowing embers. It took a moment or two before he recognised Margaret. He wanted to turn her away, would have turned her away, but she was crawling towards him, past him and into the darkness of the lean-to. He shuffled up into a sitting position, half-expecting the girl to reappear. The comforts of a woman were something Luke only ever received upon payment and he wondered what was expected of him, and then thought of what she could offer. He ducked his head and crawled in beside her.

She lay naked on his bedroll. Her long limbs stretched out as if in supplication, her hair spread about her like a halo. The campfire showered filaments of light across her body as her right hand fluttered like a small bird on her stomach. Luke studied the slight mound of her breasts, ran a finger down her chest to her hollow belly, encircled the angular hips with a fascinated sweep. Slowly he removed his shirt and trousers. All he could think of was lying atop this warm brown body, feeling the press of his skin against hers, tasting the sweetness of youth and trust. He moved slowly, so worried of crushing the fragile creature beneath him that his thighs and calves grew tight with control. As if aware of his reluctance, Margaret lifted her head, clasped her hands to the side of his face and brought their lips together. When the lengths of their skin met, a sheen of moisture sealed their limbs together.

Later that night, when stillness descended to engulf the creek's inhabitants, Margaret crept from the lean-to, dragging her maid's uniform behind her. Luke watched her silhouette from within the lean-to. She lifted a hand, delicately brushed back her hair and slipped the tortoiseshell hair comb in place, before dragging her dress over her head, wriggling her hips as the shapeless form obscured her. Although Luke couldn't see her eyes he knew Margaret was seeking him within the dark of his bark shelter; then she was moving, skirting the campfire and running into the night. He tried to listen to her leaving, strained his ears for the soft *shush shush* of her slim brown feet in the sand of the creek bank, but a void crept in and around him. He coughed, the noise sounding recklessly loud in the night's shadows. For all the wistful moments he'd spent dreaming of Claire Gordon, there had been an equal amount spent in silence in her company while she had spoken. Margaret had wanted him, not asked for anything and had barely uttered a word.

Midwinter, 1989

Wangallon Station

At the stables Sarah unsaddled Tess. Picking up the curry comb she removed her gloves and blew on her fingers before brushing down the mare; long rhythmic strokes that ran the length of the animal from neck to rump. Tess whinnied and shook her head from side to side. Bullet barked from his position on the cement step leading into the tack room. There was only a grudging respect between dog and horse; Sarah knew that friendship did not enter their respective animal vocabularies. Bullet wasn't one for sharing and Tess's comradeship only extended as far as letting Bullet benefit from a ride home after a busy day.

'Sshh, the two of you.' Filling the feed bucket, Sarah walked into the stables. Tess followed her, snuffling in anticipation, her nostrils breathing in the hair of Sarah's ponytail. Once Tess was inside and eating, Sarah slid the bolt on the half-gate. Immediately Bullet was by her side, wagging his tail and giving his best impersonation of a dog grin. Sarah patted him. 'Cheeky bugger,' she commented. Tess stuck her head over the stable door and whinnied once. Bullet barked. Next door four other stalls were full. Toby Williams and Pancake had their horses stabled in readiness for the big muster tomorrow. A mob of five hundred cows was in the road paddock and they would be joined by the Boxer's Plains' cattle tomorrow before being walked out to the stock route. As Sarah roughly calculated the cost of keeping Wangallon's cattle alive, a Landcruiser pulled up. In the half-light of approaching darkness she recognised the owner by the sheer number of dogs on the tray.

Toby Williams flicked off the headlights and shrugged on his fleecy-lined jacket. 'Damn cold out here.' He slammed the car door, setting the dogs off barking and Bullet growling. 'Friendly, that mutt of yours.'

'Protective,' Sarah answered. 'You should have called. I would have fed them for you.'

Toby pulled a hessian bag off the vehicle's tray and lugged it to the stables over his shoulder. 'Ahh, but they'd pine. My girls never did take to being apart from me for long periods of time.'

'Yeah, right.' Sarah stood back as Toby began pouring feed into a bucket. One by one he fed each of his charges, Sarah listening to his man–horse conversation. Soft murmurings to one, a reprimand to another, an acknowledgement of a good day's work to the third and then a noise that sounded strangely like a kiss. Sarah rolled her eyes. She knew drovers liked their horses and dogs, but . . .

'So now that the girls are settled, it's time for us.' Toby sat down on the cement step and patted the cold stone beside him. 'I'm quite friendly you know. Of average intelligence, but I am house-trained.'

'Comforting to know.' Sarah sat beside him.

He looked in the direction of the homestead. 'Must be lonely living all the way out here in that mausoleum.'

'I'm not alone.'

'Ah, the jackeroo. That's right, I forgot about Anthony.'

Somehow Sarah doubted that.

'But it means there is hope for the rest of us busted-arse cowboys.' He pulled out a packet of cigarettes, offered her one.

'No thanks.'

'Yeah, thought you looked too dewy to be a smoker.' He lit the cigarette and took a few deep puffs. 'So I hear you've got a few probs with a half-brother roaming the streets?'

Sarah wanted to tell Toby to mind his own business. 'Something like that.'

'Well we've all got our crosses.'

'What's yours?'

He stood, ruffling her hair. 'Women that don't have a head on them like a packet of half-chewed minties.' He stretched out his back, making a show of leaning from one side to the other. 'Something else you should know. 'Bout Boxer's Plains.'

God, Sarah thought, don't tell me the development is still going.

'Not my bees wax, I know, but,' Toby took a drag of his cigarette, looked at the glowing end of it and then stubbed it out on the bottom of his Cuban heeled riding boot. 'Long ways ago there were problems out on that block.' He stuffed his hands in the pockets of his jacket. 'There's an old wreck of a house out there in the middle of the ridge: Fenced off. Your grandfather wanted it left that way, but if those dozers get in there . . . Well, just thought you should know. Most people have either forgotten about what happened back then or they don't believe it. The thing is nothing was ever proved. I'd reckon it's better if things stayed in the dark.'

'Know what?'

'Look, it's no big deal. I just reckon people like to keep their family stuff private. Anyway, kiddo, I'll be seeing you.'

'Hang on, Toby, you can't start telling stuff like that and then leave. What else do you know and who told you?'

Toby gave a crooked smile. 'I had a great uncle who worked out here on Wangallon. Not a real family favourite from what I hear although I never met him myself. Seems there were a few shenanigans going on and there was a fight with a neighbour. From what I hear it was pretty messy, but your family would know more.' He tipped his hat.

'Wait.'

He walked up to her, close enough to go beyond the boundaries of her personal space. 'You're a good woman, Sarah. You need someone by your side that's going to support you; who understands the old ways.'

'And you'd be that person I suppose.'

'Well, I don't spend my time at the local pub playing up, girl.' Toby put his hand on the back of her head and kissed her flatly on the lips. She had the distinct impression a branding iron had just been seared into her skin.

'I'll do your droving job and then I'll be back. Not for the bloody land either.'

'Look Toby, I –'

'One day you'll need me and I'll come,' he said confidently. 'You can rely on that.'

Bullet took Toby's position on the top step, as Sarah sat heavily beside him, both of them watching as he drove away. 'Strange.' Her voice sounded inordinately loud. Bullet turned towards her, for once silent. She touched her lips as the tail-lights of Toby's truck vanished through the trees. She retied her hair, played with the zip on her jacket and wondered at the uniqueness of having only the third man in her life kiss her. Jeremy had loved her and comforted her after Cameron's death; Anthony was the man who'd been in her soul for years, and Toby? Toby was a man's man. He was tough, in his forties and . . . Bullet nudged her in the arm and huddled closer. Well, Sarah decided, I won't think about this now. Bullet snapped at something unknown in the air, the sound of Toby's truck dwindling in the distance.

'Did you see that swagger? That man gives skinny-hipped cowboy a whole new meaning.' If Shelley were here Sarah knew she would be salivating and she would be inclined to agree. 'Come on, Bullet.' She was not looking forward to returning to the homestead and she resented the fact that Anthony had made her feel unwelcome in her family home. She rubbed her shins briskly. She would be pleased when spring arrived and the days began to lengthen. The winter was nasty this year, with biting winds and plant decimating frosts and the country seemed stagnant with cold. It was a cold that seeped through her bones and into her blood. It was as if the girl of her youth was now frozen and she doubted if upon thawing she would even recognise her own reflection.

With a shake of her head she walked towards the homestead, wondering what drama had unfolded at Boxer's Plains years ago. How would she ever discover if what Toby talked about was true? It was always a bit difficult to wring reality from a good bush story. And the problem was that there was really no one left to ask. Except that Toby's concern shadowed the adamant stance of both her father and Frank Michaels. Neither of them thought a development on Boxer's Plains was a good idea. She was beginning to think that their opinions had very little to do with farming. Then she recalled the station ledgers that Angus had packed away years ago. There was a tin trunk somewhere. With a choice of freezing to death or facing Anthony, Sarah walked briskly towards the homestead. The lights were on. The winter sun, having dipped below the horizon, left a mass of cold dark earth on the moonless night and the chill penetrated Sarah's boots. She thought briefly of the deal struck with Edward Truss that afternoon, of her horse ride down to the winter stillness of the creek and the soothing quiet of a land unburdened with problems.

After her next trip to Sydney, when she had more time, she'd go out to Boxer's Plains and see if there really was an old house in the middle of the ridge.

Sarah opened the back door and took the stale mutton bone from the fridge. There was still a large portion of meat on it and Bullet hopped on his back legs in anticipation as she took the bone to the meat house. The screen door squeaked noisily on its hinges as she sat the mutton leg directly in the middle of the massive wooden chopping block and, meat cleaver in hand, struck the joint directly down the middle. The cooked bone broke apart easily. 'Presto! Dinner, Bullet.' She threw one bone on the cement path and set about washing down the chopping block with icy water from the garden hose. Bullet was waiting patiently for her to finish. 'Ferret?' Matt's dog walked stiffly along the path, the cold weather making his steps painfully slow. Ferret sniffed at the bone and then clamped his teeth around it. Bullet picked up his own and together the two dogs walked back to the sandy protection of the tank stand. In the darkness she heard them growl, crunch and whine with delight.

'Are you coming in or what?'

Sarah imagined Bullet lifting his dog brow at the tone of Anthony's voice. Stepping out of the garden shadows, she turned off the hose and dropped it on the cement near the meat house.

Anthony sat at the end of the kitchen table, a half drunk can of beer in his hand and four empty soldiers lined up to his left. Sarah opened her mouth to speak.

Anthony shook his head and lifted his hand in silence.

'That's not very democratic, Anthony,' Sarah replied, pulling her arms and head free of the thick navy cable jumper. It was damn hot in the kitchen. The old Aga was going and she was a fierce old woman who puffed smoke through cracks when she got over-heated. Sarah sniffed at the fumes gathering in the room. She'd only arrived back from the coast this morning and Anthony had ensured they'd barely talked, by making himself absent.

'Here's my summation of events.'

'Great.' Sarah sat at the table, rubbing her hands to warm them. Anthony never had been very good at holding his alcohol.

'I waited for you to come back after Cameron died, waited for you after your engagement to Jeremy fell through. Hell, I'm still waiting for you to marry me.' He took a sip of his beer and then sat the can on the table as if it had become distasteful. 'Your father and I waited for you to get over Angus's death and then –' Anthony clicked his fingers – 'ta da, suddenly you decide you aren't involved enough in Wangallon's management, suddenly you decide *you* want to be in charge.' Anthony collected the beer cans and deposited them with a tinny crash on the sink. 'But it gets better. Knowing there's a recalcitrant half-brother floating around in the ether, poor old Anthony decides to rescue the situation. He devises a sure-fire way of making Wangallon more productive, so that *when*, and I emphasise *when*, a portion of the place has to be sold to pay out said half-brother, Wangallon will survive. But does Sarah listen to him? No. In fact Sarah pulls rank and has a chat to the bank. I bet that was an interesting conversation. Did you tell them it was me putting Wangallon's affairs at risk? Did you tell them it was my fault, that I'd been overspending and now an increase was needed on our overdraft? I'm wondering, does Sarah know how offensive that is to me? Does Sarah even care how offensive it is to me?'

'Of course I care. But what did you expect me to do? You're sitting there accusing me of wanting control and your actions don't exactly scream teamwork. And for heaven's sake, Anthony, no costings? No projections for the bank? What, are you stupid?'

'Clearly I am.' From the kitchen bench Anthony pulls a sheaf of papers. 'There are the projections.' His finger stabs at each piece of paper as he sits them on the kitchen table. 'And there is the documentation. And yes I was stupid because I did it for you and for Wangallon.'

Sarah looked at the paperwork. 'My god, you used your own money? The money from your share of your family's property? You never said anything.'

Anthony stared at her. 'You never gave me the chance.'

'That's because –'

'That's because you just kept saying no, like a bloody tape recorder. God forbid if anyone, anyone should try to take the Gordon mantle away from you.' He picked up his wallet. 'You forget, Sarah, that I was only trying to help.'

'Where are you going?' She touched him on the shoulder. 'Anthony?'

He turned to face her. 'I'm having dinner at the pub. I can't do this anymore. '

'You can't do it anymore? I'm the one who's been seeing solicitors and fighting my half-brother.'

Anthony shrugged. 'Well you didn't listen to me on that score either. Good luck.'

'Good luck? Geez, Anthony, what's got into you?'

He opened the back door. 'Reality.' Then he was gone.

In the kitchen Sarah sat near the Aga. He'll come back. She cushioned her head with her arms on the kitchen table. *He will come back*, she whispered. Hadn't her grandfather told her that same thing many years ago? Everyone came back, they couldn't help themselves; Wangallon got into your soul.

That night Sarah dreamt of Wangallon. She hovered above the countryside, darting down like an eagle hawk to inspect dams and fences, swooping low over grassland to check sleeping ewes and resting cattle. She breasted the wind and let it carry her high into the stratosphere and then folded her wings against the updraft to plummet down to where men on horseback walked a single trail. The men carried their need to protect Wangallon like the rifles slung across their thighs, carefully but with determination. When she awoke in the pre-dawn Sarah understood this necessity – there was much to lose. And there was something else that unexpectedly came to her: the tin chest that contained her great-grandfather's ledgers was in her grandfather's massive wardrobe.

Midsummer, 1909

Wangallon Station Homestead

'Is it not too early for you to be wandering about?' Hamish addressed the lone figure stalking the garden as the first tinges of light illuminated the eastern sky. Claire was dressed only in her chemise and wrap. He took his wife by the elbow and together they walked the perimeter.

Claire ran her fingers across the top of the white paling fence, feeling the sharp prick of splinters in her soft skin. The fence divided their two worlds as perfectly as any boundary. 'This is a pleasant fiction,' she said evenly as her slipper-encased feet stepped over twigs. 'Have you tired of me, Hamish? Do you wish me to leave?' It was the only feasible solution unless they could come to some form of understanding.

'I will be away for some days.' Hamish steered her towards the length of bougainvillea hedge that was now large enough to block the westerly winds.

'Do me the courtesy of an answer,' she said, patting at her lack-lustre hair.

'I have tried to ensure your happiness, yet it is undeniable that we have grown apart.' The fine leather of his boots kicked at a fallen branch. 'You came here as a young carefree woman. I wonder what became of the person I admired.'

'So you do not love me?'

Hamish breathed in the earth about him, imagined the being of his land rising and falling in sleep. 'I have, during my lifetime, Claire, utilised whatever means at my disposal to carve out a place for myself in this new world. You have benefited from my efforts.'

'I do not deny that.' Her fingers clutched a little tighter at the shawl about her shoulders. 'You loved me once, I think. I remember your smile, your body next to mine for weeks on end.' She glanced coyly at his weathered profile. 'I think perhaps you liked the idea of love, of being loved. Or maybe you just like possession.' Claire felt him stiffen at her words. 'We have a divide between us, husband, one made gaping by your single-minded interest in this great property you have created.' Claire placed the slightest of pressure on his arm. 'Your obsession with Wangallon has led you away from the comforts of hearth and home, from the wife who would welcome gentle conversation. We could bridge the divide between us if –'

'When my time is over my descendants will benefit from the substantial legacy I leave. The Gordons will be remembered. I don't believe I owe anyone,' he looked at her, 'any more or less than that.'

'I see,' Claire replied tightly. Although used to his harsh demeanour, there was an unmistakeable edge to his words. 'So you care not for our small family, for those who have supported your endeavours and assisted in giving your family name a measure of respectability.'

'I am beyond caring about respectability. It means nothing. A man can raise himself up to the highest echelons and still be considered no better than a dog by some.' Having paused at the furthest end of the garden, Hamish removed his arm from hers and looked out across the wavering grassland. A mob of kangaroos was travelling slowly across his field of vision.

'Hamish, what has happened to create such a fury within you? I have seen it growing like a watered seed these last months.' His brown hands stretched wide across the weathered fence. She reached tentatively towards him, then thought better of the action. 'You are angry at something that has no bearing on our relationship. And I have not been at my best these past weeks. Between the two of us our marital difficulties have tripled through circumstances that will surely pass.'

Hamish gave such a sigh that Claire's eyes moistened. She turned aside, wiping angrily at her tears. 'We have had common interests,' she sniffed. 'Respectability for one: Why, you courted Sydney society for years and now we have friends among the most prominent families in the country. Have you forgotten the length of the time it has taken for us to be accepted? When I think of the weeks spent in Sydney during the season when only a sprinkling of invitations were ours to choose from. When I think of the effort I myself went to –'

'Then don't think, my dear,' Hamish said impatiently, continuing his walk. 'You will find it less taxing. And if we are honest with ourselves I think you will agree that the upper echelons of society are what you aspire to. In truth I have little need of such things anymore. All of our preening and amiable conversation has been for Angus, after all.'

Claire smelled the pungent aroma of tobacco as Hamish stuffed his pipe, lit it and inhaled deeply. They were standing beneath the branches of a spreading gum tree, the muted pinky-blue of dawn creeping over the countryside. 'How can you say that?' Claire's face was white, her features stiff with exasperation.

'Because there is something far more important than respectability. However, you are a woman,' he spoke a little gentler, 'and as such God divined you to see virtue in matters of little consequence.'

She bit her knuckle, glad of the half-light. What had watered this cold wedge which had so recently grown within her husband?

'Once Luke has left with the mob, may I suggest a little sojourn,' Hamish stated between puffs of his pipe. 'I thought perhaps a trip to the Blue Mountains to escape February's heat; then some sea air.'

Claire thought back to Luke's revelation, how his own mother Rose was not yet dead when Hamish became her unknown benefactor. 'You will be joining me?' Despite the mortification of the expected answer, Claire needed to know.

Hamish smoothed his moustache. 'No. You will take Angus with you. He will be attending the Kings School at Parramatta.'

Claire shuddered inwardly at the calmness with which her future was being decided. Did he really have no affection for her anymore, not even as the mother of his son and heir? Or was her current tendency towards melancholy making her presume the very worst. The very worst, she repeated silently; if the heir was no longer at Wangallon, what need was there for her?

'Many of the landed board their sons at an early age,' Hamish continued. 'The advantages are numerous. Apart from the educational and sporting benefits, the boys mix with the sons of other wealthy pastoralists, forming lifelong friendships with those of a similar social standing.' He paused and looked at her directly. 'That alone should make you agreeable.'

Now he was ridiculing her values. Dragging her feet up the verandah steps Claire attempted to formulate some last drastic retort, yet she could think of nothing that would wound him. He was beyond the understanding of mortal men. Claire lifted her head proudly as she walked towards the main door. There standing in the doorway was Angus. His face was pale.

'Mother?'

Angus's mouth opened, fat tears began streaming down his distorted face to roll across his cheeks and lips. 'Mother?' His violet eyes searched Claire's face. 'Father? W-what will I do in the city? What about Wallace and Lee and –'

'This will be the making of you,' Hamish explained. 'Now stop blubbering.'

'I'm not going,' Angus cried out, stamping his foot. 'I'm not going and I'm not leaving Wangallon.'

Hamish closed the distance between his son in three large strides. Removing his leather belt he doubled it and flicked it across the palm of his hand. 'You will quell your predilection to disobedience and accept your good fortune.'

Claire watched the adamant stance of her son and thought of his recent attempts at riding his horse. The boy had shown his determination that day.

Angus squared his young shoulders. 'Never,' he retorted as his father approached him, belt in hand. He turned on his heel and quickly ran inside.

'Please don't take Angus from me,' Claire pleaded as Hamish furiously looped his belt back around his waist. 'If you ever cared for me and I know you did once, don't take my one consolation, please don't send him away. Think about how he will pine, please think about –'

'This is ridiculous. The boy will benefit greatly from such an undertaking.'

Claire tugged at his jacket. 'I was schooled here, as was Luke. We could employ a tutor as you did then.'

'The schooling was adequate for a woman as it was for the mental faculties of Luke. Angus deserves and will receive far better.'

'For what purpose? To converse with blacks and the decrepit likes of Jasperson?' Claire opened her arms to encompass the land about them, her shawl falling to the ground. 'To contemplate sunsets and count cattle? For what reason does he need this great education other than to make my presence here redundant?'

Hamish gave her a peculiar look. Claire dropped her arms quickly, bending to retrieve her shawl. Surely Hamish understood her anger was borne of sadness, surely some slight vestige of the man she cared for lay curled within the hardened shell he'd woven about himself. Claire tugged at her shawl, gave a wan smile. In truth he'd only suggested a holiday – a sojourn, was that not the word he had used?

'I think,' Hamish said bitterly, 'you have made yourself redundant'.

Claire, having partaken of some hot water and cod-liver oil, was still dressed in her chemise. She busied herself by rummaging through the cedar wardrobe, attempting to find something suitable to her disposition. She threw various items over her shoulder, each small thud helping to eradicate the most shocking of conversations she'd ever had the misfortune to endure. The bed was already strewn with finely pintucked blouses, three skirts of varying shades of brown and two of the so-called hobble skirts. Those she would not wear again. Claire tossed the black and grey aside. The constrictions of female fashion were becoming an abomination. She decided on a fashionable morning dress of water-weave taffeta. The pink was undoubtedly a little ostentatious for a dreary bush day and was more suited to a citified soiree, however Claire was in need of cheering up. She chided at her weeping, which threatened to engulf her should she not stay angry. All manner of emotions were raking across her body. Guilt, hate and hurt being the ones she could put immediate description to. 'I hate you,' she muttered, tearing gloves, woollen stoles and boned corsets from their drawers. 'I hate you.'

Leaving the wardrobe and dresser Claire embarked on the contents of the large camphorwood chest from within which she began to yank at a selection of carefully folded evening gowns.

'Mrs Gordon, can I get you some breakfast?' Mrs Stackland's voice echoed strongly in the hallway.

Claire's fingers sorted nimbly through layers of silky material. 'No, thank you.' There were satins and silks, cottons and taffetas in all colours. With practised efficiency she swept a royal blue taffeta into her arms, the material unfolding in a shimmer to reveal a seed pearl embroidered bodice. Next she selected a burgundy satin with gold fringing on the skirt's front panel and hem. Holding up each of the gowns, she studied her reflection in the mirror above the dresser. Her skin looked sallow against the royal blue and bloodless next to the burgundy. She would need to do something about her pallor least she were relegated by the Sydney gossips to such a position of sickliness that it was deemed unsuitable to extend her a single invitation.

Dumping the gowns on the cypress floor a rip of pain surged through her. Claire buckled to her knees, clutching at her abdomen. She began to crawl towards the door, hopeful of leveraging herself up so that she could call for assistance. She slipped on the material beneath her and fell heavily as a rush of blood left her body. With a moan Claire turned onto her back, tentatively touching the wetness between her legs. She struggled upwards expecting to see some sliver of her unborn child resting amid the rich weave of the evening gowns. 'Don't look,' she chided, 'don't look, Claire.' With tired arms she wrenched the chemise from her body and wadded the material between her legs. Placing her palms on the floor she dragged herself backwards, her body sliding easily across the silk-and-taffeta covered floor until her back rested against the foot of the bed. Her head lolled back, her neck arching uncomfortably. Slowly the pain subsided, leaving behind a shallow emptiness.

Wangallon Station Homestead

Claire watched a triangle of sun enter the partially opened bedroom curtains. The elongated strip of heat travelled silently until sometime later it struck the soft flesh of her bloodied thigh. She would take the Cobb & Co coach from Wangallon Town once her recuperation was complete. Claire flinched at the unwelcome heat pricking her skin and focused on the washstand with its ceramic water jug and matching bowl. It was a long journey to Sydney, over 650 miles. On their last trip south the eight-seat passenger coach took 35 hours to travel 135 miles. Claire began to heave herself up until she was standing. The jolting and boredom of the trip south was almost too ferocious to contemplate, especially when a single 135 mile leg included an overnight stop. She took a tentative step forward as new warmth, agitated by her movement, trickled down her leg. One could expect a minimum of five nights' stopover en route as long as dry weather prevailed and the coach or horses didn't suffer a break down. At the washstand Claire poured water into the ceramic bowl and sobbed quietly. She cried for her lost baby whose soul was winding its way heavenward, and for the man who was her husband. This time, however, Claire refused to cry for herself.

High Summer, 1989

Northern Scotland

Catherine Jamieson was not a woman Maggie Macken conversed with. Indeed, on prior occasions when she could feign not having seen her approach, Maggie would fiddle with the contents of her handbag and cross the main street in the village of Tongue in order to avoid the older spinster. Today, however, no such escape seemed possible for as Maggie stepped from the curb, Mrs Jamieson followed. Maggie caught the woman's reflection in the window of the grocery store and saw the determined swing of her arms when she doubled back to the telephone booth. Attempting to give an air of an errand just remembered, Maggie scrambled in her purse for coins as she ducked in the pillar-box red door of the booth and dialled her sister in St Andrews. Maggie could usually rely on a string of complaints to issue forth from Faith with the subject, her sister's bank-teller husband, centring on ungratefulness. She listened as the telephone rang out and then stopped altogether. Damn. Unused coins fell into the change box. A sharp tap of knuckles sounded on the glass behind her.

Maggie wondered how obvious it would be if she chose to ignore her stalker and try another of her ever unhelpful sisters. Instead she took a deep breath and opened the door.

'Why, Maggie Macken. I do believe you went out of your way to avoid me,' accused Mrs Jamieson with a wave of her finger. The woman had gone grey prematurely and Maggie patted her own brown hair as a lock of grey fell onto Mrs Jamieson's brow. 'Well?'

Maggie pursed her lips and surveyed her antagonist with one unblinking stare – from the beige of the woman's sturdy walking shoes and paisley dress, to a face ruined by loneliness.

'So you sent young Jim over for Sarah's money, I hear?'

Maggie began walking along the pavement in the direction of her car. She'd parked it next to the tourist walk with a mind to visit the ruin on the hill once her errands were completed. The fortress remained Jim's favourite spot and was the place where he'd first met Sarah Gordon. Wouldn't she obliterate that day if given the chance, Maggie thought. She'd not been to the ruin herself for many a year. But now there was a need for her to return there, to revisit the very spot where two lives were altered; hers and Jim's. History had repeated itself, for Jim's life had been thrown into chaos through chance, and hers through poverty.

Behind her Mrs Jamieson puffed to keep pace. 'The village is agog with the millions he could inherit,' she called out. 'I bet you're very pleased with yourself. Having been jilted by Ronald Gordon you now manage to get your haggis and eat it as well.'

Maggie crossed over the narrow road, passed the white facade of the pub, and walked towards her car. Why the fates interceded to have Sarah Gordon bedded down for the duration of her stay at this woman's B&B over two years ago was beyond her. 'Whatever are you talking about, Catherine Jamieson?' Maggie could feel her cheeks burning.

'Revenge. You didn't get the Australian you stole from me.'

Maggie opened the rear door of her car to place her bag of groceries on the cracked upholstery. 'You lost him yourself,' Maggie said with controlled slowness. 'You with your airs, why I'm sure you chased him away.'

Mrs Jamieson grabbed Maggie by the arm. 'Ronald Gordon never would have stayed. If you'd truly listened when he spoke of his homeland, you would know that. Besides, he was already married.'

Maggie winced under the older woman's grip. She shook herself free. 'He didn't ask you to go back to his famous property either though, did he?'

Catherine Jamieson gave her such a withering look Maggie felt as if she suffered from the plague. 'He asked, Maggie Macken. But I could no sooner leave here than he could leave his blue haze.'

This was news quite unexpected. Maggie attempted to breathe evenly, but concentrating her thoughts in that department only made her more breathless.

'You should have stopped Jim from going. It's not right to steal from others.'

Maggie collected herself. She was an upstanding citizen in Tongue, well married with a son and, very soon most likely, the Mackens would be richer than all their neighbours. 'Steal? It is certainly not stealing. Besides it's you who decided to tell what lay hidden for years.'

'Because your boy hankered after young Sarah when she visited and you did nothing to dissuade him. If he'd been my boy I would have told him to stay away. It wasn't seemly the way you let them keep company. Especially when you made no bones about the company you'd kept.'

'Were it not for you, my boy would not be over there,' Maggie countered. 'None of this would be happening. After all it was you with your "holier than thou" attitude who told what never should have been spoken.' Maggie wondered once again at the logic of hiding a nasty mistake with a lie, especially when women such as Catherine Jamieson were probably shrewd enough to guess the difference. Still Maggie persisted with her argument. 'Besides, it's the grandfather who has left the will.' She fiddled with the car keys in her hand. Catherine Jamieson was still staring her down. 'It's family business now and naught to do with you.'

'You shouldn't have done it. You didn't love Ronald.'

Maggie blinked. It was strange to think that this woman talking to her may once have been young, both in looks and spirit. Maggie cleared her throat, pressed her shoulders back a little. She reminded herself that she had nothing to prove to anyone, only her family to be considered. 'Of course I loved him.'

The older woman looked at her, unconvinced, shuffled in her handbag for a tissue and pressed it against her nose. 'More than your running? More than the running shoes your own poor mother heard you lament about daily? If I didn't know better, Maggie Macken, I'd say you were lying.' Mrs Jamieson turned smartly on her heels as if dismissing an unruly child.

Maggie watched Catherine Jamieson walk away. The town gossips said the woman had been jilted, or that her man had died; whether through accident or illness no one knew. What would those same gossips say if they ever discovered that the man in Catherine's heart was Ronald Gordon? That Catherine Jamieson never married because she loved a man she could not have? That type of love was something Maggie could not even begin to comprehend. No wonder the woman hated her.

Locking her car, Maggie walked towards the sign-posted trail. The locals had always been kind to her, believing her to be a young woman who'd been taken advantage of some twenty-eight years ago. This coupled with the fact that Maggie's pregnancy coincided with enough money to finally purchase a pair of running shoes only added to the glances of pity afforded to her by neighbours and townsfolk alike. Overnight she was transformed. Maggie Macken was the promising local runner whose career was cut short by an unfortunate turn of events.

The track sloped downhill. Maggie slipped through wet grass and mud. In the distance, across the sea entrance, mountains rose enticingly. There was usually mist swirling about the peaks, while at the base the icy grip of the North Sea clutched at the rocky shoreline with each incoming wave. Maggie reached the bottom of the small valley and a pebble-strewn stream. She gasped as the cold water soaked immediately through her lace-ups and clucked her tongue at the stupidity of trying to negotiate an overgrown path in shoes meant for a morning's shopping. Scrambling over a wooden stile, she brushed rising flies from her face, hung her handbag over her shoulder and looked at the overgrown track leading uphill. Her feet were cold, her body hot and the sun was beginning to prickle her skin. She couldn't recall the distance to the ruin, nor whether the climb was a steep one. Maggie looked over her shoulder. Surely after all the years since she'd last climbed this track, hoping a young man followed, her memory wouldn't fail her. There were at least two further stiles to be crossed. And the track was a slippery one, but quite doable even when wearing questionable shoes. Maggie tucked her hair behind her ears, stamped her feet in the soft vegetation to increase her circulation, and walked on.

Midsummer, 1909

Wangallon Station

Hamish rode out towards a pinkish glare of heat and dust, refusing to look over his shoulder at the woman who had so wantonly provoked him. There was the tang of smoke in the dawn air, signalling bushfires to the south-east. Aborigines, he surmised, adjusting his arse in the saddle. He would need some of Lee's salve if he was to carry out his plan against Crawford. Age had made his backside sensitive to riding long distances. He turned his horse to the ridge and headed towards the creek, his gaze drawn every so often to the smoke hanging on the horizon. The Aborigines were adept at lighting fires to smoke out kangaroos, lizards and other campfire edibles. Hamish had observed the regeneration of trees and plants once these untended fires had burnt through the county, yet such fires on Wangallon were banned. In the heat of summer a conflagration could quickly ensue, destroying the valuable grasses so vital to his livestock's survival and Wangallon's prosperity. Of more concern was the danger to his beloved cattle and sheep. Hamish had been witness to the terrible sight of burnt sheep; the sweet stench of lanolin and the horrific burns. He wished no such pain on any creature – friend or foe. Yet out east, as evidenced by the sting to his eyes this morning, there were no such constraints.

His mount picked his way past the ridge and stepped lightly across the paddock. As if aware of the coming heat, the horse moved quickly, sensing the opportunity for faster travel would be limited in only a matter of hours. In the tree line Hamish spotted smoke streaming into the sky. This, he knew by its position, was the black's camp. He scanned to the left and right of the smoke. Sure enough there it was, downstream of the camp, a second fire; his son's. Hamish touched his horse's flanks with the heels of his boots and they moved into a trot. He leant forward in the saddle, the movement of both horse and rider causing a breath of air to brush at his face. Soon they were racing towards the growing tree line, weaving between the great coolibah gums and brigalow trees dominating the approach to the creek. As the denseness of the woody plants increased, Hamish found himself forced to slow and he picked his way carefully across fallen timber and ground made uneven by previous floods and the burrowing of rabbits.

He found Luke by his campfire, squatting like a black in the dirt. Some feet away was a reasonably solid lean-to plastered with dry mud. Luke stood as he dismounted, pulled his hat low over his forehead even though the sun was yet to breach the creek. Hamish swatted at the morning flies, noting the empty mussel shells piled to one side of the fire. One of the blacks had brought him breakfast.

'It would be helpful to tell someone of your whereabouts,' Hamish began, standing on the opposite side of the fire, his hands clasped behind his back.

Luke slurped at his freshly brewed tea, saying nothing. Hamish walked down to the edge of the creek.

'I've decided to send Angus away to boarding school: The Kings School in Parramatta.' Hamish brushed at the flies. There was rain coming for the air was humid. 'I agreed with your grandmother for your sake,' Hamish began, recalling parts of the conversation he'd faintly overheard from the sanctity of his study. He wouldn't stand to have his plans ruined through petulance.

'And how does being deprived of my inheritance benefit me?'

The brown water of the creek moved sluggishly onwards. Leaves and small twigs sailed past, caught on a deceptive current. 'A shopkeeper's life is not something you would take to, lad.' Having a conversation with Luke had always been akin to having a tooth pulled.

Luke threw the remains of his tea in the fire. 'Well that's something you have ensured I'll not know.' He picked tea leaves from his tongue, searched for his tobacco in the pockets of his trousers.

Hamish walked back towards him. 'Look at you. You can't even spend a night inside Wangallon Homestead. Not for you the constraints of a ceiling and walls. I understand that, Luke, although occasionally it would not hurt you to sleep in your room, dine with me on a more regular basis. Wangallon is your home after all, and as a Gordon you have a name and position to do credit to.'

Luke was rolling tobacco in the palm of his hand. 'It's never been my home. First it was yours. In the future it will belong to Angus. Surely I was entitled to something for myself.'

Fairness was not something Hamish had considered. 'We're landowners. You have Wangallon.' The boy never loved Wangallon the way he should have. It was as if some strange process of osmosis occurred, transferring all the bitterness and melancholy of his mother into Luke's own veins so that it flowed unbridled through his body. Hamish watched as his eldest struck a match, lighting his cigarette. 'It was your grandmother's decision.' Hamish was drawing tired of the subject. 'The drive will have to be bought forward. I've business with the Crawfords that must be taken care of. Inform the men accordingly. Tonight you and I will be riding out for the big river. We leave at dusk so you best break camp and move back to the homestead. We could be away for a number of nights so I'll leave the provisioning to you.'

Luke considered the man before him. He was tall, a bearish, barrel-chested man yet it was his imposing stare, a thousand yard stare, that made most men acquiesce to his demands. 'I'll not be accompanying you, Father.'

'This is not a subject for discussion, Luke,' Hamish answered sourly.

'I agree,' Luke dragged on his cigarette, then poked the stub of it in the dirt. 'It's not.'

'The business with Crawford –'

'Is your business. You seem to disregard my affairs so I'm reckoning it's time I repaid the favour.'

'The cattle need to be moved at the end of the week. On the wan of the full moon.'

'Look about you,' Luke countered. 'There's been little rain, the grasses are drying, already the soil floats away on the breeze. To leave a month early could find the cattle starving on the route. We will be early for any rains further south.'

'The steers must be out of this country by week's end otherwise a calamity will be upon us. Besides which, they are already being mustered up.'

'So I'm figuring you have some plan of ill that makes you push this decision.'

'They are my cattle and you work for me,' Hamish said angrily.

So there it was. One was expected to stay and work for the ongoing benefit of both the Gordons and Wangallon, even though he himself was considered no better than the other stockmen on the property. 'Then I quit.' The words came out so suddenly that Luke was momentarily stunned by his own audacity. Both men glared at each other. Luke wondered only briefly at the repercussions of his statement. What did it matter? He'd decided not to return from this drive. He looked up at his father, at the man that was like a foreign country to him. He admired him for what he'd accomplished during his life, however he never truly felt like his son, knew that he was unsure, still, if he even wanted to be Hamish Gordon's son for the man threw a long shadow and, so far, Luke had been unable to crawl free of it.

'So be it,' Hamish finally responded. 'I would never stand in the way of a man burdened by stupidity.' Hamish mounted his horse. 'I don't expect to see you again.'

Midsummer, 1909

Crawford Corner Homestead

William Crawford found his father at the dining table, a lone figure at the end of the gleaming hardwood that could comfortably seat twenty. He sat rather stiffly amid a selection of tureens arranged within ease of reach, although the food on his plate remained untouched and the crystal brandy decanter showed he had displayed a healthy interest. Billy, his page, although the eight-year-old was indeed of Aboriginal stock, waited patiently behind him dressed in the manor of an English estate domestic: breeches, waistcoat and jacket with the obligatory white stockings. The boy only needed a hand-held rattan fan to transport William back to the tropics.

'Ah, my boy. You're back. Good, good. Just in time for the evening meal although you missed a fine apple strudel at dinner today. Yes, a fine strudel.'

William took his place on his father's left, poured a generous glass of French brandy and took a more than gentlemanly sip. Mr Hamish Gordon's visiting card in the form of a garish purple and yellow bruise still graced his father's left eye and cheek, and had clearly affected the grinding mechanisms of his jaw for it was a number of days since Gordon's impudent visit and his father appeared to have lost some weight.

'This weather, really, Father, I don't know how you stand it,' William announced, taking another sip of brandy and wincing at the warmth. He had friends in both Sydney and Melbourne who benefited from those new fangled ice chests and cellars that enjoyed the bedrock virtues of a cool environment. Here he was sitting among candle-flaming candelabras, the heavy gold damask curtains obliterating any hint of air.

'The soup is excellent, cabbage, Mrs Dean informs me, with a hint of preserved orange.'

Billy ladled soup, offered William a finely rolled bun.

Oscar waited for his son to begin an oratory of the property. Having spent a number of days in the saddle, each trip longer than the one before, detail was expected. The exercise assisted with the return of his son's usual placid character, a marked feature of the youth that had been missing since Hamish Gordon's uninvited visit.

'The soup is rather good,' William admitted, finishing off the bowl and taking another sip of brandy. 'Are you still intent on pursuing your scheme?' he asked as Billy served a large slice of potato and mutton pie.

'Ah, so you have been ruminating on our discussions. Yes, my boy. You forget we were here before that Scottish brigand weaselled his way onto Wangallon. I know his type: ruthless and unforgiving; a seeker of revenge in the truest sense.'

William stretched his torso, readying his appetite for the next course. The house boy was lighting candles about the room and opening curtains with the disappearing sun. William stuck his fork into the pie. He couldn't doubt the flaky texture of the pastry, however the mutton was a little tough and the salt, well, it would drive a man to drink water until he was fit to burst. 'Exactly my point. We're not quite of that stock, Father, and . . .'

Oscar burped loudly and waved his linen napkin for silence. There really was no excuse for this type of rendering of one's opinion, not after the master of the household, and he might add the veritable brains behind their fortune, was decided on a course of action. 'William, I have discussed the situation in detail with Peters and Tremayne. Tremayne you will recall is a tracker of some repute.'

'Sounds rather African native to me.' William waited for Billy to clear his partially eaten meal before custard was served. 'You're sure he will come?'

'You may depend on it. Wetherly assures me of his plan. We don't have all the details, of course, however we know he intends to strike during the full moon. And tonight the moon will be at its brightest.'

William licked pastry from his upper lip. 'Wetherly can be trusted?'

Oscar gulped down more brandy. 'The man is indebted to me. His liaison with Mrs Constable rendered him unemployable until I offered him the position of stud master. I believe his loyalty was proved upon informing me of Gordon's counteroffer. I must say I find the machinations of life quite enthralling. Imagine Gordon having the audacity to offer Wetherly a position. Wetherly knows what side his bread is buttered on.'

William turned up his nose at the bowl of pale custard. 'A common term, Father.'

'For common people,' Oscar reminded his son. 'Hamish Gordon is not a man for paltry paperwork. He will come over the river with retribution in mind and we will be waiting, with a magistrate on hand, to witness his criminal intent.'

William doubted the plan would go quite so smoothly. Hamish Gordon, ignorant Scot he may be, was not stupid. In fact it seemed ludicrous to believe that Gordon would actually try to thieve their stock.

Oscar waved his stained linen napkin. 'I know, my lad, what you are thinking; however, we have but forty or so stray cows belonging to that brigand and they have been moved well away from suspicious eyes.'

This snippet of information sat poorly with William. Still, if his father was correct and Hamish Gordon could be made an example of, they could perhaps purchase Wangallon. The heir, after all, was under ten years of age and the eldest was beyond the mantle of managing Wangallon. He was a drover of some repute but with little business acumen. 'Very well. Certainly our plantations abroad have done very well this year, Father. The coffee trade is booming. We have, I believe, the necessary funds to purchase Wangallon.'

Oscar sucked at the spoonful of custard before waving a ruffled shirt sleeve for more brandy. Once his glass was filled and the child domestic had been sent from the room to refill the decanter, he tapped the arms of the hardwood chair. 'My boy, I'm not thinking of buying Wangallon.'

William found his spoon suspended midway to his mouth. 'What, but I thought that was what we had decided on.'

Oscar dabbed at the corners of his mouth with his linen napkin. Slowly his pale features slid into a smile. 'I said that I wanted Wangallon. I didn't say I wanted to pay for it.'

'But how then?' William stammered. He was a man of the law and should his father insist on some form of underhand deal, it would make them of no better elk than Hamish Gordon.

'Do you not see, William? Once Hamish Gordon is incarcerated and the law has dealt with him in the appropriate manner, his wife will eventually consider remarrying. Believe me, Claire Gordon is no fool. She is still relatively young and –'

William looked askance. 'You cannot be suggesting me? The woman is positively old.'

'Making you most attractive to her, besides Claire Gordon is most becoming. She is markedly younger than her current husband and youthful in appearance. And, my lad, taking this woman as your wife does not preclude you from the company of younger, more attractive, shall we say, more vigorous women.'

William nodded thoughtfully. He was beginning to understand how his father had managed to amass such a fortune. It had everything to do with tenacity and planning and very little to do with luck.

Midwinter, 1989

Wangallon Station Homestead

Sarah opened the cedar wardrobe in her grandfather's room. She was sure she recalled seeing a chest inside but blankets and plastic-wrapped woollen jumpers filled the bottom portion while suits, tweed jackets and shirts hung above. She pushed her hand between the squishy softness, smelling naphthalene and stale air and the faintest whiff of mice. She would need to set some traps to stop them from nesting among Angus's belongings. Again she pushed her hand in, this time managing to dislodge a storey-high pile of blankets. They tumbled outwards onto the carpeted floor and there, just to the left, was the glimmer of metal. Sarah stacked armfuls of folded articles to one side until finally the dented chest was revealed. She pulled it forward from the recesses of the cupboard. It landed with a dull thud on the bedroom floor, a tarnished padlock rattling with the movement. In the cupboard she found a sturdy metal shoehorn and, wedging the end in the padlock, she twisted the horn back and forth. The old lock snapped easily.

Sarah squatted down in front of the chest. She didn't know exactly what she expected to discover, except that there now seemed to be three issues at stake: Jim's inheritance and Anthony's development plan, which in turn appeared to have raised questions about the Gordons' past. The lid gave a squeak of complaint and then the overhead light illuminated a piece of folded red cloth. A musky scent pervaded the room; a hint of tobacco wafted about her. Sarah lifted the cloth tentatively, wondering whose hand had last reached for the contents and under what circumstances.

There they were. The historic ledgers her grandfather talked about: All the station ledgers since the settlement of Wangallon. Sarah carefully lifted one out. It was cloth-bound, dated 1907. She carefully turned the creamy pages. A tight hand had recorded the minute happenings of station life: dates and stock movements, weather conditions and acquisitions, supplies and sales. There were detailed lists of canvas sacks of flour and potatoes, condensed milk, cod-liver oil and beechams pills, tobacco and wooden pipes, nails, cast iron buckets, bridles and saddles, bolts of material and sewing thread. This was the year of West Wangallon's purchase and the conditions of sale, acreage and purchase price were all noted down. There was also a hand-drawn map of the property on one of the ledgers' pages and a carefully folded copy of the deeds. Searching through the remaining books, Sarah found each one meticulously filled out. This was going to be relatively easy, she decided, selecting the ledger dated 1909, the year Boxer's Plains was purchased. Sarah merely needed to know who Hamish purchased the block from and then she would have a starting point for further investigations. She ran her fingers through the entries and was stunned to find that after late January the rest of the ledger was blank. There was no reference to Boxer's Plains, no details of stock movements, not even acquisition lists of station supplies. She sat with her legs tucked under her, double-checking the ledger contents. The only points of interest were the dates noted for full moons in December and January 1909 and a remark about missing cattle thought to be on Crawford Corner.

'That's just weird.'

At the bottom of the chest were numerous letters tied with ribbon. Sarah flicked through them, discovering that many of them were either to or from Hamish Gordon's solicitor, the firm Shaw-Michaels. She sat back heavily on the floor. The Gordons had been dealing with the same firm for over one hundred years – no wonder Frank Michaels was so involved. With renewed interest she skimmed some of the letters. There were instructions regarding a will belonging to Lorna Sutton of Ridge Gully. Apparently the entire estate was to be left to a woman named Elizabeth. Sarah had never heard of her. There were also wool shipment information and proceeds, bills of sale and purchase orders for supplies including a new dray and a number of horses. But there was no deed for Boxer's Plains. Right at the bottom of the chest was a gold fob watch, a knotted dirty grey handkerchief, which appeared to have dirt in it, and a mourning card. Sarah opened the card and instantly found herself staring into the craggy face of her great-grandfather. The black and white photograph showed him as an older man although his eyes were alert, almost defiant. Beneath the picture was his name and a line from Psalm 27.

'The Lord is my light and my salvation, whom shall I fear.'

The hairs stuck up on the back of Sarah's neck as she turned the card over. On the reverse was a grainy photograph of a woman aged somewhere in her thirties or forties. How bizarre, Sarah thought, she looks a bit like me. Lifting the small photograph with the corner of her fingernail, she peeled it from the cardboard backing. A name was visible: Elizabeth.

'Elizabeth.' Presumably the Elizabeth willed Mrs Sutton's estate, Sarah decided, as she repacked everything in the tin chest except for the fob watch, and shoved the trunk back into the corner of the wardrobe. This wasn't getting her anywhere and with a return trip to Sydney looming, there were other things to concentrate on, like Anthony.

Sarah returned to her empty room. Anthony had not returned during the night and now as dawn clambered over the horizon she looked at the ruby engagement ring on the bedside table. It spoke so much of hope and the future, both Wangallon's and hers, so why couldn't she just put the damn thing on forever and say I do? Dressing warmly in a beige skivvy, matching jumper and jeans, Sarah swept the fob watch from the dresser. She flicked the small latch on the side and the cover sprung open to reveal the watch face. On the inside of the lid were inscribed the initials *HG*. Sarah touched the engraving, shut the lid and found herself looking over her shoulder. Don't be silly, she chided herself as a shiver ran down her spine. She slid the watch and chain into the pocket of her jeans.

She needed to get outside for a few hours before readying to meet the Sydney plane and she needed to see Anthony. If they didn't try to patch things up soon, there would be an awfully large hole to jump. She needed to hold out the olive branch while ensuring the development ceased. No matter what else may have occurred, Frank Michaels was right. Wangallon didn't need any bad press. Not if they went to court. The question was, should they go to court or should she take everyone's advice and just accept the inevitable.

A light fog clung to the waking day. Trees were blurred by the chilly whiteness of the air. Bullet was by Sarah's side immediately, yawning, stretching and rubbing his head against her calf muscle. 'Where's Ferret?' Bullet flicked his head towards the tank stand. Ferret was begrudgingly dragging himself upwards. 'Come on then.' Sarah tapped the dog's water bowl with a stick, cracking the thin layer of ice on top, then with the two dogs in tow, they walked across ground hard with cold. Sarah listened as the rising wind carried the sounds of sheep crying across the paddocks, calling for their early born lambs. Elsewhere the bellowing of a bull reverberated across the rustle of grasses as the moist scent of the earth mingled with whiffs of herbage: some grown brittle by cold, others gathering in intensity as they awakened to a new day.

The Landcruisers were parked in the machinery shed and Sarah headed there. She thought she'd catch up with the musterers before they dispersed across Boxer's Plains. Maybe see Matt and say hi to Pancake. She was doing her best not to think about Toby. She certainly didn't expect to see Anthony with his head under the bonnet of the mobile work truck when she walked around the corner of the shed.

'We really need to talk,' she said.

He'd not heard her approaching and bashed his head on the hood. 'Bugger it.' He rubbed his head viciously. 'When are you off?'

'Lunchtime.'

'What are you going to do?'

She shrugged her shoulders. Swallowing her pride she walked towards him, wrapped her arms about his body. 'I thought we could talk about it.' He smelled of oil and grease and the reassuring aroma of the man in her life. She kept her arms wrapped around him, willing him to hug her back. His arms hung by his sides. Sarah persevered, nestling her cheek against the raspy cold of his heavy work jacket. You have to give in, she pleaded silently. There has to be a bridging between us. She snuggled closer until her nose pressed hard against his neck. It was then he relented, with the touch of skin against skin. His arms lifted to encircle her and then his mouth touched hers. Sarah wriggled with delight at his touch. His hands pressed firm on her waist, he drew her to him roughly, bent her head almost fiercely and kissed her. She could sense the wanting between them. It hung in the air. They'd been too long apart, too long arguing. They needed to go back to the house and rid themselves of their need. Sarah's fingers plucked at his shirt tail, her forefinger touched flesh . . . and then Anthony was physically removing her hands from his body.

Sarah found herself two steps away from him, cold air encircling her, the burn of embarrassment and disappointment flooding her cheeks. They looked at each other for a long moment, and then Anthony turned away. She stood there feeling stupid, wondering what she should do next. 'Anthony?'

He slammed the bonnet down on the work truck, wiped his hands on a filthy rag.

'Anthony, I need you.'

Leaning through the window on the driver's side, Anthony turned the ignition, listened to the chug of the engine for a good minute and then turned it off. The stench of black exhaust fumes whirled around them in the increasing breeze. When he finally turned to look at her, there was something missing from his eyes.

'You only need me when it suits you.' He walked past her, got into one of the cruisers, reversed out of the shed and drove away.

Sarah waited until the last moment, sure he would stop the vehicle and come back to her. A billow of dust shadowed his departure. Moments later Bullet was licking her fingers.

Toby Williams walked his horse around the corner of the shed. 'Morning. Wondering if Ant got the old truck going? We need the welder on the back.'

Sarah wiped her cheeks with the back of her hand. 'Yep, sounds like it's going.'

He hesitated. 'Are you okay?' He fiddled with his bridle, made a show of scratching his mare between the ears.

'Fine.'

He nodded in the direction Anthony had left. 'You know what they call 'em in Wangallon Town? The jackeroo.'

'Oh.'

'I've still got a half-share in my place: a million wild acres in the territory. There's no chip on my shoulder. Hey Pancake,' he shouted. 'The truck's a goer. I'll leave it with you.'

'No worries,' Pancake yelled from somewhere behind the shed.

He rode across to her. 'Do you remember what I said to you last night?'

'Yes.'

Toby tipped his hat, gave her a look that would stop a woman at a thousand paces and rode away.

Great, Sarah thought. Just as well he was going out on the stock route. He cantered off, leaving Sarah to wonder how much of the scene between her and Anthony he'd witnessed. She figured their lovers' tiff would make good campfire talk on the route tonight, except that it was a great deal more than a tiff.

'Come on fellas.' Bullet jumped into the back of the cruiser and Sarah lifted Ferret up to join him. 'Time for a drive.'

At the sheltered clearing waking birds tweeted, fluffed and preened themselves against a background of leaves rustling in the wind. Sarah opened the latch on the wooden gate and Bullet brushed past her legs into the cemetery, bush quails fluttering upwards in fright at their sudden disturbance. The clearing, silvery with the remnants of the frost, appeared to shiver with morning energy. Sarah stared at the headstones. The ageing monuments appeared to guard each other. There was a sense of sadness here, it was true; however, more often it was hope that seemed to hover in this special place. Above her, through the canopy of trees the sky brightened with the rising of the sun. They were all here. All of those who had come before her: three generations of Gordons both known and unknown to her. Overhead, a flutter of wings accompanied the mournful call of an owl. The frogmouth left the tall gum tree to soar above her, its wings increasing in beat until the owl swooped, gliding through the tightly packed leaves that wept the scent of eucalyptus. It landed lightly, its claws grappling the headstone of her great-grandfather Hamish Gordon.

She studied the stonemason's handiwork, the height and depth of the H and G. There was no date of death noted on the gravestone, only a date of birth with a hyphen beside it, as if he was destined for immortality. Sarah squatted amid the grasses. There were too many issues in her head; too many problems that needed to be sorted and then addressed in order of importance. Her thoughts returned to Anthony. She loved Anthony yet he'd been unsupportive and inconsiderate and seemed now to be beyond discussing anything with her. She needed someone who would live with, care for and work beside her; not a man who became emotionally challenged and stubborn when his management was questioned. She was the Gordon after all. Anthony needed to understand and respect that. If he couldn't there was no future for them as a couple. Sarah twisted off a blade of grass and chewed on the pale green sweetness of it. Maybe he wasn't meant to be a part of her future. Maybe he had come into her life for a reason and now the time had come for him to leave. She wasn't the grief-stricken teenager or the ignored daughter anymore. She had grown up, was learning to live without the solid presence of her grandfather, had let go of her unstable mother and was capable and prepared to lead Wangallon into the future.

Sarah blew on her chilled fingers. There was little point compartmentalising everything; only one issue could be addressed at a time and the most pressing was the threat that Jim Macken posed. What was she to do? Sell part of Wangallon or fight to retain it all? Her hand reached automatically into the depths of her pocket to touch the ancient fob watch. 'What would you do Great-grandfather?' But of course there had only ever been one answer. It came before love and joy and companionship, for without it none of the former could exist. She loved Wangallon more than anything else in the world and she would fight to not only retain it, but control it – her forefathers wouldn't expect anything less. She was the custodian of Wangallon now. The choice was clear. Sarah whistled to Bullet and he ran through the frosty grasses like a canine movie star from a dog food commercial.

'Cute.'

Bullet gave a showman's yawn, stretching out his front legs. Together they walked back to the cruiser where Ferret was waiting. Once behind the wheel, Sarah gritted her teeth and accelerated – it was time to return to Sydney. She would call Frank before her departure and let him know of her decision.

Midwinter, 1989

Castlereagh Street, Sydney

Frank placed the telephone down on his desk and looked at the large oil painting covering the wall safe. It was a particularly good work by an early Australian artist and was similar in style to Frederick McCubbin, in that the work showed a softer, more lyrical style. It was a gift to his grandfather for services rendered on behalf of Hamish Gordon with regards to one Lorna Sutton, Sarah's great-grandfather's first wife's mother. The painting was a river scene, all blue-greens, stately trees and tranquillity. Such an illusion, Frank decided, as he pushed the intercom button. 'Rhonda, can you call and confirm the meeting with Tony Woodbridge and his client, Jim Macken, for eight-thirty in the morning?'

Instead of Rhonda's efficient voice travelling back to him, she was standing in person in his office within moments, the door closed firmly behind her. The problem with sixty-year-old immaculately groomed personal assistants that had been with an employer for over thirty years, Frank mused, was that one invariably slept with them.

'Sarah Gordon is prepared to fight?' she asked rather too enthusiastically, twisting the long strand of opera-length pearls that had been his gift to her last Christmas.

'Yes, unfortunately,' he said dourly, momentarily regretting their pillow talk, although he knew she would take everything to the grave. 'It is to be expected. Genetics will out.' He was glad to be retiring at the end of the year. 'Clear my appointments in the morning will you, until eleven. I think I'm going to need some time.'

'And her chances?' Rhonda asked.

'She will lose.' Frank looked once again at the magnificent oil as Rhonda discreetly left the room. In a yellowing folio within the safe hidden behind the painting lay Luke Gordon's hastily written letter from 1909. One needed to have the eyesight of a ten-year-old to read most of the scribble, however Frank's own grandfather had managed to decipher most of the missive and it didn't make for pleasant reading. Frank poured himself a whisky from the decanter in his cabinet and took a restorative sip. He would be the last Michaels to work here at what was once his family's business. His son, a sixth-generation Michaels, was a surgeon and his daughters had married and were living abroad.

Still, one only had their reputation in life and although his family was to soon cease association with the firm, damage was still possible to his family's name and the company. The safe needed to be cleared out.

Removing the picture, Frank sat it carefully on the floor. The work was redolent of the mythology of the Australian way of life, an artistic style that surfaced in Australia in the late 1880s leading up to Federation in 1901. The painting spoke of a life bound to the pioneer, pastoralist and explorer, all of which were displayed almost heroically on canvas. Frank turned the dial four times until a click sounded.

The safe door popped open. Reaching inside he removed the Gordon family Bible. Inside the tooled leather cover was Luke's letter. It was an incredible slice of history. An account of how business was done by driven, determined men at the turn of the century. In a leather folio beneath the Bible were the directives given by his grandfather on behalf of the Gordons. It amounted to being an accessory to . . . He wasn't even going to think the word; besides, every man eventually got his dues.

Taking another sip of whisky, Frank placed the Bible on his desk and, removing a single document for safekeeping, tipped the remaining ones into his wastepaper bin and lit the pile. 'Must be my convict blood,' he muttered grimly. He was sorry for Sarah, he guessed she had a right to know the truth, and he would tell her one day, however there were enough details burning in his wastepaper bin to fill a newspaper for a year and those media types loved a story with blood. What did they say? If it bleeds, it leads. Frank sipped at his whisky as the pile burnt out. That was it. There was no other evidence. Only what he knew and one day he too would be ash.

Midsummer, 1909

Wangallon Station Homestead

Claire sipped at tea diluted with a little sweetened condensed milk. Although only late afternoon, she'd already consumed two discreet glasses of French brandy and managed a plate of boiled eggs. The effect was one of immediate stupefaction, which, considering the morning's events, was a pleasant result. Her brain remained muddled from overtiredness and her limbs sagged with exhaustion, but she would survive. Scrunching an embroidered handkerchief between her fingers, she sent a wish of love to the slip of life so recently departed.

Claire leant her head on the arm of the couch and stared numbly at the piano and her portrait above. There were decisions that needed to be made; clothes to pack, a booking on the Cobb & Co coach and bloodied clothes to burn. Instead her mind reflected on the still clearing at the bend in the creek. Amid the drift of shadows and sunlight, a row of stone slabs marked the sleeping places of Rose's children and her own. You will have to walk away from that place, she admonished, no good can come of remembrance. A dull ache eased its way back into her heart.

When Mrs Stackland announced Wetherly, Claire was dozing. She rose unsteadily from the couch, brushing at the creases in her brown skirt, dismissing her light-headedness and assuring the housekeeper of her wellbeing. Claire wished to see Wetherly. With all that had recently transpired, she desperately required a distraction and although she barely knew the man he was most definitely that. Ensuring her balance was equal to the task of walking, Claire straightened her shoulders and tucked the wisps of hair mussed by her sleeping. She patted at her cheeks in the hope of restoring a brief glow. He'd stood in this very room with the type of intention aflame in his eyes that made women swoon. Swooning wasn't in Claire's nature although nor was she immune to such blatant signs of manly interest.

Despite her tiredness, the late afternoon captivated Claire. Light streamed through the bougainvillea hedge, its rays sweeping across the drowsy garden showering butterflies, birds and two mischievous rabbits with light. She walked directly towards Wetherly, sitting quickly in one of the wicker chairs, not quite trusting her strength.

'Good afternoon, Mrs Gordon. I trust I find you in good health.'

Claire noticed his usually immaculate attire was dusty. His shirt tail was untucked beneath his waistcoat and his eyes were shadowed with tiredness. Were it not for the fact that he only resided some half mile from the homestead proper, she would have believed he'd been travelling for some days. 'Mr Wetherly, you look quite out of sorts.'

'While you are as fresh as dew.'

Claire's cheeks coloured with the compliment despite knowing she must look ghastly.

'I was hoping to find Mr Gordon. I was left a note last night and it appears he wishes me to take charge of the cattle for the route. However I've no experience in that regard.'

What of Luke, Claire wondered. 'Mr Wetherly, if my husband trusts you to attend to this task, then clearly that is his preference.' She gestured for him to sit but he placed his hat on the wicker table, clearly distracted.

'If you could tell me where he is I would talk to him about the matter.'

'I'm sorry, Mr Wetherly –'

'Do you know where he is or not, Claire?'

Claire took a breath in anger. 'I'll ask you not to address me in that tone.'

Wetherly hesitated, took a couple of steps towards her and then smiled. 'I apologise. It is important I speak to him and I would be grateful if you could tell me where he is.'

Claire felt her body begin to ebb with tiredness, she began to feel ill. 'I cannot help you, Mr Wetherly.'

'Jacob,' he corrected her. 'Call me Jacob.' Kneeling, he took her hand. 'If we are alone . . .' His thumb circled her palm. 'I find I cannot remain in my current position.'

He was so close, flecks of dust were obvious in his moustache. He grasped her hand more firmly. 'I have already made a fool of myself in affairs of the heart. I cannot do it again.'

Claire pulled her hand free. 'Excuse me?'

'Oh I know I should not ask such a thing. It's just after our talk in the garden the other night, I felt, I thought, that you were unhappy. Am I wrong?'

Claire gave a little shake of her head. Horribly, a gasp of sadness escaped her.

He took her hand again, squeezed her fingers. 'Then in your drawing room there was this utter moment of complete surrender between us.' He paused. 'Am I wrong in my imagining?'

'I think you have mistaken...'

'It is strange is it not? We've only been alone three times and yet when I saw you at the picnic with that dreadful Mrs Webb and her poorly conceived daughters –'

Once again Claire freed herself of his grasp, 'You mustn't say such things.'

He leant towards her slowly, his fingers tracing the fineness of her cheek, slipping to touch her lips. 'If I asked you to follow me, to join me in Sydney, would you leave?' He parted her lips gently and placed his mouth over hers.

Claire pushed at his shoulders, it was a weary attempt. His was a gentle kiss, a slow languorous embrace, then he was breaking from her as slowly as he'd begun.

Claire took a long shuddering breath. 'You should not have done such a thing.'

'There will come a time when I send for you,' he continued on, oblivious to her annoyance.

'You have taken advantage of me Sir,' Claire remonstrated. The eggs and brandy were curdling together nastily in her stomach.

'It will be soon. I have debts to repay and then we shall be together. My older brother has died of consumption – the estate is now mine. I would sail late February if you were willing?'

'England?' Claire could scarcely believe what he was telling her. She leant back in the wicker chair. His hands covered hers possessively. She shook him free.

'Yes. I could make a fine life for us both.' He glanced away in a moment of reflection. 'I have not done as well as my family hoped here in the new world, Claire. I have not always been true in my life course.' He looked at her. 'However I believe I have found it now.'

Claire moved away from him. She felt she could be ill at any moment. 'If I have given you cause to think –'

From his pocket Wetherly took a gold signet ring. 'I have money coming to me soon for services rendered.' The bloodstone centre was set with a horse rampant. He placed it in her palm, folding her fingers over it. 'Here, take this as a keepsake.'

'Wetherly, I can't possibly –'

He wrapped her hands around the ring. 'When King Edward VII granted New South Wales a coat of arms in 1906 I took no interest in it. Now I understand the importance of the motto: *Newly risen how bright thou shinest*. You are my evening star, Claire, and you will guide me home.' He kissed her hand. 'You do not need love initially to be happy. It will grow. Think about what I offer you. I will send word very soon.'

Claire glanced at the ring as Wetherly mounted his horse.

'And you know not where your husband is?'

Claire shook her head, stunned by Wetherly's audacity. He spurred his horse and rode down the gravel path, breaking into a canter.

An osprey-feathered hairpiece entwined with seed pearls sat in the partially packed trunk. Claire ran her finger along the finely stitched length of pearls, recalling her presentation at Government House in Sydney years earlier. Having arrived by carriage fashionably late, Hamish and she were announced to the assembled throng with the maximum of attention. Her black hair, dressed by a maid recommended by Mrs Crawford, contrasted superbly with the pale blue satin of her gown; an effect noticed and remarked upon via a series of polite nods and indiscreet whispering behind ostrich-plumed fans. Their walk to the farther end of the ballroom was the longest and most important promenade of Claire's life.

When the musicians resumed their places and the violinists, pianist and harpist filled the room with their lilting melody, Hamish took her in his arms. He encircled her slight waist, she rested her gloved hand in his and they stepped out in time to the strains of a waltz. There was a blur of magnificent oil paintings and the rich fabrics draping the windows, a rainbow splatter of gowned women and her Hamish, tall and imposing. Light on his feet, with a steady grip that at times caused her toes to barely touch the floor, theirs was a heady evening. They twirled until breathlessness made her plead for rest, then when they retired for supper Hamish's moustachioed lips touched the pale skin of her neck. That night Claire understood what it was to be admired, what it meant to be loved. Four years later Angus was born. Long after supper, with many of the guests retired for the evening, Claire played a little Chopin on the perfectly tuned piano to a select gathering of the wealthy and the titled. It had certainly been the high point of her life.

In retrospect it was a shallow thing to lay claim to in middle age, but perhaps her time in the spotlight would assist her re-entry into Sydney society. Of course Mrs Crawford would undoubtedly prove both loyal and formidable in her support and would assist with recommendations as to household staff and a woman of standing to be her companion.

Claire reread her letter to Mrs Crawford and sealed it. Once she'd begun the correspondence she'd found it a remarkably easy thing to gild her less-than-happy ostracism from Wangallon. Residing in Sydney while her only son attended school at Parramatta was a worthy excuse, one that would have little bearing on her marital conundrum. If it were not for her frequent headaches and her predilection for conversations with herself, Claire would have considered herself to be handling her recent stresses quite well; in fact she was not. After her interview with Wetherly she could barely hold a glass of water for fear of the contents shaking to the floor. She examined the bloodstone ring where it sat near the inkwell and pondered over their few conversations. Claire was certain she'd done nothing to give him any hope of an attachment forming between them. She picked up the ring, slipped it on her finger. Jacob Wetherly offered the sort of escape she'd only dreamt about; a younger man with an English estate.

Claire angrily swiped the letter, inkwell and ring to the floor. Her father once advised that all problems were containable if superior advice could be sought. Well he'd failed to explain that some problems could not be rectified, they could only be endured. Claire clutched at the writing desk. There was a terrible pining within her; it bashed at her insides like a mad woman and wept like a willow dying for love of water. Despite what she knew, despite everything that had occurred, events were beyond her.

Closing the lid on the trunk, Claire secured the leather strapping and sat on it, exhausted. Through her bedroom window the garden was illuminated by moonlight; it silhouetted trees and shrubs, an ageing trellis with trailing beans and two rabbits frolicking under a clear summer night. Claire knelt by the window, resting her arms along the polished cedar of the ledge. A moth was bashing itself repeatedly against the gauze in an effort to reach the kerosene lamp sitting on her desk. She admired the insect's persistence while pitying the fruitlessness of its mission. It was a familiar theme.

Claire thought of her years on the property, of the great wool shipments that had departed the Wangallon woolshed, first by camel train and then by bullock teams. How many baby lambs were born for the clothing of mankind? How many cattle driven south to market? Notwithstanding the hard seasons and loneliness and distance, Wangallon had been her home for a great many years. The property had given her shelter, provided food, clothes and comfort. It was hard to leave her.

Outside the moon shone down the length of the gravel driveway. It was a splendid sight, as if a ribbon of light was waiting to spirit her away to a new life, one without hurt or loneliness. Yet despite what could await her, despite the glorious uncertainty of adventure, Claire couldn't do it. She knew she couldn't walk away and she *refused* to be tossed aside. She was a Gordon and she loved this land as if it were her own. She loved it for one reason only: Wangallon had been founded by her husband and despite her girlish fancies, despite the ruthless heart of this man who controlled her life, Claire would not leave him, could not leave him. She adored him and the love she felt for him was beyond right or wrong, it was beyond her control.

Midwinter, 1989

Castlereagh Street, Sydney

Sarah sat in one of three chocolate-brown armchairs in Frank Michaels' waiting room. Arriving twenty minutes early for the meeting with Jim Macken had done little to quell her nerves and she fought the urge to bite an already ragged thumbnail. Through the wide glass window a glimmer of colour began to spread itself across the city, slowly diffusing the monotone office building street scene from white to a musty grey. It was a rather washed-out morning sky, similar to the exhaustion edging through Sarah after a sleepless night in a strange bed. Every time sleep chanced to claim her, Anthony's face appeared, disintegrating any thought of rest. Sarah replayed yesterday morning repeatedly until she had calculated the length of their brief embrace and Anthony's forceful breaking of it. She felt queasy and her head ached from what Shelley termed a relationship event post-mortem. She rubbed at the fine skin around her eyes and looked again at her watch. It was one thing to be fighting to retain Wangallon, quite another to have to physically leave it to save her.

When Jim Macken and his solicitor finally arrived they all sat quietly at the conference table as Frank offered coffee and his secretary placed a jug of water and four glasses in the centre of the table. There were lined notepads and brand new pencils before each person while Frank had a thick manila folder at his place. Sarah noted with dismay Jim's swollen jaw with its yellow slash of a bruise and a thin line of purple beneath his left eye. The injury appeared recent, as was Anthony's. Tony Woodbridge caught Sarah's eye and smiled.

Within minutes an argument over Jim's overt demand for a share of the contents of Wangallon Homestead caused Sarah to slam her fist on the table in annoyance.

'I thought if we all met in neutral surroundings we may well be able to come to some sort of amicable agreement,' Frank Michaels said. 'Let us agree first off that there will be no claim to the contents of Wangallon Homestead.'

Tony Woodbridge had a poor way of showing his displeasure. He rubbed the dark-haired back of his hand with his stubby nails, the action making a rasping noise, and then ruffled the hair above his ear, a shower of dandruff falling on his charcoal-grey suit. 'My client doesn't need to hear this preamble. We have a legal case here, Mr Michaels.'

'Quite. However, so does Ms Gordon should she decide to contest her grandfather's will.'

'Contest the will?' Jim said, his anger rising. 'She can't do that, can she?' His head swivelled from his solicitor back across the blond expanse of wood to Frank.

Frank continued. 'If Ms Gordon decides to contest there is every possibility that your client may well lose and he would then be required to pay legal costs for both parties.'

'Is that true?' Jim asked his lawyer. His father and their Scottish solicitor, Mr Levi, had never mentioned that any of this could happen.

Tony Woodbridge spoke placatingly. 'Such occasions do occur, however I believe you have a very strong case.'

'A strong case,' Jim repeated. 'In Scotland it sounded like a done deal.' He listened as Frank Michaels listed all the factual reasons that could be presented on Sarah's behalf in a court of law. Apparently Sarah could contest based on the length of time she lived on Wangallon, her management of the property and her family's longstanding attachment.

'Of course no case is clear-cut as I'm sure Mr Woodbridge has explained,' Frank continued more pleasantly. 'Should we end up in court we will use any number of measures to cement our case.'

'Such as?' Mr Woodbridge asked.

Frank took a sip of his black coffee.

Tony read from his own pile of copious notes. 'The use of emotive elements such as, "Sarah's brother dying in her arms on the property, the floods and droughts the family has withstood –"'

'Certainly those areas are of interest and of course nowhere has your client been in sight during these tumultuous times, and' Frank twirled his blue enamel pen in his fingers, 'the fact remains there is some concern as to your client's actual parentage.'

'What?' Jim stuttered.

'Come, come, Frank,' Tony Woodbridge tutted. 'This is meant to be a conciliatory discussion.'

'Well it's all hearsay at this point, however we would require a paternity test,' Frank continued. 'In fact the court would demand it.'

Sarah knew this was part of Frank's plan. It would either delay proceedings or bluff Jim into a reduced settlement. Yet even she thought the test was a little much, after all, everyone accepted Jim as her father's son.

'I don't want my mother dragged into this.' Jim's fist hit the table for emphasis, sloshing coffee from his cup.

Frank nodded. 'I quite understand your protectiveness towards your mother, Jim.'

Tony Woodbridge lay a calming hand on Jim's shoulder. 'Paternity to my mind is not an issue,' he looked furiously at Frank, 'but my client is only too happy to comply. Consider it a necessary evil, Jim, one that will ensure your entitlement.' He looked at Jim. 'I'll contact Mr Levi in Scotland and he can inform your mother that a blood test will be required.'

'You are aware, Jim, that this case could go on for years? That there is the possibility, however slight, that your own family will be subjected to slander.'

Sarah kept her eyes glued on the middle of the wooden table. Frank sure knew how to bait a client.

'Slander?' Jim repeated.

Frank hunched his shoulders. 'It happens.'

Tony Woodbridge scratched the back of his hand, coughed politely as if clearing his throat. 'Let's keep everything above board shall we?'

'Of course,' Frank agreed smoothly, 'we can talk if you drop all claims to the house contents and stock.'

Jim and his solicitor conferred in whispers. Sarah crossed her fingers, strained to hear their words. Finally, Jim nodded.

Tony Woodbridge sat back in his chair. 'My client is in agreement to drop his claim towards the contents of Wangallon Homestead and the livestock. This is a gesture of goodwill on his part for the contents are of a historic nature and therefore valuable. However my client is cognisant of the importance of these material possessions to his half-sister, Sarah. Similarly he renounces any claim to the stock. In return my client requests his inheritance as stipulated by the late Angus Gordon.'

Frank swallowed the urge to tell the pugnacious Woodbridge to go to hell. Currently he felt they had the edge. Sarah, to her credit, remained cool following her initial outburst while Jim appeared decidedly uncomfortable. Such character differences were of major importance when it came to deciding whether court was a viable option. Frank figured Jim only had fifty per cent of the fight in him that his half-sister had. Maybe the Gordon genetics weren't that strong in the boy? Frank poured himself a glass of water and took a slow, calculated sip. 'And if we decide to contest? How does your client feel about that? He would in the short-term no doubt prefer to return to Scotland, albeit empty-handed.'

'You offered a payment plan.' Jim's voice was slow and meek.

Sarah recalled their conversation at Wangallon the night Jim flatly refused her offer and she in return had practically thrown him out of the homestead. It had been a harebrained scheme on her part. The sum needed to pay Jim out was too large. Even a payment plan would require the sale of assets.

Frank intervened. 'Ms Gordon is not in a position to offer this.'

'Why the hell not?' Jim asked.

'Then it would appear we have reached somewhat of a stalemate,' Tony Woodbridge observed. 'If your client has insufficient funds to fulfil the terms of her grandfather's will, then I would ask that thirty per cent of the property known as Wangallon be advertised for sale within two weeks. Mr Macken is entitled to his inheritance and once he is in receipt of the funds he will return to Scotland. There will be no further claims on the estate once Mr Angus Gordon's wishes are fulfilled and my client is prepared to sign documentation to that effect.'

'No,' Sarah said quietly. Her fingers closed around the gold fob watch in her hand.

'Excuse me?' Tony Woodbridge rubbed the back of his hand ferociously.

Sarah looked directly at Jim. 'No, I'm sorry. I cannot accept that a stranger can demand a share of something he has contributed nothing to. If it's proven that you are indeed my half-brother,

Jim, and you're that desperate for money – I assume because you're either incapable or too lazy to earn your own – then I can probably raise a million dollars, although I'm staggered at your lack of pride and stunned by the greed of your entire family.' Sarah paused. 'If, on the other hand, you proceed with this trial I will spend every last dollar I have fighting you and if you lose you will have to pay my court costs as well.' She leant forward in her chair. 'Take more than what I offer today, Jim, and I swear I will despise you for the rest of my life and haunt you after my passing.' Sarah clutched at the fob watch. 'That is my promise.' Sarah stared stonily at Woodbridge and Jim and then sat back in her chair, folding her arms across her chest. She knew the ramifications of the ultimatum she'd delivered.

Jim opened his mouth to speak and then, thinking better of it, sat quietly. Tony Woodbridge scribbled on his legal pad.

Frank shuffled his papers. 'There is the state of Angus Gordon's mental faculties at the time he wrote his will. Having suffered a near death accident only weeks before it could easily be argued that his mental capacity had been somewhat diminished.' Sarah had just edged them closer to a day in court.

'I want the thirty per cent that belongs to me,' Jim said flatly. 'If *our* grandfather was happy enough to leave part of his beloved place to a jackeroo then I'm sure I'm entitled to my share.'

Tony Woodbridge smiled. 'Precedent, I have always relied on such basics.' He smiled at Sarah, cleared his throat. 'If we go to court I would be entitled to bring to light certain facts. A prominent pastoralist you may be, Ms Gordon, however all I need do is establish the doubt in the jury's mind that by contesting your grandfather's will you are not being fair and reasonable in the eyes of the law. To do that I would argue that your attitude could be the result of a history of somewhat dubious activity that has occurred in your family.'

Sarah laughed. 'What? Is this a joke?'

'No joke, I assure you. Some of your property was purchased

through dubious activities. There are links to stock theft, illegal dealings and some rather shadowy speculations regarding an acquisition in the early 1900s. Although probably hard to prove, it makes for interesting discussion.'

'And you were there were you, Mr Woodbridge, in the 1900s?' Sarah asked. If she were a man she would have punched him in the nose.

'Defamation is a serious issue,' Frank countered. 'I doubt your client would have the funds to pursue a second court case.' Frank looked pointedly at Jim.

'If you could let me finish,' Woodbridge complained, 'any information that reflects on the character of Ms Gordon would, I imagine, be quite admissible.'

'You are drawing a fine line,' Frank intervened.

Woodbridge puffed out a breath of air as he collected his papers and shuffled them into a neat stack. 'And your client's offer is not acceptable, despite the passion with which it was delivered. We will have our day in court and we will win.'

Sarah stood, her hands clutching at the fob watch. 'We shall see,' she said icily.

'Oh Frank, what the hell do we do now?' They were back in Frank's office, sipping coffee and feeling glum. 'And what is this crap about dubious activities Woodbridge is talking about?'

'Forget it, Sarah. The man's an arse of the tenth degree. He loves to send a rocket out to a feisty opposition.' Frank looked across at the young woman with the great burden on her shoulders, wondering how it had befallen her generation to right the wrongs committed in the past. 'It would seem we will go to court.'

Sarah thought of the sprawling acreage that had been in her family for generations and mentally mapped out the property. Every single paddock held a story, told of the lives of those that had gone before hers. There was not one part of it that wasn't valuable in terms of productivity. Not one speck of it that wasn't important to the past and future life of Wangallon. Sarah knew she should be considering her only other option, to sell and pay Jim out. 'You do understand, Frank, why I have to pursue this?'

'Think it over.'

'I have.'

'Go home. I'll advise your father that he needs to have a blood test.'

'Unless Jim comes to the party, Frank, we won't be settling out of court.'

Hundreds of kilometres away, people not of Gordon blood were heading out to work to manage the land left in her care. It was not right, Sarah thought flatly. Her grandfather should have known better, should have done better. Everything about his life revolved around the continuation of Wangallon. Why then would he risk everything their family had built over the decades by recognising her father's illegitimate child? It didn't make sense.

'It will take a while for the test results to come through. Jim won't dally. He'll want this finished.' Frank sorted through his file and passed Sarah a business card. 'Your appointment is at 3 pm at the surgery of a specialist GP.' Frank patted Sarah's hand. 'I'm only buying time, Sarah. Everything we discussed today involves a lot of ifs and Woodbridge knows it. Our best bet remains with young Jim deciding not to drag out this business and to negotiate a reduced settlement.' He escorted her from his office through the cream and chocolate furnished reception area with its vases of palm fronds and orange bird of paradise flowers. 'Now go home to Wangallon. And here.' He gave her a parcel wrapped securely in paper and bagged. 'It's the Gordon family Bible.'

'But how?' Sarah looked in the bag and thought of the tin chest. 'Who gave you this?'

'My father.'

'Why?'

Frank pushed the button for the elevator. 'I don't know, Sarah. I wasn't born at the time. All I know is that it's been in the safe in my office for as long as I care to remember.'

'What else do you know, Frank? I know your firm has looked after my family since the time of my great-grandfather. I've seen the documents. What happened on Boxer's Plains?'

The lift door opened.

'Nothing I'm aware of. Now, my dear, you really will have to go. I have another client.' Frank forced a kindly smile as the elevator doors closed and, returning to his desk, closed the manila folder. He'd seen that forceful type of character before, in Angus Gordon: the determined chin, the ruthless streak that made words powerful, the overriding need to protect Wangallon. Frank was not surprised to see Jim Macken visibly flinching at Sarah's words during their meeting. The seeding of a forceful personality was a powerful event to witness.

In the elevator Sarah looked at the business card and thought of Anthony. What could she say to him? Her finger pressed the ground floor button for the third time. Damn it, how did someone so meticulous end up stuffing things up so badly and in the middle of when their livelihoods were at stake? He should be supporting her efforts to save Wangallon, not chasing his own reckless agenda. Sarah stepped out of the chrome and glass swinging door and turned into a strong head wind. What a mixed bag Wangallon's inheritors turned out to be. Anthony inherited a share in the property due to his ability and loyalty and because Angus hoped that one day they would marry; she'd been left a share because she was a direct descendent, and Jim? Sarah shook her head, it was all too simple. She came from a line of men that demanded testicles for succession and Jim had Gordon blood. Sarah walked down the street looking for a restaurant, any restaurant. She needed a drink and a friend.

Midsummer, 1909

Wangallon Town

Lauren spooned the rest of the rabbit stew into her mouth, scraping at the watery juices with a piece of hard bread and her finger. She couldn't recall eating such a feed before, especially one cooked and served by her mother. She lifted the plate, licking at it appreciatively until her tongue grew numb.

'More?' Mrs Grant heaved the cast iron pot from the hearth to sit it on the rickety table. She stuck the ladle into the bubbling contents and stirred the overcooked rabbit. Lauren considered another spoonful but having already consumed two platefuls she glanced guiltily at her young sister and baby brother. They were sitting on the dirt floor, grinding feathery peppercorn leaves between their fingers, smelling the pungent peppery scent before throwing the crushed leaves into the air. They would be sharing one meal tonight.

'You're sure then? You won't be getting a decent feed for a good day I'd imagine.'

Lauren prodded at her belly. 'I'm fit to bursting.'

'Good. Now dab a little of this behind your ears.'

Lauren took the glass bottle of lavender water and did as she was bidden. Then, removing the filthy towel from about her neck that served as a napkin, she stood for inspection.

Mrs Grant pulled her roughly by the shoulders, turning her from left to right. A haze of dust sprinkled the wedge of light shining through the timber walls of the two-roomed hut. Lauren imagined it to be fairy dust and flicked at the shimmering particles with her hand, stirring the air so that her mother let out a tremendous sneeze. The baby immediately began to cry, which set Lauren's young sister whining.

'God's holy trousers, Lauren,' Mrs Grant complained, blowing her nose on the hem of her stained skirt. 'Be quiet the both of you,' she directed at the squealing children, 'or I'll send you to live with your slut of a sister, Susanna.'

Lauren watched with admiration as her mother's raised hand elicited immediate silence.

'Shoes.'

Lauren lifted the olive green skirt seconded from the washing pile and pointed each of her feet in turn. Although patched with mismatched leather, the stitching was barely noticeable. Lauren had spent a brain-numbing hour polishing the leather with bees wax so that her shoes were glossy, and even her repaired gloves were benefiting from the spit and polish her mother had so industriously undertaken.

'And you've food?'

Clearing the dirty dishes, soiled nappies and needle and thread to one end of the table, Lauren opened the small traveller's bag. Inside were two changes of smalls, a new skirt made from the length obtained at the store before Christmas, a white blouse, her hair brush and a loaf of bread wrapped in calico. Her waterbag hung on the packing case chair nearby.

'Good. Now you've remembered everything I've told you, girl.'

Considering her mother's instructions were now scalded in her brain, Lauren longed to say no. 'Yes, Mother. I leave now; that will give me a good two hours of daylight by which time the full moon will be up and I'll be within Wangallon's boundary. I'll find somewhere to camp and not move until daylight. That way I won't lose my way.'

'Good. Follow the tracks, travel slowly and arrive exhausted. That way they'll be compelled to look after you.' Mrs Grant lifted the pot and sat it back on the hearth.

'Yes, Mother.'

'And don't leave once you've decided which one you're having. It will be months before the minister returns. By then we might be ready for a wedding and a christening.'

Lauren grinned.

Mrs Grant sat the lavender water in her daughter's bag and added a bottle of cod liver oil. 'Have you everything, girl?'

'I think so, Mother.'

'Good. Give me a heave with the log then will you.'

Lauren walked outside and pushed at the great length of timber that poked through a hole in the hut's wall. Inside her mother positioned the burning end of it over the fire.

'Then go with my blessing and send word when you're ready for me to join you.' Her mother sat a battered straw hat upon her head and nodded goodbye.

Lauren mussed the hair of her two siblings in a brief farewell and, with her bag and water over her shoulder, traipsed out to the waiting dray and the broken-mouthed horse. A buckboard would have been preferable. Leather seats were more to her liking. Throwing her bag into the tray she hoisted her skirts and climbed aboard. She looked about the dusty street ready to give a practised nod to anyone stickybeaking at her departure. Regretfully there was no one around. Lauren shoved at the hat perched on her head and with a jut of her chin flicked the reins. She'd never had time for the folks of Wangallon Town anyway. The dray trundled out into the middle of the dusty street. Lauren didn't plan on returning or contacting her family again unless her plans went astray. If a lady such as herself had plans to better herself, first she had to extricate herself from those who could only be a continual reminder of her less than impressive past.

Midsummer, 1909

Wangallon Station

Angus wasn't quite sure about running away now he was about to do it. It was hot and sticky and the length of the day's heat made him weary and wishing for bed. Rivulets of sweat tumbled down his back and he wriggled at the hot itch of it, irritated by the closeness of the air. Now he understood why his father always left in the middle of the night, returning either by midmorning or in the cool of the late afternoon. The moon had already risen as he stepped off a log and mounted Wallace. His horse gave a gentle whinny and shook his neck like a frill-necked lizard. Crickets were calling out and, as he walked Wallace out past the stables, Angus looked over his shoulder as the familiar building began to grow distant. He was pleased for the guiding light of the moon and for a land he knew equally well, whether day or night. Yet when he passed the ridge that was the dividing point between the homestead and the creek he reminded himself of why he was leaving and the basis of his plan.

Wangallon Town was his first stop. Once there he figured he could speak to some of the townsfolk about some form of employment. He didn't need much money, just enough to buy a bit of food for he intended to spend his nights under the stars with Wallace. Eventually he hoped his father would recognise that he had some ability as a stockman, even if he was a bit small, and decide not to send him away to boarding school. Besides, why would he want to go to the Kings School? He wasn't going to be a king and he certainly didn't want to meet any boys that were going to be kings.

He picked at the bread in the saddlebag, patted the hunk of hessian-wrapped meat and the bundle of flour. The thought of Mrs Stackland going crook at one of the maids for his thieving made him giggle. Across the moonlit landscape a number of shapes came into focus. Wallace pricked his ears. Angus figured they were some of their Aboriginal stockmen out hunting, however he recalled his father had sent them all mustering a couple of days ago. Intrigued, Angus gave the reins a flick and Wallace broke into a trot.

There was no breeze and his vision was partially obscured by trees that peppered the countryside. Whoever it was galloped away from him and there were at least three men. 'Come on, horse.' Angus pulled his hat down low, leant forward in the saddle and nudged Wallace in the ribs. The horse sped off like a whirlwind. Ill-prepared, Angus let out a yell before twisting the reins about his fingers. Wallace galloped over the ground, the eerie light of the moon-mottled bush merging together in a blur of hot rushing air. Angus found it difficult to keep steady in the saddle. His small body bounced from left to right and he became worried he would lose his grip and fall. He pulled his knees tight against Wallace's flanks and tugged on the reins to the left. Like magic the horse followed his instructions. He leant back on the galloping animal, entwined his fingers through the horse's mane and pulled hard. It wouldn't do any good if he galloped straight past them like one of those new fangled automobiles he'd seen in a catalogue.

'You damn recalcitrant,' he yelled, copying his father. Wallace slowed to a trot.

The moon, having risen to a point above the tree line, illuminated the country in a veil of white as the three riders walked their horses through box and ironbark trees. The horses moved easily through the light-flooded grasses, barely pausing in their strides as the trees grew thicker. A belt of belah indicated they had reached country subject to flooding and soon the traveller's moon shadows were lost among the close-knitted trees as they weaved through and around the woody plants. Hamish rode ahead of Mungo and one other stockman, Harry. He ducked beneath a low branch and caught his face and hat in a mess of sticky web, a large bush spider scrambling away in fright. He wiped the tacky threads on his thigh.

At midnight, with the moon suspended directly overhead, Hamish halted. Boxer, unusually reticent about joining Hamish on this escapade, had passed on his trail suggestions to his son Mungo, and the boy now turned from the agreed route mapped out days ago.

'Are you sure you know where you're going?' Hamish asked with a low growl as their steady pace led them through coolibah and brigalow timbers. One of the horses whinnied. There was the sound of equine teeth mouthing at a bit. Every noise seemed to be magnified by the night's stillness as twigs and leaf litter crunched and the soil became sandier in composition.

Mungo coughed, masking the noise with a cupped hand. Hamish sensed trouble brewing and wondered at Mungo's ability, having been unable to prevent Luke's spearing by the renegade warrior down south. A quiver settled unpleasantly in his stomach and he turned his neck from left to right. They were not the only ones travelling stealthily under guidance of the moon. Having worn the cloak of the hunted, one never forgot the feeling. At a small clearing they waited silently, their carbine rifles loaded and aiming in the direction Mungo pointed.

The noise of the unknown intruder carried through the air for some minutes; the steady clop clop and the crackle of leaf litter growing louder. The horses in the clearing shifted uneasily. Hamish reined in his mount, drew his rifle tightly to his shoulder and touched his finger to the trigger as Mungo held up his forefinger to signal one rider approaching. The moon shone down upon them like an encircling spotlight, making the timber look dark and forbidding as they backed their horses towards the shadows.

A lone figure entered the clearing. Hamish drew his forefinger down on the trigger as Mungo raised his hand. It was Angus.

'Damn it, boy. What are you doing? Do you want to get yourself killed?' Hamish rode forward, intent on chasing the boy away, but Angus was whispering to Mungo and giving practised gestures with his hands.

'What is it?' Hamish drew his horse close.

Mungo held up his hand, pointed to his right, indicated a circling motion. Hamish nodded and doubled back in the direction they'd come, Harry and Angus following. Dismounting, Mungo examined the soft imprints they left in the sand and then very carefully flicked dirt across both their entrance to and exit from the clearing. Any reasonable tracker would easily decipher Mungo's camouflage attempts however the buying of time was a valuable commodity.

'Well?' Hamish was waiting near a large coolibah tree, his rifle in his hands. They were close to the edge of the river where the force of previous floods had eroded the bank to a steep-sided drop. Angus stood to one side, his young eyes wide with anticipation. Harry looked wary.

'Someone track us, Boss,' Harry stated.

'Crawford,' Hamish hissed. He'd not expected the fool of an Englishman to guess at his plan. It was impossible to warn Jasperson.

Mungo disagreed. 'Not whitefellas, Boss. Blackfellas.'

Hamish looked at his son sitting astride Wallace. 'You must leave,' he said in a low voice. 'You were a young fool to follow.'

Mungo shook his head. 'The boy is safer with us. Besides his horse is fast and he knows how to find his way back to the *crick* and help if trouble finds us.'

Hamish considered his options. He wished he had more men. Men like Luke who knew how to move stock and weren't afraid of a fight. Still he did have Jasperson, McKenzie and Boxer across the river, a unique combination of experience, loyalty and cunning. 'Keep an eye out.'

They weaved through the trees, the moon shining down through the canopy, illuminating the tree trunks in a ghostly veil. Occasionally they caught glimpses of the river, its black glassy surface paralleling their path. Hamish said nothing of the stretch of water. Boxer's cautionary reminder of the possibility of more rains up north had eventuated. Rabbits foraging in the quietness scattered as they passed by. Overhead an owl hooted at their approach. Mungo halted. 'Here.' The riverbank sloped gradually, allowing easy access to the water's edge. It was the best place to cross for both man and animal. Mungo frowned. Dismounting, he picked up a small stick and walked quietly down the sandy bank, throwing it into the water. The piece of wood was carried quickly away on the current. Hamish looked at the river and could only guess at the pull of the water under the surface.

The cattle walked slowly across ground made uneven by past flooding. From where Jasperson rode on the wing, there was a clear view of the mob; a couple of hundred head, many of which were cows with half-grown calves. They'd gathered them up from where they wandered beneath the bright night sky as if they were catching butterflies. Jasperson almost considered increasing the numbers they took, though experience taught him otherwise. Once a man got too cocky and diverged one small step away from the original plan, trouble was the only outcome. No, he would stick with Hamish Gordon's plan and his reward would be success.

Already the moon was past its midpoint. Ahead the cattle continued their onward progression. Their current route was exposed with only a light scattering of timber across an open plain. Jasperson would have preferred to walk the cattle through a more wooded area, instead of the clear, open path they followed which was the best option for getting the cattle across the river and into Wangallon before dawn. Besides, time was getting the better of them. Behind him cows were bellowing for straggling calves. They'd dropped twenty cows and small calves three miles back and some of the old girls left in the mob still bellowed to their young, making sure they were close by. Apart from the noise, which could carry for miles on such a still night, they couldn't afford the river crossing being marred by cows looking for their offspring. At least Boxer promised the river would be easy to cross, although when they had ridden across the bridge at Widow's Nest the black had frowned at the moving water and pointed at small bubbles on its surface. Jasperson didn't need to have the brains of Charles Darwin to realise that it had rained up north. The question was, how much?

Across the mob on the right flank Jasperson made out McKenzie's slight form. The boy slipped in and out of his vision, obscured by the hovering dust cloud following the mob. He'd proved capable of taking instruction, in more ways than one, Jasperson smirked, and although he wasn't the most proficient of stockmen, the ability to keep one's mouth shut was invaluable. Jasperson twisted in his saddle, aware of his space being intruded upon. Boxer was beside him.

Jasperson's nose twitched irritably. Having told the old black to hold his position at the rear of the herd and to stop shifting about, here he was, ignoring his commands as if he knew better, sidling up to him like some shadowy spectre come to frighten the moonlight.

Jasperson twitched Boxer's arm with a short wooden crop, the action drawing blood.

'Can you not obey a simple order?'

Boxer snarled, his thick bottom lip dropping to reveal what remained of his teeth. 'Trackers.'

Jasperson lifted in his saddle, looked about the flat grassland. The cattle moved at a steady pace. Boxer pointed to the left into the wind. 'Smell blackfella.'

With the wind in their quarter they had a slight advantage, however there was precious little time. Whoever followed them would come across a trail of dropped cows and calves and immediately know they were out here moonlighting. Their best chance of success was to push the cattle hard towards the river and cross them where they could. Trying to meet up with the Boss was no longer a priority.

'Get them moving, Boxer. Head straight for the river. We will cross where we can.'

Boxer argued. 'No plan stays good once changed.' A lone stockwhip echoed.

'Damn him.' The McKenzie boy's stupidity had just given the trackers their exact location. 'Go.' Boxer galloped towards the tail end of the cattle as the mob broke into a trot.

A film of dust rose into the air. Jasperson's eyes began to water as he kept pace with the mob on the wing. Cows were calling out. Calves caught up in the rushing mob were left disorientated. The cattle reached the trees bordering the river with a crash, their hides pressed close to each other as they snorted and bellowed, foaming at the mouth. Jasperson winced at the chaotic stampede. He pictured the frightened animals as his horse kept pace through the thickening trees. He knew calves would drown, that the stock would break free of their ranks to run along the riverbank instead of crossing it. He had a disaster on his hands, one that could lead to a hanging. He was entering the tree line when something caught his eye, a flash of metal perhaps in the moonlight or a distant light, he couldn't be sure. Without hesitating he dug the heels of his boots into his horse's flanks and followed the rushing cattle through the trees.

High Summer, 1989

Northern Scotland

For the second time in a week Maggie strode towards the ruin, emboldened by the hearty walk and a sense of daring unknown to her for years. It rose above the surrounding countryside to sit proudly upon the summit of the hill, and whispered to her of bloody siege battles in one age and illicit liaisons in another. The wind whipped her hair into her eyes, stinging her with the icy scent of the North Sea as she circumnavigated the tower and approached the cliff face, exhilarated. Below lay a distant inlet and a long low bridge carrying cars across it. Beyond a sleety mist was banked on the rocky shoreline across the water. She turned back towards her own home country, the sea wind biting at her neck. Cottages dotted fields, curling smoke rose prettily from every house and chunks of peaty land were cut away from the hills as if a giant had stooped down to take a bite from a tasty morsel. She walked cautiously towards the ruin, a jumble of rocks making her leapfrog slowly from one uneven surface to another. Another day she would have jumped them. Another time she would have hitched her skirts and stretched her legs across slabs scarred by centuries. Not today. Maggie drew air slivered with cold into her lungs and whistled a sketchy tune as she stepped up onto the narrow threshold of the ruin.

She ducked her head through the opening to smell musty earth and unused space. It was dark inside. A small crack in the wall let in a line of light that crept across the dirt floor to trace the stone on the opposite side. Maggie stretched her arms wide to touch either side of the ancient doorway. It was a jump down, aye, she remembered that, for at the time excitement consumed her and she was too distracted to consider the gap between daylight and darkness. Her hands ran along the rocky walls seeking support. Gingerly lowering her body she sat squarely on the entry stones, her feet solid on the ground below. She stood unsteadily as if the light had taken her balance and with it the years between then and now. She was a girl again, her body lithe, her feet supple and her need great.

They met for the third time at the ceilidhs after Ronald's return from Edinburgh. Having enjoyed a string of afternoons together before his departure, Maggie was relieved on his return. There were whispers of him simultaneously outing with Catherine Jamieson and Maggie doubted she could entrance Ronald Gordon like the older beauty. Yet there he was walking into the white-washed hall with the other villagers, and there she was walking towards him. They met in the middle of the hall, a crinkled-eyed smile greeting her nervous anticipation. Her words of greeting were lost among a small throng of locals drawn to this strong featured, gregarious man. Having recently seen the Northern Lights, Ronald held the circle gathered about him spellbound. He talked of dazzling shafts of colour, of violets, blues and red, the enchantment in his words eliciting pride from those who'd grown up with this natural phenomenon.

They managed to dance once, then twice. His hands warm against hers, the stories of his home country floating between them like summer cider. And the words he spoke of: bush and mate, grazier and city slicker, cattle and dingoes. It was a world apart and a world Maggie needed. She cuddled up to him, oblivious to the hard stares of Tongue's matrons. Here was a man who was willing to listen, who could save her from the torment of the last few months and a difficult future. It was so grand a dance that she considered her new life in Australia a certainty. For who would not dream of leaving this rock strewn place with its town hierarchy and a population incapable of forgetting one's poor beginnings. Especially now, especially now that she owned her fine pair of running shoes – but at what cost.

So she giggled and pleaded and dreamt the Northern Lights so spectacular from the hill where the ruin was perched that Ronald laughed at her descriptions. Maggie smiled so widely that her lips ached. The ruin, she whispered into his ear, her toes straining as she stood on their tips; the ruin. This was how such things were done. How problems were rectified. He nodded, as a man to a child. He was talking to some of the menfolk. Maggie left him alone to dawdle by the hall. She pulled her cardigan about her summer frock and looked up at the stars. The night squeezed her chest with anticipation. She could be patient, although her mother doubted it, calling her silly and shrewish on occasion. She skirted the hall, kicking at pebbles and dirt, twirling in the fractured light from the hall windows.

Slowly she moved from the shadows. The dance was ending and people were spilling from the hall, some yawning, others laughing and chattering. She did not mean to grow impatient, yet she walked closer to the men haloed by the hall light. Ronald's broad back faced her and Maggie edged around the groups of people standing like cairns, squeezing through them until she was positioned in Ronald's direct line of sight. Finally she caught his eye and waved. He looked at her for a brief second, nodded and then returned to the publican who was demonstrating his fishing technique. It was enough for Maggie. It was a declaration of Ronald's intent.

I'll meet you there, she whispered to herself. And so she left, running along the main street partnered by her moon shadow, her heart skipping breathlessly as her legs carried her to the path that led to the ruin. Onwards and up she half-ran and half-clambered. She knew it were better if they went separately and thought little of her lonely race until she reached the hilltop and spied the dark silhouette of the place once inhabited by Vikings. Breathless, she clambered over the rocks strewn before the dark gaping entrance. Maggie huddled against the rock wall, deciding it better to wait outside where she could be seen than venturing into the dark of the ruin. She hoped Ronald would find his way quickly, for the dark abyss of the cliff scared her and her bare legs were freezing. She glanced back towards the path that lead to Tongue, her excitement diminishing as the minutes drew on. Then finally she saw him appearing over the rise of the hill.

Maggie sat back on the stone ledge. Remembering the past was always messy. One had a habit of sifting the good bits out so that the bad floated away with time. Here in the ruin she had laid with Ronald Gordon nearly three decades ago and to this day the seeping cold of the earth against her bare buttocks, his wet kisses and a howling wind that encircled the stone walls about them were the three things she recalled. It was hardly romantic. The rest of the night dropped away from her as surely as she'd stepped into the abyss beyond the cliff, for Ronald told her he was leaving Scotland and although she pleaded until not a shred of pride was left within her, he was to go alone. Maggie could not blame Ronald. Not then or now. He was a man like any other, and he took what she so foolishly offered. And she was the woman who believed irrationally in the strength of her wanting.

Afterwards, having begged him not to leave her, Ronald touched her cheek, wiped a tear from her clammy skin with his thumb. His own skin was tough and calloused and his tenderness left a scratch of concern where his kiss once was. 'You will be a great runner,' he praised her, lifting her clutching fingers free of his arm. 'One Scotland will be proud of.'

She'd not the heart to tell him that her cherished dream would never eventuate; she'd not yet admitted it fully to herself.

He left the ruin at daylight and Maggie followed his receding figure as if he were a hallucination. Ronald Gordon was the embodiment of many a Scot's dream. His forefathers, having left during impoverished times, were now equal to many of the lords of England in their Australian holding. They were an example of what could be done. They were what the Scottish youth in the north country aspired to; for Hamish Gordon had accomplished what seemed impossible, why couldn't another?

Not once did Ronald Gordon look back at her. Not once did Ronald show regret. But she regretted. Maggie sat on a cracked stone slab. Irregular patches of springy turf were interspersed with wind-bared soil. Tiredness was inching its way through her and the thought of the long downhill trek brought tears to her eyes. She thought of the unwanted child borne of her wishing and planning: There was real love there now. She could only hope Jim came home safe and that their lives remained intact. For her mother always believed that one couldn't escape their destiny. And that was what Maggie was most afraid of.

Midwinter, 1989

Elizabeth Street, Sydney

Sarah strode purposefully along Elizabeth Street. The rising wind whipped her auburn hair into her eyes and mouth and she plucked at the fine strands, blinking at the midday chill. She tasted the grit of smog, listening to the deafening hum of cars, trucks, people and horns as she sidestepped rolling soft-drink cans, paper, people and a small white dog. Instantly she thought of Bullet, of her horse Tess, of the birds, the space, the air. Here Sarah only sublet the space she walked in and even that was curtailed by the width of the pavement and the press of bodies. The cold shadows of a great city emphasised the towering offices and she wished for quiet and space and unpolluted air. Clutching Frank's parcel to her chest, Sarah walked on until she found a restaurant. She requested a table and then asked to use their telephone. Twenty minutes later Shelley walked into the restaurant.

'Well this is a surprise,' Shelley announced, her excited voice cutting through the air as she walked to the window table where

Sarah sat. She was wearing a blue and white hound's-tooth suit with padded shoulders, a short skirt and a silky white blouse. High-heeled white shoes completed the look. She looked very Princess Di. They hugged briefly.

'Trust you to find this hole in the wall,' Shelley glanced around the small space, 'although I like the clientele.' The restaurant was filling slowly with businessmen dressed in regulation black and charcoal grey suits. Shelley smiled brightly, enticing a couple of admiring glances. Giggling, she patted her carefully coiffed blonde hair and straightened her back. 'Boring lot. Anyway, what are you doing down here?' Sarah was gazing out the window. 'What? Something dreadful has happened, hasn't it? You look exhausted and sad.'

Sarah ordered two glasses of red wine from the disinterested waitress.

'Anyone would think we were in Europe with that attitude,' Shelley scowled as the girl sauntered away.

'Annoyed, pissed off, furious is how I am,' Sarah admitted after taking two sips of the wine. It was hot and peppery. What she really needed was a glass of water. 'Think about the very worst thing that could happen to me.' She swirled the wine in the glass and gestured to the waitress.

Shelley grimaced at the taste of her own wine and put her glass down. 'Oh, not Anthony. Don't tell me you two have had a shocking argument over that bloody property. Sarah, I've told you in the past if you want to keep him you have to defer to him just a little. Men like that.'

'Defer to him? Defer to him?'

Shelley looked over her shoulder, now they *were* getting attention, the unwanted sort. 'Shh. He adores you.'

'Waitress,' Sarah called loudly. The girl approached warily. 'This wine is undrinkable.'

The girl flattened her lips and placed a thin bony hand on her hip.

Shelley's eyes widened in surprise at Sarah's tone. 'Umm, maybe you could get us two glasses of chardonnay,' she asked politely. 'Something really chilled, and two of the fettuccine and chicken.' She glanced at Sarah for confirmation and received a dull-eyed stare in return. The waitress smiled tightly, wrote down their order and left. 'You better tell me what's going on.'

'Jim Macken has arrived in Australia. He wants his thirty per cent of Wangallon.'

Shelley found herself lifting the barely drinkable wine and taking a big gulp. Sarah's eyes were wide as organ stops, her usually tanned face devoid of colour except for two bright spots on her cheeks.

'The bastard thinks I'll just bow down and take it up the proverbial.'

Shelley spluttered. 'Excuse me?'

'Well he's got another thing coming.' Sarah's voice dropped.

The chardonnay arrived. 'Bring the bottle,' Shelley stated with an urgent nod to the waitress.

'He thinks he'll get it too. You should have seen that solicitor of his insinuating that Wangallon was built on dubious activities. For god's sake, everyone stole a few head of stock back in the 1800s. He's got another thing coming too.' Sarah met Shelley's concerned stare. 'We'll be going to court.'

'Geez, to court, Sarah? You're not going to contest your grandfather's will?'

Sarah took a sip of wine. The action calmed her.

'You're going to contest Angus Gordon's will.' Shelley could barely believe what she was hearing. Angus's word had always been law in the Gordon family. 'You can't do that.'

Sarah's eyes hardened.

'Hey, I'm on your side. Remember? What does Anthony say?'

'You don't want to know.'

'So he's against it?'

'Anthony has his own problems at the moment. I'm his and he's mine.' Sarah drained her wine glass as the fettuccine arrived. She stabbed at the steaming bowl with her fork, chewed three mouthfuls in quick succession and then pushed the bowl to one side.

'Talk to Anthony. He's always supported you in the past.'

Sarah laughed and poured more wine for the both of them. 'Not anymore. Those days are over.'

Shelley shook her head. 'Sarah, you two love each other. Surely you can work together on this. Isn't your relationship worth it?'

Sarah's love for Anthony was absolute, however a relationship fractured by deceit was difficult to repair. Yesterday morning was proof of that. 'Quite frankly, Shelley, I don't know if it is.'

'Sarah, Anthony and Wangallon are your life.'

Sarah thought about Wangallon: the expanse of sky that so totally engulfed the land, day and night; the sweet, unpolluted breath of the aged trees that stood sentinel along waterways; and the rich soil with its wavering vegetation that billowed across the great landscape like waves on the ocean. That was love, pure and unconditional. It was the type of love she once had for Anthony. Now only Wangallon remained constant.

'What are you going to do?' Shelley dabbed at the cream sauce on her bottom lip.

Outside the window the street looked cold and bleak. 'There has to be a test to confirm Jim's parentage and then we will go to court.'

'Confirm his parentage?' This was like listening to something out of *The Bold and the Beautiful*.

'It's a pretty standard thing in cases like this.'

Shelley took Sarah's hand, pulling her attention from the window back to reality. 'And what if you lose? Sarah, what if you lose part of Wangallon and Anthony. What then?'

Sarah shook her off. 'I can't think about that. I have to go to court and I have to win.'

'What about your father?' Shelley persevered. 'Surely he has some suggestions.'

'Yes, but not what I want to hear. And . . . Mum's dead. Can you believe it? On top of everything else.' She folded her hands in her lap.

'Oh I'm sorry, Sarah. Can I do anything?' Like grieve on your behalf, Shelley offered silently. She knew there was no love lost between mother and daughter yet surely there was some remaining bond left that warranted at least regret. Maybe not, Shelley decided. Sarah's violet eyes were unblinking, except that she was looking a bit like a rabbit caught in a vehicle's headlights.

She shook her head. 'Dad thinks it's best for Jim to get his share so everyone can get on with their lives.'

Shelley was beginning to think the same. 'Go home, talk to Anthony. Whatever has happened between you two, you know he loves you. Anthony has always been there for you, Sarah. He's always been at Wangallon. You can't tell me you would want to live out the back of Woop Woop without him by your side.'

Sarah drained her wine glass. 'You understand that I have to do this. I can't let some upstart from the other side of the world take any part of Wangallon. My family created Wangallon. They toiled for her, built her,' she swallowed, 'and some died for her.'

Shelley thought immediately of Cameron. 'You mean died on the property,' she corrected. 'What's that?'

Sarah opened the palm of her hand. 'My great-grandfather's fob watch.' She clutched at it. 'I'm the custodian of Wangallon. It's up to me if no one else wants to help fight to protect her. I can't help it, Shelley. I feel responsible.' She looked at the watch. 'I feel driven.'

Shelley pulled out her wallet to pay for lunch. 'Just be careful you don't lose anything precious along the way, Sarah. Be careful you don't lose yourself.' Sarah was staring out the window again. Shelley put fifty dollars on the table and sighed. She knew people eventually needed to grow up and accept their responsibilities, however surely Anthony and Ronald wouldn't let Sarah carry this burden alone. She was worried for Sarah and concerned for her future. There was a determined set to her jaw and it was with dismay that she recognised a similarity to Sarah's own grandfather, the tetchy Angus Gordon. 'Promise me you will consider things carefully before making the decision to go to court. Promise me you will talk to Anthony.'

'I have to go. I have to try to get on a flight home and I need to be at the surgery by 3 pm.'

Shelley experienced a sense of foreboding. 'Take care.' Her friend gave her an excuse for a smile. Shelley grabbed her wrist. 'Please call me if I can help.'

Sarah extricated herself and gave Shelley a brief kiss on the check. 'I will.' They both knew she wouldn't.

The chardonnay left a sour aftertaste in Shelley's mouth as Sarah walked out of the restaurant. Her friend hitched her handbag over a shoulder, clutched a brown paper bag to her chest and dipped her head into the wind. Shelley shivered, recalling the old saying about someone walking over your grave. The dictates of Sarah's ancestors were haunting her from their tree-shaded plots and Shelley knew that no matter what anyone advised, Sarah would take the hardest path. She always had. The girl was drawn to Wangallon and was clearly determined to protect it. But then with a history like the Gordons, what did she expect. There was going to be some fallout, Shelley decided as she winked at a dark-haired man near the restaurant door.

Jim waited patiently on the opposite corner of the street near Hyde Park, feeling guilty at his newly acquired skill. His decision to follow Sarah after the meeting with their respective lawyers had been borne of both anger and frustration. There was a fight looming, one he wanted to avoid if possible. He had planned on confronting Sarah without the 'suits' and suggest they try to discuss things amicably, although now he realised how naive he had been and his initial readiness to confront her had been replaced with indecision and tiredness.

Jim watched as Sarah left the restaurant alone, eventually dawdling in front of the David Jones department store window. Her long, glossy hair blew in the wind as she readjusted her handbag, before turning the corner. Jim dashed across the lanes of traffic to follow her, narrowly missing two taxis and a bus. Sarah walked quickly and Jim found himself ducking between pedestrians and apologising for his rudeness as he circumnavigated the crowds at the next set of traffic lights and stepped blindly in front of a lady in a wheelchair. Eventually he found himself in Pitt Street Mall. There was no sign of Sarah.

Jim sat heavily on a wooden bench and listened blankly as two young office workers discussed the death of a friend's parent. The widow was taking it very badly. So badly that sedatives were being used and their girlfriend was moving back home on the advice of their family doctor. Jim pulled a piece of paper from his pocket and unfolded it carefully. Tony Woodbridge had located his birth father's address in Queensland. Ronald Gordon lived on the Gold Coast and his wife, Sue, Sarah's mother, was recently deceased.

'They'll be grieving for months, that lot.' The rather rotund girl commented on Jim's left.

'You're not wrong, Kylie. Once you lose someone close it takes months for people to get over it,' her friend added, 'if they ever do'.

On the flight from Scotland, Jim had wondered what it would

be like to meet his birth father. He'd had visions of a welcoming reunion, of being literally embraced by the man who was his real father. Now he knew the reality was very different. Ronald Gordon had known of Jim's existence for years and he hadn't bothered to make his acquaintance before this. The death of Sarah's mother was unlikely to change Ronald's attitude. The real barrier between them, Jim guessed, wasn't time and absence. It was Wangallon. Sarah was obsessed with the property and she was her father's daughter, and Jim Macken was the unwanted lad from Scotland who could ruin a close family's heritage.

There was a young busker standing only a few feet away from where Jim sat. He was singing along to music from a tape recorder. His voice verged on the ordinary, yet any coin that came his way was greeted with such a wondrous smile that he invariably found the donation doubled. There was a person, Jim decided, who was happy in his own skin. He was making his own way in the world and not taking anything that he hadn't made himself. Jim thought of his Scottish parents and wished he was back home. Next week, he promised himself. Next week, after the tests are back he'd book his return flight home. He wasn't going to stay here with no friends to support him. He was paying his lawyer a fortune so Woodbridge could handle everything in his absence.

Sarah approached the busker and dropped coins in the hat at his feet. The man stopped singing and spoke to her for long minutes. Jim watched as Sarah laughed and then walked away. He followed her once again, trying to rehearse in his mind what he might say. He would like to talk to her one more time, yet somehow the words wouldn't come and instead he found himself thinking of the eerie night he'd spent in Wangallon Homestead with the sprawling paddocks beyond. When Sarah crossed at the lights, Jim didn't follow. He knew that not only did he not belong in her world, he was unwanted. He shoved his hands in his trouser pockets as the early afternoon shoppers and hurrying office workers milled around him. He should never have come to Australia at Robert Macken's urging, he decided. He should have listened to his mother.

Midsummer, 1909

Wangallon Station, adjacent to the Wangallon River

Hamish looked intently from the dark current of the river to the trees on the far bank, willing the cattle to show themselves. Removing a rope from his saddle, he borrowed both Harry's and Angus's and tied all three ropes together, securing one end to a thick-trunked gum.

Mungo shook his head. 'Better stay, Boss, mebbe cattle not cross here.'

'When they cross I want you to return with the cattle,' Hamish ordered. 'Join them up with the droving mob on the far boundary. I've got Wetherly in charge of them until you arrive, then you're in charge, Mungo. You're boss drover.'

'Me, Boss? What about Luke?'

'Luke no longer works here.'

Coiling the length of rope, Hamish walked his horse towards the water. The animal shied and reared up, begrudgingly entering the water under tightened reins and the prick of spurs. The horse found its feet on the sandy bottom and cautiously walked out into the deepening swirl. The water inched up Hamish's thighs and then the bottom of the river slipped away and the water was running over the horse's back. Hamish urged the animal onwards as his mount swam across, whispering to him, coaxing to him to keep going while simultaneously wondering how fast the water was rising. The rope was still feeding out behind them and although the current carried them diagonally, they landed on the far bank without injury. Hamish egged the horse up the sandy slope and tied the rope around a box tree, ensuring his return. The unmistakeable sound of crunching branches and a rushing tearing sound reverberated along the riverbank. His horse's ears twitched nervously. Hamish signalled to Mungo. The cattle were moving too fast. Something had gone wrong.

He managed to gallop his horse along the sandy riverbank just as the first of the cattle hurtled towards the water. The leaders ran directly into the glassy surface, while others slowed on approach. Some were pushed into the river by the weight of those behind; others thought better of the task ahead and turned either left or right to run along the bank. Casualties were immediate. Two carcasses were floating downstream while a third animal lay on its side on the opposite bank, the animal's hind legs kicking at the sand as cattle scrambled over the top. A number of calves were calling out frantically. Hamish caught sight of Boxer and McKenzie as a single rifle shot sounded. He glanced quickly over his shoulder, unsure of the direction it came from, and then headed to where the rope was tied.

The nulla-nulla hit Boxer between the eyes, the impact driving him from his young colt and sending him sprawling in the grass. Hamish watched his old friend fall to disappear behind the moving cattle. Moving quickly to the rope he charged his horse down the bank. Behind him he heard a scuffle and then a yelp. He glimpsed the butt of Jasperson's rifle and saw a white man drop to the ground.

'Go,' Jasperson yelled.

Behind him an Aborigine appeared through the trees. Hamish caught sight of a tall warrior with a skin dragged over his shoulder and spurred his horse down the bank. He entered the water as a spear entered his thigh, the impact shunting him sideways. With the spear dangling from his muscle Hamish overbalanced as his horse was swept from under him. With clenching fingers he held tight to the rope. He glanced over his shoulder. Jasperson was darting through the trees, an Aborigine in pursuit. Then the rope went slack and he sank beneath the surface. Hamish splashed uselessly as the current pushed him towards the last of the cattle crossing the river. His one chance was to grab hold of one of the cows, maybe clamber onto a back or hang onto a tail. His chances were slim. The current was pulling at his damaged leg. He tried to swim and gulped at the muddy tide, felt the water bash at the spear still dangling from his thigh. Then he was pulled under again.

Mungo watched in horror as the Boss went under. He ran along the bank, calling to him uselessly while on the far bank Aborigines were running in the same direction. These men weren't trackers. They were renegades. A rifle shot sounded. Mungo dived into the dirt, spitting grit from his mouth as cattle bellowed and lost calves cried out. McKenzie appeared on the far bank, chasing the blacks for a few scant seconds before turning his attention to a body. He dumped it in the water and returned with another, hiding the evidence of their crime. A final body appeared on the riverbank. It too was dragged unceremoniously into the water. With a stab of painful recognition, Mungo watched as Boxer floated away and for the briefest of seconds he had a terrible suspicion that his father was still alive. Lifting his rifle he cocked it, pointing the barrel across the water directly at McKenzie's stomach. Very slowly he squeezed down on the trigger.

'Mungo?'

'Go get Mister Luke. You tell him –' Mungo lowered his rifle, wondering how long Angus had been standing there. 'Tell Luke,' he hesitated, not willing to bring reality to that which he'd witnessed. 'Tell him there's bad blackfellas loose. Tell him –'

'That my father didn't come out of the river.' Angus remained rooted to the spot.

'Go. Bring him back.' Mungo helped the boy mount up and then ran back to where he'd left his horse. He still had a job to do and Boxer had told him that no matter what happened to stick with the plan.

Thick tree trunks glided by so close that Angus felt the rough tear of bark on skin. He caught sight of leaves, spider webs and low hanging branches. The ground rushed beneath him. There were ant hills, tufts of grass, rabbit holes and logs; a mob of kangaroos was startled into action. His cramping leg muscles spoke of an interminable time in the saddle and the sky now showed a dull pink where once a grey pall had hung. The moon still watched over him although now it hung low in the sky and storm clouds crossed its path. Soon a light rain began to fall.

Angus prayed for guidance, for strength for his horse; winding his fingers tighter about the reins, he lay down on Wallace's neck. Beneath his body the long extension of muscles flexed as Wallace's powerful legs sped them onwards. Wallace's sweat-heightened aroma seeped into his nostrils until Angus began to imagine that he and the animal were one. He muttered a string of indecipherable words into Wallace's ear, urging him onwards. A glimpse of a cloudy moon dipping through the trees cleared his thoughts.

'For my father, for my father,' he repeated. The phrase became his mantra. 'Go, Wallace, go.'

There was a loud gasping sound, then the horse whinnied and slowed.

Angus slid from Wallace's back, his muscles thick with tiredness. 'Maybe we walk a bit.' Wallace heaved against the reins, straining to be let alone. He was foaming at the mouth, his hide a gleam of sweat. 'We have to keep going. We have to.' Angus burst into tears. 'Damn horse.' Wrapping his arms around Wallace's neck he sunk his face into the pungent hair and sobbed. Wallace stood quietly, his head bowed. 'Damn horse'. Angus drifted back to the chaos of the river and his father sinking below the watery surface. He tugged once again at the reins and digging his heels into the dirt began to drag Wallace. The horse followed reluctantly, Angus groaning at his effort. They fought this way through acres of timbered country, disturbing sheep and cattle, frightening emus and scattering birds. Angus couldn't feel his feet anymore. They felt scraped of flesh and moist against the heel and toes of his leather boots.

As the sun rose, Angus led Wallace to the nearest stump and remounted. 'You have to do this, Wallace. I can't walk any further,' he spat bile into the dirt. 'You have to get me home.'

He wrapped the reins about his hands dug his knees in tightly and jabbed the heels of his riding boots in deeply. Wallace answered by rearing upwards. Angus held fast, patting the horse between the ears. 'Please, for my father. For Hamish.'

They galloped through trees so quickly that Angus lost all sense of direction. It was only for the red smudge of the rising sun that he knew his course remained reasonably true. Wallace nevertheless could not be steered and when the horse veered savagely to the right it was all Angus could do to hang on. Specks of saliva flew from Wallace's gaping mouth into his face. His hands were blistered from the leather reins and he was sure the soft inner parts of his thighs were red raw. Yet he gritted through the pain. He needed to find his brother. He needed Luke.

Angus woke as Wallace trotted past the stables, cutting through the orchard to Lee's vegetable garden. He could see trampled plants, heard Lee's voice rising in agitation, then he was slipping from Wallace's sweaty back into Lee's arms. He glanced over the Chinaman's shoulder. 'Thank you, Wallace,' he mouthed. His beautiful horse collapsed to the ground.

Margaret broke off a wedge of damper and added it to the plate of fried salted mutton.

'They won't miss you?' Luke thought it odd. The girl should be at the homestead. Not that he was complaining. Margaret chewed on a piece of stringy meat, a long black hair stuck stubbornly across her cheeks. The girl picked at a piece of meat deep in her mouth. 'No.' Wiping her hand on the bodice of her dress, she walked to the creek's edge. Having only seen her by the light of the campfire and in the glow of the moon, Luke halted midway in his eating as she stripped. She walked slowly into the creek, her moon-shaped buttocks clenching at the coolness of the water, her back ribboning out from the base of her narrow waist as she stretched, then disappeared beneath the surface. She emerged darkly wet. Water clinging to her shape as she dragged her dress on and returned to sit beside him, her long black hair dripping water down her back, her dress patched with wetness. She picked up the tortoiseshell comb and slipped it into her hair. Margaret nibbled on a piece of damper, watched him watching her. Luke understood the naturalness of her actions. She lived in a realm of unchanging behaviour, where the white man only interrupted what to them was utterly unchangeable. Theirs was a world governed and set out by their ancestors, where everything had its place; the stars, moon, wind, rain, animals and plants.

'Tell me about when you were little, Margaret.'

Bringing her knees to her chin, her gaze rested on the far side of the creek. 'We are spirit children.' She wrung her hair out with a series of twists, the brown creek water forming a sodden pool in the sand at her feet. 'My brothers and sisters came from many places, but we choose this tribe, our mother. They welcome us, love us and care for us. We have many mothers and fathers; we are all sisters and brothers.'

'So you were loved by and cared for by everyone.' For Luke this was a wondrous concept.

'We would all play here by the *crick*, sit by our small fires and sing our songs.'

Luke drew a line in the sand with his forefinger. 'You were lucky.'

'And you?' She pointed at him, her brown eyes enticing an answer.

His people were the ones that considered themselves civilised. 'The same.'

'After a short time,' Margaret continued, 'the women teach the girls how to gather food. We collect grass seeds, dig for the plants that live under cover of the ground, and capture scurrying creatures. Then we marry and wait for our own spirit children.' Margaret dropped her eyes.

Luke wanted to stay in the warm cocoon of her company. There was a sense of familiarity with her, a wholeness that transcended the boundary between them. She would have to stay here while he went droving once more, however maybe on his return she could join him. He considered the dangers. They would find themselves the unwelcome recipients of taunts and abuse. It would be a hard life for Margaret. He took her slim hands between his, palmed them between his own.

'They will come looking for me soon,' Margaret whispered.

'Who?' Luke scanned the creek bank in both directions.

Her eyes misted, turned glassy. 'The man I am promised to.' Margaret looked at him meaningfully.

A series of images flickered through Luke's brain. A girl with long dark hair meeting Mungo in the paddock, the same girl promised to an elder, the sullen kitchen maid Martha. 'You're not –' Luke stood abruptly. 'You're Mungo's woman?' The girl's wet hair curled messily over her shoulder. 'Why did you do this? Mungo's my friend.'

'I'm not promised to Mungo,' she almost spat the name, and then sidled nearer to him. 'If I lie down with you, the son of the Boss, then mebbe they let me be. I can cook for you,' she stoked up the campfire with a few branches. 'I'm a good cook.'

'No,' Luke said strongly. He ran his fingers through his hair, remembering Mungo's words by the creek. His friend had decided to leave Wangallon to be with this woman. Had he not told her of his plans? He moved around the campfire, placing the burning timber between them. 'You have to leave. Mungo will be looking for you.'

Margaret scowled. 'Mungo has gone with the fox; the white father.' She spat the words out.

Claire arrived on horseback moments later in a flurry of flying dirt. 'Luke, where have you been?' Angus rode with her. She didn't wait to be assisted down, freeing her feet from the stirrup she dropped to the ground, her long skirts dragging in the sand of the creek bank as she regained her balance. She frowned at Margaret.

'What are you doing here? Get back to the homestead kitchen.'

Margaret winced at the harsh words and looked to Luke.

At her glance, Claire saw a dark hallway, a dark-haired girl entering her husband's bedroom. 'Get out of my sight!' she screamed. 'Don't ever come back to my home, ever.'

Margaret skirted the campfire and took off along the creek, sand spurting out from under her feet.

'Your father is near death, you must go to him, Luke,' Claire gasped.

Luke whistled for Joseph. 'What on earth are you talking about, Claire?'

Angus spoke in a garbled voice. 'At the big river. He went under, Luke,' he gulped. 'I didn't see him come up. They took cattle, Crawford's.'

'Be damned, that man,' Luke grabbed his hat.

Willy appeared out of the bush, breathless and sweaty. 'I know a short cut. Boxer showed me.' He looked from Angus to Luke. It was obvious the boy had been running after Claire and Angus.

Luke rushed to where his saddle sat near the lean-to as Joseph trotted up the creek bank. 'You should take your mother home, Angus.' He tightened the girth strap. The boy looked ill and Claire little better.

'Never,' the boy answered.

'He's ridden half the night,' Claire argued, patting the dappled mare her son rode.

'He's my father,' Angus replied.

'Where's your horse, Willy?' Luke asked. He didn't trust Angus being much good to him. The boy looked done in.

Claire dismounted. 'You can take mine.'

Luke placed his rifle in its holster on the saddle, took his waterbag and stuffed the remains of the half-eaten damper in his saddlebag. He looked about the camp; it was a sorry place seen through her eyes. 'Sorry, Claire.' It only took a moment in her presence to be reminded of his love for her. 'I am sorry,' he hesitated, 'for everything.'

'Go,' she replied gently. 'I will walk back to the homestead. It's not more than three miles. It will do me good.'

Luke hesitated.

'Luke, bring him back to me. Bring my husband home.'

Luke knew then he'd never have won her. 'I will. I promise.'

He left Claire by his campfire, her figure growing smaller as he raced ahead with Willy and Angus. He left her knowing that one dream was ending and a new unexpected life was soon to begin. His half-brother looked beat. His trouser legs were torn in strips and dried blood showed through on his skin. It took some coercing to get the truth of the story from the boy as they cantered across the paddock, but by the time Angus finished explaining, Luke expected the worst. This was a theft of life-altering consequences. Even if his father was cunning enough to pull it off, would he survive? Luke had a feeling that men were dead already and his formidable father one of the casualties.

Midwinter, 1989

Wangallon Station

Picking up his longneck of beer, Anthony grabbed a glass and walked the length of the homestead to the verandah. He sat tiredly in one of the old squatter's chairs, poured himself a beer and took a long refreshing sip. A swirl of pink masked the late afternoon sky. It was going to be another lengthy night with another ripping frost in the morning. Through the gauze, the garden was still as the chill of the late afternoon crept from air and ground to meet midpoint a couple of feet above the earth. Anthony shivered. The logical idea would be to go inside and watch some telly in the warmth. However, these day's his brain resembled a 7-Eleven store – it wouldn't shut down.

It had taken some time to swallow Matt's unwanted advice, but unfortunately the man was right. The stories and events of the past spoke of manipulation and the type of tenacity that was single-minded and results orientated. Anthony witnessed firsthand Angus's obsessive nature regarding Wangallon: The old patriarch's refusal to hand the mantle of succession to his son Ronald, his dislike of Ronald's city-bred wife. However, being personally informed that he'd been specifically selected as a future husband for his granddaughter almost ruined Anthony's fledging relationship with Sarah. The insult of being relegated to stud bull status still rankled. Then Angus tried to bind the family together with his will. Anthony took another sip of his beer and stared at the foam. And now Sarah . . . well Matt was probably right. It wasn't her fault. It was genetic.

Stretching his leg out over the arm of the squatter's chair, Anthony sat his glass on the verandah and drank directly from the beer bottle. He gulped at the yeasty brew, trying to salve more than his thirst. He was lonely and it was a loneliness that spanned weeks. Nothing was the same or as it should be, at least not from his perspective. Every step taken by Sarah to date was akin to her holding a chisel between them. Having tried to meet her halfway by temporarily abandoning the development, he'd been accused of poor financial planning and been spoken to like an employee. Anthony understood Sarah's need to fight Jim, useless though it was, and now her grieving was done it probably was fair that she become more involved in Wangallon's management; however, pulling rank didn't cut it with him.

Anthony didn't want to work in an environment where his management decisions were continually being queried, and they didn't need the likes of Matt Schipp acting as understudy to his role. The question was, could he live with everything the way it was? He loved Wangallon. The property was more than his home, yet he no longer believed living one's life tied to a piece of dirt was all it was cracked up to be. Time changed everything. Sarah's attitude had changed. They were not a team anymore and he doubted his ability to forgive her for recent events. He couldn't help it. He still loved her, probably more than he could ever love anyone. Unfortunately he was beginning to see that it was possible love wasn't enough.

Outside Anthony fed Bullet and Ferret some dog biscuits. Pulling on his heavy jacket he walked down the cement path to the slobbering noise of munching canines. He had a mind to go into town, maybe have a few drinks and a pizza at the Wangallon Town pub. The trouble was that visiting the pub was becoming a dangerous pastime. Anastasia could sniff out a relationship domestic as quickly as any single woman. Last night after closing he hadn't immediately complained when she'd slipped onto his lap and gently prised his mouth apart with her tongue. Although he'd only succumbed for a few minutes, he'd enjoyed it. He felt for his wallet, ran his fingers through his hair and looked back at the old homestead with the outside light glowing and the scent of smoke layering the air from the kitchen Aga. Forget Anastasia, he mumbled. If it went any further the guilt would kill him. It wasn't right. It wasn't the decent thing to do. You needed to finish a relationship before you started another, even if it was just a fling.

The temperature was beginning to drop as he walked towards the worksheds. There was a sneaky southerly gaining momentum. He hadn't seen Matt today. Jack reckoned he had a woman visiting. That was all he needed. A bothersome female disrupting Wangallon's routine. Well he'd give it a week and see how things went. It could just be the excuse he needed to fire the man. Out in the west a layer of pink-tinted cloud travelled in an arrowhead formation to dip at the horizon. Too many hours cooped up during the evening made him maudlin, especially when he was alone. Somehow the house just didn't seem as hospitable when Sarah was away, or perhaps he was just no good at keeping himself company. Better to be outside. His eyes fell on the motorbike. Pulling his gloves from the pocket of his jacket, Anthony kick-started the Yamaha and with a spurt of gravel, headed away from the homestead.

He wasn't really sure where he intended to go. It felt great to be free, to have the icy air needling him awake. Soon the brain deadening effects of the beer subsided and the dirt road consumed his attention. A quick spin, he promised himself, figuring there were a few daylight minutes left. The gate out to the western boundary was open and, worried about boxing stock together, Anthony rode on. The next gate was open as well. He swore under his breath, his cursing increasing in severity when he spotted cow manure on the road. 'That bloody Toby,' Anthony muttered, accelerating as he continued westward. Obviously Matt forgot to double-check the gates. 'Typical,' he said loudly, the wind swallowing his words. 'No doubt he's holed up with his woman.'

With the remnants of the day quickly disappearing, Anthony considered returning to the homestead and swapping his bike for the cruiser. He came to a halt on the road, his legs spread wide for balance. The evening star appeared, and although he was losing the light he wanted to ensure the heifers and bulls were still safe in their respective paddocks. He flicked on the bike's headlight. It wasn't as if he had anyone waiting at home. When he rode off Anthony was unaware his wallet had fallen from his pocket.

Thirty minutes later he reached the Wangallon River and halted at the bridge. A string of twinkling lights filled the sky, merging to become an arc of light. He leant on one leg, the weight of the bike balanced beneath him. Across the wooden span the far side of the river melted into the darkness as a flash of red and white hide disappeared. Anthony rubbed his gloved hands together. 'Got you'. He crossed the bridge, aware of the void beneath, conscious of an emptiness that went beyond the space between wood and water. Despite his brain telling him to return home, Anthony rode on through the thick lignum, entranced by the sight of fossicking wallabies caught in his headlight.

At night the country looked very different. It was easy to lose your direction without a track to follow, for the darkness and depth of the landscape tended to distort distances and objects, yet it was also an enchanting time to be out. Anthony braked and, turning off the ignition, swivelled the handlebars from left to right. The beam cut through the dark of the tree-canopied bush, highlighting rabbits, ant hills and a squealing black sow with four little suckers trotting determinedly behind their mother. To his right he heard the familiar bash of heavy bodies travelling through thick scrub. With this sound his trip was rewarded, for the heavy tread of cattle was unmistakeable. Matt and Jack could return in the morning, re-muster the block and then call on the *expert* Toby Williams to pick up the ones missed. Anthony only hoped the bulls weren't boxed up.

He restarted the motorbike, passing kangaroos curled among the grass, a cow camped on the road and an owl perched on fallen timber. So taken was Anthony with his early evening adventure that on reaching the newly developed cultivation he continued on riding around its edge. The enjoyment of this night meander surprised him, especially out here on Wangallon's distant boundary. He revved the bike and leant forward into the wind. His eyes and nose were running from the coldness, the tops of his ears numb. The ground beneath was doughy with moisture and the bike fishtailed out a couple of times as a line of darkness deeper than the sky rose up in front of him. Anthony felt the change in temperature approaching the tree line. The southerly wind was blocked by the leafy giants and the air grew tranquil and moist. Slowing, he manoeuvred the bike through the timber, cautious of uprooted trees and gaping holes that lay to his left. He could smell the tang of leaves, the earthy heaviness of opened soil and then another scent, the cloying trace of a fox.

His headlight picked out the animal near a hollowed tree trunk. The fox stood with his large front paws grasping the trunk, his eyes focused directly at Anthony. He was a big animal, well fed with a glossy pelt of rusty red. They eyed each other off, each waiting for the other to move first. Anthony revved his bike, the noise reverberating through the trees as the fox crouched in anticipation and then sprung away into a clearing. Anthony followed, catching glimpses of the fox in his headlight as if playing cat and mouse. Each time Anthony accelerated, the fox disappeared, and when he stopped, the cunning animal provided a flash of tail or an inquisitive tilt of his head. 'You little bugger,' Anthony grinned, spinning dirt up behind him as the fox dived for a narrow gap between two trees. 'You win,' he decided as he accelerated out of a sliding turn, only to lose control seconds later.

The bike continued sliding at a rapid pace. Anthony caught sight of an old rusty barbed wire fence and slammed his foot on the ground, trying to find traction. The burn of his thigh muscle as he pushed his boot into the blurring dirt made little difference, and the bike hit the fence at speed, becoming entangled around his ankle, then he was falling, the heat of the bike's exhaust burning into his leg. There was a loud clash of metal hitting wood and then the stunned pain of being smashed into a tree, the bike on top of him.

It was pitch black when Anthony awoke some time later. His gloved hands touched cold, hard metal and he pushed at the object pinning him down, struggling with a haze of memory. Sweat glazed his face. Why was he so cold? Where was he? There was an insistent ache pulsating up his right leg, into his hip, and his chest hurt. He patted at his heavy work jacket, feeling strangely weak. There was a dim patch of light ahead and he focused on the relief of seeing, but nothing substantial materialised. This new world was a pastiche of unknown forms. Twisting his body to be free of the unknown weight, the grab of pain brought understanding. There was a bike pinning him down and the ancient strength of a tree walled behind his back. Anthony's pained clarity forced him to twist his body away from the tree trunk. He squirrelled out from beneath the bike as his useless right leg followed in a squeal of pain.

For a time he lay exhausted in the dirt, his teeth biting his bottom lip as if the movement would take his mind from his leg.

He guessed it was broken in at least one spot. Reaching down to straighten it out a little, he was bombarded with pain. He could stay beneath the tree where at least he was protected from the coming morning's frost or attempt to ride the motorbike home. He crawled painfully to the bike, his nerve endings contorting with pain as his broken leg bumped over uneven ground. If he could strap his leg with a couple of branches and some material he might be able to ride, if he didn't pass out from the pain. Anthony ran his hands over the motorbike's frame, touched the twisted mess that was once handlebars and collapsed, vomiting into the dirt. The few retches in him were matched with pain and a light-headedness. Great, he mumbled through chattering teeth. This was no good, just no good at all. He began crawling in the direction of the fence as his eyes grew accustomed to the dark. The shadowy forms of timber, tufts of grass and trees surrounding him.

Anthony placed one hand after another, dragging himself slowly across the rutted ground. Every movement was agony but he couldn't just lie there and hope someone would come looking. No one knew where he was. Eventually his search for timber became an odyssey to keep moving, an odyssey spurred by a knowing. He was aware of something deep within him that wasn't right. It was a sensation that went beyond the excruciating jabs from his leg or the pounding headache that threatened to stop all movement. He was having problems breathing and there was a terrible weakness sucking at his body. At least the pain drew him on, kept him awake and focused. If he could make it to the edge of the cultivation by morning he could rest. Perhaps he could crawl straight across the new cultivation to the bridge. Small steps, he reminded himself, as his face hit dirt for the hundredth time and he spat dry granules from his mouth. Small steps, he repeated, his mind forming the words yet his mouth too tired to speak them.

The dull thud of kangaroos echoed through the trees. There was a slight swish of air through leaves. He sensed open space and relished this slight victory of distance over pain. He grimaced through the final erratic grasps of his hand, his fingers ready to close around newly tilled soil. Instead he reached for loose dirt and looked directly into the eyes of a fox. The animal was very close to him. He sat as if waiting and showed no signs of moving from Anthony's path when he continued onwards. And continue Anthony did, crawling forward as the animal backed away. Crawling forward in the path of the fox he'd followed so carelessly earlier. Was there a lair ahead, Anthony wondered, some hungry cubs waiting to be fed? He was beginning to expect the worst of the quietly patient carnivore, when the remains of a building rose up from the clearing. He paused breathlessly, his mind scrambling to decipher the unknown structure. His eyes traced the fallen roof and the broken gutters. Most of the house was wrecked. The large verandah was about the only element still intact, although the boards were rumpled like an untidy blanket and saplings grew through the wood like spiky chin hairs. Anthony let out a moan of despair. He had no idea where he was. He was lost.

Giving a weak chuckle at the stupidity of his accident, Anthony burrowed his cheek in the dirt, his breath shallow. He could see the fox from where he lay, sitting on the ruined verandah, his head tilted to one side. There was an ancient hitching post to the left of the animal and wavering trees. The ground grew colder. The increasing chill and accompanying shivering began to surpass the excruciating pain in his leg. He prayed silently, wishing for help, wishing to be found. His breath sent bursts of dirt from the ground near his mouth, the same soil creeping steadily into his nose. Anthony sensed that even with the temperature dropping to zero and a nasty frost looming, exposure wasn't his main concern. He tried to turn over, however the earth rose up like a billowing sheet and he collapsed. There was something seriously wrong and although he could only guess at the extent of his injuries, his eyes pictured a black and white film running to the end of a flickering negative. When the next river of pain struck him, his fingers gripped at the unyielding dirt. 'Sarah,' he whispered weakly. 'Come home'.

Midsummer, 1909

Wangallon Station, eastern boundary

Lauren woke late, a thin line of drool forming a wet patch beneath her cheek. A curtain of spindly needlewood leaves obscured her vision and she lifted her legs from where she'd hooked them over the side of the dray, struggling into a sitting position. Her clothes were damp from last night's rain and her lower back argued nastily with the abrupt change in her position. The old nag still tethered to the dray complained briefly by snorting and striking the earth.

'Shhh. You're lucky you've still got a job.' Rubbing away sleep from the corners of her eyes, Lauren dragged the dray free of the obscuring stand of needlewoods. Miles of lightly timbered country spread out in all directions; a flat monotone of space made busy by hopping kangaroos, emus and darting birds. Lauren sniffed at the silence, lifted her skirt and, squatting in the dirt, relieved herself.

Dawn had long disappeared. The sky was a blue haze. There were thin tails of smoke in two directions and a background of grey–blue clouds in another. It was in this direction that she believed the rutted track led. Having followed it till near midnight she figured there were only a couple of hours' travel left before she arrived at the homestead. She walked in a circle, fanning out from the dray in search of the track. Surely she couldn't have strayed so far off course, yet there was no sign of her own tracks let alone the one that hopefully led her to Wangallon. 'Damn rain,' she cursed, spitting onto the ground. Returning to the dray she swigged down a mouthful of water, swished it around her mouth and spat it out before swallowing a good measure of the liquid. Lauren refused to admit she was lost. It wasn't possible. Climbing into the dray, she twitched the reins and headed away from the thin streams of smoke. She was positive Wangallon wasn't in that direction.

Two hours later Lauren stopped to check her bearings. There was a dense tree line to her right and the clouds on the horizon were gone. She sipped at her waterbag, wondering if there was a creek or river nearby, for she wasn't the only one greedy for a drink. Her horse seemed to be getting slower and the wooden seat was bruisingly uncomfortable as the dray bumped across the uneven ground. By noon Lauren admitted she was lost. She stopped under a towering belah tree, certain her horse would drop dead if she didn't rest. Lying flat in the dray, the sun filtered through the leaves onto her face, the heat pricking at her skin. She supposed she would have to wait it out until the late afternoon and then continue onwards.

'God's holy trousers, you'd think someone would live out here.' There had been such grand images in her head: A homestead rising from amid the wilderness like some ancient monument, a fine building, long and low with an impressive garden surrounded by a paling fence. That's what she imagined Wangallon to be like.

After all, everyone knew the Gordons had money and folks like that knew how to carve a home for themselves in the bush. 'Much good it will do me now.' Lauren tipped the waterbag up and moistened her tongue with the few remaining drops. It was turning out to be a real bugger of a day.

It was the soft lowing of cattle that woke her. She'd been dreaming of her mother standing over her, calling her a silly fool as she kicked at her bones polished white by the sun. Lauren licked at her sunburnt lips, barely able to raise any spit. She was going to die. She knew she was going to die. And that would be just her luck. It was fine for her mother to be calling Susanna a slut, but Susanna wasn't the one lost in the scrub. Susanna wasn't the one deserving of a better life. The sound of cattle grew closer. Lauren scrambled into a sitting position, wiping at her tears and licking the moisture from the back of her hand. She concentrated all of her attention on the noises about her. There was wind she could hear, the odd bird, a clicking sound in the tree above her, the laboured breathing of the old nag and there, it was a crack. Rifle fire or stockwhip, she wondered? There was a cloud of dust in the distance. Lauren watched the low hanging pall move steadily onwards. Another whack sounded and this time she knew it was the crack of a rawhide whip. The growing sounds of cattle spread about the countryside. Lauren patted uselessly at her sleep-creased clothes and, spitting in her palms, smoothed her hair. Pinching her cheeks red she tugged at the reins, turned the dray and drove the stumbling nag towards the dust.

'Holy frost, Lauren, what are you doing here?'

Lauren gave her best smile as McKenzie rode to where the black stockman had suggested she wait; like she had anywhere else more pleasant to go to.

Wangallon Station, eastern boundary

'I've had the most terrible time of it,' Lauren sniffed. 'I came out to join you specially and then, then,' she gave a little hiccup, 'I got lost. You wouldn't have a little water to spare?' She asked demurely. She accepted the waterbag and, taking two great gulps, was about to swipe her arm across her face when she stopped and dabbed politely at her chin.

The herd of cattle was about half a mile from them. Lauren covered her nose as the wind changed direction and blew sheets of dirt across them. 'You look like you've been up half the night.' Lauren patted McKenzie on the arm. 'It's good to see you.'

McKenzie scratched his head, the action tilting his wide-brimmed hat. 'I can't take you back to the homestead, Lauren. Mr Gordon's given us a job to do. Besides, we're already two men down, what with Wetherly and Mungo pissing off into the wind. Wetherly never showed and Mungo reckoned he was bringing a cook from the black's camp but he came back empty-handed and then pissed off. Not that I can't handle it.'

Like all this meant anything to her. Lauren batted her eyelids. Wasn't it clear she was in distress?

'You'll have to come with us.'

'What, with that raggedly mob of blacks and a bunch of cows?'

McKenzie pushed his hat back on firmly. 'That *mob* is the best herd of beef this side of the mountains.' He looked at her nag. 'So you can stay here and die or,' he gave a crooked smile, 'you can come with me as my woman. I'll tell the men we're married and they'll see right by you.'

Lauren kicked at a stick lying in the dirt – so much for the big house.

He handed her a tortoiseshell hair comb.

'Oh McKenzie, it's beautiful.'

McKenzie unhooked the horse from the dray, tying the reins to his chestnut mare. 'Got it off Mungo. Said I should give it to Mr Luke and tell 'em that he knew, something like that. Reckoned you'd like it better.'

'Where are we going?'

Hooking his arm under hers, he pulled her up onto his horse. 'Sydney.'

Lauren wrapped her arms tightly about his waist and pressed her cheek to the back of his shirt. 'Ohhh, sounds lovely.' She never had gone much on Luke Gordon.

McKenzie trotted his horse towards the herd, leading the dray behind him. 'There's someone I want you to meet. His name's Jasperson.'

Midsummer, 1909

Wangallon River

Hamish broke off some branches, peering through the dense foliage. He couldn't recall his escape from the river's currents nor how he'd arrived at this hole of bushy camouflage. His hands were ripped and bleeding, suggesting he'd clawed his way into hiding. There was pain throughout his body, shoulders, back, head and leg. With a gasp he leant against a gnarled tree trunk and surveyed his leg. The shaft of the spear was broken neatly about one handspan out from his flesh. In frustration he bashed his head against the tree trunk behind him, cursing Crawford for his artfully arranged, ambush. It was likely his men had been captured, even killed in last night's skirmish. He hoped no one had been recognised for that was the prime method of conviction.

Either way he had to presume the worst. Pulling his pocketknife free of the pouch on his belt, Hamish placed a stick between his teeth and began to slowly prise at the flesh of his thigh. He made two straight cuts, grimacing through the pain, and then grasped the shaft of the spear and pulled it free. Blood gushed from the wound. Spitting the twig free of his mouth, he ripped a length of material from his shirt tail and did his best to tie something of a bandage. Pain radiated through his leg. There was precious little time to salvage his failed plan and there was only one way to do it.

The snapping of twigs halted his ministrations. He pulled back from the noise, his shape merging with the shadowy trees. Hearing the lone whinny, Hamish stuck his head out from amid his bushy cover – the horse was riderless. He staggered over to the rangy brown mare and, coaxing her softly, dragged his body onto the saddle. There was a bloody nulla-nulla, a waterbag and a spray of dried blood patterning down the horse's girth. Hamish drank thirstily and walked the horse along the edge of the riverbank. The signs of the cattle's crossing were obvious. Hamish hoped the herd was well away.

About a mile downstream the river narrowed. Tracks marked where riders had crossed from the other side; two men only. Hamish hoped it was McKenzie and Jasperson. He'd seen his old friend Boxer go down during the fracas so the number made sense. 'Boxer dead.' He rolled the words around on his tongue, tasting its sourness. 'Dead because of a bloody-minded Englishman.' He spat in the dirt, swatting at the flies massing about his bloody wound. He thought of his old friend, envisioned his night black face. Boxer had been with Hamish from the very beginning. Together they'd travelled the breadth of the country they both loved. Boxer advised Hamish when the rains would come, taught him to study the directions the birds flew at sunset if he needed water, showed him where the best waterholes were. More importantly he was a guardian of the old ways, of the customs of his people. His was a great loss.

'The rainbow serpent came from the mother earth,' Hamish said clearly, 'and caused the waterways to form in his wake. Where he rested he made a billabong.' A wind lifted the branches about him. 'I hope you're in that place where the water is still and shady, my old friend.' To Hamish, Boxer was the last of his kind: a full-blood Aborigine with a bond of love for this land that would remain unbroken, even in death.

Hamish directed his horse down the sandy bank. The horse stepped gingerly off the edge and, with his hind legs partially bent, half-slid down the embankment. Hamish held himself steady, leant back in the saddle and relaxed his body so that he matched the horse's gait. In the centre of the river, rivulets of water ran across a sandy bar. These were the type of odds he could work with, he decided. Hamish tied a rope from his waist to his saddle and urged his horse into the water. 'Come on then, lad,' he coaxed, rubbing his neck.

The bottom deepened quickly, the water reached his thighs and then they were climbing up onto the sandy bank. The horse whinnied softly and snorted. They were stranded on an island. Realising that he had little choice but to go onwards, the horse plunged into the water at Hamish's urging. This part of the river was much deeper and the horse struck out to swim to the bank. The current caught at them and once again Hamish felt the push of water, felt the horse being propelled sideways. They were carried one hundred feet downstream into the path of a fallen tree, which stopped their progress with a jolt. Hamish grimaced as his good leg was buffeted, the horse thrashing against the timber. Finally the animal gained his footing and, finding traction on the river floor, scrambled out of the water.

Regardless of his exhaustion and the pain of his useless leg, Hamish gave a grim smile. If Crawford could prove the events that unfolded last night, he could destroy everything. Nonetheless there were two things he had in his favour. One was the involvement of the renegade blacks, especially the fur-coated warrior of last night whom Hamish assumed was the marauding Aborigine Wetherly spoke of, and secondly, Crawford would not be expecting Hamish Gordon to pay him a visit.

It was midafternoon. Through the tree canopy edging Oscar Crawford's homestead, the sun was a blinding orb. Luke hid quietly behind a stand of belah saplings and squinted across the short distance between the line of trees and the paling fence surrounding the homestead. The open space provided little cover. If he was going to make a run for it he had to be prepared. He pulled his carbine closer, running his hand protectively across the metal barrel. Overhead, crows called out soullessly. A black sulky remained parked at the front of the house, and he counted three, perhaps four horses. He ducked back under cover, his rifle grasped to his chest.

A number of hours spent searching the riverbank had yielded no clues as to his father's whereabouts. There were the obvious tracks of where men and cattle crossed the river, but apart from a quantity of manure and trampled undergrowth, there was no sign of any men. A severed rope tied to a tree and two dead beasts, already torn apart by wild pigs, marked what must have been a frenzied crossing. It was only on Willy's insistence that they'd travelled further downstream. Here along the edge of the river they'd found hoof marks. Willy, holding his palm above a boot print in the dirt, nodded once and pointed across the river. He sensed a white's energy and considered it strong. Luke left Willy and Angus on the bank as Joseph and he battled the short swim to the other side.

At the homestead there was movement. Men were mounting their horses. There were blacks among them, trackers, he presumed. The sulky was pulling away, the horse trotting along after the riders. At least he hadn't recognised his father, for Crawford would surely have him bound and parcelled up for the coppers in readiness for his appearance before the magistrate. Luke rubbed his eyes against the glare, pulled the brim of his hat down lower. The thought of his father no longer in charge of Wangallon left him hollow.

'Bloody hell,' he muttered.' The unmistakeable figure of his father was thrown into relief against the white-washed mud brick of Crawford's homestead. He was moving slowly, edging along the side of the building. 'Damn him, what the hell does he think he's doing?' Luke let out a low groan as his father disappeared through a window. Luke blinked twice in disbelief and then, crouching low, began to run towards the homestead.

Closing the window Hamish lifted his rifle, hoping it was dry enough for action. If not he had a nulla-nulla jammed through his belt. If he were accused of the crime, Crawford would ensure he was jailed. Unable to rely on Luke to safeguard Wangallon until Angus came of age left Wangallon at the mercy of any number of prospective buyers, including Crawford. He walked across the polished floorboards, his injured leg was weakening and the blood loss had not lessened. Through the partially opened door he looked down a long hallway to where a black stockman was standing with William Crawford, his father and Wetherly.

'Damn nuisance that magistrate, telling me to leave it in the hands of the police. Time was when a man's word was good enough. By the time they catch up with the mob they'll probably be mixed up with a thousand of Gordon's. Wants proof, he says, before we can charge the likes of Hamish Gordon. Tells me he's in receipt of a letter of complaint from Gordon about that damn water business last year. Warns me, *me*, to ensure my own doings are without tarnish. I've a mind to ride out there myself, confront Gordon and take him into Wangallon Town myself.'

'Mebbe he's dead,' the stockman announced.

'And maybe not,' Oscar yelled. 'Just because you find a man's horse drowned doesn't mean he's dead.'

'He was speared, Father,' William reminded him, 'and not by our men. Some renegade savage had the pleasure.'

Oscar brushed worried fingers through his hair, 'True, true. I should never have got the magistrate involved. Should have handled matters myself,' he mumbled. 'Anyway, at least it's a spear. We can't be held accountable for that.'

'I wonder if I could impose on you for payment,' Wetherly enquired.

'Payment? Yes, of course payment. You had better make yourself scarce, Wetherly. Here.' Crawford shook hands and Wetherly deposited a sum of money in his coat pocket, walked briskly to his horse and galloped off.

'Now, you lads go about your normal business and we'll see what transpires.'

William and the stockman walked out onto the verandah. A few minutes later Hamish heard horses trotting down the dirt path, then the room began to spin. He clutched at his wound, waiting for the dizziness to pass, his rifle sliding to the floor so that the wooden butt struck the boards noisily. In an instant the door was flung wide.

'So you come to us, Gordon.' Oscar looked considerably pleased with himself. 'You're not exactly dressed for a visitation, old man.' He confiscated the rifle. 'Had a bit of a night of it, haven't we? I must say I find it interesting the way you manage your affairs.'

Hamish leant against the doorframe for support. 'You've no need to concern yourself with that.'

Oscar laughed, 'Oh, but I do. Some years ago it was common knowledge you were sleeping with the blacks, under your own roof no less,' Oscar tutted. 'Not really the gentlemanly thing. But now I hear you were speared by one.'

Hamish winced at the pain that crept through him. 'Only because your men couldn't get to me first.'

Oscar coloured. 'That is an unprovable accusation, while the theft of my cattle is easy to verify.'

'You have no proof,' Hamish was beginning to feel feverish, although his clothes were still damp. 'Although I do have proof that my cattle, fifty head or more, have been wandering on your land since well before Christmas,' Hamish lied smoothly. 'I have also informed the relevant authorities about the diversion of the drain.'

'A clever tactic, I'll grant you that, Gordon. It will not help you though. My trackers will have your men rounded up before the police arrive.'

Hamish laughed. 'And my men will tell the constabulary that marauding blacks herded your escaped cattle onto my land. '

Crawford spluttered. 'The thing is, Gordon, your reputation condemns you. Especially now you are wounded and standing here in my house uninvited. I know of your early dealings in Ridge Gully, of the pedigree of your first wife's family.'

Hamish struck out with his hand and, even with his strength failing him, managed to wallop Crawford such a blow that the portly man crashed against the wall. A painting fell to the ground. 'That is the second time in as many months that you have caused offence. There will not be a third, you foppish turd.'

Oscar ran a hand over the livid mark on his cheek. 'I'm betting your dear wife doesn't know of your messy history.'

'We'll have it out now,' Hamish limped after Oscar as he walked to the verandah. 'With my wound we should be evenly matched,' he snarled.

Oscar walked twenty feet away from Hamish and then turned on him. The rifle was loaded and cocked. 'I'll say that you tried to attack me and that I shot in self-defence.'

'You arrogant, trumped-up Englishman. Always thinking yourself better than others with your airs, but if the truth be told you don't know how to fight fair. You never have.'

Crawford lifted the rifle.

Hamish didn't wait for the shot to be fired. He rushed at

Crawford, brandishing the nulla-nulla, immediately the sharp crack of gunfire echoed and Hamish felt hands pushing at him, slamming him into the wall. He looked across to see Luke, thrown backwards by the closeness of the shot, lifeless, his red blood staining the wooden boards.

With an almighty roar Hamish crossed the short distance to a stunned Crawford and, grabbing his pudgy neck, wrapped his hands about his throat. He lifted the Englishman into the air, oblivious to the torture of the added weight on his injured leg. He held on as the man spluttered, dropped the rifle and didn't let go until Crawford's eyes bulged and the stink of a bowel release stenched the air. The man fell to the ground, dead. Hamish stared at the corpse. This was not his first murder, but it was one that could lead to the undoing of his family.

He staggered back to Luke, gently turning him over. The bullet had gone clean through his shoulder. Luke, momentarily stunned into silence, looked up at his father's ragged face. Hamish gave the briefest of smiles before collapsing.

'Father.' Angus ran to his father's side.

'Holy frost, Angus,' Luke growled, leveraging his body up into a sitting position. 'Can't you do one thing you're told?'

The boy ignored him. Hamish was breathing heavily, Crawford was dead. Luke wondered how the hell he was going to get everyone out of here.

'Angus, you got your horse?'

The boy nodded between his tears. He was stroking his father's face. Willy popped his head up from the end of the verandah. 'Mebbe take my horse.'

There was the sound of running feet. Luke reached for his own rifle, pointed the barrel towards the doorway. Willy ducked out of sight. A beak-nosed man and three black faces showed themselves before screaming and running in the opposite direction. Luke sat for some minutes, considering unfeasible options. Flies settled on his wound, and massed also about his father. He pulled himself closer to where Hamish lay. His father's clothes were muddy and torn; there was a bloody wound to his thigh.

'Horses,' Willy yelled. 'Two.'

Luke rested his rifle across his legs. Payback was coming.

'Burn the place.' Hamish's voice cut strongly across his thoughts. Luke watched his father lift a bloody hand to Angus, cup his boy about the neck and draw him close. 'Burn it,' he growled.

'Do it,' Luke agreed. 'Willy, go with Angus. Start a fire. A big one. Stack all the wood you can find in the kitchen and light it up.'

As the men galloped to the homestead gate, Angus picked up Crawford's rifle and ran behind the house with Willy. Luke guessed that the rather flashily dressed white man was none other than Crawford's son. The boy had drawn a pistol and with a black by his side, ducked behind a tree.

Luke cocked his rifle, pointed it in the two men's direction. 'Stop there.'

'Where's my father?' A pronounced English voice called.

Luke looked at Crawford's prone body, then at his father's still heaving chest. 'Dead.' Through the trees to the left of the homestead, black maids were running off into the bush. Luke leant his head against the cool of the mud brick wall. There was no way of getting out of this predicament, it was either fight or see his father jailed for murder. Crawford's son and the black began to walk towards them. Their boots crunched dry dirt. Luke wiped his sweating hand on his moleskin trousers, took hold of the rifle more firmly. His hands were shaking.

Crawford's son scanned the verandah, pointing his pistol at Luke's chest. 'I'll see you hang for this.'

The impact of the shot drove William Crawford backwards. He fell squarely on his arse before falling down dead.

Angus dropped the rifle, a determined look on his face.

'Whitefella business.' The black stockman backed away, holding his hands high in surrender.

Luke let him go. No one would take his word. He turned to stare at his unflinching half-brother.

'Is it done?' Hamish turned his neck to where William Crawford lay.

Luke helped his father into a sitting position. 'Yes, Father, it's done.'

Hamish clutched at Luke's good shoulder. 'Throw the bodies in the fire and then get me over the river, Luke. I need to die on Wangallon.'

Luke checked the wound on his father's leg. The trousers were soaked through with his blood. 'You won't be dying, Father.'

Hamish gave a weak chuckle and placed his hand on his elder son's shoulder. 'This time we both know better.'

Midwinter, 1989

Wangallon Station

Sarah arrived home as a weak sun struggled amid cloud for midday prominence. Her flight had been delayed from Sydney by fog and she was overtired, with a boot load of groceries to unpack. Struggling up the back path with plastic shopping bags twisted around her fingers and Frank Michaels' package squeezed under her arm, she dumped the bags on the kitchen table, her blood supply nearly cut off. The kitchen was freezing, the sink empty except for one plate and two empty longnecks of beer. Sarah held her palm over the black cooktop, the Aga was cold, which was unusual considering they always kept the slow combustion stove lit during winter.

Outside she loaded the wheelbarrow with kindling and split logs from the wood pile at the back gate. Some feet away Bullet sat patiently in the dirt. 'Hey,' Sarah called to him, expecting his usual ferocious excitement. Instead Bullet looked briefly over his shoulder, gave a single bark and rushed a few hundred metres away from her. 'Bullet, come here.' The dog obeyed reluctantly, accepting her petting before dashing off again and then turning towards her. 'Hey, what's up? I'm sorry I've been away.'

Bullet whined. Some feet away Ferret was sunning himself like a Florida retiree. He was lying on his back, his four paws extended in the air, his head lolling to one side. He opened one eye at Sarah's voice and then clambered unsteadily to his feet, the black tubing making his gait stiff and ungainly. Bullet looked at his mate once and then stared straight ahead.

'I get it. Anthony wouldn't let you go with him?' She scruffed him between the ears. 'Well, how about you and I go for a ride later.' Bullet gave a series of barks, walked a few paces away from her and whined. 'Later,' Sarah promised.

With the Aga stoked up and burning well and the groceries unpacked, Sarah made a quick coffee. Spending another evening alone as she'd done last night was a quick fix for her anger, especially when Shelley's lecture on the importance of her relationship with Anthony had eventually, albeit reluctantly, seeped in. Shelley was right, of course; Anthony and she could fight and moan and groan, however they'd supported each other for a long time. The very least she could do was respect their relationship by not remaining angry with him. There wasn't any point; yet clearly neither was trying to bridge their disagreement with affection. 'There must be a way around this.' Draining her coffee mug, Sarah poked another split log into the Aga. There was steak for dinner, tinned mushrooms and frozen French fries: Anthony's favourites. 'One fence at a time,' she decided, opening the paper bag on the table and unwrapping the Bible Frank handed her yesterday. They could start with dinner and then attempt reconciling their differences; she needed him and she couldn't believe Anthony could still be angry with her. After all, there was fault on both sides.

The bible's black leather cover was cracked with age, the pages edged in gold. Sarah flicked through the pages and then read the neat printing on the inside.

Wangallon Station – 1862

A folded piece of paper slipped to the floor.

'Are you there, Sarah?'

Inserting the loose page back inside the Bible, Sarah closed the book and sat it on the kitchen bench.

Matt was being accosted by Ferret, who could now manage a running walk that resembled a three-legged man with a single crutch. Sarah wondered briefly how much the head stockman needed to know about events in Sydney, before deciding to tell him everything as she pulled on her riding boots. 'It'll be a court job,' she finally revealed after a rather abbreviated listing of events. There was little point in not telling him; he was her grandfather's man.

Matt grimaced. 'Sorry to hear it.'

'Well, you know what they say, Matt, it's not over till the fat lady sings.'

'I guess. What do you need me to do?'

They walked companionably to the back gate. 'Nothing. We wait and see how things unfold. Everything going okay?'

'Pretty much. All quiet on the western front,' he said, glibly nodding in the direction of Boxer's Plains. 'Toby's walked the cattle down Marshall's Lane. The feed's pretty good actually.'

'And Anthony?' Sarah asked. Not wanting to rush a showdown, yet knowing it was going to happen sooner rather than later.

'Haven't seen him. Actually there's something I wanted to talk to you about. I was hoping you'd give me a bit of leeway. I've got a friend staying and was wondering if it was all right with you if she moved in. Permanent like,' Matt scratched his head. 'That is, while it lasts. Want to have a look at the steers?'

'Sure.' Sarah lifted Ferret into the back of the tray as Bullet jumped in. She climbed into the Landcruiser beside Matt. 'What's her name?'

'Tania. She was my missus before I came here.'

'True love eh?' Sarah grinned.

Matt cleared his throat, moved through the gears more than necessary. 'Yeah well, at the moment it's working.' He thought of the last two nights. A man could die of exhaustion when it came to Tania's appetites. He'd have to try a bit of restraint otherwise he wouldn't be able to function properly. As it was he'd forgotten to double-check the gates after they shifted the cattle from Boxer's Plains to the route, and only remembered to do the job this morning. Just as well too. They were all open and it looked like some idiot on a motorbike, probably a hoon from town, had been the cause.

The cattle were feeding into the wind; the curve of their bodies above the oats obscuring their heads and legs so that they resembled a herd of Stone Age animals. Ferret barked delightedly, limping from one side of the tray to the other and snapping at the two ramps they crossed. In contrast Bullet sat at the rear when they headed east and on their return he faced the west. Sarah patted him when they stopped at a gate. 'What's the matter, boy?' They were near the woolshed where an avenue of aged peppercorn trees stood sentinel above the long drafting race. Bullet jumped from the back of the Landcruiser and, ducking through the wooden fence, ran across the yards. 'Great,' Sarah muttered as they continued home. 'Something's wrong.' Bullet was running up the road and then veering towards the west.

'He just hasn't been for a run for a while.' Matt inspected the dash of the Landcruiser, digging through a layer of Coopers notebooks, screwdrivers, pens, a carton of bullets and a bag of melted chocolates; the object of his search.

'I don't know. I think I should follow him.' Sarah watched Bullet become a speck in the distance as Matt turned north through the house paddock boundary gate and stopped at the machinery shed.

'The ranger from the PP Board is coming out this afternoon to check on Toby. I said I'd meet him out on the route to discuss numbers. I was hoping to put out another couple of hundred head. You want to meet him?' He offered Sarah a chocolate from the perpetually heater-melted and winter-refrozen selection.

'No thanks, don't want to deprive you.' The chocolate looked like squashed sheep droppings. 'Think I'll leave you to it.' Her decision not to go was based on letting Matt do his job and had nothing to do with Toby Williams.

'Righto. By the way, Tania can garden if you're interested.'

'Sure I'm interested.' Sarah doubted Matt would take any rubbish from a woman and he certainly wouldn't recommend someone if they weren't capable, male or female.

'I'll bring her over next week some time.'

'Sounds good. Well I might go find Bullet before it gets late.'

'You need anything from Wangallon Town? Jack and Tania are going in to get a few things later.'

'No thanks. We're fine.'

Sarah drove out through the house paddock gate with Ferret for company. The local radio station was playing a run of hits. Between Smoky Dawson and Dean Martin she was more than ready to start opening gates, even with the nippy breeze. She scanned the bush, expecting to hear Bullet yapping away at a roo or an emu. A year or so ago he'd often bailed up odd unsuspecting wildlife, however with age came maturity and the novelty of the chase appeared to have worn off. She drove on, stopping to open a third gate. In the dirt in the middle of the road she stooped to pick up a wallet. It appeared to have been run over for it was flattened into the dirt. Sarah recognised it instantly as Anthony's. A fizz of worry spiked through her. Turning off the Landcruiser's ignition, she cupped her hands around her mouth. 'Anthony? Coo-ee?' Her voice echoed hollowly. 'Bullet? Coo-ee?' A distant bark answered. Ferret pricked his ears and barked in reply.

A kilometre further on Sarah found Bullet waiting patiently on a fallen log. The dog jumped in the tray and they drove on, their progress slowed by the opening of gates, and Sarah stopping to call out Anthony's name. She couldn't understand how Anthony's wallet came to be in the middle of the road, or why her stomach was feeling increasingly as if it were lined with stone. At the last gateway there were cattle hoofs, quad bike tracks, relatively recent Landcruiser tracks, which appeared to have circled back towards the homestead and . . . Sarah touched the motorbike track which led through the gateway: Anthony on a motorbike, out this far? It was possible, she supposed. This was the paddock Cameron died in and she gave an involuntary shiver as she thought of Bullet's agitation, the lost wallet and the stone cold aga she'd arrived home to. 'At least I have a track to follow,' she reassured herself as she drove past the ridge, over the river and into Boxer's Plains.

'I should have guessed,' Sarah mumbled as the vehicle bumped out from between the lignum and trees to where the cultivation began. She stopped the vehicle, expecting to hear the rumble of heavy machinery; instead the rustle of leaves and Bullet's low whine were the only audible noises. The cultivation spread out before her like a chocolate slice, bordered by the browns and greens of timber. Along its edge the bike track was obvious in the soft soil. It must be Anthony, Sarah decided, but it didn't seem to be particularly auspicious catching up with him on this part of Wangallon. They needed to meet somewhere neutral. 'The United Nations building perhaps,' she quipped. Yet for all her sarcasm, things still didn't seem quite right.

Bullet let out a long howl, which set Ferret off, and together the dogs made such a cacophony of noise that birds, kangaroos, an emu and five head of cattle bounded from the scrub behind them. Sarah experienced a falling sensation, as if she'd entered a deep hole, and then she heard a faint voice, a voice she knew better than her own. She accelerated in a screech of soil and engine revs to drive madly along the edge of the cultivation. The vehicle bumped over logs, careered around trees, the tyres falling down potholes and tree holes, even becoming airborne at times. She gripped the wheel tighter, oblivious to the shower of articles falling from the dash and Ferret's yelping as she sped over the rough track. She manoeuvred the vehicle through the pushed timber yet to be formed into burnable heaps, and skirted the untouched impenetrable areas. With a desperate yank of the steering wheel Sarah side-swiped the rear-vision mirror off the driver's door as she angled between a belah tree and the upturned roots of a mighty gum.

Even before the mangled bike appeared at the base of the ironbark tree, Sarah knew that some form of payback was being extracted from her family. Something unmentionable had occurred out here many years ago and the spirits of those affected were seeking retribution. Why else had the 1909 diary entries ceased? Why else were people against any development out here? God, even Toby Williams had an opinion on Boxer's Plains. It may only have been a gut feeling on her part, however it was strong.

Sarah slammed her foot on the brake, screeching to a halt as the trees closed in, obstructing any further passage. Anthony's bike lay near an immense tree, a run of rusty wire entangled around the rear tyre. She ran to the bike. Bullet passed her in a flying leap, jumped two logs and ducked through a maze of saplings, leaving Sarah to reconcile the mangled mess of the bike and the drag marks which led further into the dense timber. She ran then, as fast as she could across the uneven ground, noticing that the thickness of the trees began to thin until suddenly there was a wreck of a partially burnt house in front of her and a fox. Bullet was snuffling the animal as if greeting an old friend. Sarah knitted her brows together, then she saw Anthony, sprawled, face down in the dirt.

'Anthony.' She dropped to her knees beside him, noticing that one leg was propped out at an angle. Placing her hand on the middle of his back, she half-expected to see bite marks or worse on Anthony's neck. There was nothing. She turned him over carefully, expecting a groan. Bullet left the fox to join her, whimpering softly. 'Anthony.' His hands were freezing, his face blue. Congealed blood matted his forehead and hair. The worst of it was the thin line of blood and saliva that ran from his mouth on movement. 'Jesus! Anthony, answer me!' Gingerly Sarah put her cheek to his mouth, dreading not hearing a breath or feeling the moistness of warm air. The slightest zephyr grazed her cheek. 'Thank God. Thank God.' Removing her jacket, she placed it over his chest and then wedged her jumper between his head and the cold earth. 'Watch him,' she commanded Bullet, who immediately sat by Anthony's side.

Sarah was back at the Landcruiser within minutes. She spun the vehicle around, reversing over the top of stringy saplings until she was away from the thickest of the trees and driving until she had line of sight to the open cultivation. She lifted the two-way radio to her mouth.

'This is Sarah at Wangallon. Can anyone hear me?'

Silence. She revved the vehicle driving until she hit the expanse of open cultivation and hopefully a better reception. 'This is Sarah at Wangallon. Does anyone copy?'

Static drifted over the airway.

'This is Sarah at Wangallon. Please, can anyone hear me?'

'Yeah gotcha, Wangallon. What's the prob?'

'It's Anthony. There's been an accident. Can you help me?'

'Hey kiddo, it's Toby. Where the hell are you?'

'Boxer's Plains. It's bad, Toby, really bad.' Sarah choked back tears. 'I don't think he'll make it.'

'You hang tight. We're on our way.'

'Anthony, can you hear me?' Sarah lay beside him in the dirt; the cotton seat covers from the Landcruiser tucked around him for extra warmth. His breathing was ragged. Now and then there would be the slightest of movements from him: a twitch of a finger or a slight relaxation of his neck. Sarah wondered what internal injuries he'd sustained for he was still blue despite her best intentions at keeping him warm. A good fire was burning thanks to the matches she'd found on the dash of the Landcruiser and the plethora of leaf litter and branches. A branch of green belah leaves gave off a steady stream of white smoke from it. Each time the smoke lessened Sarah replaced it with another branch, hopeful it would help guide the men to their rescue. She didn't dare risk trying to move Anthony for fear of worsening his condition and neither would she leave him to call on the two-way again. Sarah placed her head on Anthony's shoulder and her arm across his chest. Bullet and Ferret were lying beside them.

Sarah tucked her jacket under Anthony's chin and hugged him closer. Bullet's head was resting on his uninjured thigh; Ferret huddled close to his mate. Although the sun's rays ceased to penetrate the clearing, the spot where she lay with Anthony was warm with love. Sarah could feel it flowing into the man beside her, even as she willed her own life force to help him. They were family. They both belonged on Wangallon.

'Don't take him,' she sobbed quietly, almost expecting a phantom to stride from the nearby ruins. She pictured the stone cold Aga, hating the thought of him lying out here in the cold, alone as he had through the night. Anthony's hand was barely warm, his breath tentative, as if he were deciding whether a continuation of his suffering was worthwhile.

Sarah thought of the years they'd been on the property, of how her life altered from a fretful, unexceptional existence to one of renewed possibility following Anthony's arrival. They'd been such wonderful friends, she, Anthony and Cameron; however, the fates were unstoppable in their intercession and Cameron was taken from her. She squeezed her eyelids closed. The thought of losing Anthony stunned her into action.

'Anthony, wake up.' His forehead was clammy. 'Wake up.' Sarah shook him forcefully by the shoulders. 'Remember our endless rides. Remember how much you love Wangallon.' Her tears splashed onto his cheeks. 'I love you. Can't you wake up so I can tell you how much?' She stroked his hair, touched the slight scar on his cheek. What would she do without him? What would she do if she lost her Anthony?

There was the slightest of noise similar to wind rustled leaves. Sarah leant down towards Anthony's moving lips.

'Sarah.'

She reached for his hand, willing him to life.

'You came back.' His words carried the barest breath of life.

She wrapped her arms around him. 'Of course I came back.'

Anthony coughed. 'We were fighting for the same thing you know. We've been fighting over Wangallon,' he stuttered between clenching teeth. 'You don't understand.'

'What don't I understand?' Sarah rubbed his cold hands.

'That I love Wangallon too.' His eyes closed.

'Come back to me, Anthony.' She took his face between her hands. 'Come back to me.' A dreadful pain shot through her. A pain so soul rendering that no noise escaped her lips. Sarah rocked on her knees, the tears spilling down her face. After everything they'd been through, after everything she'd been brought up to believe in as a Wangallon Gordon, she realised that she could never be sure again that she loved Wangallon more than the man lying in the dirt at her feet.

Bullet and Ferret were barking, the sound of vehicles and people carried through the still air. Toby Williams lifted Sarah effortlessly into his arms.

'You'll be right, girl. We're here now.'

As the clearing grew smaller, Sarah clutched at Toby's arm. Over his shoulder she watched the fox walk the length of the wrecked homestead's verandah before sitting, quietly contemplative. The clearing emptied of people.

Late Summer, 1989

Northern Scotland

'What do you mean the lad's not getting the money?' Robert threw his jacket across the table, scattering the local newspaper and the uncleared luncheon dishes. 'Bloody solicitors. No doubt the Gordons have employed some big time lawyer. A barrister perhaps, or a Queen's Council. That would be right. They start off like us. Oh yes and everyone admires them for what they've achieved.' He stamped his socks on the rug. 'Left the North they say; made a fortune in the new world. Well I tell you they're no better than the bloody English.' He threw his cap on the couch, rubbing his chin vigorously. 'A bit of money and they think they can tell everyone how high to jump. Well, not me,' Robert stabbed at his chest with a rampant thumb, 'no, not me. We'll get ourselves a flashy estate man. We'll join the fray and the cost be damned. By the time I've finished with the likes of Sarah Gordon they'll wish they'd played fair.' Robert glared at his wife, the vein in his neck pulsating like a thick worm.

Maggie busied herself by picking up the machinery catalogues

Robert spent half the morning reviewing, and placed them on the table. She hung up his jacket and cap, folded the newspaper and set about tidying the luncheon dishes.

'How can you be so damn disinterested, Maggie?'

She wiped her hands on her apron. 'He's not entitled to the money. He's had a second opinion from a good man in Sydney and he just won't be getting it.'

Robert scratched his head. 'But how? I don't understand how that could happen? Do you?'

Maggie looked her husband squarely in the eyes. 'No, Robert, I don't.'

'What the blazes happened? It was a done deal, Maggie. I've signed the papers for the John Deere tractor, ordered the laying hens and the material for the new henhouse. What happened?'

Maggie shook her head. 'I can't tell you more than I know, Robert dear.'

Robert ran his stubby fingers through his hair. 'I told Lord Andrews we didn't need his contract. I've signed the papers for the tractor. I told the lads down the pub.'

Maggie touched her husband's shoulder. 'You must ring them, Robert. Tell them there was a mistake, that you can't be buying these new things.'

'I'll be breaking the contract. The finance company will make me pay.' Robert sat heavily on the couch. 'And I've nothing to pay with.' He looked at her. 'We'll be ruined.'

'You must blame the Australian law, Robert. That good Mr Levi will help us.'

'It was him that told us it was a done deal.' He covered his face with his hands. 'I'll never be able to show myself again. I'll be the laughing stock of the North.'

'No you won't be, Robert. People will understand.'

Robert squeezed her hand. 'I'll do you right, Maggie. I'll find out the cause of it and set our family square again.'

Maggie kissed her husband lightly on the cheek. That was exactly what she was afraid of.

⁂

Maggie took the box from the seat of her car and tucked it under her arm. There was a sleety mist coming in from the east and the halo around the waxing moon was a transparent white. She slipped around the corner of the pub and turned on the torch. The tourist signpost was instantly illuminated some feet away and she quickly found the trail and began the walk to the ruin. Her lace-ups slipped in the dewy vegetation as she slid towards the stream and then she was crossing the rocks, climbing the stile and trudging uphill to where everything had begun. The moon shadowed her progress as she mounted the incline, her torch beaming a path through the springy turf until the scent of the ocean was in her nostrils and the outline of the ruin rose starkly against a void of blue black sky.

At the entrance to the ruin Maggie sat on a crumbling block of stone, cradling the box in her lap. Propping the torch up, she untied her laces and removed her shoes. She lifted the lid and tipped out the running shoes. They were beige and yellow. At the time she'd had her eye on a pair of white and black ones, however these ones were the very best and although she was almost a whole pound short, the shopkeeper in Thurso let her buy them. Even he'd heard that Maggie was going to be a great runner.

Maggie put her feet into the running shoes, squeezing her heels in so that the skin bulged uncomfortably around the top. She ran her finger around the inside, pulling at lining frayed by time, and then tested her weight. The shoes pinched her and shortened her, so that her toes curled under like a hermit crab backing into a shell. Lifting one foot and then another she ran on the spot, briefly lifting her knees as high as possible. She laughed, breathless, at the folly of her exertions.

The running shoes were worn every day by her for two months. She had left off practising in the hills and took to the dusty roads. Every step she pounded went some way to ameliorating her guilt. Every mile run convinced her of her actions. As her strength grew and her pace quickened, she argued less with her sickly mother and ignored her more. How could she be expected to cook and clean for the young ones and work two jobs when she was training to eventually stand on the winner's dais in Edinburgh? There was just enough time in her self-imposed training schedule to cook up the oatcakes for breakfast, see to her mother's morning cuppa and send her younger siblings off to school. Maggie spent her lunch-time practising her starting technique outside the general store where she worked, tucking her skirt in her knickers and heading straight as a die down the centre of the bitumen road. She left her job carding wool in order to chop vegetables for tea, leaving the cooking to her poorly mother. The rest of the time she ran. Maggie ran so fast that she overtook the post boy on his bicycle and the milkman in his chugging truck. She even passed Robert Macken in his clapped-out utility, carting sheep back to Lord Andrew's estate. When the day came that the storekeeper reluctantly agreed to time her with his fancy watch, Maggie exceeded the winner of the previous year's 400 yard dash in Edinburgh. She was ready. The next day the vomiting began.

Maggie walked slowly about the ruin, thinking of another night long ago.

She was walking down the road from work one spring evening. There were three miles to go before she reached the crossroads that would lead her home and she was tired and annoyed. Having been up since three am with the youngest suffering from croup, she'd then endured the pitiful ranting of her mother as she complained of the leg ulcer which would not heal and the husband who left them all for a job interview and didn't return. For once Maggie wanted to sit by the fire and have someone bring her a bowl of broth. For once she wanted to hear the wind whistle around the thick walls of their crofter's cottage instead of the ceaseless arguments and crying and tantrums that filled her siblings' lives.

When the car slowed Maggie barely hesitated. There was no other traffic, either in front or behind, and as she wriggled into the black leather of the passenger seat, her work roughened hands stroked the soft leather. The car's headlights filtered the roadside inhabitants, scaring a black-faced sheep whose eyes shone a yellow green for an instant, and then they were accelerating down the narrow road. In Tongue they parked beyond the pub and its wooden shingle and in an instant she was following him.

Maggie began to jog around the ruin. Mr Levi had contacted her today about the required paternity test. The landscape merged into an unending circle of stone walls, uneven ground, and a void of empty air that joined land, sea and sky in an unblinking swirl of night. What she'd done could not be undone. For what could be her excuse? Could she blame the gossips for convincing their village-bound inhabitants of the identity of Jim's father? Could she seek forgiveness under the guise of wanting more of her life? And what of the family on the far side of the world? Maggie experienced a tightness in her calf muscle. There was a dull jab in her side. Pushing her fingers deep into the pain she continued jogging. She thought of Robert waking from where she left him by the fire. Upstairs he would undress quickly, dropping his clothes on the ground in a crumpled heap and then crawl into bed, kicking at the tucked-in sheets until they came askew with impatience. He would expect her to be there as always: meek and agreeable, grateful for having been taken in by him those many years ago. Maggie was pitied then and she worked the misery of her condition, becoming somewhat defiant of anyone who suggested compliancy on her part. What else could she do now she was faced with the undignified truth? With youthful determination, Maggie pumped her arms and increased her pace.

It was a straight agreement. An understanding based on mutual need and he wasn't so ugly or so old to make her shudder or reconsider her actions. At the ruin Maggie removed her knickers, resolved not to appear immature or, worse, a virgin.

'You've done this before?' he asked, pulling at her buttons roughly until her arms were pinned down by the stretch of material and her breasts shone nakedly in the Vikings' domain.

'Of course,' she answered as his mouth touched her nipple and his hands gripped her buttocks briefly before exploring further. She held him by the shoulders, biting her lip until it bled. Maggie experienced a shudder of pleasure, not once but twice.

'Well you are a greedy little thing,' he whispered, kissing her briefly as she leant back against the stone wall. If that was all it was, it hadn't been so bad. Not so very bad at all.

He undid his belt and dropped his pants. Maggie was staggered. 'Surely we've finished?'

'You may have sated yourself, my virile little mite,' he pushed her against the wall, 'but I've just begun. And running shoes are worth more than a few pound.'

Maggie moved from a jog to a run. Having broken through the pain barrier her breath grew easier. She lifted her arms high so that the air whizzed about her, her hair lifting into the shape of a butterfly's wings, and she threw her head back and embraced the pleasure of freedom. She gave a last fleeting thought to Jim's father, Lord Eliot Andrews, and the brief explanatory note left on her son's pillow. And then she was running again, running faster than she'd ever been able to in her youth. Maggie ran so fast her feet barely touched the ground and when she leapt from the cliff face she finally knew she'd been born to fly.

Midsummer, 1909

Wangallon Station

Only the buffeting from the horse's ceaseless trot kept Hamish conscious and for once he was grateful for pain. Having awoken him once they were safe on Wangallon, Luke had stayed by his side. His hands grasping the reins when Hamish's strength failed, talking to him softly, coaxing him with descriptions of the countryside they passed through. Hamish breathed in the scent of the land he loved and it was the land that propelled him onwards.

Through a haze, snippets of Wangallon seared themselves into his memory; an ironbark tree, a woolly ewe, the contemplative stance of a cow. 'Tell me what you see, Luke.'

'Open country, miles of it, Father.'

'What else?'

'A streak of blue sky. Do you need water?'

'What else, Luke?'

'Birds. There's a great flock in the air. Probably sulphur-crested cockatoos and in the trees I see pigeons. Oh, and a chicken hawk. He's diving for something in the grass.'

'It's late then.'

'Late afternoon. Can't you feel the sun on your face?'

Angus flanked his father on the opposite side. He reached out a hand and touched his father's arm. 'We're nearly home, Father. Lee will be able to brew up some potion. He'll make you better.'

Ahead lay a body. Luke slowed their passage as he recognised the suit and the spear sticking out from the man's back.

'What is it?' Hamish asked.

Luke rode on quickly. 'Wetherly. Dead.'

'You're sure?'

Luke nodded. 'Yes, Father.'

'The man was a traitor,' Hamish said gruffly. Angus's eyes were wide.

Luke held up a hand to shade his eyes and peered into the far horizon. 'I can see dust, Father, great balls of it travelling across the sky.'

Hamish slipped a little further in the saddle. 'Good. That'll be the herd. Are they far enough away?'

Luke reckoned the distance at about 15 miles from the river. 'Yes, Mungo's done a good job. We're safe.'

They rode on, Luke becoming more hopeful as they grew closer to the homestead. It was possible that Lee would be able to brew up a potion to help ease his father back to health. Against the background of dust he glimpsed the shimmer of the homestead.

They propped Hamish up in his bed. Luke opened the window.

Lee prodded at Luke's shoulder.

'Leave it, it's only a flesh wound. The bullet went straight through.'

'Let me help you, Luke,' Claire offered as Lee ministered to Hamish.

Luke brushed her away. 'No. It is an old scar, Claire.' He looked at her intently. 'It will heal. Such things always do, with time.'

Lee cut away the bloody cloth so that Hamish's thigh lay like a beached yellow belly on the pale sand of the sheets. Poking a bony finger at the sodden material, he began to wipe away the blood from around the wound. The stench of rotting flesh was overbearing.

'What do you think?' Luke leant over him.

Lee muttered something indecipherable, wringing out the cloth. The water in the bowl turned a dirty red. Hamish's entire leg was covered in congealed blood while fresh blood seeped steadily from the wound. Lee picked at two small maggots inching their way up Hamish's thigh.

'Jesus,' Luke turned to the open window and took two deep breaths.

Finally Lee spoke. 'How long wounded?'

'Sometime last night.' The shadows were lengthening, stretching their way through the bush like a long yawn. 'Can you save him, Lee?'

Lee clucked his tongue and continued his probing. 'Very much blood lost.'

'But can you save him?'

A trickle of yellow pus seeped from the wound and curved down Hamish's thigh. Lee poked at Hamish's cheek. The skin was dry. 'He must drink water.' Lee opened the bedroom door. 'You get him sit up and drink water. I get herbs.'

In the hallway Angus waited. Luke beckoned him in and Angus rushed to his father's side; Claire took Hamish's hand, gave it a squeeze and then sat quietly on a high-backed chair. Luke lifted a glass of water to his father's lips, forced some into his mouth, the liquid dribbling down his chin. 'How can I give him the blasted water if he won't wake up?'

Claire took a clean rag from the bundle near the basin and soaked it in the glass. 'Help me sit him up a little.' They lifted

Hamish and propped another pillow behind his back, watching as Claire gently opened his mouth and squeezed water onto his tongue. 'It is better than nothing,' she assured them.

Lee returned with a green-tinged poultice that he pushed deep into the wound, layering it over the top and binding it with narrow strips of rag.

Angus reached out a hand and rested it on Lee's shoulder. 'Can you save my father?'

'I will try,' Lee sniffed.

Mrs Stackland appeared with steaming water. Into it Lee mixed various herbs that he retrieved from the pockets of his tunic, stirring the concoction with a long yellow fingernail. Luke turned up his nose at the stink of it.

'I cannot say if he will last,' Lee admitted as he held the stinking brew under Hamish's nose. 'Very much blood gone and the flesh is going bad. Maybe if younger . . .'

Hamish woke, coughing at the steaming concoction. Before he could attempt speech Lee managed to get most of the contents down his throat.

'Vely good,' Lee grinned.

Hamish pushed the bowl away weakly. 'Tastes like shit,' he growled softly. He eyes looked groggily about the room. 'Take me outside, Luke.'

'No, Hamish, you are too ill,' Claire protested.

'Luke?'

Between them Luke and Lee half-dragged and half-carried Hamish out onto the verandah. They sat him down gently, placing his legs on a wicker chair. Hamish stared at the evening star risen above the hedge and remembered the stars so very long ago that had guided him to Australia and then from the goldfields northwards. 'Sit,' he waved his hand tiredly as, one by one, Luke, Angus and Claire sat in a half-circle around him. 'You too, old friend.' Hamish extended his hand to Lee. 'You too. You must forget about what has happened,' he said through stilted breaths. 'Purchase Crawford's block and change the name of it to Boxer's Plains.'

Luke nodded.

'You are the custodians of Wangallon now. You must protect her, honour her for she has fed you and clothed you and honoured you by demanding your tenacity. Wangallon is the home of the Gordons in this new country and you must fight to keep her. You are all a part of her future as I am now of her past. Don't desert her,' he looked at Claire for a long moment. 'Don't resent her. Luke and Angus, you most of all must love her. Love her like a man has loved no other and marry well.' Hamish clutched at Angus's arms. 'Until you marry and produce an heir you are the very last of us.'

Angus touched his leg. 'But Father –'

'Protect her with your life, as I have done. Protect the right of the Gordons to be treated as equals in a new land and look after those who have died and lay buried within her soil, for they have earned your respect.' Hamish held out his hand to Claire. 'If I have loved this land too much –' his fingers squeezed hers – 'forgive me.'

'But Father,' Angus cried, 'you can't go. What will we do? What will I do without you?'

Hamish ruffled the hair on his young son's head. 'Why, Angus, you shall take my place. You will run Wangallon and your brother, Luke, will help you.'

Luke gave a single solemn nod.

Angus rested his head against his father's chest and sobbed.

'Remember, boy, it is better to have lived for something than to die for nothing.'

Hamish watched the moon rise, a shaft of pure light illuminating the garden and extending outwards across his beloved property. He could hear the whistling of the rising wind through the grasses and the myriad sounds of a night growing active with scurrying creatures. He was certain there was a fox at the end of the garden and Hamish experienced a rush of desire to follow the animal out into the timber-draped landscape. He longed to walk away from the homestead and into the moonlit night, if only they would let him go.

It was surprising, this strength of his family. They were like myriad hands holding him still. Hamish faltered, momentarily confused. There was something coursing through his veins, something he'd refused to acknowledge during his lifetime for fear of pain. He gazed upon the faces of those he cared for most in the world and found himself agonising over his leaving. It was the strangest of sensations, yet his body, having failed him like any other mortal man's, now ached for the most intangible of needs: their love. He drifted somewhere between dusk and dawn, considered returning to the cluster of people on the verandah, however the shadows of his forefathers were calling and he could hear the pipes sounding from beyond this world, drawing him into the next.

Guard her, guard my Wangallon, Angus, Hamish whispered. As he stepped from the verandah out into the light, he knew Angus had heard.

Summer, 1990

Wangallon Station Homestead, New Year's Day

Sarah, Ronald and Frank Michaels were sitting on the top verandah. The sky was overcast. Heavy clouds threatened rain. Out on the lawn, Bullet and Ferret were chasing each other in ever-decreasing circles as thunder rumbled above them like a mighty God exhaling, the noise growing steadily closer. Bullet slowed his pace. Ferret gained a couple of feet and was almost close enough to give him a nip on his tail, then Bullet accelerated again.

'Stop teasing him, Bullet,' Sarah called out between their barking. As if on cue, both dogs came to a standstill. Their momentary truce was lengthened by a topknot pigeon which flew low over their heads before reaching the safety of the orange tree. A roar of thunder echoed around the homestead, followed by a loud bang. 'Lightning strike,' Sarah called out, automatically scraping her chair further back towards the wall. Bullet and Ferret bolted for cover as light rain began to fall.

Ronald flipped through the pages of the Bible on his lap before returning to the detailed family tree inscribed on the first page by Hamish Gordon. With a pencil he added the generations of Gordons since 1909. The pencil hovered over the page, then Ronald added Anthony's name. Sarah patted her father's arm. 'Thanks, Dad.'

'Well, it's only proper, considering.'

Sarah ran a hand over her baby bump. She was due in a little over two months. In a fortnight they were travelling north to the Gold Coast, where Sarah intended staying with her father until the birth. It had been surreal to discover she was pregnant. Having relegated the few queasy sensations and changes in her body to stress, Sarah missed the early signs of the new life within her. Yet acknowledging her altered state and reconciling her abilities and personality versus those of her mother eventually salved her fears. Now she was to be a new mother, a mother determined to provide for her child on every level. Reaching for the platter of chicken sandwiches on the low table, Sarah silently thanked her father for coming home to Wangallon. It had been a tough few months for both of them and she doubted if alone she would have been able to muster the fortitude to deal with everything that had occurred.

Ronald studied the aged photograph of the woman in his hand. 'She does look like you, Sarah.' He checked the name *Elizabeth* written on the reverse with the entry noted in the Bible for what must have been the twentieth time.

Frank took a sip of his whisky. 'She was Luke's elder sister. Baby Elizabeth was left in the care of her grandmother, Lorna Sutton, when Hamish and Rose moved north to Wangallon. The details are sketchy however it would appear Hamish wanted his daughter tutored in Ridge Gully, which, considering Wangallon's isolation in the 1860s, was understandable.'

Sarah offered Frank a sandwich. They'd waited months for this promised visit to Wangallon, which on Frank's advice could only occur after Christmas when his retirement was official. He'd refused to discuss anything before then.

'When Rose and Luke's brothers passed on, Hamish thought it appropriate Elizabeth stay with her grandmother. I suppose there was little point moving the young girl north with Hamish a widower. Eventually she was given her grandmother's surname. I don't think she ever saw much of Hamish so it was only fitting she receive her grandmother's estate.' Frank took a bite of his sandwich, breadcrumbs falling down his pale green shirt.

'What happened to her?' Sarah could feel the whole saga creeping up on her again. Distant cousins, cock relations . . .

Frank waggled a finger at her. 'I know what you're thinking, my dear, however there's nothing to worry about. Elizabeth married quite late and there were no children. Her husband died in the 1920s.'

A surge of relief flooded through her.

'A small part of the estate,' Frank continued, 'was meant for Luke. My grandfather doctored the papers. If he hadn't done so Luke would have queried who the beneficiary was.'

'Why on earth would Hamish do his own son out of his inheritance and keep his sister a secret?' Sarah asked, although she was equally intrigued with the level of complicity that bound the Michaels and the Gordons.

'I doubt it was for Elizabeth's benefit,' Ronald turned to Frank. 'Luke must have been furious'.

Frank selected another sandwich. 'He never knew, which was why Angus was so determined to ensure Jim Macken was made aware of his birthright. Guilt, I guess. Angus wanted Jim to have what his older half-brother had been denied: his share of his inheritance and his family. Imagine thinking all your family were dead, which Luke did, except for a much younger half-brother and a steel-edged father who ruled with the proverbial iron fist. It was Claire who eventually discovered Elizabeth's existence. She forwarded the majority of the illegal documents she'd found back to my father, including the family Bible, which mentioned

Elizabeth. I guess they wanted the family history safeguarded by someone they could trust.'

'So Claire agreed with Hamish.' Sarah rubbed her tummy. The baby was practising his rugby kicks. 'I don't get it.'

Closing the bible, Ronald passed it to his daughter. 'Sure you do, Sarah. As the years passed it was easier to leave Elizabeth in the care of her grandmother. Why? For succession purposes, of course. He didn't need a married daughter arriving with a demanding husband and complicating his inheritance plans. And Hamish had a new wife and family. Elizabeth took her grandmother's name and was raised as her ward.' Ronald shrugged. 'That's what happened back then.'

'But why not tell Luke?' Sarah argued.

'They wanted Luke to stay at Wangallon. Angus was still a boy at the time. They did it to safeguard Wangallon. If he'd learnt of a sister floating around in the ether do you think Luke would have been happy to stay? He would have been furious he'd never been told of her existence.'

'To quote your grandfather, Sarah,' Frank brushed crumbs from his lap, 'the end justifies the means.'

Sarah took a sip of water. Today of all days she could have quite easily consumed a bottle of merlot. 'And Boxer's Plains?'

'As you saw from the document I left in the bible, your family purchased it legally from the estate of Oscar Crawford following his death and that of his son in an Aboriginal uprising.'

Sarah lifted an eyebrow. 'What Aboriginal uprising?'

Frank returned her suspicion with a smooth smile. 'Anything else is innuendo,' he instructed her. 'Gossip'.

Sarah scrunched her lips together. 'You won't tell us?' The rain was steadily increasing and for a moment Sarah thought Frank may not have heard her.

Frank looked out at the garden. 'I could tell you there was a dispute over stock.' He took a sip of his whisky, which was so filled with ice it was nearly clear. 'And that Hamish was of an unforgiving nature. I can also tell you that as a Scot he loathed the English with a passion capable of retribution.' He stared dispassionately through the rain-flecked gauze. 'Lives were lost, Sarah. Including Boxer's, the old Aborigine Hamish treated as a friend.'

'So Hamish named the new block after him.' Sarah thought it all sounded a little simplistic. 'Truth is stranger than fiction.' She looked at the deeds to Boxer's Plains.

Frank drained his glass. 'The truth, Sarah, is that the events of 1909 left such an impression on your grandfather's mind, that Angus never purchased land again.'

'Yet Grandfather went to extraordinary efforts to ensure Wangallon's continuation.'

Frank gave a chuckle and looked at Sarah. 'It's genetic.'

'And what of the Michaels' family?' Ronald asked.

Frank sat forward in his chair. 'A long time ago an impoverished Scot by the name of Hamish Gordon rode into Ridge Gully with a Chinese man. Some months later my great-grandfather's signature appeared on the deed transfer when Hamish purchased the general store, which eventually grew to become Lorna's Emporium. I believe my great-grandfather hoped never to meet Hamish Gordon in a darkened street.' Frank widened his eyes for emphasis. 'Many years later when the Boxer's Plains' sale took place,' Frank continued, 'the required paperwork was completed quickly and efficiently. Oscar Crawford was a descendant of the magistrate who sentenced my forefather to penal servitude in Australia. So you see, Sarah, eventually everyone gets their due.'

It was pouring. The rain was driving through the gauze horizontally. Sarah lifted the ceramic platter and carried it inside to escape the torrent of water beginning to run across the verandah's floorboards. She thought grimly of the losses experienced during her life. Sarah didn't feel deserving of any more grief. Surely she'd also paid her dues; particularly in one regard. Ronald and she barely broached Maggie Macken's suicide. It was a shocking thing to happen. All they could do to reconcile the damage Maggie's single lie had caused was to try to forgive her. Yet it was a difficult lie to forgive; it had affected far too many people and spanned nearly three decades. Sarah wondered how Jim and his father were coping. Jim had left Australia within a day of learning of his mother's death. Mr Levi had then told Frank about Maggie's suicide note. The Mackens were proud people and they too had been unsuspectingly woven into Maggie's imaginary life. If it had been appropriate she would have written to Jim, but the words between them had been too acrimonious and it was better for their relationship to be sealed forever by silence.

'So how's the patient?'

Toby Williams was standing at the back door, the rain pelting down so hard that his wide-brimmed hat resembled a waterfall.

'Come in,' Sarah held the door wide.

Toby shook his head, the action spraying a ring of water from his hat and sending streams of it down his Driza-bone jacket. 'Just wanted to let you know that all the cattle are back in their respective paddocks.'

The rain was growing heavier. 'One minute we're praying for rain and the next we're hoping we don't get too much,' Sarah commented.

Toby looked down the back path. 'Reckon you can do with a bit of this for awhile, especially being summer and all.'

'You're probably right,' Sarah agreed. 'Toby, I want to thank you for everything. For looking after the cattle on the route, for –' her eyes moistened – 'sorry, you know what I mean.'

'Sure, kiddo. Actually I've got something for you.'

Sarah opened the handkerchief-wrapped object. It was a small tortoiseshell hair comb.

'It belonged to my great-aunt Lauren. Figured you'd like it.'

'It's beautiful, but really I can't accept it. It looks like an antique.'

Toby smiled. 'Consider it a loan then. I'll be seeing you, kiddo.'

She leant forward and kissed him on the cheek. Sarah would miss him terribly, however she couldn't ask him to stay. He was heading north to the territory and he wanted to get back in time for his brother's wedding.

'Call if you need me,' Toby chuckled. 'Actually that won't happen. How's about I just pop down and check on you myself one of these days.'

'Anytime.'

Removing his hat, Toby placed it against his chest. Instantly his face was saturated. 'Now she gets interested, right on leaving.'

'Go,' Sarah grinned. She watched him walk down the back path. With the rain lessening, she shrugged on a wet jacket and plodded out to the back gate. Toby's vehicle revved through the mud and drove away to a chorus of barking dogs.

Beyond the gate the house paddock was a sea of water. Bullet and Ferret were out playing in the rain. They raced around in circles, splashing muddy water in dog-high arcs until eventually Ferret began to whimper. Matt's dog had managed to get himself caught on a small island. Sarah watched as Bullet traced a path to his friend and then, having reached him, led him back through the wet grass to dry land.

Years ago Anthony had done the same thing. He'd rescued her and together they'd built a life together. Sarah placed a hand on her stomach. There would be a fifth generation on Wangallon and her unborn boy would be called Cameron. Sarah would like to have thought that only she and Anthony could be congratulated for the achievement, however she knew better. Sarah could just imagine her grandfather sitting up there in his squatter's chair, accepting applause from all of those intrinsically connected to the property, shaking his gnarled hand on the fruition of all his convoluted planning. Sarah guessed Angus deserved some recognition, although at times she wondered what had occurred in her grandfather's life to make him so obsessively protective of Wangallon. 'Come on, baby. We better have ourselves a nap.'

Tomorrow was a busy day. Sarah was flying to Brisbane to see Anthony and her obstetrician. The doctor said there was every chance he'd be out of traction and able to hold his newborn son when the time came, and although it was a tenuous thing to cling to, it had given Anthony something to strive for during his recovery. Sarah studied the engagement ring on her finger and smiled, recalling Shelley's suggestion she take on the role of wedding planner. The new year was going to be a busy one. With a sigh Sarah took a long lingering look at her land. They were assured of a good summer and autumn with this fall of rain. A kookaburra was laughing in the distance and as the rain eased, a distant rumble sounded in the west. There were knobby clouds deep on the horizon and the blue–grey tinge heralded further storms.

Sarah thought of the men and women who'd lived and died on the property, of those who'd been unhappy, and others who'd been unable to envisage setting foot beyond her rich soil. Wangallon was an intriguing legacy to be part of. No wonder the old homestead never felt empty. It was filled with the thoughts of her ancestors and she suspected they would have much to say over the coming years. Jim's thirty per cent share of Wangallon had passed to her following the news that he was not remotely related to them, so that Sarah now controlled sixty per cent of the property. This was how it was meant to be, Sarah mused. One descendent in every generation, one strong-willed Gordon to act as custodian until the arrival of the next. Now she was on the verge of creating her own family, of producing an heir, she was beginning to understand the lengths her forefathers were prepared to go to protect their heritage. In the future Sarah knew it would be no different for her.

Acknowledgements

No book such as this can be written without acknowledging the pioneers of this great country, Australia. Their tenacity and determination to forge new communities in an unknown, harsh environment continues to provide inspiration for those of us attempting to tell a little of what their lives may have been like. *A Changing Land* is the sequel to *The Bark Cutters* and in writing it I have once again drawn on my rural landscape, although the work is entirely fictional.

My parents, Marita and Ian, like many of their generation, have a strong oral storytelling tradition and I thank them for their love, guidance and humour. Thanks to my agent, Tara Wynne, and my sister, Brooke; between the two of them they have covered every business element I could think of, and then some. And to David, thank you for your ongoing support.

To Random House and the wonderful team within: publisher Larissa Edwards, editor Chris Kunz, rights manager Nerrilee Weir, marketing strategist Tobie Mann and PR stalwarts Karen Reid and

Judy Jamieson-Green, thank you for your continued assistance and professionalism.

Thank you to Margaret Adams for advice on the Kamilaroy tribe and to the enthusiastic booksellers across Australia who continue to support me.

Lastly, to my readers and friends, both old and new who have joined me within the pages of my novels. By reading my work you have made it come alive for me, thank you.

About the Author

In the course of her career Nicole Alexander has worked both in Australia and Singapore in financial services, fashion, corporate publishing and agriculture. A fourth generation grazier, Nicole returned to her family's property in the late 1990s. She is currently the business manager there and has a hands-on role in the running of the property. Nicole has a Master of Letters in creative writing and her poetry, travel and genealogy articles have been published in Australia, America and Singapore.

Visit www.nicolealexander.com.au

Reading group questions

1. Succession planning – the passing on of the family property to the next generation – is a major issue in Australian agriculture. In *A Changing Land* a strong succession plan is vital to Wangallon's longevity. Do you believe Sarah has a right to be offended when she learns she must share the property with others?

2. Do you think Claire makes the right choices in *A Changing Land*? In what ways is she different to Hamish's first wife, Rose?

3. Lauren and McKenzie each have their own agendas throughout the course of the novel. Did you feel empathy for them at the end of the novel? Why?

4. Do you agree with Anthony's decision not to tell Sarah immediately of his development plans? Discuss.

5. Consider the role animals such as Bullet, Ferret and the fox play in *A Changing Land*.

6. What significance does the tortoiseshell hair comb play throughout the novel?

7. To what extent do you blame Maggie Macken for the events that unfold in *A Changing Land*?

8. What do you make of Luke's feelings for his stepmother? Do you think Hamish is aware of these feelings?

9. The spirits that roam Wangallon are tied to it for many reasons. Discuss.

10. The author uses an interwezaving narrative involving different timeframes in this work. Why do you think she chose to write the novel in this way?